Christmas at Liberty's

Fiona Ford is the author of the Liberty Girls series, which is set in London during the Second World War.

Fiona spent many years as a journalist writing for women's weekly and monthly magazines. She has written two novels under the pseudonym Fiona Harrison, as well as two sagas in her own name in the Spark Girls series.

Fiona lives in Berkshire with her husband.

Christmas at Liberty's

Fiona Ford

arrow books

1 3 5 7 9 10 8 6 4 2

Arrow Books
20 Vauxhall Bridge Road
London SW1V 2SA

Arrow Books is part of the Penguin Random House group
of companies whose addresses can be found
at global.penguinrandomhouse.com.

Penguin
Random House
UK

First published in Great Britain by Arrow Books in 2018

www.penguin.co.uk

A CIP catalogue record for this book is available from the British Library

ISBN 9781787461376

Typeset in 10.75/13.5 pt Palatino
by Integra Software Services Pvt. Ltd, Pondicherry

Printed and bound in Great Britain by Clays Ltd, Elcograf S.p.A.

For Rebecca Irwin and Karen Shaw, my very own
Liberty Girls

Acknowledgements

There are so many people who have helped bring this novel to life, that I think I could write an entire book full of thank yous. However, as that would not only be dull but quite an expensive way of doing things, I will endeavour to keep it brief.

First of all, huge thanks must go to all the wonderful staff at Liberty's who were patient with me to the nth degree. This book is of course fictional and in no way represents the real events of the store in wartime. However, the kindness they have all shown in allowing me to take liberty with Liberty's and create my very own fictional wonderland is something I will be forever grateful for.

To Rene Hudson, thank you for revealing so many wonderful secrets about Liberty's during your time working at the store. Your stories about crystal ashtrays in toilets and Russian princesses were so entertaining – I think you should consider a career as an after dinner speaker.

Huge thanks must also go to Martin Wood and Julie Summers, your help and assistance on all things Liberty, fabric and rationing was invaluable.

And while we're on the subject of huge thanks I am indebted to staff at the Westminster Archives who spent weeks dutifully finding and chatting about long forgotten Liberty's treasures, staff records and general memorabilia – thank you for making the job such a pleasure.

Naturally, I couldn't have written this novel without my wonderful agent, Kate Burke, fantastic editor, Emily

Griffin and the entire team at Arrow. Thank you all for your patience in helping to create this story.

Very special thanks must also go to The Saga Girls, a unique band of fellow saga writers who understand the highs and lows of all things saga as we chat daily on our special secret site! In particular, Elaine Everest, Jean Fullerton, Nancy Revell and Kate Thompson – I owe you all a rather large drink or two for your guidance.

To Chris and Sylvia Lobina, many thanks to you both for sharing the reality of life in Elephant and Castle, and reminding me of the importance of tea, not dinner!

And of course my parents, Barry and Maureen Ford, thank you for all the plot ideas, suggestions for character names and generally just being an incredible source of help. My lovely friends who frequently put up with too many of my stories which begin with, 'during the war', your support is not something I ever take for granted and I'm lucky to know and love you all.

Finally, thanks to you, lovely reader, for choosing to spend some time in the land of Liberty's. There are endless wonderful sagas out there and the fact you picked this one up means the world – thank you.

Prologue

December 1925

As the familiar pinpricks of light danced invitingly up ahead, the little girl stopped in the middle of the crowded street, unable to tear her gaze away. The sight of the sparkling shop windows always sent a thrill down her spine and she wanted to drink it all in.

Every Christmas, together with her mother and sister, Mary visited London to buy gifts for the family, and this store was always the highlight of the trip. The black and white mock-Tudor building looked like it belonged in a fairy-tale rather than in the heart of London. She was eager to step inside.

Glancing up, Mary realised her mother was too busy telling off her younger sister to have even noticed where they were. She bit her lip in irritation. Clarissa was always spoiling things, and this time Mary had had enough. Before she could change her mind, Mary let go of her mother's hand and dashed through the crowds of Christmas shoppers, determined to claim her prize.

Ignoring her mother's cries, she charged on, darting through legs, dodging shopping bags and rounding perambulators. Finally reaching the window, she let out a gasp of delight. Up close the display was even more magical and she pressed her face against the glass. At the centre of the window was the largest Christmas tree Mary had ever seen. It towered above her, ablaze with fairy lights,

1

each bulb sparkling like the brightest stars in the sky. In between the lights, glittering tinsel in hues of red, gold and green hugged the branches, while glass baubles in every colour dangled tantalisingly from the pine. The girl had never seen anything so beautiful and, as her gaze strayed to the mound of Christmas presents elegantly wrapped in red and green paper and topped off with a silver or gold ribbon, she shook her head in wonder.

Just then, she felt a hand clamp down on her shoulder. Startled, she looked up at its owner, only to come face to face with her mother.

'Mary! You mustn't run off like that,' the woman exclaimed.

'I'm sorry, Mummy,' the girl said in a small voice, 'I just wanted to see the lights. They're so pretty.'

The woman's face softened as she turned away from Mary and gazed back towards the window. 'They're rather special, aren't they?'

'I've never seen anything so magical, Mummy. I want to climb inside.'

Mary's mother turned her gaze back to the child and smiled. 'Well, why don't we see if they'll let you and Clarissa do just that?'

'Do you really think they will?' the child gasped.

The woman winked, holding out her hand for her daughter to hold. 'This is Liberty's, darling. Dreams come true here.'

Chapter One

September 1941

Glancing up at the thick black clouds that had suddenly gathered ominously overhead, Mary Holmes-Fotherington quickened her pace along the narrow London street. Although she had been a frequent visitor to London as a driver in the women's army, the changing landscape still took her breath away. The grimy streets were covered in soot and mounds of rubble surrounded shelled-out buildings, so that the place looked more like a ghost town than a capital city. With only one good coat to her name she was eager to resist the late summer rain she knew would surely soak her straight through. Spotting her final destination just yards away, Mary ran the last few steps, her suitcase banging painfully against her shins at the sudden change in pace.

Seconds later she arrived at the two-up two-down terraced house not far from the Elephant and Castle Tube station. Raising her hand to rap loudly on the door she became aware of her racing heartbeat and clammy forehead. Pausing for a moment to smooth down her hair, she tugged at the collar of her coat to ensure it was straight, then took a deep breath to steady herself. Now more than ever she needed to make a good impression and she was darned if she would allow nerves to get in the way.

Lifting the knocker again, the door swung open before she had a chance to use it, almost causing Mary to lose her balance and fall straight into the open doorway. Instead she did her best to compose herself as she came face to face with a heavily pregnant young woman with thick blonde hair and rosy cheeks. Her sapphire-blue eyes gazed at Mary with undisguised curiosity as she rubbed her bump.

'You must be Mary,' she said in a broad South London accent. 'I'm Alice Milwood. Well, don't stand on ceremony then, come on in before the heavens open.'

Without waiting for an answer, Alice turned her back on Mary, leaving her with no choice but to step inside and follow her down the dimly lit passageway.

Reaching the kitchen, Mary saw Mrs Hanson, the landlady who had placed the advert seeking lodgers whom she had met a week ago. On her hands and knees scrubbing the tiled floor, locks of greying chestnut hair falling in front of her face, she looked for all the world as if she were preparing for a visit from the King, rather than a new lodger.

'Dot,' Alice interrupted, taking a seat at the kitchen table and gesturing for Mary to do the same. 'Your latest waif and stray has arrived.'

At that Dot looked up and, spotting Mary, broke into a broad smile. 'Still want to move into the madhouse then?' she chuckled, getting to her feet.

Mary returned Dot's grin with a tight smile before setting her suitcase beside her feet. 'Yes please.'

At that Alice grunted and she picked up her knitting. 'You won't say that when you've been woken up by Dot's tuneless wailings at five in the morning. She thinks she was born for the stage, don't you, Dot?'

'Hey, lady!' Dot scolded. 'Respect your elders. Besides, my warblings used to earn me an extra couple of quid up the King's Head on a Saturday night.'

4

''Til it was bombed,' Alice teased. 'I reckon that's why Jerry raided the place, put the punters out of their misery.'

At that the two women burst out laughing, the affection they held for each other as obvious as the barrage balloons over Tower Bridge. The sound was a welcome one and gave Mary a moment to glance around the kitchen. It was obvious how Dot loved and cared for the place. Although not large, the kitchen was spacious enough to house a large table under the window that looked out on to a small courtyard garden. The floral-print curtains that formed the front of the kitchen cupboards were immaculate, as were the neatly ironed teacloths that lay folded on the wooden work surface ready for use.

For the first time since arriving at the Air Ministry's South London airstrip a week ago, Mary felt a little of her anxiety start to shift. It already felt like a lifetime since she had emerged from the tiny plane, bleary-eyed and bewildered at this sudden new direction her life was taking. With nobody expecting her, and nowhere to go, she had spent hours sitting on a bench outside a nearby train station, pondering her future. Mary couldn't recall a time she had ever felt so lost and lonely. She had realised just how alone she was now. After all, nobody knew where she was, and worst of all nobody cared. The tears Mary had successfully kept at bay since she began her journey back to the UK spilled down her cheeks. Ignoring the looks of passers-by Mary gave in to the wave of self-pity that had engulfed her and let the tears flow. She wasn't sure how long she had remained on the cold wooden bench sobbing. But by the time she'd finished her cheeks felt red raw and her eyes stung from all the salty water. Wiping her face with the hem of her navy skirt, she saw a stray newspaper someone had left

5

behind and reached for it. Idly she flicked through the pages, until like a bolt from the blue an advertisement had called out to her.

Widow seeks clean and tidy female lodger for room to rent near Elephant and Castle Tube, the notice had read.

With a sudden surge of optimism, Mary had taken the next train to London, and arrived at the address. Knocking tentatively at the door, Mary almost broke down in tears when Dot welcomed her inside. Over a much-needed cuppa, Dot revealed she had been widowed in the last war and now made ends meet by renting out two rooms to lodgers. To Mary's surprise and delight, Dot hadn't asked her many questions as they drank their tea in the sunshine-filled kitchen and had merely nodded when Mary explained she had just returned from living with her sister in Ceylon. Now she was back in England she needed to find board and lodging. Dot had smiled kindly at Mary and said her luck was about to change. She had a room that was about to become vacant in a week once the current occupant had left to become a Wren.

Choking back her disappointment that she couldn't move in immediately, Mary had asked Dot if she could recommend anywhere for her to stay in the meantime and had been directed to a nearby bed and breakfast not far from the Walworth Road.

'So have you been living here long, Alice?' Mary asked now as their giggles subsided.

'Since the spring, but me and Dot go way back, don't we?'

Dot nodded as she filled the kettle and placed it on the range. 'I've known Alice since she was a nipper. She was a cheeky little brat then 'n' all.'

Rolling her eyes, Alice smiled at Mary. 'When me and my husband Luke's place was bombed out in the spring

6

raids we were homeless and Dot took pity on a poor pregnant woman and invited me to lodge with her.'

'And I've regretted it ever since,' Dot chuckled, setting a fresh pot of tea on the table between them. 'The only reason I did it was because I knew you'd not want to move up to Scotland to stay with your in-laws. Oh, and of course I wanted your Liberty's discount.'

Alice laughed. 'She's not joking.'

'You work at Liberty's?' Mary gasped.

Alice gave her a genuine smile. 'Certainly do.'

Mary's eyes widened at the news. She and her mother had loved visiting the store every Christmas, but she had never considered the people that worked there had lives outside of the shop. In her mind they were as much a part of the store as the gorgeous fabrics and beautiful interiors.

'How long have you worked there?' Mary asked.

'About ten years,' Alice replied. 'I joined as a Saturday girl in the stockroom and worked my way up to become a deputy in the fabric department, though I'm only part-time now.'

Dot poured the tea and handed them each a cup. 'Wanted to become an ARP warden, didn't you, love?'

'Got to do your bit for the war effort,' Alice said firmly. 'They're ever so good up Liberty's though; most of the male staff have joined up, so us women have had to step into the breach, means we've got a lot of vacancies to fill. Nobody wants to work up a shop when there's so many factories crying out for pairs of hands.'

Mary nodded. 'I thought that's what I might try to do actually.'

Dot raised an eyebrow. 'You want to work in one of the factories? I didn't think you'd be suited to that sort of thing.'

'Why not?' Mary bristled.

'Well, I thought you said you'd just come back from Ceylon or something?' Dot said, narrowing her eyes in confusion. 'Sounds a million miles from a life in a factory.'

'As Alice said,' Mary said quietly, taking a sip of tea, 'we all have to do our bit.'

'What were you doing in Ceylon?' Alice asked.

'My sister Clarissa lives there. She runs a tea plantation with her husband Henry.'

Alice raised an eyebrow. 'Fancy! I've never been further than Bognor Regis.'

Dot chuckled. 'And you won't be going any further for a while in your condition either, Alice.'

'How far along are you?' Mary asked, gesturing towards Alice's bump.

'Six months.' Alice smiled, rubbing her hands over her extended belly. 'And I'm hoping he or she doesn't get any bigger. My back's killing me as it is.'

Mary shot her a sympathetic glance. 'I don't imagine life is any easier with your husband away. Dot mentioned he was in the RAF.'

'That's right. Luke's a flying officer,' Alice said proudly. 'We've been wed coming up five years now. This baby will be our first.'

'Do you have any children, Dot?' Mary asked politely, turning to her new landlady.

Dot shook her head. 'No, me and my George weren't blessed before he was killed in Flanders, God bless his soul.'

'I'm sorry,' Mary said quietly.

'You weren't to know.' Dot smiled kindly. 'I'd have loved a house full of nippers, but it wasn't to be. Still, I'm looking forward to Alice's baby coming along.'

'And you'll be honorary grandma,' Alice grinned. 'Let's face it, you're about as close to one as he or she is going to get.'

'Are your parents far away?' Mary asked.

'You could say that,' Alice said, lips pursed. 'Me mum died just after I was born, and me dad, well, he's in America. Has been for years now.'

Now it was Mary's turn to raise an eyebrow. 'Have you ever visited?'

'We don't have that kind of relationship,' Alice said tightly. 'Besides, Liberty's wages don't go that far.'

'Anyway, enough about us, we want to hear about you. You said you were in the services yourself,' Dot said, gesturing to the khaki jacket that hung on the back of Mary's chair.

'Yes, the women's army, the ATS,' Mary replied, feeling a sudden heat creep up her neck.

Dot narrowed her eyes. 'You never said.'

'No, well, to be honest, it's not something I talk about,' Mary said, shifting uncomfortably in her seat. 'I was discharged, and that was why I went to my sister's in Ceylon, to make a fresh start.'

'So why didn't that fresh start work out then?' Alice asked bluntly. 'Cos I warn you now, we don't want no trouble.'

Mary couldn't miss the warning glance Dot shot Alice across the table. 'And we don't want none of your stirring either, Alice,' her landlady said sharply. 'It ain't none of our business. We've all got things in our past we'd rather not talk about, don't you think?'

At that, Alice looked meekly at the table before glancing back up at Mary. 'Sorry. I shouldn't have said that. I blame the pregnancy: it's making me say things I shouldn't.'

9

Dot roared with laughter. 'And the rest, Alice Milwood. You've always been a mouthy mare; that baby in your belly hasn't made a scrap of difference.'

At that Alice started to giggle and this time Mary joined in, finding their laughter infectious. After a few moments they settled down and Mary smiled at each of the women she was about to live with. It was only fair she told them a little of her situation; they deserved that at least.

'The truth is that as well as being discharged from the ATS, my family don't talk to me any more,' Mary sighed. 'I won't bore you with the details but my parents and my sister dislike some of the decisions I've made and as a result they have cut me off. Now I'm jobless but at least I'm not homeless any more, and I can assure you, Dot, I intend to get work as soon as possible. I won't be taking advantage of you.'

There was a sharp intake of breath at Mary's bald statement of the facts and Alice and Dot exchanged looks.

'Well, I can't say it's ideal,' Dot said gently. 'But you strike me as someone what needs a helping hand and I think there are times where we all need one of those. What do you think, Alice?'

The pregnant woman wrinkled her nose as she looked Mary up and down without saying a word. Nervous under Alice's scrutiny, Mary felt her head spin. The girl before her might well be her own age, not to mention short and pregnant, but Mary had come up against plenty of women like Alice before, especially in the ATS. She was under no illusions: Alice was not someone you would mess about.

'I want to agree with Dot,' Alice said eventually, 'really I do, Mary. You seem like a nice girl, you've got a posh accent, seems like you'd never put a foot wrong.'

'Thank you,' Mary murmured.

'But the thing is,' Alice continued, 'we don't know anything about you, you could be anybody, and even if you're not anybody and you are who you say you are then you've still shown up here at Dorothy Hanson's door wanting board and lodging without a job.'

Mary coloured, about to protest, but it was clear Alice hadn't finished. 'I understand you've had a rough ride, Mary, none of us under this roof can say we've had a smooth time of things, but what concerns me is that you don't take advantage of Dot.'

'I would never do that,' Mary said vehemently. 'I would rather leave here homeless and jobless before taking advantage of anyone.'

'Well, you say that,' Alice replied evenly. 'But what I don't get is why you don't want to tell us about your past. Seems to me if you were as straight as a die you'd want to tell us about yourself.'

Dot raised an eyebrow. 'That right, Alice? Want to tell Mary all about the skeletons in your cupboard when you've just met?'

At that Alice coloured. 'Well, no, but you can see the point I'm making.'

Mary's heart was banging like a drum against her chest. She could understand why Alice would feel nervous about letting her stay in their home and she wanted to reassure her, but it would be impossible to tell her the reasons that had brought her here. Mary knew that if she revealed all now her fresh start would be over before it had even had a chance to begin.

'You're right, Alice,' Mary said earnestly, her green eyes meeting Alice's blue ones. 'I could be anybody, here to rip you off and cause you trouble. All I can do is give you my word that I'm not. I've had some problems but I want to

11

start again: move forwards now, help with the war effort. I promise you and Dot I won't let either of you down.'

There was a pause before Alice gave her a tight smile. 'Good. In that case, Dot, I make you right. It's clear Mary does need a helping hand. As I said earlier, we do need people up Liberty's if you fancy it? You won't earn a fortune and of course if your heart's set on working up a factory, I won't try and change your mind, but I could put in a word for you if you like.'

Mary looked at the two women in astonishment. 'That would be wonderful, but I don't have any retail experience.'

'Would she need any, Alice? I thought you said they were desperate now,' Dot put in.

'We still have standards,' Alice exclaimed. 'The Liberty family and the board would have kittens if they thought we were going around taking on just anyone. That said, Mary, Dot is right. You're clearly a bright girl, you could learn on the job.'

Mary felt her head spin as she took in this unexpected offer. When she had been discharged from the ATS she'd realised she would never have the pick of the jobs; indeed, she would be lucky to get anything at all. But now she was being offered the chance to work in the store she had adored as a child. A store that had been filled with happiness and magic.

'Don't worry if references are a problem,' Alice said. 'To be completely honest with you, Mary, Liberty's is that short-staffed at the moment they'll be glad to get their hands on anyone who can add up and string a sentence together.'

Mary raised an eyebrow and Dot roared with laughter. 'She don't mean it like that. She just means you could probably stick a couple of references down and by the time they get around to checking 'em your feet'll be well under the table.'

'You'd really do that for me?' Mary said eventually.

Alice leaned forward and gave Mary a curt nod. 'I would. Though I warn you, mess me about or show me up in any way and you'll find it'll be me that'll be at liberty to make you pay.'

Chapter Two

The gold weathervane perched on top of the mock-Tudor building glinted in the morning sunshine, filling Mary with a sense of anticipation. Pausing suddenly on London's Argyll Street, much to the annoyance of passers-by, she drank in the scene. Although it had been over five years since she had been to Liberty's, she was delighted to see how little had changed. In fact, she thought, casting her gaze over the criss-cross windows and the coats of armour that hung either side of the heavy wooden door that formed the main entrance, the store seemed a lot larger than she remembered.

Mary realised the building was so big it was all you could see from this point in the street, making the whole place seem even more grand and imposing. Despite the unexpected warmth of the autumnal morning, she shivered with excitement. Was it really possible she might end up a Liberty girl herself?

The day after she had moved in, Mary had been in the kitchen washing up when Alice had marched in and slapped a sheet of paper on the wooden table.

'Application form,' she announced firmly. 'Fill that out, give it to me and we'll get you an interview as soon as possible.'

Wiping her hands on a tea towel, Mary glanced nervously at the form. Although Alice had assured her she would help her get work, Mary hadn't been convinced that she would. After all, Alice hadn't exactly offered her the greatest of welcomes when she arrived.

'Are you really sure this is all right, Alice?' she began. 'I mean I don't want you thinking you have to do me a favour just because we share accommodations.'

Alice rolled her eyes and took a seat at the table. 'How many more times? I offered to help you and I meant it. Now fill this in tonight and I'll take it back with me tomorrow.'

'And you're really sure references aren't a problem?' Mary said, taking a seat opposite Alice and reaching for a pen from the dresser.

'Not at all. To be honest, your biggest problem's going to be Mabel Matravers,' Alice said, stifling a yawn.

'Who's that?' Mary asked puzzled.

'She's the deputy manager,' Alice explained. 'And a right pain in the arris she is 'n' all.'

Despite the warning, Mary couldn't help chuckle at Alice's choice of words. 'I've come across a few of those in my time.'

Alice raised an eyebrow. 'I don't doubt it but they don't make 'em like Mabel any more. She's been there over twenty years. Worked her way up from Saturday girl just like I did and was made up to deputy manager when Jerry Beale, the original deputy manager, was called up.'

'So she knows her stuff then?' Mary said thoughtfully.

Alice nodded as Dot burst through the front door laden with gas mask and shopping bag. 'Dot knows her from way back, don't you?'

'Who?' Dot looked blank as she set her bags down.

'Mabel Matravers, or Partridge as was,' Alice said.

'Oh, her.' Dot nodded. 'Yes, that's right, I knew her and her brother David as kids when they lived round here. She was ever such a lovely girl. At least she was until her mother disappeared.'

'What happened to her mother?' Mary asked.

'Took up with a fancy man, didn't she,' Dot said in hushed tones. 'Had an affair behind her Paul's back, fell pregnant and left her two kiddies for him to raise while she set up shop north of the river and played happy families with a new baby and new fella. Not that I blame her for cheating on her husband, he was a right sod, always womanising and gambling.'

'Dot,' Alice hissed. 'You'll put Mary off.'

'No, really, it's fine.' Mary smiled. 'It won't go any further. Poor Mrs Matravers though, what a thing to bear.'

'Became tough as old boots overnight,' Dot said authoritatively. 'Mind you, she had to really, she was only twelve and her little brother was five years younger than her. With their dad barely on the scene she had to fill her mum's shoes pretty quickly, running a home and bringing up David.'

'She's a hard grafter is what Dot's trying to say,' Alice explained. 'She's nobody's fool either. Loves Liberty's, has devoted her life to it. The family, along with our store manager Mr Button, adore her.'

'And will she be the one interviewing me? Not this Mr Button?' Mary asked, filling in the form.

'Yes.' Alice leaned over the table to examine what Mary was writing. 'She rules the shop floor with an iron fist, but although you wouldn't want to cross her she is fair.'

Alice delivered her final pronouncement and left Mary to complete the rest of the paperwork. Once Mary was finished Alice ran her eye over it with military precision, leaving Mary feeling rather hot under the collar. By the time she was satisfied, Alice was confident she would be able to organise an interview for Mary. It hadn't taken long, and now, just three days after moving into Dot's home, Mary was on her way to meet the infamous Mrs Matravers and was feeling more than a little nervous.

Steeling herself for whatever lay ahead, Mary propelled herself towards the store and was just about to walk inside when she felt someone tap her on the shoulder.

'Alice!' Mary gasped, turning round to find her new friend grinning.

'Thought I'd try and catch you before you went in. Wanted to wish you luck,' she said, giving a half-shrug.

The gesture wasn't lost on Mary and she felt a surge of gratitude. 'Thank you, that's extremely thoughtful. I would have waited for you to catch the Tube but, to be honest, Alice, I was so anxious about this new start I felt I was better off on my own.'

Alice nodded in understanding. 'Well, what are you waiting for? Best get inside.'

'I was just about to,' Mary admitted. 'But I was looking for the doormen to make themselves available to me. Where are they?'

Throwing her head back with laughter, Alice roared so hard, passers-by turned to stop and stare. 'Sorry, darlin',' she snorted, steadying the hat that was about to fall. 'But the doormen are long gone. What with the war 'n' all, they've all joined up.'

'So what do customers do then?' Mary asked, her eyes filled with bemusement.

'Well, it's a funny business, Mary,' Alice said, wiping the tears of laughter from her eyes. 'They have to do this thing where they open the door themselves. I know you with your airs and graces might find that a bit hard to believe but it's the way of things round here.'

Mary gave her a good-natured nudge with her elbow. 'Bally cheek! I'll have you know I'm extremely down to earth.'

Alice smirked. 'We'll see. But regardless, it don't matter to you what customers are doing with the doors.'

'Why?' Mary looked blank.

'Because this entrance is for customers only,' Alice said, guiding her away from the majestic set of doors and down the street towards a dark alley around the back of Kingly Street. 'You'll be wanting the back way.'

Within moments, Mary was looking at a very different set of doors. The narrow pathway was a world away from the grand walkway leading to the main entrance, and the back of the building looked dirty grey and, if she were honest, a little uncared for. As for the staff entrance, it was nothing like the front: just a plain black door covered with scratches and dents.

As Alice pushed open the door with one hand and beckoned Mary to follow her, Mary saw that the back of the store was in a similar state. The stone stairway that led to the floors above was cold and uninviting. The paint on the walls that had once been white was peeling while the windows that looked out on to the street below were black with grime.

'As you can see, they don't lay on the royal treatment for the staff!' Alice chuckled as she ran up the flight of steps.

'So I see,' Mary replied as she followed Alice up several flights of stairs to the top floor.

'Right, we're here.' Alice paused for breath. 'You want to go through that door there and walk straight on until you reach another set of doors, then you've reached the office. Mrs Matravers will see you in there.'

Mary gulped nervously. 'Anything I should know?'

Alice shook her head. 'She's all right really. Bark's worse than her bite. Just remember you belong here and don't take any notice if she tries to tell you otherwise. Oh, and remember what I said the other day. Don't show me up or you'll regret it. Now I'd better get on. Dreary Deirdre the floor walker'll have my guts for garters if I'm late. My tea break's just after ten; come and find me and let me know how you got on.'

Without waiting for a reply, Alice dashed back down the stairs towards the shop floor and left Mary to her own devices. As the sound of Alice's footsteps drifted away, Mary squared her shoulders, lifted her chin and made her way to the office as instructed.

At a small desk sat a petite bespectacled girl with long auburn hair inexpertly curled into a victory roll. Although Mary knew that, at twenty-five, she wasn't old, from the way this girl was anxiously scribbling away in her notepad, tongue hanging slightly out of her mouth, Mary had a feeling she was a good bit younger than herself. She suppressed a smile. There was something about the girl's earnestness that reminded Mary of her old friend Peg, and for one brief moment she had a pang of longing for her old days in the ATS and the friends she had made.

Enough of that, Holmes-Fotherington.

'Excuse me,' Mary said politely to the girl. 'I'm here to see Mrs Matravers about a position in the fabric department.'

At the sound of Mary's voice the girl jumped. 'I'm so sorry, I didn't see you there. Mrs Matravers is expecting you. I'm to ask you to fill in this test, then show you straight in.'

'Marvellous. Thank you. Am I all right to sit here?' she asked, gesturing towards the stiff-backed wooden chair by the door.

'Oh yes, of course,' the girl stammered. 'Mrs Matravers says you have ten minutes to complete it, then I'm to show you in.'

Nodding, Mary sat down. Running her eyes over the sheet she saw it was simple addition and subtraction and breathed a sigh of relief. This she could do in her sleep.

Finishing in less than ten minutes, Mary stood in front of the girl behind the desk who was now engrossed in writing some very long list. Mary touched her shoulder gently to catch her attention.

'Should I go in now?' she asked, making the girl jump once more.

The girl got to her feet, but she paused for a second. 'I'm so sorry I made you wait. Please don't tell her I didn't see you straight away. She's ever so particular, and it took me such a long time to work my way up to this position.'

Mary frowned. Was this Mrs Matravers really so terrifying that the girl couldn't admit to making a mistake, albeit an incredibly minor one? 'Of course I won't,' she said kindly.

The girl flushed with relief. 'Thank you so much. I'm Rose, by the way.'

'Mary,' she said as Rose knocked timidly on the door.

'Come in,' a voice called.

Walking inside, Mary was surprised to come face to face with a short woman about ten years older than her, with dark brown hair tied back in a severe bun and sallow skin that made her look tired.

'Mabel Matravers, I'm the deputy manager,' she said, holding out her hand and shaking Mary's hand without getting up from the hard-backed chair. 'You must be Mary, I've heard a lot about you. Please sit.'

Noticing an uncomfortable-looking wooden chair opposite, Mary sat as Mrs Matravers leafed through her application form.

'Any experience?' she asked without looking up.

Mary blanched. 'I'm sorry?'

'Do you have any retail experience?' Mrs Matravers asked again, her tone impatient.

'No,' Mary said, a hint of defiance in her voice.

Mrs Matravers lifted her face to meet Mary's eye. 'And it says here you live in the Elephant and Castle. You don't sound as if you grew up there?'

'No, Cheshire,' Mary said bluntly.

Mrs Matravers nodded before looking back down at her notes, giving Mary a chance to look around the tiny, stark inner office. She noticed that the walls in here were just as uncared for as they were in the stairwell, and aside from the chairs, desk and filing cabinet in the corner, there was very little to make the place feel like the home she knew Arthur Liberty, the founder, had so wanted his store to be.

'So why do you want to work at Liberty's?' Mrs Matravers asked without looking up.

Mary cleared her throat. 'Well, I've always loved the store, ever since I was a young girl—'

'That it?' Mrs Matravers interrupted in a bored tone. 'You always loved the store?'

'Er, no,' Mary began, only for Mrs Matravers to interrupt once more.

'Only we're looking for girls with a bit more about them than that they love the store,' she said crisply. 'We're looking for girls who are committed to the arts and crafts movement. Who adore the cutting edge, have a passion for excellent customer service and the finer things in life.'

'Well, of course …' Mary trailed off as Mrs Matravers put her hand up to silence her.

Bending down to look at the sheets of paper again Mrs Matravers ran her finger down the page then paused. 'I see you were in the ATS up until recently.'

Mary nodded. 'That's right. I was a driver.'

'So what are you doing here?' Mrs Matravers barked. 'Shouldn't you still be in the army? We've had several girls from here join up.'

Mary gulped nervously. 'Yes, Mrs Matravers.'

Leaning forwards, Mrs Matravers fixed Mary with her steely gaze. 'And so why aren't you still a private driving for the army? There's a war on; it's not as though your services aren't needed.'

Mary let out a deep sigh. She should have known this moment was coming; how stupid she was not to have prepared for it. Biting her lip, she realised that she had been focusing so hard on worrying about whether her mental arithmetic was up to scratch she hadn't prepared an answer as to why she had left the ATS.

Mary was just about to answer when Mrs Matravers saved her the trouble. 'Reading between the lines here it seems as though you were sacked. That right?'

She felt the chill of Mrs Matravers' words run right through her and nodded.

'Speak up, girl. Were you dismissed?'

'Yes. I was discharged,' Mary replied, her cheeks pinking with shame.

Mrs Matravers said nothing, but Mary couldn't help notice the small smirk of satisfaction.

'I don't know an awful lot about the army, Miss Holmes-Fotherington, but what I do know is that to have been discharged from the army, particularly during wartime, you must have done something dreadful,' she said eventually.

Mary looked at the floor. Afraid that if she glanced up she might burst into tears and reveal everything.

'What I have to decide now is whether or not I think you deserve a chance to be a Liberty girl,' Mrs Matravers continued, her face not giving anything away. 'You've clearly got an unsavoury reputation which we here at Liberty's do not condone. Our name, our reputation, is of exceptional importance.'

Miserably, Mary lifted her chin to meet Mrs Matravers' eyes. 'I understand that more than anyone. I would have no desire to bring Liberty's into disrepute.'

Mrs Matravers, with her thin lips pursed and grey gaze focused, ran her eye over Mary once more as if looking for some other discrepancy. Mary felt a sudden chill in the room and huddled into the navy cardigan she wore over the red floral tea dress she had carefully pressed that morning.

As the floor manager returned her gaze to the paperwork on her knee, she took her time reading her notes and finally glanced at Mary's arithmetic test, nodding at each sum. Then she pursed her lips while she read Mary's references. As Mrs Matravers' finger hovered over the made-up entries, Mary gulped, sure she would be found out.

'Well then, Miss Holmes-Fotherington,' Mrs Matravers said, dropping the sheaf of papers to the floor as she stood up. 'Congratulations, your application has been successful.'

Mary's hands flew to her mouth in shock. She had been braced for rejection. 'Thank you, Mrs Matravers, I can assure you I will not let you or the Liberty family down,' she gushed, standing up to shake Mrs Matravers' hand furiously with gratitude.

'You can start tomorrow. Florence Wilson runs the fabric and haberdashery department; Alice Milwood is her second in command, though of course she is part-time. You will receive commission of one and a half per cent on top of your basic pay. You may choose your own clothing to wear as your uniform but we will not tolerate loud garments,' Mrs Matravers said, giving Mary's best floral dress a withering stare. 'On your way out, see Rose who will give you your handbook and explain to you the rest of your duties.'

'Thank you so much, Mrs Matravers,' Mary said as the deputy store manager began to usher her out. 'I can promise you will not regret this.'

With her hand resting on the doorknob, Mrs Matravers paused for a moment before opening the door to show Mary out. 'I'd better not, Miss Holmes-Fotherington. Because rest assured if I hear of just one misdemeanour on your part, you will be out of Liberty's faster than you were thrown out of the army.'

Chapter Three

Mary followed Mrs Matravers out into the office, doing her best to keep up as the deputy manager pulled out a variety of documents from a steel filing cabinet and thrust them into Rose's hands.

'Give Miss Holmes-Fotherington the tour, a copy of the staff rules and ensure she understands her hours of work.'

'Yes, Mrs Matravers,' Rose said meekly as the deputy manager stalked back to her own office and slammed the door shut. Rose pushed the glasses back up her nose, tucked a loose strand of hair behind her ears and fixed Mary with a beaming smile. 'Congratulations, welcome to Liberty's.'

'Thank you, dear,' Mary replied, finding the younger girl's enthusiasm infectious.

'I've got so much to show you. Please say you've got time now to go through everything otherwise Mrs Matravers'll make mincemeat of me,' she said, rifling in her desk drawer for some paperwork.

'Of course.' Mary smiled as the girl found what she was looking for and triumphantly pulled out a sheet of paper clearly marked 'Liberty Rules'.

'This is for you,' Rose said, handing her the sheet. 'Now follow me and I'll show you what's what.'

'All right,' said Mary, following Rose out of the door. Quickly Rose rattled off a list of things Mary needed to know including her pay, hours of employment and how each department was referred to with a letter of the alphabet rather than by name.

Listening while she read through the rules Rose handed her, Mary couldn't help smiling as she realised how many similarities there were between Liberty's and the ATS. Any absence through illness had to be reported to the superintendent's office before ten in the morning. No private letters were to be received at the store; there was a 25 per cent staff discount and any staff purchases had to be made before quarter to eleven in the morning. Additionally Mary would be given three weeks' holiday but her employment could be terminated with one week's notice.

'It says here that there's no eating or drinking in the stockrooms as well as on the shop floor.' Mary frowned as she continued to follow Rose down the dark corridor. 'I can understand why it wouldn't be pertinent to drink or eat in front of customers but why not in the stockrooms? In the ATS we always enjoyed a sneaky cup of tea when we could.'

Rose turned her head and smiled. 'Mice.'

'Sorry?' Mary shook her head in confusion.

'The building's made of two nineteenth-century ships. If we start eating in the stockrooms then that means we get mice,' Rose explained brightly as she pushed her way through another set of double doors. 'Here we are: this is the staffroom, where we can sit and eat sandwiches.'

Mary looked around at the canteen. She had to admit it was a nice room with wooden tables and benches spaced evenly across the tiled floor. Noticing how the sun streamed through the large windows, Mary couldn't resist opening one of them. Craning her neck out of the window she could see halfway across London, but the scenes of devastation from the raids left her speechless. Buildings stood without roofs or walls, piles of rubble lined the city's streets and you could even make out washing left abandoned in what was left of people's former homes. She looked across to the streets of Soho below, and let out a horrified gasp at the devastation. Amongst the ruins she could just about make out the old Patisserie Valerie, where she and her mother had spent many a happy hour after shopping in Liberty's, indulging in cream cakes and endless cups of tea.

'It's a bit different when you see the bomb damage from up high than when you're on the ground, ain't it?' Rose called cheerfully.

'It is rather,' Mary said softly. 'This bird's eye view of the city is not one I've seen before.'

'But you weren't bothered about the height, were you?' Rose persisted.

'No. Why are you asking me that?' she said, shutting the window.

Rose walked across the staffroom to a little blue door Mary hadn't seen before. 'Because part of your duties will be fire-watching. Two days on the floor, two nights on the roof keeping watch. Nearly everyone takes a turn, even the chairman, Mr Blackmore hisself.'

Mary nodded her head in approval. If even the head of Liberty's could sit on the roof for two nights then she could hardly object.

'What else do I need to know?'

Rose thought for a moment, her blue eyes appearing almost cat-like behind her glasses. 'I think that's everything. I imagine Alice told you about all the different societies there are here. If you're good at swimming, for example, there's a ladies' team. We compete against all the other big stores like Harrods and Selfridges. Usually beat them every time too.'

Mary chuckled at the girl's obvious sense of loyalty. 'Swimming's not really my area. I'm more of a horsewoman, but I can't imagine there's an awful lot of call for that.'

'Not really.' Rose grinned. 'But there's a sports day every year, usually down in Merton – you know, where we have our print works. Maybe if you're good with horses, you'd like to try some of the other competitive races?'

'Maybe,' Mary conceded as she followed Rose back out to the stairwell.

'Let's go and introduce you to Miss Wilson. You're so lucky, she's ever so lovely, I wish I worked for her instead of Mrs Matravers,' Rose admitted as she skipped down the steps, only to stop suddenly. 'Oh my days! Did I just say that out loud?' she gasped, clearly horrified by her gaffe. 'I'm so sorry. I didn't mean to be so disrespectful. Mrs Matravers'll string me up if she hears me talking like that.'

Mary took a step towards Rose and squeezed her arm. 'Rose, you really must stop worrying so much. It's perfectly acceptable to let off a bit of steam every now and then. We used to do it all the time in the army.'

'So you won't tell her what I said?' Rose begged, her face stricken.

'Of course I won't. Though you might not want to make a habit of saying things like that if you're that much of a worrier.'

'No, you're right,' Rose agreed as she carried on walking down the steps. 'Thanks, Mary.'

'Anytime,' she grinned, before asking: 'Have you been at Liberty's long?'

'A year, ever since my husband Tommy was called up into the army. It's like a fairy-tale working here. I love it.'

Mary covered her shock at the fact the girl who couldn't have been more than twenty was already married and instead concentrated on asking about the business. 'Didn't you want to work on the shop floor though?' she persisted.

'Not really,' Rose sighed. 'I'm better off back of house; at least that's what Mrs Matravers says anyway. I love the Liberty's fabrics though.'

'I imagine that must be a bit difficult though, with fabric rationing. How long has it been since it was introduced? Three months?' Mary pointed out.

'It definitely makes things harder,' Rose admitted. 'But Miss Wilson's ever so kind. She started a little sewing circle in the summer and now some of us sit down together once a week and make new things out of our old stuff. If there's any scrap left over we all club together and make something out of that too.'

Mary raised an eyebrow as they reached the bottom of the stairwell. 'I'm afraid I'm rather a dunce when it comes to sewing.'

Rose smiled as she held open the door that led to the shop floor. 'Oh, don't worry about that. Miss Wilson will soon have you sewing like a dream.'

Privately Mary doubted that very much, but as she followed Rose across the floor towards the fabric department she didn't have the heart to tell the young girl the truth. Instead she focused on looking around the store, and was delighted to see it was just as wonderful as she remembered. The hum of activity from shoppers admiring all the gorgeous things on offer made her feel alive and she remembered the pull of excitement she used to feel when she visited with her mother.

She also felt a sense of relief that so much was the same, even during a war. The floorboards continued to gleam like silk, the highly polished glass counters still boasted the same beautiful silver and pewter pieces,

29

while items of jewellery filled with rare rubies and peridots continued to catch the eye of elegantly dressed customers.

As Rose strode across the floor, out towards the atrium, Mary felt a rush of excitement when she caught sight of the sparkling chandelier that still hung from the ceiling. It all seemed a world apart from the bomb damage that lay just yards away. With a start Mary remembered how charming the store had always felt, and was grateful to realise that despite the very worst of times they now found themselves in, Liberty's hadn't lost that sense of enchantment.

Once they reached the fabric department at the back of the ground floor, Mary stopped dead in her tracks. She had never seen anything so beautiful. There was roll after roll of fabric in every print and hue you could imagine. The colours glittered like jewels, and Mary couldn't tear her eyes from gorgeous blue paisley, teal seagulls and bright pink peacocks. As a child this had been her favourite department to visit: she'd loved imagining the things she could do with all the pretty prints. Now she thought of spending her days admiring the gorgeous creations that lined the department she would be working in. Aware that Rose was saying something, Mary brought her attention swiftly back to the present, just in time to be introduced to Miss Wilson.

Immediately Mary could see how right Rose had been. Miss Wilson's warm and open face radiated friendliness and Mary had a feeling that the two of them would get on like a house on fire.

'Mary, it's such a pleasure to have you in my department,' Miss Wilson smiled, holding out her hand to shake Mary's.

'It's marvellous to be here,' Mary replied, taking her supervisor's hand.

Mary noticed immediately how unlike Mrs Matravers' handshake it was. Whereas the older woman's grip felt almost cobra like, Miss Wilson's was softer and more welcoming.

'Now, I insist you must call me Florence or, better yet, Flo. I can't stand all this Miss Wilson business.' She giggled as they broke free from each other's grasp. 'It's something Liberty's insists upon but I can't abide it, can I, Rose?'

Shaking her head, Mary was amused to see Rose was as enchanted with Miss Wilson, or Flo as she now chose to think of her, as she was. Miss Wilson appeared to be perhaps a couple of years older than her, Mary thought, but with her twinkling green eyes, peaches and cream complexion and chestnut hair twisted into a chignon, she looked more like a film star than a shop girl.

'I can't wait for you to start tomorrow; in the meantime, can I just introduce you to some of our best-selling fabrics so you'll have a bit more of an idea what's what in the morning?' Flo asked kindly.

Mary nodded. 'I would love you to.'

'Wonderful. And can I ask how much you know about pattern-cutting and the type of fabrics that best suit each particular garment?'

'Sorry?' Mary coloured in confusion. 'I don't quite know what you mean.'

The welcoming smile Flo had worn just seconds earlier vanished. 'Surely you know how to cut a pattern?'

Mary shook her head. 'I'm sorry, I can barely thread a needle.'

A flicker of disbelief passed across Flo's face. 'And Mrs Matravers sent you here? When you know nothing about sewing?'

'We're short-staffed in this department. Plus, she lives with Alice,' Rose put in quietly.

'I see.' Flo pursed her lips as if mentally running through the situation in her mind. 'Very well, if Mrs Matravers and Alice think you're suited here then I'll trust their judgement. But I warn you, Mary, we cannot afford mistakes. Every bit of fabric is as precious as the Crown Jewels and so I will need you to pay attention and learn quickly. We'll give it a month's trial and see how things work out; if you can't learn in that time I'm sorry but we will have to let you go, no matter how short-staffed we are.'

'Yes of course,' Mary said, the joy she had felt just seconds earlier replaced with fear.

As Flo made a note on the personnel file Rose had brought down with her, Mary felt a flash of despair. She wanted nothing more than to make a new start, but it seemed she still had a long way to go.

Chapter Four

Mary was astonished to find that it was almost the middle of the afternoon when she finally left the store. Stepping out of the Tube train at Elephant and Castle she made her way up the stairs to the surface and blinked at the daylight.

Once Mary had got over her initial dismay that Flo hadn't wanted to take on someone as inexperienced as her, she had gritted her teeth and done her best to make the best of the situation. She couldn't blame her new supervisor for feeling the way she did, but Mary knew she was a quick learner, and that, coupled with grim determination, meant she was able to push her disappointment aside and concentrate on every word Flo had said.

Not only had she learned how to cut a basic pattern, but she had also discovered how different fabrics hung. Rayon was a thinner material and draped well with the dressier skirt patterns compared to cotton, Mary had discovered. By the time Flo had dismissed her, Mary had felt exhausted and all she could do was hope that her boss hadn't been let down.

After the day she had endured, Mary couldn't wait to get back to Dot's terrace in Bell Street. It wasn't long before the place she now called home came into view, with its black front door and traditional London brick. She couldn't resist a smile. The house was a world away from any ATS billet or even the old Cheshire pile she had grown up in. For a moment, the image of her parents standing on the doorstep flooded her mind. She knew they would gape in astonishment at the size of the place, unable to believe that three adult women could live together in what they would consider a shoebox but was actually palatial for most people.

Then of course there was the fact it always looked so smart. Dot was frequently found leading the front step or scrubbing the door and its frame. Until the bombs started to fall, Mary knew that Dot had always washed her windows with similar frequency. But now the windows had brown tape stuck all over them to prevent injury from flying shards of glass should the house ever be hit. So far much of Elephant and Castle had been decimated, and what had once been referred to as the Piccadilly of the South, thanks to its numerous shops, theatres, dance halls and cinemas, was in danger of losing its title after so much had been destroyed during the spring raids.

Mary felt a pang of sadness. Nobody had expected the war to last this long, and she felt especially sorry for those who had lived through or served in the last one. Dot had lost her husband George in 1917 and Mary was aware that she felt her husband had given his life in vain. It was understandable.

Shaking her head bitterly, Mary pulled out her key and let herself in. She knew better than most that there really was no justice in the world. Opening the door, Mary stood in the dark, narrow hallway and shucked off her sodden raincoat, resting it on the banister to dry. 'Hello, Dot, are you home?'

'I'm in 'ere,' a voice called from the kitchen.

Mary followed the delicious smell of baking wafting through the house. 'What's all this?' she asked, catching Dot elbow deep in flour and egg powder.

Dot turned and smiled. 'Thought we'd need cake either way, so I'm having a go at a seed cake! Come on then, how did you get on?'

'I got it! I got the job!' Mary burst out excitedly, unable to keep her good news to herself any longer.

'That's wonderful, love.' Dot thrust her cake-floured arms towards Mary and enveloped her in a hug, sending clouds of dust everywhere, and Chalky, Dot's ancient moggy, fleeing for cover. 'I knew you'd do it.'

Mary stepped back and raised her eyebrows. 'Did you? Because I wasn't sure myself.'

'Oh, twaddle!' Dot shrugged, turning back to her cake batter and expertly tipping it into a tin. 'I had every faith. So when d'you start?'

Walking towards the kettle that stood on top of the black-lead cooking range, Mary filled it with water, unable to wipe the smile from her face. 'Tomorrow at eight.'

Dot placed the tin in the steaming oven. 'What's your boss like?'

'She's nice,' Mary smiled, reaching for two cups from the little green dresser that stood next to the sink. 'Her name's Miss Wilson, but she told me to call her Flo.'

'Local girl, is she?'

Mary pursed her lips. 'I believe so. She lives in Islington.'

'Watch 'er,' Dot said, raising an eyebrow. 'Trust nobody north of the river.'

As the kettle whistled, Mary removed it from the heat and filled the teapot, watching the leaves swirl around the scalding water. 'I swear I will never understand this North–South London divide,' she chuckled. 'What does a river matter?'

'Spoken like someone who ain't a Londoner!' Dot grumbled, pouring milk into a striped creamer. 'Anyway, enough of all that now, tell me more about what happened today. I want to hear everything.'

Taking their tea, the two women sat either side of the small wooden table that overlooked the courtyard garden and Mary told her landlady all about Mrs Matravers and Flo.

'She seemed a bit unhappy that I didn't know one end of a needle from the other,' Mary said carefully, taking a sip of tea.

Dot frowned. 'But how can you know so little about stitching? Didn't you learn as a girl?'

'My parents didn't think I needed to know about anything practical,' Mary sighed. 'The only thing I was expected to do was marry well, so my sister Clarissa and I were taught French and German and the history of art by a governess, all in preparation for our debutante balls of course. All we were supposed to do after that was go to finishing school in Geneva.'

Dot arched an eyebrow. 'Fat lot of bleedin' good any of that'll do you when your rations have run out and you've got a filthy great hole in your stockings.'

'There was a reason why I took such great care of all my clothes in the ATS. I had a feeling if I started darning my socks I'd end up with a bigger hole than when I started.'

At that the two women broke into laughter before falling into a comfortable silence. Taking another gulp of her tea, Mary's eyes roamed hungrily over the dresser and its array of vibrantly colourful mismatched plates and cups.

'You've got quite a collection there.' Mary gestured towards the dresser.

Dot smiled. 'Full of memories, each and every one. That blue and white one was a present from George's parents when we wed.'

'Do you still see them?'

'No, they passed on a couple of years after he died,' Dot said sadly. 'I put it down to the shock of losing their only child. They adored the bones of him, just as I did. We were all heartbroken when we got word he was killed.'

'You must miss him,' Mary said quietly.

Dot's gaze met Mary's and she couldn't miss the look of anguish in the older woman's grey eyes. 'Every day,' the landlady replied sadly. 'It's been over twenty years but there isn't a day that passes when I don't think of him. Every one of those plates on that dresser over there carries its own story. Those white ones on the top shelf were wedding presents from my mum and dad, God rest their souls, and the striped creamer George gave me himself on the day of our marriage. Said it was to hold all the love we had for each other so every day we could always be sure to pour a little out.'

A surge of warmth flooded through Mary. 'Oh Dot, that's lovely.'

'It is, and my George was lovely,' Dot said firmly. 'The world lost a great man when he passed over. It still feels so cruel we only had two years of marriage together, and one of those saw him away at war.'

'I'm sorry.' Mary clasped her hand.

Dot wrapped her palm around Mary's. 'Don't be. He was a fine man; we crammed a lifetime of happiness into those years. My only regret is we never had children, but it was the price we paid.'

The sadness written across Dot's face was obvious.

Mary felt Dot's sorrow as keenly as if it were her own. 'I'm sure you would have made a lovely mum, Dot.'

The landlady blanched with surprise. 'Do you think so?'

'I know so,' Mary said softly. 'You're full of love and common sense.'

Patting her hand, Dot gave it a final squeeze before letting it go. 'That's a very kind thing to say. What about your mum? Was she like that before you had your falling out, if you don't mind me asking?'

Mary thought for a moment. Had her mother ever been full of love? 'When I was very little, but then the governesses came, and my sister and I grew up.'

'What's that got to do with it?' Dot looked puzzled.

'We hardly saw our parents after that. Perhaps before we went to bed when Nanny would send us downstairs to kiss our parents goodnight but other than that, very rarely,' Mary admitted.

Dot looked at her in shock. 'And that's the only time you saw your parents? No wonder you fell out! Some people don't deserve to have lovely children like you.'

Privately Mary agreed, but felt it was too early in their relationship to share her true feelings about her family and instead she smiled and took a sip of tea.

'Come on then, are you keeping me in suspenders all night or what?' Dot said, changing the subject.

Mary looked at her blankly, causing Dot to sigh. 'Liberty's! I mean I know you said you don't know one end of a needle from the other, but does that mean they're keeping you on?'

'Yes,' Mary nodded, setting her cup back down on the table. 'I've got a month's trial, but Flo wants to make sure I know everything. She started to teach me about patterns and different fabrics today but honestly, Dot, it was as though she was speaking a different language at times.'

Dot chuckled. 'I thought you were good at learning those.'

Mary rolled her eyes. 'Yes, but I got the feeling Flo was rather surprised I had been hired at all. I think she would rather they had employed someone who knew about the fabric trade.'

'You will,' Dot said kindly. 'You've got a month to prove yourself, and from what I've seen so far I can see you're bright, capable and a joy to have around. Give it time, love, work hard and I'm sure this Flo will soon come round.'

'Do you really think so?' Mary asked, visibly brightening at Dot's statement.

'I wouldn't have said it if I didn't think so,' Dot said firmly. 'Rome wasn't built in a day, and you won't become a seamstress overnight. Now, stop fishing for more compliments and tell me more about the store. Alice tells me nothing, says it's all too boring!'

Chuckling at her landlady's impatience, Mary told Dot everything, from the shabbiness of the staff quarters to her interview with Mrs Matravers and then on to her training with Flo and the beauty of the store itself.

'What I don't get is how Liberty's is still selling fabric?' Dot mused. 'I mean it's all rationed now, isn't it? You can't even get scraps from the remnants pile no more, otherwise the War Office'll have your guts for garters.'

'We're still relying on a lot of old stocks,' Mary explained. 'It takes over a week to make new fabric in Merton as it's all done by hand.'

When the timer for the oven pinged, Dot got to her feet and pulled the seed cake out. 'So even Liberty's is making do. Mind, those prints are ever so lovely. You can always spot when someone's wearing one.'

Mary nodded. 'They are, but now the War Office has reclaimed half the factory space down in Merton, and almost three-quarters of the boys have joined up.'

Dot shook her head. 'This war, robs you of everything.'

Mary sighed; she couldn't disagree. She knew that after everything she had seen during her time in the army, feeling sad about a lack of Liberty print may seem trivial, but it was trivial things that made many other things in life more bearable.

'I remember my George saved up to buy me a Liberty scarf years ago,' Dot said, carrying the cake across to the table and setting it between the two of them. 'We'd been up the Derby together in Epsom one year, and in those days Liberty's would always make scarves with the winner's name printed in the middle that day. I've still got it; it's beautiful.'

Mary looked across her teacup at Dot in surprise.

'Don't look at me like that, young lady,' Dot bristled, catching Mary's glance. 'My George had an eye for class, and we might not have had the money most Liberty customers have got, but we knew a pretty thing when we saw it.'

'I'm sorry,' Mary rushed. 'I didn't mean to offend you. Your eye for detail really is extraordinary.'

It was true. Dot might have been reliant on George's war pension and the money she made from letting out her rooms, but she was a master at achieving a lot with very little. The handmade cushion covers that sat on the settee in the parlour were made from a pair of old floral curtains, while the tea cosy had been knitted by Dot herself to match the colour of the lilies she had planted in the garden. The little touches Dot arranged made the tiny South London house feel like a home, and nothing was ever wasted.

'I'll let you off this once,' Dot grinned. 'Mostly because I'm hoping you might get me a bit of fabric at discount!'

'Why didn't you ask Alice? She's been there for ages now.'

'She's part-time so won't get such a big allowance,' Dot said wisely. 'Besides, she don't owe me one for her cheek like you do now!'

As Dot burst into laughter, Mary couldn't help joining in. The older woman's mirth was infectious.

'Anyway, did you see Alice after your interview?' Dot asked, bringing her giggles under control.

Mary nodded, just as the sounds of the front door being opened echoed through the hallway.

'Did she tell you?' Alice asked, flinging her bag in the corner with one hand and peeling off her coat with the other.

'She told me,' Dot replied. 'And I'm delighted for you girls. It'll give you the chance to get to know each other as you work together.'

'Well, it's more a case of Mary working for me,' Alice pointed out as she pulled up the chair and helped herself to tea and a slice of Dot's seed cake. 'Oh, this is so good,' she cried, devouring the moist, sweet cake. 'I dunno how you do it with no eggs or sugar.'

Dot tapped her nose and grinned. 'I have my ways. So are you going to be showing Mary the ropes or what, Alice?'

Alice nodded, crumbs falling from her mouth. 'Yes. Flo was very unimpressed I'd recommended someone with no sewing skills whatsoever.'

Mary coloured at the baldness of Alice's statement, waiting for her to continue.

'But I said she was all right really, and told Flo she was a quick learner.'

'Did you?' Mary looked at her in undisguised shock. Amazed that after all of Alice's warnings about letting her down she was now coming to her rescue.

'No need to look so surprised,' Alice grinned. 'I got you the interview so it's my neck on the line as much as yours if it doesn't work out, which it will of course. The one thing she did think was good was your accent.'

'What's her accent got to do with anything?' Dot asked, clearly bewildered.

'She sounds posh.' Alice brushed the crumbs from her lap. 'She don't have to put on no airs and graces like the rest of us.'

41

'It's not my bally fault I learned to speak the King's English,' Mary replied, her eyes flashing with mischief. 'Anyway, if it's that much of an advantage, that surely means I'll make more than you in commission.' With that she threw her head back and laughed at Alice's outraged expression.

'She's got a point there, darlin',' Dot chuckled. 'Might want to brush up your p's and q's!'

'I think it's mind your p's and q's,' Alice groaned.

Dot stood up to clear the plates. 'Well, whatever it is, you might want to start doing it, otherwise our Mary's going to wipe the floor with you.'

Alice threw Mary a mutinous look, which only made her laugh harder. 'Cheer up, Alice, you may not have my accent, but you do have a lovely husband. Any news from Luke?'

At the mention of her husband, Alice's face lit up and she scrabbled about in her pocket for a letter. Pulling it out of the Liberty print shift she wore with such pride, Alice held it aloft, her eyes brimming with excitement. 'He wrote to me this morning,' she squealed. 'He's coming back for Christmas. He'll be here in time to meet the baby.'

Mary clapped her hands in delight at her friend's good news. 'That's wonderful. How long for?'

Alice rubbed her growing belly affectionately. 'Just seventy-two hours. But it will be wonderful to have him home, so we can be a family, even if it is for a short time.'

'He'll be over the moon hisself!' Dot smiled. 'What a Christmas present.'

'It's the best present in the world,' laughed Alice.

'Where did you and Luke meet?' Mary asked, brushing the crumbs from her top.

'At the Coronet,' Alice smiled bashfully. 'I was with my friend Maureen, and was a farthing short of the cinema seat.

Luke was behind and offered to give it to me, and, well, we've never been apart since then until this flippin' war.'

As Alice's face darkened, Dot reached out and squeezed her hand. 'We're all making sacrifices, sweetheart. Make the most of today because we don't know what tomorrow's got in store.'

Alice patted Dot's hand gratefully. 'Ignore me. My moods are all over the shop at the minute. I blame Mrs Matravers giving me the work of six members of staff instead of one.'

'We've all got our crosses to bear, Alice love,' Dot went on. 'But anyway, it seems to me that we've all had some good news today.'

'What good news have you had?' Mary asked.

'I've got a new job myself,' Dot said proudly.

'Have you?' Alice exclaimed. 'You never said.'

Dot wiped her hands on her floral apron and shrugged. 'It's not a proper job, not like you girls. It's just one morning a week down the hall on the Old Kent Road, giving sewing lessons. It's part of the WVS; some of the girls need a bit of encouragement, so I volunteered.'

'But that's brilliant,' Mary smiled. 'We're all in the fabric trade now in one way or another.'

'Just as long as you don't want to give Mary any more sewing tips,' Alice teased. 'Flo had a devil of a job even getting her to hold a pair of scissors the right way round.'

Mary's eyes widened in mock horror. 'Alice—'

'Now, now, that's enough, the pair of you,' Dot said, cutting Mary off before the two launched into a row. 'As we've all had a good day, how do you girls feel about celebrating?'

Alice and Mary exchanged looks of surprise. 'I don't know, Dot. I mean I don't want to feel dreadful tomorrow for my first proper day,' Mary protested.

'Don't be daft,' Dot said, raising her eyes heavenwards. 'I'm suggesting a night up the pictures, not a night tripping the light fantastic. It's so rare we get any good news I think we should celebrate.'

Watching the light begin to dip behind the clouds, Mary could see everyone start to shut their blackout blinds. She knew the older woman was right, there was so little to celebrate during these difficult times, even the minor moments of joy deserved to be marked. Turning back to Dot, she grinned. 'Why not?'

'Grand,' Alice said, rubbing her hands together with glee. 'I think *Atlantic Ferry* is on at the Coronet.'

'Come on then, girls. What better way to celebrate Mary's success than with a decent film! My treat.'

With that the trio of women descended into the London night to toast their success and look forward to the promise of new beginnings.

Chapter Five

During Mary's first few days at Liberty's she felt as though her feet hardly touched the ground. There was so much to learn, there were some days she felt as though her head would never stop spinning.

Each day she would rise at dawn, wash and dress, then sit down to a breakfast of porridge made with water to power her through the day. This morning marked her first full week in the job and Mary was delighted to find each day was becoming easier as she slowly started to understand the fabric department.

Despite her initial warnings, Flo had patiently shown Mary the ropes, taking the time to instruct her so thoroughly that Mary had treated herself to a notepad and pen from the gift department so she could write everything down. She had lived and breathed the world of textiles, and with Flo's help she had learned how to read a pattern, along with how to cut each piece of fabric so nothing was wasted. Although many of the Liberty's customers weren't as restricted by money as others, they still had to contend with rations just like everyone else. With one yard of woollen cloth costing three coupons and all other fabric two coupons, every inch of material had to be accounted for, and Flo insisted that ensuring there was no waste was now the most important skill of a fabric-cutter.

Consequently Mary had yet to find herself on the shop floor serving customers. Instead Flo had marched her off to the fabric stockroom and told Mary to familiarise herself with each pattern.

Alice too had been kind, Mary thought as she got off the Tube at Oxford Circus and walked down Argyll Street. Turning her face towards the late September sunshine, she felt a flush of pleasure at the unexpected burst of warmth. Winter was just around the corner and although the mornings were a little lighter now double daylight saving time had decreased by an hour, Mary knew darker mornings were just around the corner. Consequently, she had learned to make the most of the little things and as her thoughts turned to her fellow lodger she did just that. Mary knew she hadn't earned Alice's trust yet, but Alice had still taken time to give Mary clear instructions, explain about the way each fabric was stored and priced, as well as taken her through the rigorous admin system. Mary realised there was still a long way to go before she proved herself, but now, as she walked past the famous London Palladium, she couldn't help feel a surge of excitement. Last night Flo had said she was ready to start serving customers and by the time she reached the staff entrance of Liberty's she was feeling relaxed yet ready to work.

Leaving her jacket and bag in the staffroom, Mary made her way to the fabric department, smiling as she saw the chandelier that hung from the atrium twinkle in the early morning light. She didn't think she would ever get tired of the sight of it, no matter how long she worked here.

'Morning, Flo,' Mary called, spotting her superior polishing the counter until she could see her face in it.

Flo rewarded her with a genuine smile. 'Mary, love. What are you doing here at this time?'

'Thought I'd get in early as today's my first real day.'

'Well, that's very good,' Flo said, narrowing her eyes. 'But you do know there's no overtime, don't you?'

Mary nodded, aghast her new boss thought she was expecting extra payment. 'I know. I'm here because I want to be, Flo. I want to show you how much I've learned.'

Flo's face softened and her green eyes twinkled with apology. 'Sorry. That's very good of you. I know you've had a lot to learn this week, but I'm delighted with your progress. How about I make us a nice cup of tea while we get set up here?'

Mary looked at Flo in alarm. 'But we're not allowed food or drink on the shop floor.'

Flo chuckled. 'Well, I won't tell if you don't. Finish straightening the zip packets under the counter for me, will you?' Nodding, she stalked off up the stairs to the staffroom. Less than ten minutes later she was back with a steaming cup in each hand.

'Don't say a word to nobody,' she said in hushed tones. 'Mrs Matravers will have our guts for garters if she catches us.'

'Thanks.' Mary took the cup gratefully and savoured the illegal sip. 'I thought it was just me that was terrified of her.'

Flo grimaced as she took her own illicit swallow. 'Mrs Matravers puts the fear of God into all of us. She had the last girl we employed to work in this department sacked because she said she talked to the customers too loudly.'

'What?' Mary wailed, a feeling of hopelessness flooding through her. 'Then I've got no chance.'

Flo shook her head. 'The thing with Mrs Matravers is her bark is worse than her bite. Yes she puts us all on edge, but she does respect hard work, and that's what she'll like about you. I have to admit, Mary, that I still have reservations about taking you on but you've worked your socks off since you arrived, and I'm proud of you.'

Happiness flowed through Mary as she gave Flo a shy smile. 'Thank you.'

'Nothing to thank me for,' Flo said matter-of-factly, 'I can see you've made an effort and I'm prepared to give you a chance.'

'So, what else can I do?' Mary asked, unable to stop grinning.

'Enjoy your tea before Mrs Matravers starts her morning checks,' Flo chuckled. 'Didn't they teach you to enjoy your breaks when you could in the army?'

'Well, yes, but I came here early to make sure I was prepared,' she said, her tone anxious.

'Things are going well, Mary. I know you're on a month's trial and you want to prove yourself, but I want you to relax for five minutes while there's nobody here and tell me about yourself.'

Mary felt the flash of alarm she usually experienced whenever anybody started asking personal questions, in fear she would give herself away. 'What do you mean?'

'Just that now's a good time for us to get to know each other,' Flo carried on. 'You've been so busy down in the stockrooms that we've hardly had a chance to chat. Now, I know you live in South London with Alice, and you used to be in the ATS.'

'That's right,' Mary said tightly.

'So what brings you to Liberty's?' Flo pressed. 'I don't mean to sound nosey but I'd have thought a girl like you wouldn't need to work. Can't you just return to your life of balls and shopping, find yourself a rich husband?'

Mary smiled ruefully. 'I haven't led that life for a long time. And in my experience all the rich men wanting a wife are dreadful bores.'

Flo threw her head back and roared with laughter. 'You're a tonic, Mary. Have you got a sweetheart?'

Mary shook her head. 'Not me. I've been out to the odd dance and the pictures of course with men, but I never met anyone I wanted to marry, much to my parents' annoyance.'

Flo frowned. 'Why would they be annoyed?'

'Because they spent a fortune on my debutante ball and I was more interested in enjoying myself with my friends than in finding a husband,' Mary chuckled. 'All the men I was introduced to weren't for me.'

'And what about in the army?' Flo pressed.

Mary felt the hairs on the back of her neck rise, before deftly shaking her head. 'I was always far too busy. But what about you?' she asked, hurriedly changing the subject. 'Do you have a sweetheart?'

At the question Flo lit up. 'I've been with my Neil since we were children. We lived next door to each other.'

'That's lovely,' Mary exclaimed. 'What does he do? Has he been called up?'

Flo nodded. 'Navy. I'm so very proud of him. I'm still dreading getting that telegram though, you know – the one stamped by the War Office. I just keep praying he'll be one of the lucky ones and come back to me safe and sound if and when all this is over.'

Mary nodded, knowing full well what Flo meant. Her friend Kitty had gone through just the same thing when her fiancé Joe was killed in the navy. It had been the reason she had joined up and Mary had always admired her bravery.

'Still, you just keep going, don't you?' Flo continued. 'What else can you do?'

'You live with your aunt, don't you?' Mary put in.

'That's right,' Flo said. 'My mum disappeared shortly after I was born and my father and I don't keep in touch. I keep trying to persuade my aunt to come along to our stitching nights. Has Alice told you about those?'

Mary grimaced. 'Rose mentioned something.'

'They're lovely. Each week a few of us get together here after work, sew something, drink tea and have a natter,' Flo explained, ignoring the look of horror on Mary's face. 'You would be more than welcome. Especially now you've learned one end of a needle from the other.'

'It sounds really nice,' Mary said, nibbling her bottom lip. 'But I don't think I've learned enough yet.'

Flo narrowed her eyes. 'You're a Liberty girl now, Mary. I rather think it might be a good idea for you to give the stitching night a try.'

The look of displeasure on Flo's face wasn't lost on Mary. Something told her that if she wanted her month's trial period to continue then she needed to show willing.

'Actually, Flo, you're right,' she said evenly. 'My landlady is an excellent seamstress and I have no doubt she would love to show me a few things. Besides, the stitching nights sound like a good way to improve my skills.'

'Wonderful.' Flo smiled, the warmth returning to her green eyes. 'Who knows, you might even enjoy it.'

'I might,' Mary chuckled. 'I didn't enjoy it in the army, but then as children nobody taught us how to sew. Daddy always used to say it was a bally good job our daily Mrs Evans could sew a button on my things as without her no doubt I'd walk around naked.'

Putting her cup under the counter, Flo fixed Mary with a look of curiosity. 'Do you see much of your parents?'

Mary shook her head. Draining her own cup she put it next to Flo's. 'No, they're up in Cheshire.'

'You could visit, you know,' Flo said helpfully. 'We could always pop your weekly half-day on to your Saturday so you could get up there for the night. I'm sure your parents must miss you.'

'Thanks, Flo, but that's not necessary. My parents don't want anything to do with me. They told me so themselves, so there's not an awful lot of point going to see them,' Mary said in a neutral tone. She hadn't meant to say so much about her family so soon, but despite Flo's no-nonsense nature, Mary felt she could confide in her, especially after Flo had been so candid about her own family. Glancing across she could see that Flo wanted to ask more but was prevented from doing so by the appearance of Mr Button, the new store manager, who was making his way towards their department.

'Everything shipshape and Bristol fashion, Miss Wilson?' he enquired.

'Tip top, Mr B,' Flo replied in a plummy tone Mary recognised as her sales voice. 'Just finished checking the departmental sales and about to check the stock list, all with Miss Holmes-Fotherington's help of course.'

Mr Button, a kindly older gentleman who was unofficially the chairman's right-hand man, smiled warmly at the two women. 'Excellent. As I'm still finding my feet myself, I had a feeling I could rely on you.'

Mary had discovered on her first day that Mr Button had only joined Liberty's a week earlier from another department store in Kent. Since his arrival everyone had wanted to put on a good show as he always seemed so warm and approachable.

'Of course,' Flo beamed. 'You can always rely on us, sir.'

Mr Button's eyes twinkled as he turned to Mary. 'And how are you getting on, young lady? Miss Wilson here showing you the ropes, I hope?'

'Absolutely, sir,' Mary said sincerely. 'She's an excellent NCO.'

'That's right, I heard you were in the army,' Mr Button chuckled. 'Still finding it hard to lose the lingo, eh?'

Mary's cheeks flamed red with embarrassment at her mistake. 'Sorry, sir.'

'Not at all.' Mr Button smiled sympathetically. 'I know I had a terrible time of it when I left. In fact I often used to call my wife "sergeant", which drove her potty.'

Flo grinned. 'I can imagine. What's her real name sir?'

'It was Ethel,' Mr Button said sadly. 'She died last year in the raids.'

'Sir, I am so sorry.' Flo's hands flew to her mouth in horror. 'I shouldn't have said anything.'

'Don't be silly,' Mr Button said kindly. 'You weren't to know. It is a shame she's not still alive to see me working here though. She always did have a soft spot for Liberty's.'

'I expect she loved their prints,' Mary said warmly.

Sadness clouded Mr Button's copper eyes. 'She certainly did. She bought her wedding-dress material here. She was a vision when we married and said she wanted to pass it on to our daughter when she wed. Sadly we were never blessed with children either, so I kept her wedding dress. I couldn't bear to part with it after she passed away.'

'Well, I think that's a lovely memento to keep hold of,' Flo said smoothly.

'A beautiful reminder of a lovely memory,' Mary put in.

Mr Button smiled as he composed himself. 'Thank you girls. Now, I didn't come down here to give you my life story, I came here to let you know that we're expecting Princess Valentina today. I know that none of you are strangers to royal visits, but please do ensure you give her the very finest of Liberty welcomes.'

Flo nodded her head enthusiastically. 'Of course we will, sir. Is there anything else you would like us to know?'

'Nothing at all, my dear. Deirdre has completed her floor walk, but Mrs Matravers will be down presently to complete her final morning checks. I'm sure if she has any more information to impart regarding the princess's visit she will let you know.' Mr Button beamed once more before making his way to the jewellery department to pass on the good news.

Once Mr Button was safely out of earshot, Flo sank her head into her hands, all airs and graces gone in an instant. 'This can't be 'appening.'

'What's wrong?' Mary asked, her face a picture of concern.

Flo lifted her head to face Mary. 'Princess Valentina, she's half Russian, half Georgian, and a daughter of some Eastern nobleman. She lives over here and she's lovely. But she adores the Liberty prints, Mary, loves them.'

'Surely that's a good thing?' Mary said, her eyes narrowing in confusion.

Flo cast her gaze heavenwards. 'Ordinarily yes, but we're in wartime. We can't sell rationed goods to those that aren't British and the only fabric available off ration now is blackout material. I don't think she'll want to leave here with armfuls of that.'

'She'll understand, I'm sure,' Mary persisted as Alice stalked across the floor to join them.

'I don't know,' Flo sighed. 'I didn't ever want to be in the position of having to say no to a princess.'

Inspiration surged through Mary. 'Well, how about we hide some of the fabric then?'

Flo and Alice exchanged puzzled looks.

'Hide what where?' Alice asked eventually.

'Some of the more precious rolls of fabric.' Mary shrugged. 'That way there's less for her to fall in love with.'

'You know, that's not a bad idea.' Flo's eyes danced with merriment. 'We'll have a word with Larry, ask if we can hide some of the rolls in the menswear stockroom just until she's been.'

'Who's Larry?' Mary quizzed.

'Number two in menswear and also does all the deliveries for his sins,' Flo replied. 'Does anything for anyone and a general lifesaver.'

'Pssst, look out, Mabel's about,' Alice hissed.

Spinning around, Mary saw Mrs Matravers stalking towards them, her heels clacking across the wooden floor, closely followed by Rose.

'I take it Mr Button's told you about our special visitor?' she barked sharply, her dark eyes glaring at the girls, not waiting for an answer. 'I'm sending Rose here down to work with you, because as you know the princess does rather favour our Liberty prints and we expect her to want to spend a lot of time in this particular department.'

As she pushed Rose towards Flo, Mrs Matravers smiled before adding, 'I myself will also be on hand to ensure the princess's visit goes smoothly.'

'Wonderful,' Flo simpered again.

Once Mrs Matravers was out of sight, Rose, Mary and Alice crowded around Flo.

'Oh Gawd,' Rose groaned. 'Princess Valentina is going to be so upset.'

Mary laughed as Flo quickly outlined their plan to remove much of the stock. Together the girls made a start on the stack of Sungleam fabrics, prints made from a rayon and wool blend. Mary knew these fabrics were so popular that before the war when stock was plentiful they had been given a mini-department in their own right.

Just over twenty minutes later, with more than a dozen fabrics safely stored in the hands of Larry, who thankfully had asked no questions, Flo looked a lot calmer.

'Thanks, girls.' She smiled, straightening the display so that it looked just as inviting as it had before half the stock had been removed. 'I hate doing things like that. I dread to think what Mr Liberty hisself would say, but it's for the greater good.'

'Definitely,' Alice agreed, standing next to Flo and admiring the rack. 'You know, unless you knew how many rolls we stocked here, you'd never know we'd half-inched some.'

Mary chuckled. 'It's one of those occasions where you could say the war has come in useful for once. I heard Mr Button only the other day telling the silver department to spread the goods out to make it look as though we stocked more. The last thing anyone wants is to go the way of D H Evans and start closing floors.'

Running a hand across the counter to check for any speck of dust she might have missed, Flo sighed. 'It's all so sad. This store was the place people visited for all the beautiful things. Now we've got to pretend we've still got all the beautiful things with clever display work.'

'Everyone's in the same boat though,' Rose put in. 'Selfridges has got less than nothing, yet they're pretending for all the world stocks are high.'

'We're the only big store that hasn't been hit,' Flo mused. 'There are times when I wonder why.'

Alice giggled. 'P'raps the Jerries have got a passion for arts and crafts like the rest of us.'

'Or leather goods,' Rose said, joining in with the joke. 'Mrs Matravers says that it's only the leather goods department that's keeping us open. All the fine ladies want a leather bag, and Liberty's is still the place to come.'

Flo glanced at the clock. 'We're opening in two minutes. Mary, have you got your sales book?'

As Mary nodded, a loud bell sounded, signalling the store was open for business. Immediately the first of the day's customers began to walk through the doors and Mary watched with interest.

The first thing that struck her was how the customers had changed. When she was a child visiting the store with her mother, she had seen many girls in their twenties flocking to Liberty. Now the place seemed populated with women her mother's age. Mary knew that was probably because most of the girls her age had joined up. As usual whenever she allowed her thoughts to return to her ATS days she felt a pang of guilt she wasn't there serving alongside her friends. Mary had been good at her job and had loved her time as a driver. She had never regretted her decision to run away from home and join up. Her time in the army had been a life lesson, a greater lesson than any she had received from the endless chain of governesses that had swept through the house to teach her about languages and the arts.

But now that was all over, because of one careless, heartbreaking mistake. A mistake that had not only cost her the job she loved but the love of her family too. Watching a customer walk towards her, she caught Flo's eye signalling encouragement and Mary squared her shoulders ready to flash her best smile. There would be no more mistakes, she resolved; from now on Liberty's was her world and she would give it her all.

Chapter Six

It wasn't until past lunchtime that the infamous princess walked through the doors of Liberty's. It was the dogs Mary saw first, six beagles stalking their way through the entrance of the great mock-Tudor store as if they owned it. Then there was a hushed silence as each customer took in the sight of royalty walking amongst them.

Watching agog from her position behind the glass counter, the low autumn sunlight streaming through the windows, Mary saw the princess walk across the store and stand in the atrium, right underneath the glittering chandelier, pausing to admire her surroundings. Mary found she couldn't take her eyes from her. Unlike any minor royal Mary had encountered in the past, Princess Valentina had no entourage and was dressed simply for the English autumnal weather in an understated navy tea dress and jacket. Tall and willowy, with her jet-black hair swept up into an elegant bun on the top of her head, she stole the show as if she were the leading lady in a Russian ballet, Mary thought.

As Princess Valentina fussed over her dogs, Mr Button sprang into action, jovially welcoming her to the store.

'And you've brought all your dogs too, I see,' he enthused. 'How splendid.'

'Not all my dogs.' The princess chuckled good-naturedly. 'I have another four at home.'

If Mr Button was surprised he didn't show it. 'Well, we are extremely honoured to have you and your wonderful hounds here this afternoon. Now, may I ask your highness where you would like to go first?'

'Fabrics are the real reason I am here. But I think I should like to see the carpets first.'

'Of course, of course,' he said delightedly. 'If your highness would like to follow me, I can assure you we have some very beautiful rugs for your delectation.'

'I know you will.' The princess smiled dreamily. 'Just visiting your beautiful store makes me happy.'

As the girls watched Mr Button lead the princess towards the staircase, Mrs Matravers bounded towards them.

'I've just come to check the fabrics are all in order,' she snapped. 'As you know this is the princess's favourite department and I want to make sure you girls have got this place looking first rate.'

'Of course, Mrs Matravers,' Flo replied smoothly. 'We are more than ready for Princess Valentina's visit.'

The deputy manager cast her gaze across the rack of materials, a look of bewilderment on her face. 'What is the matter with these rolls of fabric? They don't look right.'

Flo rushed to Mrs Matravers' side, and steered her back towards the rolls of fabric that hadn't been tampered with. 'We were just having a little play with the display, weren't we, ladies? Wanted to get everything just right.'

Mrs Matravers stepped towards the rolls and ran her hand over the fabric as if searching for something she wasn't yet sure of. Finally she seemed satisfied. 'Very well then,' she replied. 'Be ready for when the princess calls.'

In fact the Russian princess didn't visit the fabric department until after four o'clock.

'Places, everyone,' Flo called as she saw the princess approach the department.

'Your royal highness,' she said as Mrs Matravers signalled her to come forward and greet the princess.'Welcome to the fabric department. How can we help you today?'

Princess Valentina beamed at Flo and squeezed her hand. 'My darling girl, you are so lucky to work here every day surrounded by such beauty.'

'Thank you, your highness. We think we're rather lucky as well,' Flo smiled, leading the princess to the remaining rolls of fabric on display.

The princess gasped in delight as she ran her fingers across each one. 'These are so beautiful.'

The girls said nothing as they watched the princess select a paisley pattern that Mary knew had always been a bestseller in the scarf department.

'How much for this?' she asked.

'I'm afraid you can't buy that,' Flo muttered desperately.

The princess's mouth fell open before she recovered herself. 'I'm sorry?'

'I said it's not for sale,' Flo told her again, looking for all the world as though she wanted the ground to swallow her up completely.

'But why?' she asked, her dark eyes filled with hurt and confusion. 'Why do you not wish to sell me these things?'

Flo looked at the rest of the fabric girls in desperation and Mary's heart went out to her. She could see that her boss was struggling to say no to a princess, and Mary bit her lip wondering if she should intervene. She had been to enough debutante balls in her lifetime to know how to handle nobility, but equally she was well aware that there were over two weeks left of her month's trial and she didn't want to do anything to jeopardise her future at Liberty's before it had a chance to begin.

Anxiously she glanced at Mrs Matravers, and saw with relief she was about to come to Flo's rescue. 'Well, it's not that Miss Wilson here doesn't want to sell you these very fine fabrics, of course we do, it's just not possible.'

Once again Princess Valentina looked bemused, glancing from Mrs Matravers to Flo, both of whom by now were unsure what to say next. In that moment, Mary felt compelled to say something.

'Actually, I'm dreadfully sorry, your royal highness,' she put in politely. 'Unfortunately, these are rationed goods, and we cannot sell them to overseas customers. It's Liberty's policy, you see.'

As Mary finished her speech, Mrs Matravers' eyes flashed with anger as she glared at the store's latest recruit and then turned back to the princess. 'Please do accept my apologies for Miss Holmes-Fotherington's inexcusable outburst,' she began, only for the princess to raise her hand as if to halt Mrs Matravers in her tracks.

'This is quite all right,' she said quietly. 'Miss Holmes-Fotherington was right to tell me. Of course I will not buy these things. I understand rationing perfectly well and would have no desire to take rations.'

As Mary and Flo exchanged nervous looks, Mary mouthed sorry at her new boss. She could have kicked herself for making such a stupid mistake. Mrs Matravers had warned her mistakes would not be tolerated and here she was making the colossal one of speaking without permission to nobility on her very first day on the shop floor.

Mrs Matravers eventually spoke. 'I'm delighted you see it that way, your royal highness. However, Miss Holmes-Fotherington should have known her place and not addressed you when she had not been given permission. She will be reprimanded later. Please accept my humble apologies.'

The princess shook her head. 'There is no apology or reprimand necessary. Miss Holmes-Fotherington was just giving me the answer to my question and I am grateful. Now, I will bid you farewell, but thank you for letting me look at your beautiful fabrics and I will be back soon to take another look.'

With that the girls curtseyed as the princess left the department, guided by a scowling Mrs Matravers. Once they were safely out of earshot the girls turned to Mary.

'Well done,' Flo beamed. 'I had no idea how to tell Princess Valentina she couldn't buy anything. Thank you so much for knowing just what to say.'

'I should cocoa,' Alice gasped. 'You got us all out of a hole speaking up when you did.'

Just then the unmistakeable sound of Mrs Matravers' heels clacking determinedly back across the wooden floor sounded above the gentle hum of shoppers. As the deputy manager came into view, Mary could see her face was puce with anger and she had a horrible feeling the woman's rage was about to be directed at her.

'Mary Holmes-Fotherington,' Mrs Matravers hissed. 'A word, now.'

Without waiting for an answer, the Liberty stalwart gripped Mary's arm and steered her down the stairs and towards the stockroom. Slamming the door behind her, Mrs Matravers looked at Mary as if she was about to pounce.

'I ain't never been so embarrassed,' she began, her plummy tones disappearing, only to be replaced by broad cockney ones. 'You ain't been here five minutes and you got bleedin' royalty eating out your hands making me look a prize fool! I been here twenty years, had to work me way up the ladder, show the Libertys I was good enough to be here! I've worked hard where I am; even when war broke out and I was promoted well above my station, I knew they'd done it because they trusted me. But today all

61

that was gone up in smoke, the moment you spoke to that princess.'

Mary's eyes widened at all her manager had said. 'Mrs Matravers, I can assure you I meant no disrespect. I didn't mean to speak out of turn, I just wanted to help. Flo and Alice, well, they said I had just helped them out of a hole.'

'My point exactly.' Mrs Matravers' steely grey eyes flashed with anger. 'The moment that princess told you that you wouldn't be reprimanded after your insolence, all my authority was gone. The staff won't respect me now. They'll respect you though, with your posh accent and silver spoon sticking out your gob. You've got the ear of the great and the good; the only ear I got's riddled with tinnitus.'

'Mrs Matravers, please—' Mary tried again, only for the manager to cut her off.

'Listen to me, girl,' she thundered. 'I got the measure of you. I'd sack anyone else for their outburst earlier but you, well, you've probably got the whole Liberty family eating out the palm of your hand. Just know this: I've got my eye on you. I'm going to make it my business to find out the real reason you were flung out the army and when I do, I'll make sure everyone here knows about it; then you'll be out of here faster than you can say Princess Valentina.'

With that Mrs Matravers flounced out of the stockroom. As the door slammed behind her, Mary sank miserably to the cold stone floor and let the tears fall. It seemed that she was destined to a life of making mistakes and paying heavily for them. The new start she hoped Liberty's would bring was feeling even more tainted than ever.

Chapter Seven

That night, Mary went to bed early to try and shake off the awful mood she found herself in. Yet, as she tossed and turned, she couldn't stop going over her altercation with Mrs Matravers.

It was all such a mess, she thought miserably, running her hands over the photograph she kept of her parents beside her bed. Even though they no longer wanted anything to do with her, she found she missed them dreadfully. From nowhere the events that had led up to their estrangement flooded her mind and even though it broke her heart to do so, her thoughts turned to her final day in the army seven months ago. It had, after all, been the trigger for the situation she found herself in now.

At the time she had been stationed in Camberley. Wearing her grease-smeared khaki overalls, servicing a Lister truck that would be leaving as part of a convoy later that day, she had been bent over the engine when a brisk tap on her shoulder had made her jump. Spinning around, her heart still pounding, she had come face to face with a grim-faced volunteer.

'Sergeant Haines wants to see you immediately.'

'Any idea what it's about?' Mary asked, a feeling of dread enveloping her.

The withering look the volunteer shot her was all she needed to know. And so she had slowly walked up the hill to the office where the sergeant had read out her list of offences as if she were no more than a common criminal.

'Anything to add?' Sergeant Haines had sneered when he had finished.

'No, sir,' Mary had replied in as dignified a fashion as she could with tears streaming down her cheeks.

'Then you're dismissed immediately. You have an hour to gather your belongings and go.'

With that Mary had turned and fled from the office, running at such speed she had tripped and fallen down the muddy bank, scuffing her knee and ripping her overalls.

She had packed her belongings into her kitbag and was marched from the barracks exactly one hour later. Standing at Camberley railway station with a rail warrant for her return to Cheshire, Mary had hoped her parents would be glad to see her. Yet, as she boarded the train bound for London, she knew deep in her heart that would not be the case. Less than seventy-two hours after returning home, she was proved right. With her parents' fury still ringing in her ears, she had boarded another train that would be just one of many modes of transport that would eventually take her to Ceylon.

Now, the tears streamed down her cheeks just as furiously as they had when she had been dismissed. She pulled the candlewick bedspread up around her chin, the feel of it offering her comfort as it had been a present from Dot, who had pressed it into her hands for the colder nights when she moved in.

Just then there was a knock at the door, and Dot's beaming face appeared holding a cup of tea, closely followed by Alice. 'We thought you might like a brew, love,' Dot said, walking into the room and handing Mary a steaming cup.

'Thanks. That was very kind of you,' Mary said in surprise, sitting up and taking a grateful sip. There were times, she thought, when there was nothing a cup of tea couldn't solve.

Alice sank down heavily on the end of the bed and rubbed her stomach. 'You all right after Mrs Matravers chewed your ear off? We could hear her shouting at you from the shop floor.'

Mary nodded. 'Yes of course. It was my own fault. I shouldn't have said anything to the princess.'

'You were only trying to help,' Alice said gruffly. 'She had no business giving you a dressing down like that.'

'Don't worry about old Mabel,' Dot added. 'She'll come round.'

'I hope so.' Mary sniffed, hoping her landlady and colleague couldn't see her tears in the night-time gloom. 'All I can do to gain Mrs Matravers' trust is to continue working hard, and hope that helps adjust her view of me a little.'

Sitting on the edge of the mattress, Dot nodded. 'I'm sure it will in time, love. You've just got to give Mabel a bit of room. She's got her own crosses to bear.'

'How do you mean?' Mary's eyes danced with curiosity in the half-light.

'Well, you know I told you how she had to bring up her brother when her mother left?'

Mary nodded as Dot continued. 'What I didn't tell you is that Mrs Matravers' weak spot is her husband Alf, a good-for-nothing who used to run the Elephant and Castle pub 'til a few years back. He was thrown out by the brewery for thieving, but our Mabel loves the bones of him, which is just as well as he lost his job up the cinema as an usher not so long ago.'

'What for?' Mary asked, taking another sip of tea.

'Thieving, just like her father lost his job down the docks years before,' Alice said brusquely.

'That's terrible.'

'It is,' Dot sighed. 'Poor woman, she's terrified now Liberty's will sack her as well for some reason, though why

65

they would when she works herself into the ground I don't know. She hasn't half gone through it, mind. It's a wonder her brother turned out so well. David's a doctor, would you believe. Works in Guy's Hospital nearby, another one that's worked his socks off.'

'My word,' Mary breathed, trying to make sense of all Dot had just told her. 'But why hasn't Mrs Matravers' husband been called up?'

'He's too sick,' Alice grimaced. 'He's eight years older than her anyway at forty-four but I heard he's got a gammy leg from the last war.'

'So she's the sole earner for the family once again?' Mary sighed in understanding.

'Got it in one.' Dot smiled, patting Mary's hand. 'She might have had a few difficulties in the family but she's a grafter is old Mabel. She brought up David on her own while holding down a job and running a home. She respects hard work.'

Mary nodded, remembering how Flo had said much the same earlier. 'I'll remember that.'

'Just because she raised her little brother on her own doesn't give her an excuse to be a tyrant,' Alice grumbled. 'I may not want Mary making a show of me, but she did nothing wrong earlier.'

Now Dot patted Alice's hand. 'We know that, Alice love. I'm just saying Mabel probably doesn't think about Mary having crosses of her own that brought her here. All she thinks when she sees Mary is a posh little madam that was born into a world of privilege and doesn't know the meaning of hard graft. We know she's in the wrong, love, and deep down I expect Mabel does too. Don't be too hard on yourself. I expect Mabel will forget all about this in the morning.'

'You mean once she's given Alf his beer money for the night,' Alice glowered, before rubbing her eyes with the heels of her hands. 'Sorry, ignore me, girls. I'm tired, and Joy came in to see me at work today wanting cash herself.'

'Cheeky little brat,' Dot breathed. 'I thought she had a new job up Claridge's.'

'She has.' Alice sat upright, trying to get comfortable despite her ever-expanding belly. 'But she hasn't had her first wage packet yet. Asked me for a few bob to tide her over.'

'I hope you sent her away with a flea in her ear,' Dot said, narrowing her eyes.

Alice looked at her hands. 'You know I can't do that. I'm all she's got.'

'Who's Joy?' Mary asked, only for Alice to flinch. 'Sorry, I didn't mean to poke my nose in.'

Alice ran a hand through her hair and smiled at Mary. 'You didn't. Joy is my sister, though really I was more of a mother to her. I raised her after our mum died in child-birth and our dad went off to America. He was a common criminal and a lifetime of thieving and hanging about with gangs eventually caught up with him. Let's just say he had to disappear quickly ...'

'Alice, I'm sorry,' Mary whispered.

'Not your fault,' Alice sighed.

'Well, Joy's young yet,' Dot consoled, seeing that Alice was becoming quite upset. 'She may change her ways now she's got a job.'

Alice let out a snort of disgust. 'She was thieving at seven, and I bet she's still thieving now.'

'It's like a sickness with her,' Dot mused. 'But you've got to think of your own family now. Whatever would your Luke say if he knew you was giving out your hard-earned to that good-for-nothing sister of yours.'

Alice pinched the bridge of her nose, and to Mary's dis-may she saw tears stream like rivers down her face. She had never seen Alice cry and honestly thought she never would. Alice seemed untouchable somehow, as if she were so strong she were made of iron.

'I miss Luke and I just wish he was here! I know it's self-ish, I know women up and down the country are expecting like me and their husbands aren't by their sides either, but there are days when it all just feels too much, especially when Joy comes calling.'

Mary couldn't help herself. She quickly got out of bed to slip an arm around Alice. 'You need to let it all out, you'll feel so much better.'

To her surprise, Alice leaned into her and sobbed her heart out. Exchanging worried looks with Dot over the top of Alice's head, Mary stayed there, pleased to finally be able to help. After a few minutes, Alice sat up and dried her eyes with a hankie Dot pressed into her hands.

'I'm sorry, Mary, I've soaked your nightie,' Alice said with a watery smile.

Mary shrugged. 'I think that's the least of our worries at the moment, don't you?'

'I should say so,' Dot chuckled. 'Some of us have to go to a stitching night tomorrow and don't know one end of a needle from another.'

At the reminder, Mary groaned and sank her head into her hands. 'Don't remind me. I want to show Flo that I'm a team player, but honestly I think it might do me more harm than good if she sees me actually attempting to sew.'

'I've been thinking about that,' Alice said, getting to her feet. 'How would you like to join us tomorrow, Dot? You could give Mary here some pointers.'

Dot's face flushed with pleasure as she stood up beside Alice. 'I'd love to. I've been getting on ever so well teaching those youngsters how to sew up the Old Kent Road.

I'm sure I can show Mary a thing or two and it'll be nice to meet Flo.'

A rush of gratitude surged through Mary. 'Would you really do that for me, Dot? I've been worrying about it all day.'

'You mustn't. I know you've only got a month to prove yourself, but I could show you a few stitches, help you find your feet.'

'That's very kind of you, Dot.' Mary smiled appreciatively.

'It's nothing,' Alice replied, as she and Dot waved her gratitude away.

But as they wished her goodnight and left her alone with her thoughts, Mary hugged her knees to her chest, a feeling of contentment beginning to flood through her bones. This was the first kindness she had been shown in a long time, and Mary fervently hoped it was a sign of better things to come.

Chapter Eight

Despite her talk with Dot and Alice, Mary still felt nervous when she arrived at work the following day. Although she had a little more understanding of why Mrs Matravers felt so hard done by, Mary was fully expecting to be hauled over the coals for some other misdemeanour. Yet, waking that morning, she had already decided not only to be more diligent but to try and hold her tongue as well.

It wouldn't be an easy task, but it was one she was prepared to try if it meant she could keep her job. She was loving life in Liberty's far more than she could ever have anticipated and as each hour passed without incident or interference from Mrs Matravers, Mary allowed herself to relax, discovering she was good with the customers and enjoyed helping them find the right fabric. Whether it was introducing them to the timeless Liberty Peacock print or spotting a new customer who might prefer a more traditional paisley, Mary found she had an instinct for working out what customers wanted.

Yet there was still so much to learn. From day one, Flo had told Mary that there was a strict hierarchy in each department. Every sales assistant served in order of seniority and given Mary was the newcomer that meant she was expected to wait her turn. Then there was the fact Liberty sales assistants were expected to know every customer by sight so when she wasn't serving, Mary was rifling her way through the sales slips, putting a name to every face that bought something, a challenge she relished.

By the time the clock struck six, Mary felt exhausted. Nervously biting her lip, she wondered if Flo would forgive her if she made her excuses and got out of the stitching night.

Catching her wary look, Flo roared with laughter. 'Forget it, darlin'! You're coming to the workroom with us, and you'll enjoy yourself.'

Mary shot her a pleading look. 'Please, Flo. I'm dreadful at needlework and I'm exhausted too.'

'She's not still whinging, is she?' came a voice across the shop floor.

'Dot,' Flo cried, whirling around to face Mary's landlady and enveloping her in a warm hug. 'I'm so pleased to meet you finally!'

'Well, nothing else to do of a night, so I thought I'd come and join you girls, especially with your latest recruit. Don't want her giving you any of her cheek!' Dot chuckled, breaking free from Flo's embrace.

Mary rolled her eyes and returned to the packets of buttons she was sorting, while Flo led Dot to a chair behind the counter.

'How are you anyway, love?' Flo asked warmly.

'Right as ninepence,' Dot smiled. 'Least I will be when I can get someone to help out with the Morrison shelter I've had cluttering my garden since time immemorial. I know Hitler's not spread his barrel-load of hate for a while, and air-raid sirens aren't going off every five minutes at the moment, but I don't trust him not to do it again, and I want to be ready for him.'

'I thought you were going to ask one of the neighbours?' Mary called over her shoulder.

'I don't like to yet,' Dot replied sagely before turning to Flo and giving her a warm smile. 'You make sure Neil puts a ring on that finger of yours before long, love. If only so

71

you've got some bugger to put a shelf up without having to ask the entire street.'

Flo giggled. 'We've only been together twenty years, Dot! I think it'll be me asking him at the rate we're going. But listen, why don't you ask Mr Button to help? He don't live far from you.'

'Who's Buttons?' Dot asked, perplexed.

'Mr Button. Our new store manager,' Mary sighed. 'I did tell you, Dot.'

'You can't expect me to keep up with all your comings and goings,' Dot grumbled.

Just then the sound of footsteps stalking towards them made the girls look up.

'Hello, ladies, just thought I'd see how you're all getting along?' Mr Button called cheerfully, as he performed his usual evening checks. He paused by the rolls of crêpe and let out a gasp of shock. Mary gazed over at him, and caught him looking at Dot as though he had seen a ghost. 'Dorothy Banwell, is that really you?'

Dot swung around. 'Edwin?' she breathed.

Mary watched aghast as the blood drained from her landlady's face and exchanged an awkward glance with Flo. It was clear to them both that Dot and the store manager knew one another somehow, as they stared at each other for what felt like an eternity, clearly rattled.

'You two know each other then?' Flo said eventually, breaking the silence.

'Yes, we go way back ...' Edwin's voice trailed off hesitantly.

'I haven't seen you in over thirty years,' Dot whispered, as if Flo hadn't spoken. 'I never thought I'd see you again once you left for Kent.'

'Nor I you.' Edwin smiled softly, recovering slightly. 'It's good to see you. You haven't changed a bit.'

At that Dot seemed to snap out of whatever trance she was in. 'We both know that's not true. What are you doing here anyway? Last I heard you was in the army driving ambulances.'

'Where did you hear that?'

'I got my sources,' Dot said coldly. 'Anyway, you ain't answered my question.'

'I left three years ago now,' he explained. 'My eyesight was getting so bad I was struggling to see so I was put out to pasture and as you know I used to be a Saturday boy in Bourne and Hollingsworth, so found my way here.'

'Well, you look like you've fallen on your feet now, Edwin,' Dot said, her composure returning.

'You always did like to get right to the point, Dorothy Banwell,' Mr Button said softly.

'It's Hanson now,' she bristled.

Edwin raised an eyebrow. 'You're married?'

Dot shook her head sadly. 'Not no more. My George was killed in the last war, serving his country.'

'I'm sorry,' Mr Button replied, his voice rich with sorrow.

'It was a long time ago,' Dot sighed. 'What about you? You wed?'

'Widowed,' Mr Button said softly. 'My Ethel died in the Coventry blasts. She'd been visiting her sister.'

At that, Mary couldn't help but let out a gasp of horror. She remembered how her old ATS friend Kitty had been dangerously caught up in the city's raids, managing to not only escape with her life, but her integrity intact.

'Well, seeing as you two already know each other,' Flo said, a hint of mischief in her eyes, 'perhaps you wouldn't mind helping Dot assemble her new shelter then, Mr Button?'

'Oh no, love, I couldn't—' Dot began, only for Flo to shush her.

'It's no trouble at all,' Mr Button insisted. 'I'm in Bermondsey, Galleywall Road.'

'That's not far from us at all,' Mary grinned. 'We're on Bell Street just down the road from the Tube.'

Mr Button cleared his throat. 'I would be happy to help if you would like me to, Dorothy. It might give us a chance to catch up.'

'It's very kind of you, but I don't want to put you to no bother,' Dot said firmly.

'It's no trouble at all. Tomorrow's my half-day if it's not too short notice?' Mr Button tried again.

Dot paused for a moment before giving an almost imperceptible nod of her head. 'Only if you'll let me give you your lunch by way of a thank you.'

'I would like that.' Mr Button brightened. 'Are you joining the ladies for their stitching night?'

'I certainly am. Mary's going to learn how to thread a needle at the very least.'

As Mary groaned, Mr Button offered Dot a kindly smile. 'Well, in that case I'll leave you to it. Flo, if you could just make sure that the blackout blinds are secured in the pleating room, please, before you start work. I'll see you tomorrow, Dorothy.'

When he was out of sight, Dot's expression hardened as she turned to Flo. 'I cannot believe you put me on the spot like that, lady.'

Flo's smile slipped. 'I'm sorry, I thought Mr Button was an old friend of yours. I would never mean to put you in an awkward position.'

'Well, you have,' Dot snapped.

'I'm truly sorry.' Flo bowed her head. 'I thought I was helping and you perhaps just needed a bit of encouragement.'

There was a pause before Dot relented. 'Ignore me, it was just a shock seeing Edwin after all this time.'

'Right, shall we go then?' Flo said, sensing the subject needed changing.

'Shouldn't we wait for Alice?' Mary asked.

'She'll be along later, she's on ARP duty,' Dot said as Flo chuckled.

'Yes, you don't get out of it that easily,' she said, reaching for a large canvas bag, and snapping out the lights. Using her tiny electric torch, she led the way across the shop floor, heels clattering briskly, almost as if she were Mrs Matravers.

'Where is it we're going?' Dot asked as Flo led them down the stairs.

'The pleating room,' Flo called.

'Get away,' Dot breathed. 'A whole room just for pleats?'

Flo laughed as she led them across the bridge that connected the new shop to East India House in Regent Street. 'We used to have a beading room as well, Dot.'

'Never in this world,' she cried, tripping over a step in the dark. 'How far's this place, Flo? I'll have broken both me arms at this rate and will be incapable of showing anyone anything.'

'We're in here,' Flo said, coming to an abrupt stop.

Throwing open the door, she led the women inside and snapped each of the blinds down before throwing on the large light.

As a warm yellow glow flooded the room Mary looked around the huge workspace in awe. Large wooden tables stood in rows with long benches at either side while pendant gas lamps suspended on what looked like string hung over each work station. Towards the back of the room there were jars lined up on shelves filled with threads in every colour, while on another shelf stood jars of needles in a variety of sizes along with scissors.

'It's a seamstress's dream,' Flo declared as she walked over to a bench, dumped the bag she'd been carrying in the middle and snapped on one of the lights.

'What have you got in there?' Mary asked, her voice full of curiosity.

'Old clothes that are past their best,' Flo explained, tipping the contents on to the table.

'Cor, you've a lot of paisley in here,' Dot marvelled.

Flo nodded. 'I thought we could make a patchwork quilt out of it. It'll be an easy thing for Mary to start on, and a nice relaxing task for the rest of us.'

'Lovely idea,' Dot agreed.

Only Mary looked unconvinced. 'I'm not sure about this. I don't want to make a mess of this fabric and waste it.'

Just then the sound of doors clattering broke the girls' train of thought as Rose pushed her way through and smiled at the collected ensemble.

'Sorry I'm late, Mrs M wanted my help sorting out the stock-take rota. Have I missed much?'

Flo smiled. 'Not a thing, love. We were just saying we thought we'd make a quilt.'

'Oh, lovely. I've brought some old bits of material myself.' As Rose tipped her own bag out on the table alongside Flo's, Mary found herself admiring the haul along with everyone else.

'Ooh, look at this one, Rose!' Dot picked up an old dress that had clearly seen better days. 'This seagull print's beautiful.'

'It's Liberty,' Rose admitted shyly.

'So it is,' Flo gasped. 'That's much too good for quilting: why don't you make yourself a nice frock or skirt? We've got loads of patterns over on the bookshelves, and it'll give Mary a chance to practise her fabric-cutting skills.'

Rose shrugged. 'I think it's too worn. I'm sure it's the only reason Mother let me have it.'

Dot snatched the fabric from the table and held it up to the light, examining it with the seasoned eye of a professional. 'There's plenty of life in this yet. Why don't we make you a nice skirt. Flo's right, this fabric's far too pretty to hack up for a quilt.'

'Do you really think I could?'

'Yes,' Flo insisted. 'You come and sit with me, and we'll find you a nice pattern that'll be perfect for this skirt.'

Rose perched happily next to Flo and together they searched through patterns, leaving Dot and Mary to make a start on the quilt.

'Come on then,' Dot grinned, reaching for a jar filled with needles. 'Time to thread that needle, my girl.'

Opening her mouth ready to protest, Mary was all set to make her feelings on the matter clear, when something in Dot's face stopped her. With a start she realised that her landlady looked excited about helping her and all previous shock over Mr Button had been temporarily forgotten.

'All right, Dot, I'm in your hands,' she said, picking out a needle with a large-looking eye.

Twenty minutes later and Mary was feeling pleased and frustrated with her progress in equal measure. She had mastered the art of threading the needle with various different colour threads as long as she craned her neck and held the eye up to the light. But the moment Dot had excitedly suggested she start sewing on to the fabric, things had gone wrong. She had been unable to master even the most basic running stitch, and the thread was so rough and uneven she had no idea how anybody could sew a seam in a straight line. She had also ended up stabbing her thumb repeatedly in her attempts to get her needle through the fabric so she was now bleeding all over the cotton.

'Look at this,' she grumbled, sucking the blood from her thumb. 'The War Office will charge me with waste if they catch sight of what I've done.'

'It's not a waste,' Dot replied patiently as she unpicked Mary's handiwork. 'Now have another go, and this time try not to get so much bleedin' claret everywhere. Blood's a sod to get out.'

Handing the fabric back to Mary, Dot turned to the other girls. 'You found a pattern for that lovely bit of material yet?'

'Yes.' Rose smiled excitedly. 'Look, I'm going to make this A-line.'

'Beautiful,' Dot replied. 'That'll suit you down to the ground. You can wear it when your Tommy comes home.'

Rose giggled in anticipation. 'Not sure Mother would like that. She's never really cared for Tommy. It's silly really, I don't think anyone would have been good enough for me if I'm honest.'

'Still, she gave you both a roof over your head when you married,' Flo put in. 'She can't hate him that much.'

'I never thought of it like that before,' Rose mused as she turned to Mary. 'What about you then? Don't you want a sweetheart?'

Mary turned her attention back to her fabric and kept her gaze firmly on her work. 'No thanks, Rose dear. I'm not remotely interested in courting.'

'Oh, you should be, Mary,' Dot said firmly. 'What about one of the textile workers over at Merton Abbey?'

'What about them?' Mary said, a look of horror flashing across her face.

'Well, would you like to go to the pictures with one of them?' Rose urged.

Mary shook her head. 'I've more than enough to occupy my time, thank you.'

'Give over,' Dot said, her eyes twinkling with merriment. 'You're only young – where's the harm?'

'Really, Dot, thank you for your interest but I'm happy as I am,' Mary said firmly.

'But there's plenty of fellas out there for you, love,' Dot continued. 'You might want to take one to the Liberty's Christmas party. That's happening this year, isn't it, Rose? Alice always goes on about how lovely it is.'

'I haven't heard anything about it,' Mary replied stiffly.

'Oh, it's wonderful, Mary,' Rose exclaimed. 'Liberty's hire out the third floor of the Lyons Corner House in Piccadilly and we have ever such a nice time. Actually, we need people to help organise it – why don't you join the social-club committee?'

Mary smiled as politely as she could. 'Thanks, but I'm just the new girl. I'm not sure I would be welcomed.'

'Of course you would,' Rose insisted although Mary studiously ignored her.

Noticing Mary's indifference, Dot piped up, 'Sounds lovely, Rose. And look, you'd have somewhere nice to wear your skirt.'

'Do you think so?' she asked, admiring the fabric. 'It's a shame my Tommy won't be home this Christmas to see it, but I'll keep it nice for him.'

Flo turned to Mary. 'So will you come?'

Mary shook her head. 'Dances aren't really my cup of tea. It does sound like a marvellous affair though.'

'So come,' Rose insisted. 'It's ever so Christmassy. Last year Mr Blackmore sang carols with Mrs Matravers.'

'I'm not sure …' Mary's voice trailed off awkwardly.

'Don't be like that,' Dot teased. 'You must know your way around a ball or two what with your upbringing and time in the ATS.'

Mary paused for a moment. More than anything she wanted to be like all the other girls her own age and enjoy dances and courting. But she couldn't entertain the thought of it, and she had a feeling she might never be able to again.

'Do you miss it then?' Rose asked bluntly. 'The ATS, I mean.'

At the question, Mary felt a wave of nausea as she remembered the last dance she had attended. It had been the previous Christmas in the mess room of the barracks in Camberley. It had all started as such a wonderfully happy affair. She and the other girls had gathered together and pressed their ghastly khaki army knickers, better known as passion killers, and shined their brogues. One of the girls had even taken out her lipstick and insisted the girls all made themselves up.

Walking into the mess that night, they had given the boys who were all clustered around the makeshift dance floor a little wave as a sergeant put the gramophone on. As the notes of 'All Over the Place' wafted through the room, Mary felt a drink being pressed into her hands and happiness flood through her as the evening took hold. Until later, that was, when the last thing she felt was happy.

As the memory threatened to engulf her, she forced herself to return to the present. This was her new life and she would not allow the past to ruin it.

'I do, I had some wonderful times, which is why I think you're right, I'll come after all. And, Rose, if the committee will have me I would love to join in.'

Rose's face lit up at the news. 'You won't regret it, I promise, Mary.'

'Lovely,' Flo agreed. 'It's a great night. We even get some of the Liberty agents from outside London to come down.'

'Do you remember that fella from last year?' Rose giggled. 'He tried to do magic tricks with a Liberty print and never got it to work.'

Flo laughed. 'If I were you I should think about your own Liberty print. I think Dot's right though, Rose. That dress will make a smashing skirt for the occasion.'

Rose beamed as she admired the fabric with fresh eyes. 'What about you, Flo? Will your Neil be home for the dance?'

Flo shook her head sadly. 'I doubt it. Last I heard he was in Malta. I'll still be going though, even if I do just have to dance with the girls.'

As she smiled at the girls, Mary caught the glimmer of sadness behind her green eyes. In that moment she realised just how awful it must be for your best friend and soul mate to be away fighting in the horrors of war. She had seen and experienced enough herself in the ATS, though she had never lost a loved one herself.

'And I'm sure Neil will want to hear all about it,' she said, clasping Flo's hand in comfort.

As Flo flashed Mary a grateful smile, she bent down and caught Mary's handiwork. 'Would you Adam and Eve it, our Mary's only gone and sewn a straight line.'

Swivelling her head down to look at her latest effort, Mary was thrilled to see that Flo was right. She might have treated her hands like a pin cushion but she had at last mastered the running stitch.

'I can't believe it,' she said in shock. 'Never did I think I'd be able to sew.'

'I had every faith,' Dot grinned. 'You've done some nice work there, you should be proud of yourself.'

'You certainly should,' Flo said, her eyes dancing with delight. 'We'll make a Liberty girl of you yet, Mary Holmes-Fotherington.'

Continuing to admire Mary's stitching, the door suddenly burst open and Alice stood at the door, her coat buttoned up wrongly, her cheeks pinched and eyes brimming with tears.

'What's wrong?' Flo gasped. 'Did something happen when you were out on duty?'

Alice shook her head. 'I haven't been on duty. I've been at home. Girls, I had a letter this afternoon from the RAF.'

The girls exchanged nervous glances. Dot immediately rushed to Alice's side and Mary's eyes strayed to her friend's hands. She couldn't fail to notice she was clutching the letter tightly in her hand.

'What does it say?' Flo asked quietly.

'Luke is missing,' she sobbed, her knees buckling beneath her.

As Alice sank to the floor, the rest of the girls exchanged glances.

'Are they sure?' Rose asked, her voice thick with shock.

Alice nodded in despair. 'They're sure – look here.'

She thrust the monogrammed notepaper at her friends; Mary took it from Alice's outstretched hand and scanned the contents.

15th September 1941

Dear Mrs. Milwood,

Please allow me to express my own and the squadron's sincere sympathy with you in the sad news concerning your husband Flying Officer Luke Milwood.

The aircraft of which he was Pilot took off to attack Boulogne Harbour on 31 August 1941 and nothing further has been heard.

You may understand that in many cases aircrew reported missing are eventually reported prisoner of war, and I hope this may give you some comfort. Your husband was a most proficient Pilot and his loss is felt by us all. We shall of course forward your husband's belongings. Please accept the deep sympathy of us all, and let us hope that we may soon have some good news of the safety of your husband.

Yours with regret,
Howard M. Rogers

Wing Commander Howard M. Rogers
RAF Station
Biggin Hill

'Oh Alice, I'm so sorry,' Mary whispered.

She and the rest of the girls wrapped their arms around their friend, and they remained silent as the enormity of the news sank in. Mary clasped Alice's arm more tightly then. She of all people knew how precious life could be, and she made a silent vow to provide a shoulder to cry on for her new friend, come what may.

Chapter Nine

The following morning, Mary was surprised to see Alice not only up, but washed and dressed in her work clothes. Sitting at the kitchen table, with a bowl of porridge and cup of tea as usual, Alice was clearly ready for a busy day at work.

'What are you doing?' Mary gasped, pouring herself a cup of tea from the pot on the table and sitting opposite her friend. 'Surely you're not going to work?'

Alice squared her shoulders and lifted her chin defiantly. 'Why not? Best thing to do in a crisis is work, and that's exactly what I intend to do.'

'But what about the baby? You must be exhausted,' Mary put in, topping up Alice's cup with fresh tea.

Alice looked at Mary coldly. 'I'm over six months pregnant: I'm always tired. Today is no different. I can't sit here all day, Mary, I'll go mad, wondering "what if".'

Mary understood and said nothing. She too knew the healing power that work could offer in a crisis and understood there was nothing better than getting stuck into a task when your heart was breaking. Yet she also knew that the grief and worry Alice was going through wouldn't wait forever. Taking a sip of the scalding yet comforting liquid, she fixed her eye on Alice. It was impossible to miss the sallow skin and bags under her eyes that no amount of Pan-Cake make-up would cover. Mary made a mental note to keep an eye on Alice.

'Morning, girls. How are you feeling, Alice?' Dot asked gently as she appeared in the kitchen wearing her favourite floral housecoat. Sitting down between the girls, she poured herself a cup of tea and exchanged a look of worry with Mary.

'I'm all right,' Alice sighed. 'I didn't sleep much, but I feel better knowing I'm going into work.'

'As long as you're sure,' Dot said. 'Mary, make sure Mabel goes easy on our Alice today.'

Alice snorted. 'It's not me that has to worry, it's Mary she's had it in for.'

Mary couldn't help smiling at Alice's teasing. 'You know, I've been thinking all night about Luke,' she began, ignoring the look of fear on her friend's face. 'In the army we would hear of people going missing all the time only for them to turn up alive.'

'Really?' Dot asked, her eyes agog.

'Really,' Mary confirmed. 'Alice, I don't want you getting your hopes up, but all is not lost yet, I promise.'

As Mary finished her speech, Alice smiled weakly. 'I appreciate you trying to help me, Mary, but honestly I think it's better if I face facts. It's unlikely Luke's ever coming home, and I can't afford to fall apart with a baby due in less than three months.'

'Nobody said anything about falling apart,' Dot went on softly. 'All Mary's trying to say is that there's hope, that's all.'

At the kindness of Dot's words, Alice gave in to the tears she had so bravely kept at bay. 'I can't stop thinking about where he might be,' she wailed. 'What if the Germans have made him a prisoner of war like the letter says and they've hurt him? What if he's in pain or scared? What if he's dead?'

As Alice spoke the words Mary and Dot had considered but hadn't like to say, they each scrambled to Alice's side and wrapped their arms around her.

'You don't know anything yet,' Mary said soothingly. 'And there's no point allowing your imagination to run riot at this point: it won't change anything and it won't make you feel better.'

'She's right,' Dot agreed, reaching into her pocket for a hankie and wiping the tears from Alice's face as if she were no more than a child. 'And your Luke is precisely the reason we've all got to keep fighting this bleedin' war.'

'But it's not fair,' Alice cried, tears still cascading down her cheeks. 'We've got a baby on the way. This was supposed to be a happy time, now I don't know if I'll ever see him again and my baby could grow up without knowing its father. How am I ever supposed to come to terms with that ...?'

As Alice trailed off, she gave in to great racking sobs, leaving Mary feeling powerless to do anything but hold her friend.

By the time Alice had finished sobbing, Mary could see the girl looked as though she had been put through an emotional mangle, but she still looked better for it.

'Anything I can get you, love?' Dot asked kindly. 'More tea? You've got to keep your strength up.'

Alice sat up straighter. 'Go on then.'

As Dot poured yet another cup of tea Mary could only stare at her friend in concern.

'Mary,' Alice snapped eventually. 'I'm not made of china, I'm not about to break.'

'Sorry,' Mary replied hurriedly.

Alice sighed. 'No, it's me that should be sorry. I know you're both worried about me and I appreciate it.'

'We just want to help you, love,' Dot said.

'Then let's please talk about something else,' Alice pleaded. 'How about you and Mr Button? That'll take my mind off things.'

'Yes, go on,' Mary grinned. 'How do you know each other?'

Dot rolled her eyes. 'I don't want you gossiping about me and him up Liberty's.'

'We won't,' Alice promised, making the sign of the cross with her fingers.

'All right. We used to court each other. We met when I was fifteen and he was seventeen. We went to a dance up the church hall, and when I saw him, I got butterflies. Edwin had already started an apprenticeship as a cobbler. He had eyes as inviting as a chocolate puddle and hair to match, but ever such a kindly way about him,' Dot said wistfully.

'Don't stop there,' Mary begged, pouring out yet more tea for them.

'I don't know what you want me to tell you,' Dot shrugged. 'We met, we courted, I thought he was lovely and we went out.'

'Why did you lose touch?' Alice quizzed.

'He moved to Kent with his parents, and I was heartbroken,' Dot stated baldly.

'Did you not think of marrying him?' Mary asked.

'We were just kids really. Too young. We wrote, of course, for months.'

'So why didn't you keep writing if you thought he was so lovely?'

'We just didn't,' Dot sighed, avoiding their gaze. 'There was no big row, we just grew apart and the letters stopped. Then I met George up the Electric Theatre one night. I suppose I felt guilty I'd met someone else, until I bumped into Edwin's sister up East Street Market one day and she told me he'd gone and got engaged to some girl called Ethel and he was going in the army.'

'Sounds like it all worked out then,' Mary mused.

'I suppose it did. Me and my George – well, there was nobody like him.' Dot smiled at the memory.

'But what was it like bumping into Mr Button after all this time?' Alice pressed. 'I cannot imagine what you must have thought yesterday. You looked horrified.'

Dot shifted uncomfortably in her chair. 'It was a shock. I didn't expect to see him. Not only that, he hasn't changed a bit.'

'But he's all grey,' Alice pointed out.

'The *essence* of him hasn't changed a bit.' Dot squeezed her eyes shut, bringing her childhood memories to the fore. 'He's still that young lad, and seeing him took me right back to when I was fifteen.'

Mary giggled. 'So are you looking forward to his visit later this afternoon then?'

The landlady silenced her with a look that would sour milk. 'I don't want to hear no saucy talk. Me and Edwin courted donkey's years ago and that's the end of it.'

With that Dot took what was left of her tea and marched back upstairs, leaving Alice and Mary to get ready for work.

By the time Mary got to the Tube station – without Alice who wasn't starting until eleven – she was feeling keyed up about the morning ahead. The store was always busy on Saturdays as shoppers prepared for the weekend, and Mary was bracing herself for whatever lay ahead.

As the train roared along the platform sending clouds of black grime into the air, Mary boarded the carriage and found a seat by the window. Sinking into the red and green velour seat, she let out a sigh so deep she blew the pages of the newspaper held by the man sitting opposite her.

As he rustled his pages, the man glared across the top of the paper, which screamed the headline *Russia Needs A Year's Output*.

Screwing up her eyes she did her best to read the *Herald*'s main story but could only make out a few of the words. Whatever the details though it was clear that Russia was in dire need of help now Hitler had declared war on the country that used to be its ally.

Mary shook her head sadly as the train pulled up at Oxford Circus. With the bombs rarely falling over London any more it sometimes felt like peacetime; walking through the city the sight of sleepy squares, cats yawning on windowsills and errand boys' bikes propped up against kerbs meant she could almost pretend the war was over. But then she'd see a queue for the butcher's along with bare shelves in the shops and be reminded the war was getting worse not better.

Mary arrived on the shop floor and started serving her first customer before she caught sight of Flo, whose face was full of despair.

'Have you seen Mrs M?' Flo asked as Mary bade her customer goodbye.

'No! Why?'

Flo pulled a face. 'She wants to see you first thing. I said I'd get you straightaway.'

'Oh no!' Mary wailed. 'What have I done now?'

'I don't know,' Flo said quickly. 'But just get up there quick as you can.'

Immediately, Mary jostled her way through the crowd of customers that had now gathered in fabrics and marched across the floor towards the staircase. As she ran up the flight of wooden stairs she couldn't help but marvel at its sheer beauty. Everything in the store was so lovely, from the curved architraves and stained-glass windows to the little wooden carvings depicting life in Elizabethan times.

By the time she reached the top she was so out of breath she could barely utter a word to Rose who was sitting behind her desk. At the sight of Mary in front of her looking so flustered, Rose didn't know whether to laugh or cry.

'Mrs Matravers has had to go out on an errand,' Rose said, getting up to offer Mary her seat. 'She says she will see you after work.'

With a groan Mary sank on to the hard chair and wiped the sweat from her brow. 'I rushed up here for nothing! Do you know if she was going to tick me off about something?'

Rose gently patted Mary on the back. 'She did have a face of thunder, yes, but that doesn't always mean much. Half the time it's because she's had a row with Alf, but you never heard that from me.'

Mary lifted her chin. She wasn't sure the younger girl was right, but she admired her optimism if nothing else. Turning her attention to Rose's desk she saw a mountain of paperwork spread out. She poked a forefinger at a sales docket. 'You look busy.'

Rose sighed. 'Yes. Mr Button wants me to have a look at some of these outstanding invoices. Honestly, there just aren't enough hours in the day or members of staff. I shouldn't complain but I'm doing the work of five!'

'I know it's not easy.' Mary walked across to the window and looked out at the grey rooftops across Soho and beyond. 'But we've all got to make an effort while this war's on.'

'I know, I know. Sorry, I've just done two nights' firewatch duties; I'm ratty, that's all. That and Mum's thinking about joining up! At her age!' Rose sighed.

Mary raised an eyebrow as she turned back from the window. 'Your mum wants to join up?'

'Yes. She's been to the WRNS recruitment office this week,' Rose said in a small voice. 'Normally I'd be all for it, but who's going to take care of my dad?'

'What's wrong with your father?' Mary asked, amazed she'd heard nothing about this before.

'Dad can barely walk after he was shot in the last war,' Rose said, her voice breaking. 'He can get about with a stick, but he's in agony much of the time. Mum's always cared for him, and my wages help put food on the table. But Mum says Dad can manage, that she can do more good by fighting for her country and going off to war than she can being Dad's carer.'

'My word,' Mary whistled. 'But why does your mother want to join up *now*? Isn't it a bit sudden?'

Rose blew her nose noisily. 'She says it's all to do with Russia. That this war's getting worse now Hitler's gone against Russia; he'll be back with more hate before long. Those barrage balloons aren't going anywhere anytime soon and so we need more able-bodied people to ensure that it ends sooner rather than later. I know it sounds silly but I'm clinging to the fact she's thirty-nine and they may not take her. How am I going to take care of my dad and work here too? This job's our lifeline.'

Privately Mary thought Rose's mother was doing a very brave thing, but one glance at Rose's tear-stained face told her that was not the right thing to say. Instead she squeezed the girl's shoulder.

'Don't worry, I'm sure it'll all work out,' Mary offered. 'I know things seem a bit bleak, but there's always hope around the corner. Are you coming out with us fabric girls tonight? We're going to a Chinese restaurant.'

Rose shook her head sadly. 'I can't. I've got to get Dad's tea on. Mum's late back on Saturdays from WRVS duties. And in the meantime I've got all this paperwork to sort out.'

As the tears started to fall down Rose's cheeks, Mary took control. 'How about I come back with you after work and help you with your dad? Then once he's settled we'll join the others. What do you say? You look like you need a night out.'

Rose smiled brightly. 'Would you really come back with me?'

'Of course,' Mary grinned. 'What else are friends for?'

Chapter Ten

The rest of the day sailed by, and as Mary threw herself into her duties she almost forgot she had a meeting with Mrs Matravers later that day. Together with Alice and Flo, she served customers, cut lengths of fabric, held a yapping dog while her owner admired a roll of Tana Lawn, and measured and remeasured fabric for trousers and siren suits that customers had their hearts set on, thanks to the fashion bible *Vogue*.

The magazine's latest issue had caused something of a stir as it had suggested women's wartime musts included a white mac, to make it easier to be seen in the blackout, along with trousers as they were more practical than skirts.

By the time Mary's mid-afternoon break came around, she and the rest of the girls were more than ready for a rest from women all demanding to know how to make and wear the latest fashions.

'Shall I make us all a cup of tea?' Mary offered. 'We could hide the cups in the stockroom.'

Alice looked at Mary as if she could kiss her. 'I know I should say no, but yes please, I'm dead on my feet.'

'That would be wonderful. I saw Mrs M go out about ten minutes ago as well, so you've plenty of time,' Flo hissed over her shoulder as another customer caught her attention. 'You're an angel, Mary Holmes-Fotherington, an utter angel.'

As Flo carried on serving, Mary allowed a little burst of delight to run through her. She felt as though a miracle had happened: even though there was still a fortnight left of her month's trial, it was as though she had turned a corner and was on her way to being accepted into this new life she was trying to carve out for herself. As she bounded up the stairs, excitement burning in her lungs, she revelled in this unexpected surge of pleasure.

Reaching the staffroom, she got to work quickly making cups of tea for all. Once she was sure the coast was clear she made her way back down the stairs, taking care to keep the tea in the cups rather than on the shop floor.

She had just reached the jewellery counter when she heard the unmistakeable sound of Mrs Matravers' heels clacking their way towards her. Heartbeat roaring in her ears Mary ducked behind a mannequin in ready-to-wear, hoping against hope Mrs Matravers wouldn't see her. If she was caught with a tray of tea no doubt there would be even more of a dressing down later during their chat.

But despite her best efforts, the sharp tap on her shoulder told her she had been found. Straightening up, she swung around and came face to face with her deputy manager, cheeks flushed with anger and eyebrows pinched. Mary didn't think she had ever seen her boss look so furious.

'A word. Now,' she said in a menacing tone.

Unsure what to do with the tea, Mary deposited the cups on the jewellery counter and followed Mrs Matravers to her office.

As she walked back up the stairs, Mary's heart was in her mouth; she desperately tried to think of ways she could endear herself to Mrs Matravers, but knew it was pointless. What would be would be, she thought as her boss stalked past Rose. Offering her new friend a petrified smile, Mary followed the deputy store manager into her office, all her new-found hopes of acceptance dashed.

Once she was inside, Mrs Matravers slammed the door so hard that the floor vibrated and whirled around to face Mary. 'What is it about following orders you don't understand, Miss Holmes-Fotherington?'

Mary shrank back; her boss's grey eyes were filled with so much fury, she half expected to see sparks. 'I really am so sorry I missed you, Mrs Matravers. But it's been such a busy day, and Alice of course needed sustenance so I offered to fetch the girls a cup of tea.'

'"I offered to fetch the girls a cup of tea,"' Mrs Matravers mimicked cruelly. 'Well, that's all right then. Why am I so upset, I wonder? Miss Holmes-Fotherington, you seem to spend your life letting me down. You were told to come and see me first thing and yet you failed to find me before I had to leave on urgent business. Time and time again you deliberately flout the rules and I cannot help wondering if you really need a job here?'

'I do, I love it here, Mrs Matravers,' Mary cried desperately, refusing to give her boss the satisfaction that she privately thought her boss's order that morning a little unreasonable.

Mrs Matravers said nothing. Instead she returned to her desk and sat down. Picking up a pair of glasses, she put them on her nose and leafed through a notebook on her desk.

'I've already warned you, my girl, about showing me up,' she hissed, all airs and graces gone in an instant. 'Yet that's what you do, day in day out. Well, I've had enough. You posh lot think you're better than the rest of us. You don't know a thing about hard graft like what we do, but I'm here to make sure you work twice as hard as everyone else, understood?'

Mary observed the woman sitting opposite her. She was only around ten years older than her, Mary thought, but she had the appearance of a woman much older, who had been beaten down by life and consequently was more than used to blaming everyone around her. Since she started Mary had been happily working her fingers to the bone, anxious to prove herself to Flo, Alice, Dot and Mrs Matravers that she was worthy of being a Liberty girl. There was a war on and it was all hands on deck. But she didn't see why she should be penalised for having a posh accent. Suddenly she felt very tired of having to put up with Mrs Matravers' disapproval. She knew her boss had not had an easy childhood, and that with her husband out of work she was perhaps struggling for money, but despite their difference in upbringing Mary would argue that life hadn't been a bed of roses for her either.

Drawing herself up to her full height, she eyed Mrs Matravers coldly. 'I appreciate that you're my boss and a certain degree of respect is required. But I rather think you've got a bally nerve singling me out. I'm sorry you disapprove of my accent, I'm sorry you disapprove of me, but in no way do I see why that allows you to pick on me each and every day. I am more than happy to take my turn and go above and beyond where necessary, but I will not be your whipping girl. Now, I'm genuinely sorry about the tea, I can assure you it will not happen again, but I think we've both said all that needs to be said.'

Spinning on her heel to turn and leave, Mary registered the look of shock on Mrs Matravers face. She had one hand on the doorknob when her deputy manager's voice boomed loud and clear.

'Nicely said, Miss Holmes-Fotherington.' Her voice had taken on a steely edge. 'But before you leave my office in a fit of pique, you think on. I know things about you, things you probably don't want getting out. Not if you want to keep your reputation intact anyway.'

Slowly Mary turned round to face her boss. A creeping sense of nausea rose up within her. 'What do you mean?'

Mrs Matravers got to her feet, her grey eyes gleaming like the cat that got the cream. 'I mean, Mary, you'll do exactly what I say, when I say it. Normally I'd have some shop girl out on her ear for what you've just said to me, but I think I'll keep you on. Not only are we more short-staffed than Marksies, but I reckon I'll have more fun that way. Besides, nobody else is going to employ you, are they? Not when they find out exactly why you were sacked from the army.'

'I don't know what you're talking about,' Mary said, her voice faltering.

Mrs Matravers walked around to the front of her desk and leaned against it, arms folded as she offered Mary a lazy smile. 'Yes you do. You know exactly what I mean and I know why your family want nothing more to do with you 'n' all.'

Mary trembled with shock. 'How do you know about my family?'

'I know everything, my girl, it's my job,' she said pointedly. 'Given what you did I can't say I blame 'em. Just imagine what would happen around here if folk found out a posh girl like you had gone and got themselves pregnant out of wedlock and lost the baby too.'

Chapter Eleven

The wind whipping around her head, Mary huddled deeper into her coat as she walked through the streets of Soho. Over a week had passed since Mrs Matravers had called Mary out and she'd felt bereft ever since. Knowing that someone had identified her private pain and wanted to use it against her had left her feeling broken. Now she had no idea which way to turn.

Over the past few months she had done her utmost to block out the agony she felt at losing her job, her baby and her family in such quick succession. Now it was as though someone had held up a mirror to all she had endured and was forcing her to relive it day after day. Turning the corner, Mary wrapped her scarf tightly around her neck and took a deep breath. It may have been the first full week of October, but temperatures had plummeted as quickly as the happiness she had newly discovered. She had no idea how Mrs Matravers had managed to find out her secret. Mary could only assume she had gone to the ATS and told them she needed to know why an employee had been discharged, and the army had accommodated her request. Mary shuddered at the lies Mrs Matravers must have told, no doubt promising whomever she spoke to that the matter would of course be handled with discretion and delicacy.

The only consolation Mary found for herself was that Mrs Matravers didn't appear to know everything, and for that Mary was beyond grateful. Now, as she hurried along

Greek Street towards the French Pub, Mary found herself wishing she had someone to confide in about all of this, but she knew there was nobody. Mary remembered how she had naively thought her sister Clarissa would be the one to help her when she arrived in Ceylon. Clarissa, to her credit, had asked no questions, welcoming her older sister with open arms. But then of course when she discovered that her sister was pregnant, months later and in the most horrifying way possible, she too had turned her back. It was the first time the sisters had fallen out and, sadly, Mary knew that it would be the last. All of her family had made it very clear that she had brought nothing but shame upon their name, and she could never return. Instinct told Mary that it was just a matter of time before Mrs Matravers blurted out her secret, and at a time when she could be sure of causing maximum damage as well.

In the meantime, her boss had made it clear that she would be working Mary to the bone, if she wanted a guarantee of silence. Consequently, Mary had performed four nights of fire-watching and had also been roped into a stock-take as well as made to sit on the leisure and amateur athletics committees. She had missed out on not just one but two nights out with her colleagues at the Chinese restaurant, and had been unable to help Rose with her father as promised, which left her racked with guilt. Now she had been roped into the Christmas party organisation and it was fair to say Mary was exhausted and in no mood to meet Mrs Matravers and the rest of the committee members to discuss ideas.

Arriving at the old pub, she pushed open the door and stepped into the warm, foggy atmosphere. Condensation steamed up the blacked-out windows as crowds of men and women gathered around tables drinking beer and port, chatting about their days together.

Mary couldn't help smiling as she pushed her way through the throng. Since the Luftwaffe had stopped its nightly bombing campaign back in May the city had a renewed, albeit subdued, vigour.

'There you are!' Rose got up to wave at Mary. 'I got you a port and lemon.'

'Wonderful, thank you,' she said, taking a seat opposite Mrs Matravers and smiling at the assembled group. As well as Rose, Mr Button, Larry, Flo, Alice and Mrs Matravers, there was a lady she recognised as Betty Johnson from gifts, though they had never spoken. Everyone was deep in conversation, apart from Alice who was staring blankly through the crowds. Mary's heart went out to her as she leaned over and clasped her hand, forcing Alice from her reverie.

'How are you?' Mary asked sympathetically.

Alice shot her a watery smile. 'As well as can be expected. Isn't that the phrase?'

'Still no news then?' Mary asked in a low voice.

'No, and I don't expect it,' Alice said, taking her hand from underneath Mary's so she could stroke her bump. 'I just feel so lost, Mary. I don't know what to do or how to carry on. I feel like I'm in limbo.'

Mary's eyes strayed to Alice's growing stomach. Her friend might feel as though her life was on hold but the growing baby inside her wasn't going to stay still. Mary knew that though Alice might not like it, her life was about to change and she was going to have to make the best of it for her child's sake.

Mary was about to open her mouth to say as much when Mrs Matravers clapped her hands together.

'Now that we're all here,' Mrs Matravers said, pointedly staring at Mary, 'let's begin. I imagine we're all in agreement that we do the same thing as usual? The Liberty family is of course keen to show the staff their gratitude for all their hard work – isn't that right, Mr Button?'

The store manager looked at Mrs Matravers and beamed. 'That's right. The board and the family all feel that although there may be difficulties in the world, and of course with so much on ration now provisions are poor, the Liberty staff still deserve a jolly good Christmas.'

At that there was a round of applause before Mrs Matravers brought proceedings to order. 'So, Rose dear, I wonder if you would talk to Lyons about the menu. Just what we usually have, I think. A few hors d'oeuvres, a fish course perhaps?'

Larry cleared his throat. 'Actually, Mrs M, I wondered if we ought to do something a bit different to the traditional dinner and dance that we usually see at the Corner House.'

There was a collective intake of breath as Larry made his suggestion. Mary peered at him across the table. Short, stocky and with a strong jawline, Larry looked as though he was a lad you wouldn't want to meet in a dark alley, but she also knew he had a heart of gold after the way he had diligently helped hide the fabric from their Russian friend.

'Why on earth would we do that, Larry?' Mrs Matravers thundered. 'The annual Christmas dinner is a time-honoured tradition.'

Mr Button raised a hand warningly. 'Now, now, Mrs Matravers, I'd like to hear what Larry has to say. Go on, son.'

'Thank you, sir,' Larry replied gratefully. 'I just thought that with the war taking a turn for the worse now, perhaps we ought to spend a bit less on our own party and give a bit of money to the Russians.'

All eyes were fixed on Mrs Matravers as she let out a gasp of horror. 'The Russians? Why would we give money to them? They were our enemy up until recently. Now

Hitler's invaded them they suddenly want our help. I don't think so.'

'Quite right,' Mrs Johnson agreed.

As the deputy manager made her pronouncement Larry looked defeated and Mary's heart went out to him. His idea was undoubtedly a good one, and they all ought to be doing more to help the war effort. She knew many people's feelings had been mixed about Germany's former ally but now things were different.

'I think Larry's right,' Mary said boldly, ignoring Mrs Matravers' glare.

Mr Button put his pint glass on the table and nodded thoughtfully. 'Yes, I think Larry's hit on something here. Nobody wants our staff to go without, Mrs Matravers, but although Russia was our enemy they're on our side now. If we help them, they'll have greater strength to help us and there's a chance we'll finally win this war.'

Rose met Mary's eyes and smiled. 'I agree. What about a rubber or aluminium drive? We could organise a fundraising appeal immediately and announce how much we've raised at the party. I read in the paper the other day that's what Stalin needs more than anything and he's appealing for other allied countries to help.'

Flo clapped her hands in delight. 'Wonderful idea. We could make some banners at the sewing circle, urging people to help. What do you think?'

'I think that's a marvellous idea,' Mr Button exclaimed as Mary and Rose nodded their support.

Larry, buoyed by their encouragement, carried on. 'So are we all agreed? I mean let's not forget some of our best customers are Russians. Wasn't our very own Princess Valentina in the store recently?'

'She's not strictly Russian,' Mary pointed out.

Rose shrugged. 'She's as good as.'

'And she took rather a shine to you, didn't she, Mary?' Mrs Johnson said pointedly.

Mary took a sip of her port and lemon as she met the older woman's gaze. This woman clearly didn't like her and as she looked from Mrs Matravers back to Mrs Johnson something told her they were thick as thieves. She wouldn't give either woman the satisfaction of letting them upset her, so instead: 'The way I see it, ladies, is that we are all enemies of Hitler and we are stronger together than we are apart,' she said, faking a smile.

'Well said,' Mr Button agreed.

Mrs Johnson looked mollified by this and nodded. 'Well, what do you think? Perhaps we could have a prize for the department who was able to collect the most scrap.'

Mrs Matravers stiffened. 'We are not like other department stores.'

'No we're not,' Mr Button replied with a frown, 'but Marks and Sparks did raise enough money to fund a Spitfire recently, which was extremely worthwhile.'

'Does that mean we should start doing everything they do? My goodness, you'll have us in uniforms in a minute.' Mrs Matravers shuddered at the idea.

'I think this is a noble cause and would motivate all the staff into doing even more for the war effort,' Mr Button said diplomatically.

Mrs Matravers sighed. 'Very well, then perhaps we should take a vote on it, if Mr Button agrees.'

As Mr Button nodded, everyone's hand went up in favour of a new dinner dance along with the aluminium drive and Mrs Matravers made a note in her jotter.

'Very good. So who wishes to liaise with Lyons?' she asked.

This time Mary raised her hand. 'I don't mind doing that.'

Mrs Matravers nodded. 'Fine, and who would like to organise the catering?'

'I'm ever so good with a ration book my mum always says,' Rose grinned. 'I don't mind, Mrs Matravers.'

The deputy manager smiled and patted Rose's hand. 'That's very nice of you, dear, but I rather think Miss Holmes-Fotherington would like to take that on as well.'

'No, really, I don't mind,' Rose protested, a strand of auburn hair falling into her eyes.

Mrs Matravers laid her hand warningly on Rose's arm. 'That's enough. Mary will do it. And she can also organise the entertainment. In fact,' she said with a hollow laugh. 'I rather think Mary can organise the whole thing. She's certainly well connected, as we've seen already, thanks to the way she got on with Princess Valentina – I'm sure this will be nothing to her.' As she threw her head back with laughter Mrs Johnson joined in, her high-pitched giggle jangling throughout the pub.

Flo and Rose exchanged doubtful looks. 'I think that might be a bit much for Mary ...' Flo began.

'Yes, I rather think that's a bit too much responsibility for such a new member of staff,' Mr Button cautioned.

Mrs Matravers shook her head. 'Nonsense. Oh, and while I think about it, Mary, I shall need you to accompany me to Canterbury next Saturday.'

Mary looked at her quizzically. 'I'm sorry, I don't follow.'

'We've an agent there,' Mrs Matravers explained. 'I need to visit them to ensure they are selling our products to standard, and you can assist. Flo will be busy running the department and Alice can't make such a long journey in her condition. Larry here has a delivery in Whitstable to make and will be our driver.'

At the thought of spending the entire day in her boss's company Mary felt a sick feeling burn in her stomach.

'That's very kind of you, Mrs Matravers, but I wonder if Flo can spare me for the day?'

Flo waved her hand. 'Of course we can manage.'

'It will be good for you to see some of the other areas of the business, Mary,' Mr Button added. 'At Liberty's we're very keen to develop our staff.'

'With your probationary period almost up it will be good for me to see how you've progressed,' Mrs Matravers added.

The colour drained from Mary's face. 'It's you that makes the final decision then?'

Mrs Matravers gave Mary a curt nod. 'Yes. Is there a problem with that?'

'None at all,' Mary said quickly.

'Then that's settled. We need to leave early on Saturday morning. You'll have my decision about whether or not your employment will continue after our visit,' Mrs Matravers said smugly as she glanced at the group's empty glasses and gestured at Mary. 'I rather think it's your round, dear.'

Almost immediately Mr Button was on his feet. 'I shall not allow a lady to go to the bar in my presence. I insist on getting the drinks.'

Without waiting for an answer he pushed his way through the crowds and made his way to the bar.

'Blimey, Mary, you're ever such a trooper,' Rose said admiringly. 'You sure you don't mind taking on all that work?'

As Mary opened her mouth to speak, Mrs Matravers interrupted. 'Of course she doesn't. I can tell you she thrives on hard work. Isn't that right, Mary?'

'That's right, Mrs Matravers,' Mary replied, doing her best to look enthusiastic.

'Well, that's settled then.' The deputy manager smiled. 'Mrs Johnson, Larry, would you be so kind as to assist me with helping Mr Button at the bar?'

With that the trio got up, leaving Flo, Alice and Rose gazing doubtfully at Mary.

'Are you really sure you're all right with all this work? It seems ever such a lot for Mrs M to pile on you,' Alice said.

'She's right, I like to be busy,' Mary replied firmly.

'But there's busy and there's busy,' Flo put in, draining her drink. 'I don't want you to feel overwhelmed. She's already got you on all the leisure clubs and now the Christmas committee as well.'

Mary held Flo's gaze and smiled with what she hoped was more confidence than she felt. 'Really, I'm fine. But I am sorry I had to miss helping you out with your dad the other Saturday, Rose. And I'm sorry I missed the Chinese too.'

The girls batted her concerns away. 'It can't be helped,' Flo said.

Rose nodded in agreement. 'It wasn't your fault. I just felt sorry for you missing out like that.'

'Oh, I didn't mind,' Mary lied. 'Anyway, I know you've both got enough on your plates at the moment. When is it Neil's coming back, Flo?'

At the mention of her soul mate she flushed with excitement. 'Christmas. I can hardly believe it.'

Rose whistled. 'That's such lovely news, Flo.'

There was a pause then as the girls turned to Alice and saw her eyes fill with tears. 'Girls, don't mind me,' she said firmly. 'You should talk about your sweethearts. It's what keeps them alive in here.' She touched her heart and then her head.

Flo gave Alice a sympathetic smile. 'Oh Alice, I just wish there was something I could say or do to make you feel better.'

'We all do,' Rose whispered. 'I don't know how you're getting through the days.'

'Because I have to.' Alice shrugged sadly. 'We none of us know what this war will throw at us.'

The girls fell silent at Alice's statement. The fact was that she was right. Nobody had any idea what would happen next, or when or whether this war would ever actually end. The constant threat of danger and the unknown was now normal, and all any of them could do was try to get through the days with grace and hope in their hearts.

'Is there any news on Tommy's leave?' Alice asked, breaking the silence.

Rose shook her head. 'He says he thinks they're heading overseas again but of course he doesn't know where. Everything's always so last minute with Tommy.'

'That's the joy of being a driver in the army,' Mary smiled wistfully. 'I used to get unexpected stops with my family if I had to make a delivery up north and of course it made sense for me to stay with them rather than in a strange billet that would cost the army money.'

'You must miss them,' Flo said in a low voice. 'I don't want to pry and ask why you don't talk to each other any more, but is there really nothing you can do to make things up?'

'Family is everything,' Rose said softly.

Mary shook her head. 'No, and I don't mind a bit. Of course I miss them, but well, as we've just been saying, you don't know what life is going to throw at you in this war. It's better this way.'

'But, Mary,' Rose said, her eyes brimming with tears. 'The idea of never having anything to do with your family again's heartbreaking, ain't it? I know I've been moaning about Mum lately but I wouldn't be without her.'

Flo whipped her head around to face Rose and gave her a firm stare. 'That's enough. Sometimes families don't get on. Mary's right, things are better left.'

Mary raised an eyebrow. 'You sound like someone who knows.'

'Dad only turns up when he wants something. He's like a bad penny, always getting into trouble,' Flo said angrily. 'I've lost count of the times he spent my wages on booze or let me down.'

'I had no idea,' Rose murmured.

'Well, some things are private, aren't they?' Alice said firmly. 'Look at my dad. The best thing he ever did was get on a boat to America to escape his troubles back here. It's just a shame he didn't take Joy with him!'

Flo frowned in sympathy. 'I hope she's not been looking for money again?'

Alice shook her head as she took a sip of lemonade. 'Not yet, but it's only a matter of time with Joy.'

'And does she know about Luke?' Rose asked gently.

'No.' Alice's eyes flamed with fury. 'And I don't want her knowing either. She'd only invite me to live with her and try and sell my baby or something.'

Mary gasped. 'She can't be that bad.'

'You wanna bet?' Alice said, raising an eyebrow as Mr Button returned with a tray of drinks, closely followed by Mrs Matravers.

Mrs Matravers sat back down on the hard wooden bench and raised her glass at Mary mockingly. Mary took a sip of her own port and lemon and locked eyes with her boss. Mrs Matravers might think she had a hold over her by knowing her secret, but, as Flo rightly said just moments earlier, some things were private and Mary was determined that the biggest part of her secret stayed that way.

Chapter Twelve

As Larry and Mrs Johnson returned to their seats with the rest of the drinks, Mary couldn't help noticing another man she hadn't met before had joined them.

'David Partridge,' he announced, smiling broadly at the girls.

'He's my brother before any of you go getting any ideas,' Mrs Matravers called warningly.

'Lovely to meet you, David.' Flo leaned across the table to shake his hand, and Rose followed suit.

By the time he reached Mr Button, Mary had managed to assess his strong jaw, thick dark hair and twinkling blue eyes. He looked younger than his sister, she thought, placing him at about thirty, and also seemed completely different.

'You're an army man, I hear,' David greeted the store manager pleasantly.

'That's right, thirty years' service,' Mr Button said proudly.

David bowed his head slightly as he released the store manager's hand. 'The country is honoured, sir.'

'Now, now.' Mr Button coloured. 'It was a vocation for me. Loved every moment. The honour was all mine.'

'What was it you did?' David asked.

'Drove ambulances mainly,' Mr Button replied, taking a sip of his pint. 'But of course I'm not the only one that's ex-army.' He smiled, gesturing towards Mary.

As David's eyes met Mary's her heart skittered. 'Mary, a pleasure,' she said, composing herself just in time to shake his hand.

David grinned and wagged his finger at her. 'My word. That's brave. Why did you leave?'

'She got thrown out for poor behaviour,' Mrs Matravers said in a flash.

As the words hung in the air, Mary felt a surge of panic as she looked at Mr Button. Did he know? He was chatting away to Larry now and she breathed a sigh of relief that he didn't seem to have heard. Turning back to David, she saw he didn't appear to have heard either as he continued listening to his sister.

'What are you doing here, David?' Mrs Matravers continued. 'Soho's not exactly your area, is it? Surely you weren't just passing?'

'Can't a man bump into his sister?' David said, holding up his hands in mock horror as Mabel shot him a playful, disbelieving glance. 'No, I was visiting a patient and saw you in here. Thought I'd pop in and say hello.'

'Well, it's lovely to see you,' Mrs Matravers said in a warm tone Mary had never heard before. 'But don't be too late. There may not be bombs dropping left, right and centre at the moment, but you hear all the time how people are falling over in the dark because they can't see. I bet your hospital's full of people that have hurt themselves that way.'

David smiled affectionately at Mrs Matravers. 'Thank you for your concern, sister dearest, but I have managed to get home in the dark before now.'

'Sorry,' Mrs Matravers said meekly, 'I just worry about you.'

'Good,' David chuckled, hanging his wool coat on the back of his chair.

'What is it you do, David dear?' Mrs Johnson piped up.

'I'm a doctor. Work in Guy's Hospital, to be precise,' David replied, taking a sip of his beer.

Larry stuck his chin out. 'You wouldn't have a look at my tonsils, would you, doc? They've really been giving me trouble lately.'

As he opened his mouth Rose started to laugh, only for Mrs Matravers to issue him with a firm stare. 'He will most certainly not look down the back of your throat in a public house, Larry.'

David shrugged good-naturedly. 'I don't mind. But, er, perhaps Mabel's right; the pub isn't the best place.'

'So have you been a doctor long?' Mary asked, sensing Larry was about to push the issue.

'About six years now,' he replied.

'Isn't it dangerous with all the bombs?' Mr Button asked doubtfully.

David smiled. 'All the operating theatres were moved to the basement for safety. But when the first lot of bombs dropped we were operating on a chap and there was no hot water, so all we could do was sterilise equipment on Primus stoves.'

'No!' Rose gasped. 'Weren't you frightened?'

Mrs Matravers rolled her eyes. 'Of course he wasn't frightened, Rose. He's a trained professional.'

'Actually, there were times when we were a bit scared,' David admitted. 'Not necessarily for ourselves, but for the safety of our patients.'

Mary felt a jolt of surprise. It was unusual to hear someone speak so frankly about working during the raids. She remembered when she had been caught out in a blast while driving in London, delivering papers to Downing Street. She had sought a public shelter immediately, but had been terrified all the same. Naturally, nobody ever confessed to fear, so it was refreshing to hear someone being so open.

'So do you live on site?' Mary asked eventually

'Yes, it's very comfortable. We're well looked after.'

'And you enjoy what you do?' Flo asked, leaning forwards to make herself heard over the chatter in the pub.

David nodded, pausing for a moment to take another sip of his beer. 'It's all I ever wanted to do since I was a little boy, though I think of it more as a calling than a job.'

'How lovely,' Flo replied. 'I feel that way about Liberty's.'

'Do you?' Rose asked, astonished.

Flo leaned back and sipped her drink. 'I do. I used to peer in the windows as a little girl, wishing I could afford to buy something.'

'I think that's something Mary knows all about,' Mrs Matravers smirked. 'Only she's gone the other way. Once upon a time she was all high and mighty, buying things left, right and centre in our shop, now she can barely afford a pair of shoelaces.'

As she and Mrs Johnson roared at her joke, David narrowed his eyes while Mary shifted uncomfortably in her seat. Opening her mouth to reply, Mary caught sight of David slipping her an awkward glance. In that moment she felt drawn to him, and as her eyes met his she felt something inexplicable pass between them.

Mrs Matravers didn't notice the exchange as she set her glass down on the table with a loud thud. The action made Mary jump and she couldn't miss the deputy manager's steely gaze. Mary didn't miss the subtext, and got to her feet.

'Well, if we've concluded our Liberty business, I must get home, girls. I promised Dot I'd help her sort out her jam jars to take to the rag-and-bone man in the morning. I don't want to let her down.'

A flash of disappointment crossed David's face. 'So soon? Surely you can stay a bit longer? You've barely touched your drink.'

'If Mary says she has to leave, David, then she has to leave,' Mabel hissed while Mrs Johnson nodded her head.

Mary put on her coat and smiled. 'I'm so sorry. It really was a pleasure to meet you but I must go.'

As Mary was turning to leave, Alice piped up. 'I'll come with you. I might not want to help Dot with her jam jars, but my back's killing me. See you tomorrow, all.'

As the girls walked out of the pub, Mary couldn't resist one final glance behind her and was delighted to find David gazing back. Giving him the briefest of smiles, she felt something pass through her that she hadn't felt in a long time – hope.

Chapter Thirteen

The following morning, Mary found herself tackling one of the less glamorous tasks that was part of her duty working at Liberty's. She stood in the alley out by the staff entrance, the cold wind biting at her fingers, diligently going through the bins, sorting out all the scrap that could be saved for the war effort along with any food waste that could be composted.

With the last of the bags sorted, Mary wiped her sticky hands on the teacloth Flo had thoughtfully offered her, and tried not to heave at the smell of what she was sure was leftover fish. Mary had no problem doing her bit, but Mrs Matravers was asking her to take a turn sifting through the rubbish far more than the other girls.

She didn't usually feel sorry for herself, but today she was tired and fed up. Mrs Matravers was not only keeping her nose pressed to the grindstone, she was humiliating her as well. The comments in front of her brother in the pub last night had been rude. Mary hadn't missed how protective she was over her brother either, checking what time he was leaving as if she were his mother, but there had been no reason to embarrass her employee; Mary was just glad that neither Mr Button or David seemed to have heard what Mrs Matravers had said about her army discharge. In another world Mary would have told the woman precisely what she thought of her. Yet given Mrs Matravers wasn't just her boss, but the keeper of her secrets, she knew she had to do everything the woman asked.

Getting to her feet, she looked at her wristwatch, a gold Rolex her father had given her when she turned twenty-one, and saw with a faint thrill that it was almost five o'clock. Tonight the stitching circle was meeting, and if there was one thing she was looking forward to it was letting off a bit of steam with the women she now considered friends.

Nodding to the men who worked in the loading bay, she returned to the shop, smiling. If you'd told her a few weeks ago that she would be looking forward to a night with a needle and thread she would never have believed it. But as she caught sight of Alice striding across the shop floor towards her she suddenly realised how one's life could change in a heartbeat.

'Are you all right?' Mary asked urgently, convinced she'd seen a look of pain flash across Alice's face. The fact she was due in less than two months wasn't lost on her or Dot, who both privately thought that with the amount of strain Alice was currently under, she should have given up work by now to rest.

'I'm fine. Honestly, if it's not you fussing over me it's Flo.'

'We're just worried about you,' Mary said quietly.

Alice paused by the atrium, took her friend's hand and smiled. 'I'm honestly all right. I know you all think I'm mad putting on a brave face—'

'We don't think you're mad,' Mary insisted, cutting Alice off mid-flow. 'We just want to help you, make sure you're not doing too much, that you know if you want to talk, then we're here for you.'

Alice's face softened. 'I know, and I'm grateful. But I'm better off working and throwing myself into things to take my mind off Luke. And I can do that a lot better if I know you're not watching me like hawks.'

'Fair enough.' Mary gave Alice's hand a quick squeeze. 'Now, did you want me for something?'

'Yes! Your favourite customer's in the shop and she's asking for you. Nobody else will do!' Alice giggled.

'Mrs Hunter's here? It's not Thursday.' Mary raised her eyebrows in surprise.

Alice linked her arm through Mary's and propelled her friend across the store. 'No, but she's got a new *Vogue* pattern she's desperate to try and wants help choosing the right fabric. She says you know which fabrics suit her best.'

At the sight of Alice's eye roll, Mary couldn't help laughing. 'What can I say? Some of us have got it, and some of us haven't.'

'Well, whatever you've got can you please hurry up and give it to Mrs Hunter. I don't want us to be late for the stitching circle tonight,' Alice hissed as they neared the fabric department.

Sure enough there was Mary's favourite customer standing with her hands on her hips, auburn curls bouncing on her shoulders, looking bemused at all the rolls of fabric on display.

'Mrs Hunter,' Mary greeted her, doing her best not to breathe in the clouds of Rivers of Paradise her client always insisted on wearing. 'How can I help you?'

'Oh thank God! Mary darling, I've got this blasted pattern and I need help choosing the right fabric. It's one of those siren suits I've seen Churchill wearing. The girls are mad about them of course and I want to get mine ready before Jane Merryweather holds her beastly dinner party on Saturday night.'

Mary smiled. Once upon a time these were her mother's concerns, and with a jolt Mary found herself wondering if they still were. She felt a surge of horror as she realised there was every chance her own mother might find herself in Liberty's shopping for something similar. What would she do if she came face to face with her?

'Mary dear, are you quite all right?' Mrs Hunter asked, her voice rich with concern.

Suddenly Mary came to. 'Yes of course, I'm so sorry,' she said. 'Now let's have a look and see if we can find you the perfect material.'

Much to her delight, Mary found that her knowledge of fabrics was improving by the day and she could talk extensively about the way certain fabrics draped, suiting some patterns more than others.

'Oh, this is gorgeous,' Mrs Hunter said, pouncing on a roll of floral Sunbeam fabric.

'It is beautiful,' Mary agreed. 'It's very light, though, so it might not be suitable for a siren suit.'

'But it will show Mrs Merryweather up a dream,' Mrs Hunter frowned, running her fingers over the material.

Mary stifled a smile. 'It is beautiful, but siren suits are meant to be warm so they keep you cosy in a shelter.'

'In a shelter!' Mrs Hunter let out a horrified gasp. 'But I want to wear this to a dinner party, not underground.'

It took every ounce of self-control Mary possessed not to roar with laughter at Mrs Hunter's statement. But remembering she was the customer and that the customer was always right, she pulled out the roll of Sunbeam and cut out the required length of fabric.

As she bade Mrs Hunter goodbye, Mary saw Dot, Alice and Rose on the shop floor looking at her, a mixture of disappointment and urgency in their eyes.

'What's up with you three?' she asked, filling out the sales docket ready to take to the counting house.

'We want to get on with the sewing circle,' Dot urged.

'Why the rush?' Mary queried.

Dot pursed her lips and looked knowingly at Rose, who immediately caved in. 'I told Alice we wanted to make baby clothes!'

'I thought we were making a quilt?' Mary asked, bemused.

'I know,' Rose wailed, her spectacles falling down her nose. 'But me and Flo were talking after you and Alice left the pub last night and thought it might be nice to get some baby things made for Alice. After all, it's not long, is it?'

'Nine weeks,' Alice confirmed. 'He or she should be with us by the middle of December, all being well.'

Mary shook her head, a lock of raven hair falling loose from her victory roll. 'I think it's a lovely idea, but I don't know how much help I'll be to you. I've only just got the hang of sewing in a straight line.'

'I know that,' Rose said kindly, 'but it's more about us all coming together to do something nice for the baby. You know, a new start.'

From nowhere, Mary felt as if she had been punched in the stomach. Despite living with Alice, who was blossoming each day, Mary hadn't given any thought to her own baby. She simply hadn't allowed herself to, choosing to neatly separate the two things. But now, as Rose's words of a new start hung in the air, the memory of the day she had said goodbye to her own child cut her as surely as if she were being sliced with a knife. What chance did she have of a new start when this torture, this agony, was always at the back of her mind, just waiting to pounce?

She opened and closed her mouth, unsure what to say, only for Alice to come to her rescue.

'Rose, why don't you go on down with Dot and we'll see you in the old pleating room. I've just got to run through this bit of paperwork with Mary,' Alice said quickly. 'Where's Flo?'

'She's with Mrs Matravers, said she would see us down there,' Rose replied. 'Are you sure you don't want us to wait?'

Alice shook her head and smiled. 'You two go on; we won't be long.'

Once Rose and Dot were out of earshot, Alice rounded on Mary. 'Are you all right? I couldn't help notice how your face fell when Rose mentioned a fresh start. Is there anything you want to talk about?'

'I'm fine,' Mary replied, doing her best to rally. 'Really, I'm just a bit tired.'

There was a pause as Alice cocked her head and regarded her. 'I know you and I didn't have the easiest of starts, Mary, but I've become quite fond of you lately. I'd hate for you to feel you haven't got anyone to talk to. It's taken me a while to say this but I consider you to be a real friend ...'

As Alice trailed off joy bubbled up inside Mary at an unexpected pace. 'Alice, I don't know what to say.'

'I mean it,' Alice smiled. 'I know what it's like to keep things bottled up. When my sister fell in with a bad crowd and turned to thieving just like our old man I was so ashamed I didn't dare tell anyone what she'd done. Thankfully I had my Luke to talk to; without him I'd have gone under. I just want you to know that me and Dot, well, we're here for you if you change your mind. Now, I'd better get down to the pleating room and find Rose before she has kittens.'

With that she turned on her heel and without a backward glance left Mary reeling at the unexpected sentiment. She might still be dealing with her own private battles, she thought, but the new friends she seemed to be making were helping her cope with that pain. Reaching under the counter for her black sales book, she leafed through the pages. At the end of every working day she had to ensure every part of the sales slip was filled in, complete with her sales number to ensure she got her commission. She had just filed the final part away when she looked up and saw Mr Button hovering over the counter clutching a posy of white nasturtiums.

'Mr Button,' she said warmly. 'You all right?'

The store manager nodded gravely. 'Mary dear, I know you will be seeing your landlady Mrs Hanson at the sewing circle later and I wondered if I could trouble you to give her these?'

As he thrust the flowers towards her, Mary caught a fleeting look of embarrassment crossing his features.

'Of course,' she said gently. 'Is there any message or would you just like me to give her these gorgeous blooms?'

The heavy floral scent wafted through the air as Mr Button hung his head and paused for a moment. 'Just the flowers ... No, wait!' Taking a deep breath, he looked at Mary beseechingly. 'Please also add that I'm sorry.'

Resting the flowers on the counter, she saw a look of despair flash across his face. Mary knew it wasn't her place to pry, but at the same time she had become quite fond of Mr Button, and hated to see him looking so upset.

'Are you sure there's nothing you would like to talk about, Mr Button?' she asked. 'Do tell me to mind my own business if you would like.'

'Oh Mary.' Mr Button's face fell as he ran his hand through his greying locks. 'I rather fear I upset Dorothy earlier when she popped in to see me. I asked her if she would like me to accompany her on a walk in Hyde Park next Sunday.'

'Well, that sounds very nice,' Mary murmured, unable to see the problem.

'That's what I thought,' Mr Button wailed. 'And after we had such a nice lunch the other day when I made the

Morrison shelter for her I had hoped we might be able to renew our friendship.'

Mary smiled sympathetically. 'I'm sure it will just take time. Dot's been on her own a long while and her husband George ... Well, she adored him.'

'I know.' Mr Button nodded sadly. 'But, you see, Dorothy and I were engaged. I thought we might have been able to tap more easily into some of the closeness we shared before.'

Mary couldn't help it; she let out a little gasp of shock before composing herself. Dot had never said a word about being engaged to Mr Button; the way Dot had told it, she and Mr Button had been little more than friends.

'I'll tell her,' Mary said, giving the store manager her best smile. 'You can rely on me.'

'Thank you, Mary,' Mr Button said earnestly.

With that he stalked quickly out of the fabric department and back up the stairs. Picking up the flowers, which were in full bloom, Mary buried her nose in them and inhaled their scent. She had a feeling her landlady wouldn't appreciate them quite as much as she did.

Chapter Fourteen

It was a full twenty minutes before Dot acknowledged the flowers that Mary had rested next to her work station when she joined the girls in the pleating room. Mary had expected her landlady to be as intrigued as everyone else when she tried to press the blooms into her hands but as Dot studiously ignored her and focused on her work, Mary got the hint and sat down opposite Flo. Taking the scissors Alice thoughtfully thrust at her, she concentrated on unpicking the seams of what had once been a very pretty Liberty print blouse, and said nothing.

In fact Mary was so caught up in her work that she barely heard Dot mention the flowers. 'Sorry, did you say something?'

Dot sniffed. 'I assume he gave you those.'

'If by "he" you mean Mr Button, then yes he gave me the flowers to give to you by way of an apology,' Mary replied, unable to resist a smile.

'Oooh, what's he done?' Alice asked.

'Surely he can't have done anything,' Rose cried. 'Mr Button's ever such a kind man. He gave me a day off that wasn't part of my holiday allowance when Dad had to go into hospital the other day.'

Dot said nothing and carried on stitching what looked to Mary a seam over and over again.

'Come on, Dot,' she said in a low voice. 'It can't be that bad.'

Dot lifted her chin and Mary was astonished to see tears pooling in her eyes. 'Oh, it's not, I suppose. We got to talking about George and Ethel and he told me that I broke his heart when I broke off our engagement.'

At that the girls put down their stitching, and looked at Dot, agog.

'You were engaged?' Alice said in disbelief.

'To Mr Button?' Flo added.

Dot nodded sadly. 'Yes, he asked me to marry him and I said yes. He asked my father and we was all set to get wed.'

'So what happened?' Mary wondered.

'We was both under twenty-one at the time, and, well, Edwin's father got a job over Kent way and insisted Edwin and his sisters went with him. His mother was sick, you see, had TB, and they thought the sea air would do her good.'

'So why did that mean you broke off your engagement?' Rose asked, puzzled. 'Surely you could still see each other?'

'We did for a while,' Dot explained. 'But then my father made me break it off with him and that was that. I was devastated.'

'But I don't understand,' Flo protested. 'Why would your dad do that if the two of you were engaged?'

'I was upset George stopped writing to me. Dad said that if a lad could do that then he wasn't that interested and he didn't want to see me with a man that would treat me so casually before we wed so he withdrew his permission,' Dot said. Her tone was firm, implying she wasn't about to say any more on the subject. 'Then I met George and knew he was the one for me.'

'Did you never tell Mr Button about George?' Mary asked quietly.

Dot met Mary's eye and shook her head. 'No, I didn't. I thought it best to move on. My father thought so too and I knew better than to disobey him.'

The girls fell silent as Dot finished speaking. Mary felt there was more to the story than Dot was prepared to share, but she, together with everyone else, had far too much respect for the landlady to pry any further and let the matter drop.

Instead, she leaned over to give Dot an affectionate squeeze, only for her landlady to back away. 'Sorry, sweetheart, I don't mean to be rude but is there a reason you reek of fish?'

At that the girls burst out laughing as Mary's face fell. 'I had to clear out the bins again.'

Dot raised an eyebrow. 'Didn't you do that just the other day?'

'Yes, and fire-watch duty too,' Flo put in grimly. 'I'm tempted to have a word with Mrs Matravers, Mary. There's no reason for her to be throwing all these terrible jobs at you.'

Alarm at the very idea pulsed through Mary. 'No! I mean thanks, Flo, but honestly, I'm fine. I'm sure she'll get bored of it all soon enough.'

Rose shook her head. 'I've never seen her like this before. Usually she just sacks the floor girls she can't stand, but you, well, it's like she's playing a game.'

'I don't know, girls,' Mary sighed. 'I hope she might come round in the end. She's got to make a decision about my probation on Saturday. I hope that once she's done that she might stop toying with me.'

Flo patted her hand. 'I'm sure she will. You work hard enough and that's what she's always valued.'

'Not only that but she's put you on most of the shop committees going. She wouldn't do that if she was planning on getting rid of you,' Alice pointed out.

'Don't forget she's got a lot on at home at the moment,' Dot frowned as she tied a knot at the end of her thread. 'Mabel's the breadwinner at the minute with Alf out of work, and given he likes to spend all of Mabel's hard-earned down the boozer I imagine she's worried about money as well.'

'So I'm the scapegoat?' Mary said forlornly.

'For the moment,' Dot said bluntly. 'She'll get over it, trust me.'

'She hasn't told anyone Alf's lost his job,' Rose put in, unpicking her stitching.

Dot snorted with laughter. 'Course she hasn't! If there's one thing Mabel's got in spades it's pride. She wouldn't tell you if she was dying, however much it hurt. No, she'll be keeping this one close to her chest.'

'And in the meantime, enjoying watching me fail,' Mary mused.

Alice looked up from her needlework. 'Well, me and Flo have been talking, and we think we can help you sort out some of the organisation for these committees Mrs Matravers has saddled you with.'

'Oh girls, that's very kind of you but you don't have to do that.' Mary sighed heavily, feeling as if she were adding to her friend's problems. 'Besides, Alice, you'll have enough on your plate with the baby.'

Alice narrowed her eyes. 'I told you, Mary, it's better for me to be busy.'

'And I certainly am now Mum's gone,' Rose admitted.

'I know it's hard,' Mary sympathised, 'but your mum's gone off to do a rather brave thing. Try and feel proud of her.'

'Oh I do,' Rose gushed. 'I just don't know how me and Dad will cope, and with Tommy off fighting in the army, well, it just feels like the empty chairs at our table outnumber the people sat around it.'

'You'll manage,' Alice promised. 'And we'll all help out when we can, won't we, girls?'

Together everyone nodded earnestly, assuring Rose that she wouldn't be on her own.

'I think that's the nicest thing about working at Liberty's,' Mary smiled warmly. 'It's a bit like in the army where we all mucked in to help each other.'

Dot chuckled. 'If that's the case, do any of you think we ought to make quilts as well as baby clothes this winter? What with the coal shortage this year, this little nipper's going to need as much help as he or she can get.'

'Yes, because it's not like he or she is likely to have a father to help out,' Alice wailed, all the happiness from earlier gone in an instant.

As Alice broke down in tears, the girls gathered their friend in for a hug.

'I'm sorry,' she said, her voice muffled through the various arms and jumpers. 'I didn't mean to cry. I've been trying so hard not to cry.'

'Better out than in, darlin',' Dot soothed.

'I knew it was all too much for you,' Flo scolded good-naturedly.

'That's what I said,' Mary murmured. 'You need to take care of yourself, Alice.'

'We just want to help any way we can,' Rose said tenderly.

'And I'm grateful,' Alice said through her sobs. 'But I'm scared I'm going to have to raise this baby alone.'

'But lots of women are doing that while their men are away fighting,' Rose pointed out.

'I know,' Alice said shakily. 'I know that looking after babies is women's work and that Luke wouldn't be changing nappies even if he was here. I know that with this war on he would still be in the RAF away from home, fighting for God knows how long. But not knowing where he is, wondering if he's alive, makes the idea of bringing up a baby alone like that seem all the more terrifying. We've been together for so long; he's my world. I don't think I can do it, girls.'

There was a pause before Mary spoke. 'I can't begin to imagine what it must be like to be in your shoes right now, Alice. But I do know a little about grief, and what I know is that it gets a tiny bit easier to live with each day, this anguish you carry around with you like a talisman.'

'Mary's right,' Dot added, her South London tones rich with sorrow. 'When my George died I thought I'd never survive. But I did. I took it one day at a time, and that's what you must do. You will never get over this, darlin', but you will live with it, and when that nipper comes along in a few weeks your Luke will feel all the closer to you as you'll have a little piece of him beside you all the time.'

Lifting her chin, Alice smiled gratefully at the girls. 'Thank you.'

As the clock above the table chimed eight o'clock, they broke apart.

'Time to go, girls. Mrs M will have our guts for garters if we stay here any longer,' Flo exclaimed. 'See you again next week?'

'Where else would we be?' Rose chuckled. 'Do any of you fancy a drink before we go home? One of the neighbours is with Dad tonight so I don't need to hurry back.'

'Where were you thinking of going?' Dot frowned. 'Not the Frog and Parrot, I hope – you heard what happened the other week?'

'No,' the girls replied in unison.

Dot leaned forwards and spoke in hushed tones. 'Well, it seems the landlord Jimmy Allan's been selling dodgy beer.'

'What do you mean "dodgy"?' Alice said, wrinkling her nose. 'You mean off?'

'No, I mean illegal. Apparently there's some hooch ring selling homemade booze up the West End at the minute.'

Rose frowned. 'But why? Beer's not been rationed.'

'No, but the ingredients that make it have been,' Mary said knowledgeably. 'I've heard of this before. There was a similar racket down in Surrey when I was stationed there. Some poor lad even went blind.'

'Get away!' gasped Alice. 'Blind?'

Mary pursed her lips, causing her chin to dimple. 'If you use too much alcohol it can cause blindness apparently.'

The girls looked aghast as they put on their hats and coats ready for the night air.

'I think I might give that drink a miss tonight, Rose,' Dot mumbled. 'I'm a bit tired.'

'Me too,' Flo put in.

'And I'm exhausted,' Alice yawned.

Mary smiled at Rose kindly, 'Nice idea, love. Another time perhaps?'

Rose nodded as she wound her woollen scarf around her neck. 'Yes, I think I've rather lost the taste for it myself now.'

Together the girls left the pleating room and walked back across the bridge and out into the shop. Once they'd ensured all the lights were off and the blackout blinds were in place, they walked out of the staff entrance and Mary slammed the door hard behind them.

Turning around she expected to come face to face with one of the girls but they had all walked just up ahead and instead she saw a man looming over her.

She screamed in shock, only for the girls to hurry back towards her.

'Mary, Mary love, are you all right?' Dot cried, her voice rich with concern.

Suddenly Mary felt the man reach for her arm, and then heard the sound of a familiar voice.

'I'm so sorry,' he said. 'I didn't mean to scare you. It's David, David Partridge. Do you remember me? I'm Mabel's brother.'

As Mary's eyes got used to the gloom, she found herself staring into the whites of David's eyes.

'Yes of course,' she said, heart still pounding. 'I'm so sorry to have screamed at you like that, but you gave me quite the fright. Whatever are you doing here?'

'Yes, who are you and what d'you want?' Dot said fiercely.

Even in the dark, Mary could tell David looked taken aback at the sight of so many women.

'It's all right, Dot, I know him,' Mary said, suddenly feeling sorry for David. 'But what I don't know is what you're doing here.'

'Well, I wasn't sure where you lived and I wanted to see you again, Mary, so I thought I'd wait for you after your stitching night. I'm sorry to give you a fright,' David said nervously. 'I wanted to ask if you might be free for a drink sometime.'

Mary stood rooted to the ground in shock as the rest of the girls giggled like teenagers.

'Are you asking our Mary out?' Flo said archly.

'I rather think I am,' David smiled. 'You all rushed off so quickly the other night that I hardly had the time to get to know you properly.'

Mary felt a rush of blood to her head. After losing the baby in Ceylon she had vowed never to get involved with another man again. It only led to trouble and heartbreak. Then again, there was something about David that made her feel drawn to him. She had felt the spark between them the moment he sat beside her, but could she afford to take the risk of having more to do with him? After all, if he ever found out the truth about her, he would more than likely run a mile, and Mary couldn't honestly say she would blame him.

'Oh, for heaven's sake, Mary,' Flo chided. 'Don't keep the poor lad in suspense. Go out with him for a drink if nothing else.'

'Just make sure it's not Jimmy Allan's place,' Dot muttered darkly.

'Will you come?' Mary begged.

'No I won't!' Flo exclaimed. 'And David never asked me neither.'

'You would be more than welcome to,' David said suddenly. 'If that's what you'd like, Mary?'

Dot took control of the situation. 'No it isn't! What Mary is trying to say, David, is that you seem like a very nice young man, even if you do go around scaring people half to death, and she would very much like to go for a drink with you.'

David grinned. 'When would you be free?'

'Now?' Mary blurted. Something told her that if she didn't pluck up the courage to go right this moment then perhaps she never would.

Chapter Fifteen

The French Pub was eerily quiet compared with the previous night, Mary thought as she took her first sip of the port and lemon David bought for her. Tonight they were sitting in the cosy snug rather than the open bar where it was much more sedate. The early October night was as chilly as if it were the middle of winter and Mary was glad of the warmth the snug provided.

'So how is life at Liberty's?' David asked, interrupting Mary's train of thought.

'Marvellous,' Mary smiled. 'I'm really enjoying it.'

'Hope my sister isn't giving you a hard time. She has a tendency to pick on the new girls. See if they're made of Liberty's material, so to speak,' he said gruffly.

Mary laughed, a lock of hair falling from her victory roll. 'Is that what it's called? All I'll say is I'm surviving and Mrs Matravers hasn't put me off yet.'

David chuckled. 'I still can't get used to calling her that. She's always been Moaning Minnie to me!'

'You and your sister are close then?' Mary asked diplomatically, raising her voice over the roaring fire burning in the grate.

'Yes, I think so,' David replied, shucking off his coat to reveal a smartly fitted grey suit, 'even though there's five years between us. But of course we had a rotten upbringing so that brought us closer together.'

Mary nodded. 'I'd heard something about that, but not much from Mrs Matravers.'

'There's not too much to tell.' David leaned forwards in his chair, the sparks of the fire dancing in his clear blue eyes. 'We were both miserable, but both had a strong work ethic and got out in very different ways. I worked hard at school, hard enough for them to take pity on me and allow me access to the scholarship fund to do my Higher School Certificate. I was fortunate enough to gain a scholarship to go on to university and train to be a doctor.'

'That's impressive,' Mary said admiringly.

'I don't know about that,' David replied, looking bashful. 'We just did what we had to. Mabel took elocution lessons – from a woman who sang in the Elephant and Castle pub would you believe! From there she managed to get a Saturday job in Liberty's and she worked her way up. Never forgot where she came from though, and married the chap who ran the pub.'

'You mean Alf?' Mary asked.

David shook his head despairingly. 'The one and same. Let's just say her husband hasn't got Mabel's work ethic.'

'You don't approve?' Mary ventured.

'Not much, no. He's a lazy shirker, always has been,' David admitted. 'Always on to some get-rich-quick scheme. He used to be an usher over at one of the West End cinemas up until recently. He was on sick leave more often than he was at work and now he's been sacked for thieving, leaving my sister the only one putting bread on the table.'

Mary raised an eyebrow. 'From what I know of your sister she's a stickler for hard work, so I find it hard to believe she'd put up with that.'

'That's the trouble with Alf: he's her blind spot. He can do no wrong.' David sighed in despair. 'Sorry, ignore me, the last thing I want is to talk about my sister, and given she's making your life rather miserable at the moment, I imagine she's the last thing you want to talk about as well.'

Mary smiled. 'How about we talk about you then? What made you want to become a doctor?'

'My grandmother was very ill with scarlet fever when we were small,' David explained matter-of-factly. 'She was the only one that ever really tried to take care of us, and when she died it felt like my world had collapsed around my ears. From then on I vowed I would always take care of the people I loved, and somehow becoming a doctor seemed the best way to do that.'

'My word,' Mary breathed admiringly. 'How very noble.'

'Not as noble as fighting in the army like you,' he said softly.

At the mention of the ATS, Mary felt her cheeks flame with embarrassment. She wasn't ready to tell him about how and why she had been discharged. 'It is,' she pointed out. 'But I didn't do so for very long. And let me just say that serving in the ATS was nothing compared to the battles I had with my friends, who were all wretched bores when they realised I had joined up.'

David threw his head back with laughter, before regarding Mary carefully. 'And what about your family?'

Mary froze, her drink halfway between the table and her mouth. The easiest thing in the world would be to brush off David's enquiry, but to her surprise she found that she didn't want to. In fact she wanted to be candid, even if it was only about a small part of her life story.

'To be honest, my family and I aren't close,' she said carefully. 'We had a falling out some time ago, and we no longer speak.'

She could sense David watching her as if waiting for her to reveal more of her story, but although Mary was happy to share something of herself, she didn't want to say too much.

'That must be tough,' David said eventually.

'It is,' she replied with a sigh. 'I really miss them.'

'Were you close – before?'

At the thought of her family, Mary smiled. 'Oh yes. I was a real Daddy's girl. Mummy always used to say I was rude and headstrong, just like my father.'

David chuckled. 'I haven't seen much evidence of rudeness yet.'

Mary made a face. 'You will if you're around me long enough. Mummy always used to say I couldn't help myself!'

'Then I fully intend to be around for long enough to see it,' David said, staring into her eyes.

Despite Mary's best intention of staying only an hour, the couple stayed in the snug until almost closing time where they swapped stories about their lives. Mary learned that not only did David have a keen interest in fishing but he was also quite the seamstress thanks to his medical training; he offered to show her how best to use a blanket stitch when they next went out.

By the time the landlord rang the heavy bell behind the bar to call last orders, both looked as surprised as the other that the evening had come to an end.

'Well, that was great fun,' David smiled as he got up to help Mary on with her coat.

'Yes, it was,' she agreed, turning round to face him only to find his smile had been replaced with a grimace as he looked over at a tall, thin man standing by the bar.

'Is everything all right?' she asked gingerly.

'Fine,' David muttered. 'It's just Alf.'

'Mrs Matravers' husband?' Mary gasped.

'The one and the same,' David replied, walking towards him. 'Alf, how are you?'

Mary watched as the man turned round at the sound of David's voice and grinned with a smile that didn't reach his eyes. His face was full of lines, while his black-as-coal eyes gave off an air of menace.

'I'm all right, ta, Dave,' he said in a broad South London accent. 'I'd be even better if you refreshed me glass 'n' all, what with me being out of work and that.'

As he gestured to his empty pint glass, David nodded grimly at the barman, and dropped a handful of coins on to the bar.

'Who's this then?' Alf asked, looking Mary up and down.

'My friend Mary,' David replied. 'She works for your sister at Liberty's.'

Alf smirked. 'You're not that posh tart she's taken on recently, are you?'

Mary opened her mouth to speak, but David beat her to it. 'Don't talk about a lady that way.'

'From what I hear, she ain't no lady,' Alf chuckled, taking his fresh pint from the barman.

Suddenly David flew at Alf, and held him by the collar of his tattered coat. 'Don't you ever talk like that again,' he growled, 'do you hear me?'

A look of surprise and fear flashed across Alf's face. 'All right, all right, it was just a joke.'

'Then apologise to Miss Holmes-Fotherington for your crassness.'

Alf made to laugh, as if he thought David was joking before realising that he wasn't. 'Sorry, no harm meant.'

Mary said nothing; her heart was roaring in her ears at what she had just heard, and it was all she could do not to flee from the pub in horror.

Shooting him a withering look before releasing him, David turned to Mary. 'Are you all right?'

When Mary gave a curt nod, David stalked towards the exit, held the door open for her, and then let it slam as he helped her outside. 'I'm so sorry about him,' he said earnestly.

Mary shook her head sadly as they continued walking down Dean Street. 'It's not your fault,' she said quietly.

'And it's not yours either,' David replied grimly. 'He's always been rotten to the core. I have no idea what my sister ever saw in him.'

Mary shrugged. 'Love is blind.'

'Can I walk you home?' David asked hopefully as they reached the bus stop that would take Mary back to the Elephant and Castle.

'I think it's a little out of your way and the bus stops directly outside my house,' Mary said gently. 'And I'm sure that like me you have to be up early tomorrow.'

David looked at his feet. 'That's true. But if you won't let me take you home, will you allow me to take you out again? Properly this time. To the cinema perhaps?'

'Where Alf used to work?' Mary asked doubtfully.

David chuckled. 'I think we can go to any other cinema.'

'Then I would like that very much,' Mary replied quietly.

As she uttered the words he hoped to hear, David's face lit up. 'Wonderful. Does Saturday suit?'

'I'm not sure what time I'll be back,' Mary sighed. 'I'm going to Canterbury with your sister to visit a Liberty agent. I've no idea how long these things take.'

'Sunday then?' David asked, his voice full of anticipation. 'I have patients to see at the hospital but I will be free from around two?'

'Perfect,' Mary beamed, her face lighting up at the thought of another night with Mrs Matravers' brother.

As her eyes met David's she found any trace of worry or nervousness had disappeared. Lost in his piercing blue eyes, she felt something stir and realised a passion she thought was long since dead was beginning to come back to life.

Chapter Sixteen

That Saturday Mary woke to a cool, bleak morning. Drawing back her blackout blind she was astonished to see that through the darkness she could make out the first frost on the rooftops visible from her window.

Quickly, she washed and dressed, mindful of the fact that today was no ordinary day. This would be her first visit out of the store as a representative of the Liberty brand. Mary hurried along the dark street, aware Mrs Matravers would have her guts for garters if she was even a minute late. Skipping breakfast, she hurried to the Tube, then made her way to the store.

Seeing the familiar black and white Tudor building that looked just like the Chester Rows she had adored frequenting as a girl always put a spring in her step, and despite the almost ungodly hour she still felt that same surge of excitement as always that she was a Liberty girl. Though of course, she realised with a sudden jolt, there was every chance that after today she might not be a Liberty girl for much longer. Her future depended on whatever decision Mrs Matravers made at the end of her probation period. As Mary rounded the corner to deliveries, where she had promised to meet her boss and Larry, she realised just how nervous she was.

She thought back to how David had told her that his sister always gave trouble to the new girl, and wondered if that was true. As another image of David flashed before her, she felt a sudden thrill pulse through her body. The drink they had had together in the French Pub, along with the sparks that flown between them afterwards, had been so unexpected, yet felt so utterly natural. Mary still had to pinch herself to believe it had really happened.

It was only the thought of Alf that left a bitter taste in her mouth. She had been blindsided at the way he had spoken to her, and was under no illusion: Mrs Matravers must have told him everything. Mary shook her head; how little the woman knew, she thought bitterly.

Now, as she hoisted herself up into the the van and took a seat in between Larry and her boss, she glanced across at Mrs Matravers, who appeared engrossed in her notes. For a brief second she wondered what would happen if she were to suddenly tell the woman the truth about her baby. How she still felt the pain of the loss as keenly each morning as she had when it had happened, and just how much she still missed her family who had chosen to turn their backs just when she needed them the most. Would that shame her and her husband into treating her with less disdain?

'Mary, did you familiarise yourself with the guard books I left for you to go through last night?' Mrs Matravers snapped, interrupting Mary's thoughts.

Reaching down into her bag, Mary pulled out the precious books showcasing the Liberty range of prints that she had been entrusted with the night before. 'Yes, I examined them thoroughly just as you asked.'

'Good.' Mrs Matravers nodded. 'I need you to talk to the agents.'

Mary gasped in astonishment. 'Why me?'

'I want to see how much you've learned,' Mrs Matravers said tightly.

Privately, Mary felt the only reason Mrs Matravers really wanted her to talk to the agent was so she could watch her make a fool of herself. Mary gritted her teeth; she wasn't prepared to give her boss the satisfaction of saying she hadn't passed her probation.

'You will also need to make them understand how wonderful Utility fabric can be,' Mrs Matravers continued, 'and how Liberty's customers can still enjoy the prints they know and love if we move forward with that next year.'

Mary frowned. 'Have you met some resistance then?'

'A little. Some of our agents think that the new Utility clothing scheme that the government is talking about introducing will be a disaster,' Mrs Matravers admitted. 'They just want us to keep making prints from the archives; you know there are thousands of them. But of course we can't do that.'

Larry glanced up from the steering wheel and burst out laughing. 'The problem is some of our customers, shall we say, don't want to be like nobody else. I s'pose you'd call 'em snobs!'

'Larry!' Mrs Matravers admonished. 'Do not say such things.'

'Sorry,' Larry muttered. 'But you must admit, Mrs M, our customers aren't typical of other stores.'

'And that's precisely why they are so very special,' Mrs Matravers replied. 'And precisely why Utility clothing will be such a hard sell.'

'Surely everyone can see we have to do our bit for the war effort,' Mary ventured. 'It's just change, that's all; nobody likes it.'

'Very true.' Mrs Matravers nodded. 'But retailers don't always see it like that, and so it's our job to convince our agents that Utility clothing and the Utility fabric we can offer is the way forward. In fact I rather think it's the only way forward.'

'How d'you mean?' Larry asked.

Mrs Matravers let out an exasperated sigh. 'I mean that it cannot possibly have escaped anyone's attention that goods are in short supply with every last scrap concentrated for the war effort. Nobody's got anything for us to sell!'

'I knew things were tight, Mrs M, but not that bad,' Larry protested.

'We're surviving, Larry, just like other shops, but I've no idea how long for. We're rearranging goods left, right and centre to make it seem as though we've got more than we have. And of course our customers expect so much more from us,' Mrs Matravers wailed. 'Why on earth do you think we're still making home deliveries to our most revered customers even though petrol's rationed?'

'We may not have plentiful stock,' Mary reasoned, 'but the one thing we can give them is excellent customer service and attention to detail, and we can share their passion for beautiful things. Liberty's is synonymous with quality after all.'

Larry let out a low whistle at Mary's speech while Mrs Matravers looked shocked before she spoke. 'That's a very wise statement.'

Mary offered a tight smile. 'But it's true, isn't it? I consulted the guest book the other day and saw several comments from our customers who said how wonderful Liberty's still is, that it's a breath of fresh air, a world away from the horrors of outside. That's what we have to offer. Liberty's is a landmark, an icon; there's nowhere else like it.'

Mrs Matravers gave Mary the first genuine smile she thought she had ever seen from her. It lit up her entire face, Mary thought, and it was a real shame she didn't do it more often.

'And that is what you must tell our Canterbury agent!' Mrs Matravers exclaimed.

In fact, Mary told the Canterbury agent at the department store, Beaths, a lot more besides during the hour-long meeting she attended with Mrs Matravers. After the women arrived, they whiled away the morning enjoying a tour of the store and meeting the staff that sold the Liberty prints, before moving onto lunch. Afterwards, they met a lady named Mrs Elm, who was standing in for the store manager. Together they drank coffee and Mary talked about her view of Liberty's and why it was so special. As she spoke, Mary felt a depth of passion for her work that she had never experienced before.

By the time she had finished the agent looked as enthused as Mary and agreed that it would be a wonderful opportunity to keep the Liberty name, spirit and passion for beautiful and artistic things alive.

Leaving the store and stepping out into the late afternoon breeze, Mary huddled into her coat and felt as if she were on cloud nine. Even Mrs Matravers had the good grace to congratulate her on a job well done.

'I must say, Mary, you handled that rather well,' she admitted. 'You surprised me.'

Mary smiled at the compliment, but knew it would be in her interests to remain modest. 'You prepared and trained me well, Mrs Matravers.'

'Yes, I did rather,' Mrs Matravers mused as she pulled her navy pillbox hat firmly over her head. 'And now we must find Larry and make our way back to London. I've a mountain of paperwork to get through.'

Mary frowned as they headed down the narrow Canterbury street and back towards the staff entrance of Beaths. 'You haven't forgotten Larry has a delivery to make in Whitstable?'

'Yes I had!' Mrs Matravers groaned. 'Oh, Alf will have kittens if I'm not back in time to make his tea. I promised him I wouldn't work late tonight and that I would bring back fish and chips. He has a rare night off from the cinema.'

'Sorry,' Mary shrugged, choosing not to question Mrs Matravers over why she was lying over the fact Alf was still working. 'It's almost four now, so perhaps we will be back in time just after store closing and you can take your paperwork home?'

Mrs Matravers charged ahead, all friendliness from earlier forgotten. 'Perhaps. Come along, Holmes-Fotherington, I won't be even later because of your dawdling.'

Arriving at the staff entrance, Larry took one look at Mrs Matravers' face and leapt into action. Sprinting over to the cab of the purple truck, he opened the door for his passengers.

'Hurry, Larry,' Mrs Matravers ordered. 'We need to get back to London as soon as possible.'

'Yes, ma'am.' Larry all but saluted as he fired the engine into life and began the long drive back to London, determined not to incur the wrath of Mrs Matravers any longer.

Chapter Seventeen

As the van rumbled through the city, Mary couldn't help noticing the stony look on her boss's face. Tutting and grumbling under her breath as Larry drove them through the winding countryside that led to Whitstable, any hope Mary might have had of the two of them reaching a new understanding fell by the wayside. Mrs Matravers would always have a problem with her, she realised, and no amount of hard work could change that.

With a sigh, she stared straight ahead out of the window, enjoying the scent of the sea air that filled the van through the crack in the window. The burnt orange leaves on the trees looked fiery against the darkening skies, and the nip in the air reminded her that winter was just around the corner.

Eventually, after getting stuck behind a tractor and a flock of sheep that seemed in no hurry to move anywhere despite Mrs Matravers opening the window and demanding they get out of the road, they arrived. Although it was pitch black, Mary could tell they were near the seafront and clambered out of the van to savour the salty sea air.

Mrs Matravers glanced at her watch. 'Oh hell's bells, it's gone seven. Not only have I missed store closing but it will be too late to get that wretched paperwork, and of course Alf will be furious.'

As Mrs Matravers sat in the cab pulling faces like a petulant child, Mary sighed. It wasn't as though any of this could be helped and it was rather foolish of Mrs M to promise her husband the earth when she knew she had such a busy day ahead of her.

Wisely choosing to keep her opinions to herself, she was just about to ask if there was anything they could do to help when Larry beat her to it.

Mrs Matravers shook her head sadly. 'No, Larry dear. If you could just make your delivery as quickly as possible I would be most grateful.'

'Do you need a hand?' Mary asked as he got out of the cab.

Larry shook his head. 'No, it's just a small piece of furniture for a regular customer. I won't be long, but how about you go and get yourselves some fish and chips for when I've finished. We can eat them in the cab on the way home.'

Mary smiled at the suggestion and turned to her boss. 'Good idea. How do you fancy a walk along the front to the chip shop? You might be late but there's no reason why you should miss out on your supper as well.'

Lifting her chin to look at Mary, Mrs Matravers flashed her a sad smile. 'Why not? To tell you the truth I'm starving.'

Together the two walked along the seafront, the roar of the sea providing the perfect backdrop. Mary found she was enjoying the chance to breathe in some fresh air after the events of the day. She hoped she had done enough to secure her probation and that she wouldn't end up sacked like so many of the other girls who had fallen prey to Mrs Matravers' whims before.

'How about this one?' Mrs Matravers suggested as they rounded the corner, finding themselves in Victoria Street.

Mary looked up at the fish and chip shop and saw a queue of people snaking out of the door and around the street corner. The aroma of the fryers filled her senses and right on cue her stomach gurgled noisily. 'It must be good if the queue is that big,' she said with authority.

Joining the back of it the two women stood in companionable silence as they waited their turn, the scent of fish and vinegar getting stronger the closer they got to the counter. By the time they reached the shop's front door Mary could almost taste the fish and chips she was looking forward to devouring, when suddenly she heard a noise above her head. It was only a very soft rumble at first, followed by a high-pitched whine that sounded like a menacing army of wasps.

Glancing up at the inky black sky, Mary felt her blood run cold as her well-trained eye caught what looked to be the outline of a lone plane, flying perilously low. The telltale shadow meant only one thing to Mary – it had to be a German raider, intent on destruction.

'I don't like the look or sound of that,' Mary said, urgently tugging at the sleeve of Mrs Matravers.

'What?' the deputy manager frowned.

Mary pointed at the sky. 'That. Let's leave now.'

Mrs Matravers wrinkled her nose, her grey eyes narrowing. 'I don't think so, Mary, we're about to be served. That plane is just flying across the water. We're in Kent; there are all sorts around. The Jerries haven't dropped a bomb for ages. I find it hard to believe they would start now.'

'For crying out loud,' Mary roared over the drone of the plane as it grew louder still. 'Come on!' She grabbed her boss by the hand when she heard the all-too-familiar scream of a bomb falling through the air.

After that everything seemed to happen as if in slow motion.

'Hurry,' Mary cried.

'Wait!' Mrs Matravers screamed, clutching her stomach, eyes wide in terror.

But this was no time to pause or offer comfort or words of hope. Mary knew if they were to have any chance of survival they had to run as fast as they could before the bomb blasted through the street. The whistle grew louder and louder, and Mary felt a sickening sense of dread as she all but dragged her boss over the road, her lungs burning and her heart pounding, adrenaline pumping through her body, urging her to find safety.

Reaching the other side of the road, Mary threw herself and Mrs Matravers against the grass verge just in time as the bomb Mary had heard only seconds earlier rocketed to the ground.

Almost instantly debris and rubble fell from buildings all around, trapping Mary and Mrs Matravers beneath the wreckage. Clouds of dust filled Mary's mouth and lungs and she coughed furiously, doing her best to remember her army training. Instinctively she knew to protect others around her and so she threw herself on top of her boss to shield her from any more falling rubble. As the buildings continued to tumble down Mary noticed Mrs Matravers remained mute, but her body was shaking so violently, she could tell her boss was terrified. Mary paused for a moment in surprise. This couldn't be the first time the deputy manager had found herself seeking shelter during a raid: she had endured the Blitz, for heaven's sake. Yet now she lay on the ground, her clothes ripped, her right leg cut and bruised, and Mary felt a wave of sympathy for Mrs Matravers crash over her.

Again acting on instinct, Mary leaned over to clasp her boss's hand, and was surprised to find Mrs Matravers gripped it as hard as if she had offered her a life raft.

'You're going to be all right, I promise, Mrs Matravers,' Mary shouted over the din, her voice hoarse from the dust she had inhaled. 'We'll get you out of here in a jiffy, then you'll be back home in no time, reunited with your Alf.'

'I won't,' Mrs Matravers began to moan. 'My leg hurts, Mary. I think it's broken. I'll never see my Alf again. This is how I'm going to end my days, here in this rubble.'

'None of that now, Mrs M,' Mary said kindly. 'We just have to wait for the all-clear to sound and then we'll get you out of here. Look, it's not that bad, we might have what feels like a ton of rubble on us, but I promise you it's no more than a few bricks. We'll easily get out of here, just you wait.'

'Do you really think so?' Mrs Matravers asked, her voice thick with emotion.

'I know so,' Mary said firmly. 'Now let's think about something else while we wait for those blasted Jerries to stop their funny business.'

'All … right …' Mrs Matravers panted.

In a flash Mary knew her boss was going into shock and she had to free her from the wreckage as soon as possible.

Quickly but gently Mary eased herself up by picking her way through the bricks that had propelled them to the ground. With what little room she had created, Mary bent down to check her boss's airways were clear and then put her into the recovery position.

'You'll be absolutely fine, Mrs M,' Mary called, working quickly to create further space by throwing more bricks and rubble to one side.

But there was no reply as Mary continued tossing debris out of the way. Within minutes she had made a large enough gap to drag Mrs Matravers through. Taking a deep breath, she gingerly grabbed her boss under her armpits and pulled her out to what she hoped was freedom.

Chapter Eighteen

Just as Mary dragged Mrs Matravers into the open air, the welcome ring of the all-clear siren sounded. Pulling off her good wool coat – which was now badly torn, she noticed – Mary placed it under her boss's head to keep her comfortable while all around them pandemonium continued to rage. The shops and homes that had once proudly lined the street had been reduced to nothing more than burning rubble. As for the fish and chip shop they had been standing in moments earlier, it was hard to believe, Mary thought, glancing across the road sadly, that it had once been anything other than a burning mound of bricks and mortar.

With the scent of scorched wood filling her nose, Mary glanced down anxiously at her supervisor. Thanks to the glow from the fires burning all around them, she could see that aside from the graze to her knee, her boss seemed to be all right. Mary clasped her hand, and felt at once how cold the woman was. She needed to get Mrs Matravers' temperature up, and without a second thought peeled off her cardigan and wrapped it around her boss, taking care to tuck it under her chin as if she were no more than a baby.

'Help will be here soon,' she promised. 'We'll get you looked at and then straight home.'

'I'm fine,' Mrs Matravers muttered. 'If you wouldn't mind helping me up.'

Alarm coursed through Mary as she watched her boss struggle to lift herself from the ground. 'No, don't,' she cried over the roar of the flames. 'Don't move a muscle until a first-aider has assessed you.'

'I'm fine,' Mrs Matravers repeated weakly, 'I'm just so tired.'

'I know. The best thing you can do is rest,' Mary said firmly, crouching beside her.

'I can't rest,' Mrs Matravers insisted, her grey eyes flickering open with urgency. 'I need to get back. There's so much to do.'

'You need to stay where you are,' Mary said, more determinedly this time.

Mrs Matravers offered Mary a watery smile. 'I'm sorry, Mary, I haven't been very kind to you.'

Mary spluttered, unsure if it was the dust from the explosion or the unexpected apology that caused her to falter. 'That's not true.'

'It's generous of you to say, but we both know I haven't. Will you forgive me?' Mrs Matravers asked. 'I'm sorry, I shouldn't have judged you so harshly, and I shouldn't have tried to use your mistakes against you; you must have suffered enough.'

There was a silence between the two of them then as Mary let Mrs Matravers' words sink in. Lifting her gaze to meet the eyes of the woman who had tormented her, Mary suddenly found the courage to voice the words she had kept hidden for so long. 'Yes, saying goodbye to my child has been the hardest thing I have ever had to endure.'

As the rumble of tyres thundered over the din of the blaze, Mary looked up to see scores of vehicles arrive at the scene. Civil Defence Volunteers had arrived to clear the scene and take care of the wounded. Mary couldn't help marvelling at the way they worked together with all the finesse of a military operation.

Householders were standing in the street screaming and crying at all they had lost, while one young girl, Mary noticed, was squeezing the life out of a mewing cat that had just been discovered under a mound of bricks. If only everything in life could be remedied with a cuddle from a cat.

Mrs Matravers coughed, catching Mary's attention. Turning back to look at her deputy manager she was startled at the haunted expression across her face.

'Are you all right?' Mary asked, her voice shaking, concerned the Liberty stalwart was in more pain than she was letting on.

'I lost a child myself once,' Mrs Matravers said shakily. 'She was only six weeks old but she was my world. I never got over losing her, and I can't imagine it's any easier for you.'

'No,' Mary replied, tears brimming at the memory. 'My child didn't even live for one day. But I shall never forget her and she will always hold a special place in my heart. Losing her will always be the worst thing that has ever happened to me.'

Mrs Matravers groaned in anguish. 'I know. Ruby was the beginning and end of my world. I never thought I would find happiness again after she died, but slowly I learned to rebuild my life, and now, just as I think I've found happiness again, it looks like it's all about to be destroyed. I'm pregnant, Mary, and I'm going to lose my child here, amongst all this rubble, I can feel it.'

At Mrs Matravers' shock announcement Mary's chest tightened with fear. There might be no love lost between the two women, but Mary wasn't about to let her lose another baby.

Getting to her feet, Mary saw a group of first-aiders working their way around the scene. Quickly and efficiently they were assessing the injured and treating them in order of priority. Waving her hands frantically in the air, she caught the attention of a female first-aider who immediately rushed towards them both.

'My boss here is pregnant and has hurt her knee rather badly,' Mary said hurriedly, gesturing to Mrs Matravers.

'How far along are you?' the first-aider asked quickly.

'Four months,' Mrs Matravers rasped. 'I lost a baby years ago. I can't lose another.'

'Don't you worry, love,' the first-aider smiled. 'Now let's have a look at this knee.'

Gently assessing Mrs Matravers for any further injuries, the first-aider paused and turned to Mary to do the same.

'I think you need to go to hospital. Just for observation,' she announced.

'Both of us?' Mary asked in surprise.

The first-aider shook her head. 'Just your boss here. I want her in so we can keep an eye on that baby. But you'll freeze to death, love. Let me get you a blanket to wrap around you. No sense you catching your death.'

Mary didn't protest as the woman quickly but efficiently wrapped a blanket around her shivering shoulders. 'Now, do you think you can help me get her to the ambulance? Then we'll get her across to the hospital.'

Mrs Matravers moaned as she leaned on Mary for support. 'I can't go to hospital, I've got to get back. Liberty's needs me.'

'Your baby needs you more,' Mary said firmly. 'I will ensure Alf knows what has happened.'

Reaching the ambulance, Mary helped Mrs Matravers settle into the back, and turned to the first-aider. 'Thank you for all you've done.'

'My pleasure.' The woman smiled before her expression turned to concern. 'Are you all right to get home?'

'Yes, we had a lorry a few streets away. I'm sure Larry will still be there wondering what on earth's happened to his fish and chips,' Mary said wearily.

At that Mrs Matravers moaned. 'Oh heavens, I'd forgotten about poor Larry.'

'Leave him to me,' Mary reassured her. 'In fact, leave everything to me. No doubt I'll see you on the shop floor bright and early Monday morning.'

With that, Mary was about to turn and leave her to the care of the first-aiders, but to her surprise Mrs Matravers gripped her wrist. 'You've more than passed your probation, Mary,' she said, her voice loud and true. 'Thank you for everything you have done for me. I was wrong about you, and I'm sorry. You are just the kind of girl we need at Liberty's.'

Chapter Nineteen

It was well after midnight before Larry and Mary returned back to London. Exhausted by her ordeal Mary had fallen asleep as soon as Larry had started the van's engine, and she had woken up bleary-eyed to find she was outside the home she shared with Dot and Alice.

Larry had helped Mary inside, and then insisted on driving to see Alf immediately to break the news about his wife. Rest was what she needed, Larry insisted, and Mary didn't argue.

That night Mary slept like the dead, not waking until gone three in the afternoon. Coming to, she had forgotten all about the events of the previous day, until the memories hit her like a tidal wave and she realised with a start how close she had come to being snuffed out like a candle.

Throwing back the covers she examined her reflection in her vanity mirror and groaned. Her face was still covered in soot and grime and she looked as though she hadn't slept in weeks. Every part of her ached as she washed and dressed, then hurried downstairs only to find there was nobody in apart from David, sitting at the kitchen table, the sunshine highlighting his lovely face. Mary jumped in shock.

'What are you doing here?' she gasped.

David smiled and got to his feet. 'I'm here to take you out for lunch. Your landlady Dot let me in.'

'Where is everyone?' Mary asked, looking around the kitchen as though Dot or Alice might be hiding under a chair or behind the range.

'They've gone for a walk along East Street. I was told to make myself at home, then make sure you had tea and something to eat.'

Pulling out a chair Mary sat down without question, then smiled as a steaming hot cup of tea was pressed into her hands and a plate of hot buttered toast was set before her.

'Where did you get so much butter?' she gasped, letting the salty juice dribble down her chin and savouring the taste.

'It's Dot's. She told me you would need beefing up after last night's antics and to fill you up, rationing or no rationing.'

As David sat opposite her, she felt his eyes upon her and suddenly felt shy. 'Are you all right?' she asked.

David grinned. 'You really are a treasure, Mary.'

'I don't think so,' she said, refusing to meet David's eyes.

'I do,' he said firmly. 'After the way you rescued my sister last night, you're a heroine to me.'

Shyly Mary peeped out at David from under her fringe. She still felt as drawn to him as she had done the other night, but all this talk of heroism was making her feel ill.

'Is there any news on Mrs Matravers at all?' she asked, moving on to safer territory.

David's eyes never left hers. 'Yes, I managed to telephone the hospital this morning,' he said. 'My sister is doing well.'

'And how is her leg?' Mary ventured. 'She seemed to have hurt it quite badly.'

'Just a sprain. Alf is driving down in my car to get her as we speak.'

Mary raised an eyebrow as she finished the last mouthful of toast. 'Didn't you want to get her yourself?'

David shook his head, a lock of brown hair falling into his eyes. 'I wanted to thank the girl that saved my sister in the first place with lunch. Assuming you're not too tired, that is?'

A flicker of alarm passed across his face and Mary smiled sympathetically. 'I'm not too tired at all.'

He grinned, leaping to his feet. 'Then shall we? There's a little place I know.'

Shyly, Mary let David escort her out of the house and together they walked towards the Tube station. The autumn sunshine was still bright, despite the fact winter was just around the corner, yet it could do nothing to disguise the horrors of war that were evident everywhere.

What had once been a row of houses was now nothing more than a pile of rubble, while shops and buildings stood in partial ruin, though Mary noticed with a smile that some of the shopkeepers had done their best to remain open for business. One shoe shop had cleared out the rubble and posted a sign in the broken window, declaring they were more open than shut. But what haunted Mary the most was the sight of fragments of lives half lived with half-bombed-out homes exposing wallpapered rooms and cupboards hanging from walls.

'You never get used to it, do you?' David said sombrely.

Mary shook her head, knowing just what he meant. 'No. I was only thinking the other day that sometimes it's possible to believe that the war's over. Sights like this prove that no matter how hard you want to pretend, the Jerries aren't going anywhere.'

David nodded grimly as he quickened his step. 'What was it like? When you were caught out with the bomb like that yesterday?'

'Horrific,' Mary replied as they carried on walking. 'I thought I would be more prepared, given my army training, but despite the continued raids of the past twelve months I had never been involved directly in a blast. I had always heard the siren and taken shelter.'

'I have always been fortunate too, but when you see sights such as this one' – he pointed to another block of houses that had been decimated – 'you wonder why not me? There but for the grace of God.'

'You can't think like that,' Mary said earnestly, 'you just have to get on with life, make the most of every opportunity. Don't worry about why you haven't been in a blast or when you will be, worry about how to make each moment count, so if you are, well, then you have no regrets.'

Stopping abruptly in the middle of the street, David cocked his head and smiled. 'So are you telling me that's what was going through your mind last night? The fact you had no regrets?'

Mary could have kicked herself. She didn't want to lie to David, but nor did she want to tell him any more than she had done about her past. 'I've plenty of regrets,' she replied honestly. 'But I wasn't thinking about any of that last night. I was focused on keeping your sister alive.'

'And I still cannot believe you single-handedly pulled her from the wreckage like that,' David said, letting out a low whistle.

Mary laughed as they continued past the Tube station and headed in the direction of the river. 'Before I joined the army, I might have told you I was bally heroic to have done such a thing. I'd have sent Daddy and Mummy a telegram informing them of my bravery and letting them know what a jolly marvellous daughter they had.'

'And now?' David asked.

'And now, this is daily life,' Mary shrugged. 'I'm not special or different or, God forbid, heroic. I'm just like everyone else.'

Together they walked across Southwark Bridge, past the damaged buildings at the northern end and out into the City itself, shuddering at the skeleton-like state of Cannon Street Station. They continued past the craters and piles of rubble that lined the streets around Ludgate Circus, pausing only to marvel at the fact St Paul's Cathedral was still standing amid so much devastation.

'So where are you taking me?' she asked, feeling as if they had been walking for hours.

David's face broke out into a broad smile. 'We're going to see a friend of mine. Do you like Italian food?'

'I love it,' Mary gushed.

'Well, then you're in luck, because today I'm taking you to a little family-run eatery,' he replied, steering her into a narrow street.

After more than two hours on their feet, Mary realised they were now in the heart of Soho and felt a pulse of delight. She had always adored this area, feeling strangely at home amongst the narrow streets and dark brickwork. Reaching a bright red door with dark windows, Mary took in the nondescript building in front of her. It didn't look like much, she thought, but then it struck her how Italians now probably had to try to disguise who they were. When Mussolini had announced Italy was at war with Britain and France last June, mobs had stormed the streets where Italians lived, hurling rocks and throwing stones at Italian shops and homes.

Pushing open the door, David led her inside and she was stunned at how different the restaurant was. The place was heaving with people crowded around tables covered with white cloths, and a band in the corner played traditional Italian music. With laughter and gaiety at every table, Mary felt as though she had been transported across the continent to Rome, a city she had once visited with her father when she was small. Memories of happier times came flooding back, hitting her squarely in the solar plexus as she remembered a time when she and her father had been so close. Wrenching herself back to the present, she took in the scent of fresh tomato, oregano and garlic and licked her lips in anticipation of what was to come.

'Giorgio.' David greeted an olive-skinned older man weaving his way through the tables with a smile for all his customers.

'David! You come!' Giorgio replied, beaming at his friend and welcoming him with a kiss on each cheek. 'And who is this?'

'May I present my very good friend, Mary Holmes-Fotherington,' David said, giving Mary a little push forward.

'Delighted to meet you,' Mary said as Giorgio also kissed her enthusiastically on each cheek.

'Please, come with me, I save for you the best table,' he cried, leading them to an intimate table in the corner.

Pulling out a chair for Mary, he placed a menu in each of their hands. 'For you, David, I have kept back a little of the minestrone and the lasagne I know you love,' he explained, before opening a bottle of what looked to Mary to be a very good red wine, and filling their glasses. 'Sshh,' he said, tapping his nose.

As he walked away, still wearing a large grin on his face, Mary couldn't help laughing. 'How do you know Giorgio?'

'I used to work for him when I was in medical school.'

'You're not serious?' Mary looked at him open-mouthed in shock.

David nodded, taking a sip of wine. 'It's true. Giorgio needed a pot washer, and I needed to pay my way. I've been grateful to him ever since, and consider him family.'

Mary smiled affectionately at the passion in David's voice. 'Do Giorgio's family help him run the restaurant?'

'His wife Giovanna does,' David replied, 'his children are in Italy. You know for them family is the most important thing in the world.'

'But not for you?' Mary asked, feeling emboldened by the wine.

'What makes you ask that?' David said in surprise.

'I just thought that with your sister being in hospital you would have rushed down to see her, rather than pop out for lunch with me,' Mary replied.

David played with the stem of his wine glass. 'Mabel and I have a complicated relationship. We've always been close, but she can be rather possessive, as you perhaps witnessed when we first met.'

Mary raised a knowing eyebrow. 'I did notice she mothered you a bit.'

David laughed. 'Kind of you to put it that way. She's always been the same. Never afraid to fight my battles for me. When I got in trouble at school she was straight into the headmaster's office and when she got wind I was courting a young lady named Vera at university she took great pleasure in telling her she was not to trample all over my heart!'

'And did she?' Mary giggled.

David shook his head. 'We only went out once. I dread to think what Mabel might have done if she knew I'd taken a girl out *more* than once.'

At the ridiculousness of the statement, they broke into laughter, only stopping when Giorgio arrived with a steaming bowl of minestrone soup for each of them.

'And you don't feel as protective of Mabel?' Mary asked, smiling her thanks at Giorgio.

'I adore Mabel, but I see her faults,' he replied, picking up his spoon. 'She can be judgemental and bitter, and I

160

have seen the way she and Alf talk to you. It's not something I approve of.'

The rich smell of tomatoes was making Mary's mouth water and she took an appreciative mouthful. It was easily the best thing she had eaten in years and she couldn't resist taking another large spoonful before she spoke. 'It doesn't matter, David. And besides, I hope that things will be different after yesterday. Your sister told me I'd passed my probation, so it looks as though I may be staying at Liberty's for some time.'

'I sincerely hope so,' David replied softly, 'because I rather like you, Miss Holmes-Fotherington.'

As he reached over and clasped Mary's hand, she felt a sudden thrill at the feel of his skin against hers. 'I rather like you too.'

Once David and Mary had finished their soup, Giorgio placed a lasagne in front of David and a large tomato and olive pizza in front of Mary. The size of the dish had Mary's eyes out on stalks as she wondered how she could eat something so large.

But as she and David continued to chat about their lives Mary found she had no problem devouring the pizza, or the vanilla ice cream that David had thoughtfully asked Giorgio to prepare especially for Mary. It was funny how rationing didn't seem to have touched this particular restaurant, and as Mary finished off her dessert, she found she didn't want to know just how Giorgio sourced his ingredients or indeed where from.

'That was the best meal I have ever eaten,' Mary sat back and sighed once they had finished. 'And I don't think I'll ever need to eat again.'

David laughed as he got to his feet and helped Mary on with her coat. 'So are you too full for a stroll around the park?'

Mary was delighted at the thought of spending more time with David. 'I would love to.'

'Then shall we?' he asked, holding his arm out for Mary and waving a fond farewell to Giorgio.

Outside they walked through the labyrinth of streets that eventually led them to St James's Park. It was now almost seven o'clock, Mary realised, and the night was drawing in. As she looked back up at David she found him looking at her intently and instantly recognised her own desire mirrored in his gaze. The two of them were so swept away by one another that words were no longer necessary as David pulled Mary into his muscular arms and showed her the depth of his affection with a sensuous kiss. The feel of his lips against hers set what felt like a small explosion off inside and as Mary lost herself in the moment she enjoyed every fizz and sparkle, never wanting the kiss to end.

Chapter Twenty

Nearly a fortnight after the Whitstable bomb and Mary felt as though her world and everything in it had shifted on a sixpence. Not only had she passed her probation and become a fully-fledged Liberty girl but Mrs Matravers had returned to work a different person. Generally she had become kinder and more tolerant with the staff, and had begun to treat Mary with a great deal more respect.

As a result, Mary found she no longer woke with a feeling of dread in her stomach as she wondered whether Mrs Matravers would single her out for some new form of torture. Instead Mary felt light and happy. She found nothing could dampen her mood, not even the relentless downpours, grey skies and dark mornings and certainly not the endless round of committee meetings she continued to endure.

Mary knew that much of Mrs Matravers' change in attitude was because her baby was safe and well and the deputy manager had announced the news of her pregnancy with glee when she returned to work. Mary was delighted to see that everyone clapped and cheered at the idea of a baby Matravers and found herself hoping this signalled a new start for all of them. Knowing she had the approval of Mrs Matravers and Flo meant Mary felt more confident. Not only was she able to advise customers more efficiently but she was also beginning to get more out of Flo's weekly sewing circle, taking pleasure in learning the basics from Dot and even managing to start a little romper suit for Alice's baby.

Since her Italian lunch with David the two of them had become inseparable and there was barely an evening she and the doctor hadn't spent together. However, the couple were keeping their fledgling relationship under wraps with neither one keen to invite anyone into their private world. Mary had not even confided in Dot or Alice. She knew it was silly, they would no doubt be delighted for her, but Mary didn't want to cause Alice any pain. The baby was due in seven weeks' time and Alice was no longer spending much of her day in tears. Yet there was still no news of Luke and Mary knew her friend must be feeling bereft. The last thing she felt that Alice needed was the sight of love's young dream taunting her as she prepared to give birth without her husband, and so she and David agreed to keep things to themselves.

Now, as she took her place for the weekly sewing circle, she felt a flush of happiness that the new life she had carved out for herself was beginning to turn out so well.

'I've been wondering if I ought to do something more useful,' Dot put in as she unpicked the stitching of a rayon skirt. 'I keep hearing how this new National Service Act of the government's means they want more men and women doing vital war work. I feel I need to do more.'

'You're doing plenty,' Flo said loyally. 'Besides, that's just for men, isn't it?'

Mary shook her head as she reached over the table for a safety pin. 'Women as well.'

'Do you fancy going back in the army then?' Alice asked Mary.

'I don't think you can go back once you've been discharged,' Mary replied, swiftly changing the subject. 'Seems as though your mum had the right idea though, Rose.'

'She did,' Rose sighed. 'I had a letter off her yesterday. She's having a whale of a time but Dad's proud of her for doing her bit.'

Mary raised an eyebrow. 'As I recall it wasn't a holiday camp.'

'Tell that to Mum,' Rose grumbled. 'She says being a Wren is the making of her.'

'Well, we need everyone to do what they can,' Mary said loyally before turning to Flo. 'You never think of joining up?'

'I have thought about it,' Flo sighed. 'I made some enquiries down the labour exchange the other day.'

At that there was a huge intake of breath.

'You never said,' Alice gasped. She shifted uncomfortably on her seat: her bump was now so large it prevented her sitting upright.

'You can't leave Liberty's,' Rose said firmly. 'The place would never cope without you.'

Flo smiled wanly. 'I don't want to leave. Liberty's is in my blood, but I have to do something more for this war. Nobody else in my family seems able to do anything.'

'What about your aunt?' Alice asked.

'She's in the WRVS like Dot, but my dad's a right shirker, he'd just take off the country rather than give anything back,' Flo said grimly. 'I don't want to be like him.'

'However did he end up with your mum?' Rose asked. 'Was he always a layabout?'

'I don't know,' Flo replied, bending her head over the outline of a rabbit she was embroidering on to a pocket. 'I don't know much about Mum either as she left when I was so tiny. Whenever I try to ask Auntie Aggie about it, she says her sister always played her cards close to her chest and she doesn't know any more than she's told me.'

'Do you think the only reason she hasn't come back is because of your father then?' Mary asked.

'Maybe,' Flo sighed. 'Strikes me that if my mum had really loved me though she'd have stuck around. What sort of woman leaves her child with a drunk father?'

Mary frowned at Flo's outburst. She could tell that the subject still caused Flo pain. 'Maybe it wasn't as simple as that. Perhaps she thought it for the best.'

'It doesn't excuse the fact I've got a sorry excuse for a father who's only ever on the want,' Flo said bluntly.

'When did you last see him?' Alice asked.

Flo set her needlework down and tried to remember. 'Must be at least five years ago now. The few times I have ever met my dad have always turned into a disaster of sorts. The last time I saw him he gave me and Aggie a hiding and threatened to do more besides after he nicked her jewellery and we went to the police,' Flo said grimly.

'Oh Flo, I'm sorry,' Mary said.

Flo managed a thin smile. 'But it's like my Neil says, he's the past so that's where I have to leave him.'

'How is Neil getting on?' Mary asked, seizing the opportunity to turn the conversation around. 'Will he still be home for Christmas?'

Alice pursed her lips. 'I hope for your sake one of us can be reunited with our sweetheart soon.' At that she burst into tears, holding the baby blanket she was stitching to her face and soaking it with her tears. At the unexpected outburst the girls exchanged worried looks before getting up to comfort her.

'Oh Alice,' Mary said, wrapping an arm around her friend. 'Please don't cry.'

'Yes, what's all this, lovey?' Dot asked kindly.

'It's me, isn't it?' Flo babbled. 'I'm sorry, I didn't mean to make you cry by talking about Neil, I'm so sorry.'

Rose rested her head on Alice's shoulder. 'What can we do?'

Alice lifted her chin and smiled sadly at the girls. 'It's me who should be sorry. Since I fell pregnant, I've been all over the shop, crying one minute and laughing the next.'

'It's never easy,' Dot soothed. 'Your Luke's still missing, you're bound to be upset.'

'I know. You're right. I'm sorry, girls.' Alice wiped the tears from her eyes with the heels of her hands. 'Come on, distract me. Mary, what's happening with you and David? And don't try to deny it, because me and Dot have seen the two of you canoodling on our doorstep twice this week at least.' At that the girls burst out laughing while Mary went bright red.

'You know?'

'We all know,' Dot chuckled. 'You two thought you were being so clever hiding things but the love on both your faces is that clear all the Elephant could see it even in the blackout!'

Mary couldn't believe the secret she thought was hers had been played out so publicly. 'It's early days,' she managed.

'Oh, don't be so coy,' Dot teased, giving her a playful nudge. 'With a war on, you should celebrate all you can. You young things ought to enjoy yourselves.'

Mary arched an eyebrow. 'Is that what you and Mr Button are doing now you've made up?'

'Me and Edwin are enjoying each other's company,' Dot said primly.

'But you have made up, haven't you?' Mary persisted.

Dot smiled. 'We have. It's been like a breath of fresh air finding one another again. I think we're both happy to see where it leads.'

'But no canoodling on doorsteps for you then?' Flo asked cheekily.

At the idea of the older woman and their store manager engaging in a public display of affection, the girls roared with laughter, only stopping when they caught sight of a gleam of excitement in Flo's eye.

'I've got some news,' she blurted, getting to her feet.

'Ooh, what?' Rose asked excitedly. 'Wait, you haven't found a new job doing war work already, have you?'

'Sssh, Rose,' Dot hissed, impatiently pressing a finger to her lips. 'Let Flo speak.'

Alice regarded her department manager warily. 'You're not pregnant 'n' all, are you? This place will be Baby Liberty if we carry on.'

Laughing, Flo shook her head. 'No, I'm not expecting. But, well, I've been wanting to tell you all this for a week or so now, but with the bomb and Mrs Matravers and Luke missing, well, there's never been a good time to say.'

Mary was on the edge of her seat. 'Go on,' she demanded.

'The other day I had a letter from Neil. He told me he's coming back at Christmas as it goes,' she said hurriedly, glancing at Alice to check her reaction.

At that the girls banged on the table with delight. 'That's wonderful news,' said Alice sincerely.

'No, wait, that's not it,' Flo called above the excited din. 'In the letter, Neil had a question for me. He asked me to marry him.'

Now all the girls bar Alice were on their feet, clapping and cheering at the good news. Yet despite their joy, none of them could take their eyes from Alice. Although she was smiling, Mary could see the tears that were brimming in her eyes.

Flo stepped forward and knelt down beside Alice as the girls quietened down. 'I'm sorry. I know this is the worst timing in the world for you.'

'What are you sorry for?' Alice gasped. 'This is the best news I've heard in weeks. Come here.'

As Alice pulled Flo into her arms, Mary exchanged smiles with all her friends. She had never felt a part of something so big and so heartfelt in all her life, and she wanted to savour it.

'So when's the big day?' Rose called, removing her glasses to wipe away the steam.

Flo pulled away from Alice and regarded the girls with a grin. 'Boxing Day, ladies, while he's home on leave. That's what I wanted to tell you all. I'm getting married at Christmas!'

Chapter Twenty-One

The following morning as Mary joined Alice, Rose and Flo on the shop floor, she found the girls huddled around the till, still reeling with delight at Flo's announcement.

'So you really had no idea at all he was going to ask you?' Rose exclaimed as she handed the weekly sales figures to Alice.

'None at all,' Flo replied, beaming. 'It was the best letter I've ever had. I can't stop carrying it around with me, it was so romantic.'

'Aren't you worried about losing it?' Alice asked.

Flo shook her head dreamily as Mary gave her a playful nudge. 'Flo, there's just nine weeks to go until Christmas, do you really think you can organise a wedding in that time?'

'That's right,' Rose agreed. 'Are you sure he didn't mean next Boxing Day?'

Flo looked up sharply from her paperwork and narrowed her eyes at the girls. 'He meant this Boxing Day and yes, I do think we can organise a wedding in that amount of time. I've already booked the church.'

Mary looked up from the fabric she had been cutting for a customer who would be collecting her pre-ordered goods later on. 'Really? My word, that's quick.'

'Yes. The vicar is an old family friend of my aunt's. He said he would be more than happy to marry us on that day,' Flo replied happily.

Rose raised an eyebrow. 'Blimey! You don't hang about!'

At that Flo let out a groan and held her head in her hands. 'The thing is, that's the only thing I have got sorted out. I haven't organised my flowers, a dress, the food or a guest list.'

Rose, Alice and Mary exchanged looks of concern before Alice spoke.

'We'll help, Flo.'

'Yes, of course we will,' Mary agreed. 'Look, I'm organising the food for the Liberty Christmas dinner. Why don't you let me have a word with the caterers, and see if they can help? It's a bit short notice, but I'm sure they'll do what they can.'

Flo smiled at Mary sadly. 'That's very kind of you, Mary, but I'm afraid we won't be able to afford caterers. I think it'll be a paste sandwich and pint of stout if we're lucky.'

'We can organise that for you,' Alice insisted. 'Let me speak to Dot. She knows everyone and anyone, and no doubt she'll be more than happy to get involved – she's very fond of you.'

Flo breathed an audible sigh of relief. 'Do you think she'd mind?'

'Mind?' Mary snorted. 'She would be more upset if you didn't ask her.'

'And what about your dress?' Rose asked gently. 'Perhaps you could buy something with your staff discount. We do get Liberty fabric at wholesale price.'

'I did think that,' Flo sighed. 'But it seems a dreadful waste of coupons. I thought I might try to do something with my aunt's old wedding dress. She lost my uncle in the last war, just like Dot. But she's always kept it and said nothing would give her greater pleasure than to see me walk down the aisle in it.'

Alice clapped her hands together in delight. 'Yes! Why don't you let us work on it at the sewing circle? We can

171

easily do two nights a week if old Buttons lets us have the pleating room.'

'Speaking of which, I thought we might do an extra night at Rose's,' Mary suggested. 'I think she might appreciate a bit of help with her dad.'

Rose flushed at Mary's suggestion. 'Mary, that's kind, but you don't have to do that.'

'Nonsense,' Alice said firmly. 'I think it's a great idea, Mary.'

'It's a lovely idea,' Flo put in. 'I'd been meaning to ask you if you were coping on your own, Rose.'

'She's not,' Mary cut across Rose. 'She's tired, fed up and needs some support.'

'Mary!' Rose flushed, clearly embarrassed.

'What? It's true,' Mary shrugged. She had privately been wondering for some time how she could do more to help the young girl. For too long now the bags under Rose's eyes and wan appearance had been left unchecked.

'That's a great idea, isn't it?' Alice said, as the rest of the girls nodded their heads in agreement.

Looking in amazement at her friends, Rose's eyes shone with tears of happiness. 'I can't believe this. How can I ever repay you?'

'No repayment necessary,' Alice smiled kindly. 'You'd do the same for us.'

Flo nodded shyly. 'And actually, there is one thing I wanted to ask you girls, but now you're all doing so much, I'm not sure you'll want to.'

'What is it?' Mary asked, wrapping the fabric tidily. 'If it's providing the entertainment for your reception, I don't mind having a go. I did a rather good Geraldo impersonation in the army, and of course my rendition of "I Don't Know Why I Love You But I Do" was legendary.'

Flo chuckled. 'That's a generous offer, but actually I was hoping you girls would be my bridesmaids.'

At that Alice, Rose and Mary fell silent as they each considered what Flo had said.

'Are you serious?' asked Alice.

'There's nobody else I would rather have at my side as I make my vows to Neil.'

'Then we would love to,' Mary said softly, looking at the rest of the girls for confirmation.

Rose jumped up and down in excitement. 'Of course we would love to! But you know what this means, don't you?'

The girls shook their heads as Rose laughed. 'We're going to need another sewing circle night to make our dresses.'

Flo glanced across at Mr Button who was deep in discussion with Mrs Matravers. 'Well, then, we'd better ask a certain someone to butter him up. He might not like the idea of staff staying on outside of working hours two nights a week.'

'I don't think you'll have to wait long,' said Alice as she caught sight of their first customer walking through the doors.

'Hello, girls,' Dot called, waving at them as she stopped beside Mr Button.

'What are you doing here?' Mary exclaimed when her landlady and store manager wandered over to the fabric department.

Dot sniffed. 'I'm meeting Mabel for a cuppa.'

'During working hours?' Flo queried. 'That doesn't sound like Mrs Matravers.'

Mr Button gave Flo a wink. 'What Dorothy hasn't told you perhaps is that it's more of an interview. Mrs Matravers feels the fabric department could do with another set of hands and who better than our very own Dot.'

Flo let out a gasp of surprise as she turned to Dot. 'You're going to be a Liberty girl! You never said.'

'Well, it's not guaranteed,' Dot said, looking at Mr Button for encouragement before she turned back to face the girls. 'And besides, it would only be part-time. I've just been up the labour exchange and signed on to do part-time in one of the munitions factories. This war means we have to do more, girls, if we want to see the back of Hitler and his band of bleedin' merry men.'

At Dot's outburst, the girls looked surprised. They knew Dot felt strongly about doing more for the war effort, but they hadn't expected her to act so quickly.

'I think that all sounds marvellous, Dot,' Mary smiled warmly. 'And it will be wonderful to have you working here alongside us all. I think Mrs Matravers is right, with your skills you'll be a real asset.'

'Won't she just,' Mr Button said, his cheeks pinched with pride.

Flo nodded in agreement. 'Exactly. Though you're making me feel guilty I'm not doing enough myself.'

As Flo frowned, Dot clasped her hands. 'Don't be silly. You're doing more than enough as it is, putting bread on the table for your family, love, not to mention the fact you've a wedding to plan.'

'I should do more though,' Mary sighed. 'I've been missing more direct action, and the incident with Mrs Matravers in Whitstable reminded me that I'm good at keeping calm in a crisis. Fire-watch duty just doesn't seem enough.'

Alice laughed. 'It may not be, but I would say you've got enough on your plate working here and with all your committee duties.'

'Yes, how's everything coming along?' Rose asked.

Mary rolled her eyes. 'Badly. I sent the football teams to the wrong venue at the weekend for their fixture against

Harrods and Selfridges have pulled out of the fun run I was trying to organise.'

Mr Button chuckled. 'Not to worry, Mary. But while I'm here, I need to talk to you girls about Christmas.'

'The party?' Mary paled.

'No, the store,' Mr Button said. 'Now, we all know that this Christmas is going to be a little more difficult than previous wartime Christmases. After all, we're not going to be getting many deliveries, with almost everything on ration. But what we can do is give everyone the hope of future Christmases that will perhaps be merrier.'

'What about decorations?' Mary asked. 'Will we have enough of those to sell, do you think? I always used to love seeing what Liberty's had every year when I was a child. The glass baubles were always so beautiful.'

Mr Button grimaced. 'It's unlikely. Everything is rationed, so I think if we do have anything that's festive it will come from past stock. We won't be having a Christmas tree either. If St Paul's can't have one neither can we, sadly.'

'So how will we make it look festive?' Rose wailed. 'Even though people have got no money, they come to us to make their world a bit nicer, don't they?'

'Well, Rose, we'll have to get our thinking caps on,' Mr Button smiled. 'I wondered if during your stitching evenings you might like to make some decorations for the shop so we can dress the store? We will of course have our older decorations in storage but it will be nice to have a few new ones. What do you say?'

'What have you got in mind?' Dot asked.

Mr Button's face went blank. 'Er, I'm not sure.'

Dot laughed. 'We'll do our best. Reindeer made from pipe cleaners will go down well.'

'Oh, and stars,' Flo chimed, getting into the spirit.

'There you are.' Mr Button grinned delightedly. 'I knew I could leave it in your capable hands. Now I must be going, I have a meeting with the board. I'll see you later, Dorothy.'

With that, Mr Button turned on his heel and hurried across the floor. Once he was gone, Rose's face dropped like a stone. 'We're never going to capture the magic of a Liberty's Christmas in pipe cleaners.'

'Course we are,' Flo said consolingly. 'It's not like you to be so pessimistic.'

'Sorry,' Rose said, her shoulders slumped. 'I'm just a bit down knowing it'll be only me and Dad round a table this Christmas. Mum won't be back, and Tommy's God knows where.'

Dot smiled at the youngster. 'You and Malcolm must come to us. We'll put on a good do.'

At the invitation, Rose visibly brightened. 'Can we really?'

'Course,' Alice smiled. 'The more the merrier.'

'Thank you. Dad will be thrilled,' Rose grinned as she turned to Mary. 'What about the Christmas party, Mary? Have you given much thought to it?'

Mary hid her face in her hands. 'Not yet. I haven't had time.'

'Well, as long as it doesn't turn out to be a damp squib,' Alice said pointedly. 'It's the highlight of the Liberty's calendar, Mary, so you might want to get to it sooner rather than later.'

'Did I just hear you say something about the Liberty party turning out to be a damp squib?' Mrs Matravers barked from behind the girls.

Mary jumped in shock as she turned around to face her boss. 'No, not at all, it's coming together wonderfully.'

'That's right,' Alice agreed. 'Mary was just telling us how the entertainment and food are all sorted out now.'

Mrs Matravers' face broke into a broad smile. 'That's wonderful news, Mary, I knew we could rely on you.'

Guilt ate away at Mary as she exchanged an awkward glance with Rose. Mrs Matravers was finally being nice to her and treating her with respect; she couldn't bear the idea of throwing it all away over a silly lie.

Mary was just about to open her mouth to tell her deputy manager the truth when Mrs Matravers drummed her fingernails on the counter thoughtfully. 'It's possible I may be able to help, if you don't mind. I was talking to some of the managers in the other West End stores the other day. They've been having problems sourcing alcohol for their various functions because of rationing. I may know someone who could source something suitable.'

Mary's face lit up in surprise at the help from an unexpected quarter. 'That would be a marvellous help, thank you.'

'I can let you know immediately,' she said, turning to Dot. 'Shall we step into my office and discuss the post?'

Together the two women turned and walked up the wooden staircase, leaving Mary beaming from ear to ear at her unexpected change in fortunes.

In fact Mary found herself beaming for most of the day. Not only did she make more sales than she had since starting at Liberty's, but she found that her knowledge was improving almost daily thanks to Flo's patience.

The big question, she thought as she stamped the ration book of her final customer, was what she, Alice and Rose were going to do about bridesmaids' dresses. With clothing rationed and money scarce, she knew they wouldn't be able to buy something new. But it was important they all looked the same, rather than thrown together – Flo deserved the very best wedding they could organise.

As she said goodbye to her last customer, she looked across at Flo who was busy sorting through a box of zips and needles. 'Have you got a colour in mind for your wedding?' she asked thoughtfully.

Flo turned and looked at Mary, bewilderment in her eyes. 'A colour? What are you on about, Mary?'

'Is there a colour you want everyone to wear?' she tried again.

Flo stopped what she was doing and rested her hands on her hips. 'I just thought we could all wear what we like. What with the war, all we want is to be together. Oh, and show Jerry he can't stop us living our lives.'

Mary smiled at her triumphantly. 'That's it! We'll all wear red, white and blue. We'll make it a British wedding to remember.'

'How do you mean?' Flo asked, clearly confused.

'I mean you'll obviously wear white and us three will wear red, white or blue for the colours of the flag. Neil will wear blue with his uniform, I've got a blue dress, I know Alice has got a darling little white suit that we can alter for her, and I'm sure Rose can find a dress that's red or blue.'

'What a wonderful idea,' Flo gushed. 'I love the idea of a proper British wedding. I had been so worried about asking you all when I know how scarce money is.'

Mary smiled. 'Well, you needn't have been. We can customise everything during our stitching nights.'

'In fact, if Rose doesn't want to wear her skirt, I've got one she can borrow,' Alice added, joining in the conversation.

'And we can accessorise with hats or scarves. I wonder if we could borrow a scarf?' Mary mused out loud, just in time for Mrs Matravers to hear.

As she walked across the shop floor towards the girls, Dot tagging along behind her, Mary caught her superior shaking her head. 'Absolutely not.'

Flo chuckled. 'It was worth a try.'

Mrs Matravers stopped by the till, and gave Flo a huge grin. 'But we could gift you a scarf each. I spoke with the Liberty family earlier on today and told them of your wedding and they not only suggested a scarf for each of the bridal party, but that we also provide you with a dinner service as your wedding present.'

Flo's hands flew to her mouth at the generous gesture. 'I don't know what to say. That's incredible, thank you.'

'Our pleasure. I've also got some good news about the party and I hope your wedding reception. I saw Alf during my tea break and he seems to think he will be able to source drinks for both. Obviously, there will be a charge, but Alf said it will be reasonable.'

Now it was Mary's turn to clasp her hands together in delight. 'I can't believe this. Thank you.'

'Yes, thank you!' Flo added, her eyes shining with grateful tears. 'I don't know what to say.'

Mrs Matravers smiled at the group. 'There's nothing to say. Coming together and supporting each other in happy or sad times, well, that's the Liberty way.'

Chapter Twenty-Two

The bare branches and the plummeting late October temperatures echoed the empty feeling that had engulfed Mary for the past few days. Since she and David had been courting they had seen each other every day, but David's job at the hospital and Mary's work and wedding-preparation commitments meant the two had been forced to spend time apart. Now Mary was counting down the hours until she saw him for lunch, and the fact that he had come to mean so much to her in such a short time wasn't lost on the former driver.

She had been so distracted by thoughts of the doctor that she had tidied up the same roll of fabric three times over, as well as handed one customer the wrong pattern to go with her fabric.

'Are you all right?' Flo asked kindly as she took the material from Mary's hands and placed it back on the shelf.

Mary smiled apologetically. 'Sorry, I've been thinking about David. He's meeting me in an hour and I can't wait to see him.'

'As I live and breathe. Mary Holmes-Fotherington soft on a fella!' Flo chuckled. 'When you first started here you told me you were too busy for sweethearts.'

'She's been out with him almost every night this week,' Alice added, after saying farewell to one of her regular customers. 'I think it's serious.'

Mary rolled her eyes. 'Alice, please. We want to keep things quiet, we're just enjoying each other's company.'

'Well, if you want to keep things quiet you want to focus less on mooning over your fella and more on your job,' Dot barked from the counter.

Despite the rebuke, Dot was smiling and Mary couldn't resist smiling back. Dot had only started in the department yesterday and was already making quite a name for herself.

'I don't know what's got into me, ladies. I have never felt this way about a man before,' Mary exclaimed.

'I think it's brilliant, Mary,' Alice grinned. 'Honestly, I don't know why you've been so coy about going out with fellas since you got here but I think you and David are made for each other.'

'He is ever so charming,' Dot agreed, snapping her sales book shut. 'When he came round to call for you that day after you saved Mabel, he was ever so polite, asking me and Alice all about ourselves. You've landed a good 'un there, make no mistake.'

'I don't think you've done so badly yourself,' Mary pointed out. 'You and Mr Button make a charming couple.'

Dot sniffed as she turned around and saw a customer loitering by the Sungleam fabrics. 'We're not talking about me. But before I go, I just stopped by to see if you're all free for your supper with me and Edwin on Saturday.'

Mary and Alice exchanged looks of surprise.

'We would love to,' Mary said, recovering first.

'Course we would,' Alice agreed.

Dot's beam at the girls' acceptance lit up her entire face. 'Wonderful. And what about you, Flo? Can you get away? Rose and Mabel will be there as well.'

'Wouldn't miss it for the world,' Flo confirmed delightedly.

'And David? Can you bring him?' Dot asked, turning back to Mary.

Mary shuffled uncomfortably on the spot. It was one thing admitting she and David were together to her friends, but she wasn't sure she was ready to sit around a dinner table with him and his sister just yet. David was going to tell Mabel about their relationship any day, as they had agreed it would be better coming from him, but Mary had no idea if she would approve.

Although her relationship with Mrs Matravers had improved since Mary had pulled the woman from the bomb wreckage, she had no idea if that would extend to her approving of Mary courting her precious brother. After all, Mary had still fallen pregnant out of wedlock and Mrs Matravers had made no secret of her feelings about that particular subject. Sensing Dot was waiting for an answer, Mary shrugged non-committally. 'I'll see what I can do.'

Dot frowned, before her face broke into another smile. 'No need to wait, we can ask him now.'

As David sauntered across the department floor, Mary's face lit up at the sight of him.

'Did I feel my ears burning then?' he asked. 'I was sure I heard my name mentioned.'

'You heard right,' Dot grinned. 'Tea at my house on Saturday. You'll come, won't you?'

A flicker of surprise passed across his face before he nodded. 'I don't see why not.'

'Lovely,' Mary replied with a fake smile. 'Are you here to whisk me away somewhere?'

At that his face lit up. 'Yes, I thought we'd have a bite in Golden Square. I've brought a packed lunch.'

Noticing the basket that hung from his arm, Mary giggled appreciatively at the idea of David, an esteemed doctor, making sandwiches just for her. 'Then let me fetch my coat and we'll go.'

Less than ten minutes later and the pair were huddled in their coats enjoying a very cold autumn picnic on a park bench. David had gone to the trouble of making not just paste sandwiches but tongue as well; Mary couldn't believe the lengths he had gone to.

'Careful, I could get used to this.'

David laughed. 'And you wondered if I would be any good in the kitchen. Well, let me tell you I can work a night at the city's finest hospitals and still put on a good lunch. Can I tempt you to an apple? Fresh this morning.'

Mary bit into the fruit gratefully. She couldn't remember the last time she had tasted fresh fruit, only tucking into tinned varieties when she was lucky enough for her rations to allow – which was rare.

'So what have I done to deserve all this?' she asked, letting the sweet juice dribble down her chin.

'What makes you think you've done something?' David asked quietly.

Mary lifted her chin and looked into David's blue eyes. There was something he wasn't telling her, she was sure of it. 'Out with it. Come on.'

David smiled. 'Rumbled, eh? Never was good at keeping things to myself.'

'Is it Mrs Matravers?' Mary asked anxiously. 'Did you tell her about us?'

'Mabel? No. I haven't had a chance yet.'

'So what is it?' Mary was puzzled.

Putting the rest of his sandwich back in the basket, David took hold of Mary's hand. 'I've joined up. The army needs medics and I've enlisted with the Royal Army Medical Corps.'

Mary felt as if she were falling as she listened to David's announcement. Of course she understood; men and women were being ordered to serve and fight for their country. She would do the same if she could. Yet there was something so painful at the idea of losing the man she adored to the services that had discharged her so dramatically.

'When do you leave?' Mary asked quietly as she glanced down at the bench to hide the tears that were forming.

'Sunday afternoon,' David replied, lifting her chin to look at him. 'I'll face six months' training before I'm posted elsewhere. I don't want to leave you, my darling, but I've got to. I have to fight for our country in any way that I can.'

Mary nodded miserably. 'I'll miss you, but I understand. We need to throw all we've got at this war.'

'I'll more than miss you,' David said, leaning forward to plant a tender kiss on her lips. 'You've very quickly become my world, Mary Holmes-Fotherington. I love you.'

Mary gasped in surprise at the sound of the words she hadn't known she longed to hear. Of course she knew that she loved him: she had known she loved him since the day they had met. But somehow, hearing the words said aloud made Mary feel happy and alive in a way that she never had before.

'I love you too,' she said quietly. 'I'll write.'

'As will I, every day,' David promised, making Mary laugh.

'You won't have time,' she said gently. 'The Medical Corps will keep you more than busy with war work, not to mention drill practice. Why don't you say you'll write when you can?'

'Do you know that's just one of the many reasons I love you?' he said gently. 'You always know how to make me smile.'

Returning his grin, Mary felt fireworks dance and fizz in her stomach as he pulled her into his arms and showed her the depth of his love with a long, lingering kiss. At the touch of his lips on hers, Mary felt as if her soul was on fire with desire and she knew that no matter how long David was away, she would wait for him forever.

Chapter Twenty-Three

Friday night and the Liberty girls were at Rose's house, enjoying their first sewing circle outside the store. A pot of tea and some of Dot's seed cake that had been made especially for the evening stood in the centre of Rose's kitchen table, while piles of fabric, thread and buttons were strewn across the four corners.

The scene made for a happy one, Mary thought as she took a sip of tea and turned her attention to the romper suit she had nearly finished. Thanks to Dot, it had taken shape rather nicely, and while Mary knew she was no sewing expert, she had to admit that she had enjoyed the experience more than she expected.

Dot smiled admiringly. 'You've done very well there.'

Mary returned her landlady's grin. 'I couldn't have done it without you.'

Dot patted Mary's arm affectionately. 'I know fine well you couldn't.'

Rolling her eyes heavenwards, Mary ignored the jibe and carried on with her sewing. After she had finished the suit, she was hoping Dot would help her take in the blue dress she wanted to wear for Flo's wedding and she didn't want to get into a row with the matriarch so early on in the evening.

As Rose arrived with yet another pot of tea, the girls looked up gratefully.

'Why don't you sit down, love,' Dot said not unkindly. 'The whole point of us being here is to help you and your dad out.'

'How is your dad?' Alice asked gently. 'Does he mind us all being here?'

'Course I don't mind,' a voice called before a man limped into the kitchen from the hallway. 'It's nice to hear the house filled with chatter again. You girls are bringing it to life.'

Mary looked up at the man leaning against his walking stick and smiled. With his auburn hair and bright white smile, he was the spitting image of his daughter, and the look of affection for his child that was as obvious as the hair on his head told Mary that he was as kind and loyal as his daughter too.

'Well, it's very good of you to have us, sir,' she said.

'That it is,' Dot added. 'Just as long as we're not tiring you out.'

'It's Malcolm,' Rose's dad smiled. 'And no, you're not getting in my way. I just came to say goodnight to you all.'

''Night, Dad,' Rose said, getting out of her chair to kiss him goodnight.

'Are you sure we're not in his way?' Flo hissed once Malcolm was out of earshot. 'It's only eight o'clock – it seems a bit early for bed.'

'That's what time he usually goes up,' Rose replied. 'He's done in by then, and I can get on with the tidying and organising his food for the next day.'

'Well, you won't have to do that tonight,' Flo said gently. 'This Woolton pie should keep you going for a couple of days.'

'It was very kind of you to bring that, Flo. You didn't have to,' Rose said, her cheeks flaming with embarrassment.

Flo waved her thanks away. 'Nonsense. I'll pop over tomorrow if you like; that way you won't have to help your dad after work, you can go straight to Dot's.'

'I was going to suggest I look in on your dad myself, Rose,' Dot said. 'I'm only doing a half-day at Liberty in the morning.'

Rose looked at her friends bashfully. 'I couldn't ask you to do that.'

'You didn't ask, I offered,' Dot said in a tone that brooked no argument. 'We're only around the corner, darlin', it's no problem to help you out.'

Picking up a needle, Rose expertly threaded it with bright red cotton and smiled gratefully. 'Only if you're sure it's no trouble. Dad's my responsibility; I don't expect charity.'

'It's not charity,' Dot exclaimed. 'It's helping folk out, something this area was famous for.'

'Well then, thank you,' Rose said shyly.

'So that's settled,' Dot grinned. 'I'll pop in when I've done the tea.'

Alice groaned. 'You're really putting me to shame, Dot. I've got a half-day myself tomorrow, and I'd planned on putting my feet up with the latest Agatha Christie.'

'Good job as well,' Dot said. 'You've not long to go.'

'I know, just six weeks and this little one will be with us,' Alice said, rubbing her hand protectively over her stomach.

'Your bump's quite neat,' Flo remarked kindly.

'I know, I've been so lucky. I've not suffered any morning sickness at all, it's more my legs that are the problem now.' She lifted a puffy ankle for the girls to see.

'Looks like you might need to sit down a bit more at work. With only a month and a half until that nipper's due you might want to have a word with your manager,' Dot winked. 'Shop work's no good for a girl in your condition.'

With that the girls chuckled while Flo blushed. 'I do try to get her to sit down more but she won't take my advice.'

'I can still pull my weight,' Alice replied.

'Yes, but there's now rather a lot of it to pull,' Mary teased.

The girls roared with laughter; then Alice cut across the giggles. 'More importantly, what's happening with David? When does he leave for the Medical Corps?'

At the change in subject, Mary felt a chill in the air and shivered. 'He leaves on Sunday.'

'I'm sorry to hear that,' Flo said sympathetically. 'Maybe he won't be gone long, what with support growing for Russia now.'

'I don't know about that,' Dot chimed in, her tone one of warning. 'We need the support of the Yanks, their lease and lend scheme's all well and good, but what we need is more help out there on the front line.'

Flo sighed. 'Until we get outside help, there's no telling how long our boys will be away for.'

The girls fell silent as they reflected on the seriousness of the situation, before Alice spoke up. 'Does Mrs M know yet about you and her brother?'

Mary shook her head. 'David said he'd tell her tonight.'

'Oooh, tomorrow'll be interesting at work then!' Flo chuckled.

'Don't be like that, Flo,' Rose wailed. 'Mrs Matravers has been really nice to Mary lately.'

'Yes, but that was before she started courting her brother,' Alice pointed out. 'She's famously protective of David; it wouldn't surprise me if she thought Mary wasn't good enough.'

Mary said nothing. She didn't want to admit that she was worried for precisely the reasons Alice had suggested.

'Why is Mrs Matravers so protective of him?' Alice asked, echoing Mary's own thoughts. 'I understand that she brought him up single-handed and she's more like his mother than his sister, but she's got him on this ridiculously high pedestal and is so suspicious of anyone that comes near him. Remember how she was with him in the pub the other week?'

At this the girls murmured in agreement.

'You can understand it,' Dot sniffed. 'It's common knowledge down East Street Market. Everyone knows what happened to the Partridge family. Their mum took up with another fella and left them high and dry to start another family when she was pregnant. David might look strong now but he cried himself to sleep for months. Mabel was petrified he'd break in two – he was heartbroken, the poor lad.'

'That's terrible,' Alice said tearfully. 'How could a mother do that to her children? Just abandon them like that? I'd never do that to my kids.'

'Edith Partridge had a tough time of it with her husband,' Dot muttered darkly. 'You don't know what went on behind closed doors, Alice.'

'Did they ever see her again?' asked Rose, helping herself to a slice of Dot's seed cake.

Dot shook her head. 'Edith left and never looked back as far as I know. Mabel's heart hardened overnight: she wanted to make sure nobody would ever hurt her or David again.'

'What does David think about all this then?' Alice asked, helping herself to more tea.

Dot shrugged. 'She's his sister, he knows she means well, but he wants his own life. He's always treated her with respect, but he's different to Mabel, softer somehow. It all comes from a place of love though, that's what you have to remember about her. Everything she's done, she's done for David.'

'It's so sad though,' Rose said quietly. 'Nobody should have to endure so much.'

'Yet some of us do,' Mary replied. 'And it seems that any headway I've made with Mrs Matravers is about to go up in smoke once she gets wind of my relationship with her brother.'

'Don't be so silly,' Dot scolded. 'Mabel will be fine. All of that was a long time ago. Anyway, even if she's not all right with it at first she'll come round. It's not like he's going to stay a bachelor forever. It's a miracle he's not been snapped up before now and he'll do no better than you.'

'I hope you're right,' Mary sighed, 'because if it's all right with you, Dot, I thought that we could make tomorrow night a bit of a goodbye dinner as well. I would like to give him a good send-off.'

'I had already thought the same thing myself, sweetheart,' Dot said, her grey eyes twinkling. 'I think that's only right and proper. We'll make sure your David goes out in style.'

Chapter Twenty-Four

As Mary stepped out of the Tube station and made her way to work, she hurried along the pavement to keep out the increasing autumnal chill. October had turned into November in the blink of an eye and the skies above were grey and uninviting. It seemed to Mary that the whole of London was as upset as she was that this was David Partridge's last night in London before he left for the army the next day.

Last night she had barely slept a wink as she tossed and turned, wondering how she was going to cope without him. She knew it was silly, they had barely been together five minutes, but in a short space of time David had taken up residence in her heart and now she found it impossible to imagine a day without him.

Walking past the tall, stone-coloured buildings that lined Regent Street, Mary couldn't help wondering if it was a help or a hindrance that she had a fairly good idea of what life would be like for David in the Medical Corps. Although Mary had been in the ATS, she remembered only too well the early mornings, the PT sessions, endless drill marches and war work that had taken her all over the country. The best thing was the feeling of doing more to help end this war, and Mary knew that the moment David put on his khaki uniform he would feel as though he were single-handedly capable of fighting off Hitler once and for all. There were times she was shocked at how much she missed the army and the friendships she had made there.

But as she turned into Argyll Street, she felt a pang of hope. Her place of work reached out to her like a beacon of light. Liberty's had offered her a home and salvation when nobody else would. Here she was rebuilding herself; here she was carving out a new life and here she had found friendships where she never expected to.

In that moment Mary understood that Liberty's was exactly where she wanted to be. Standing in the street admiring the iconic store Mary realised for the first time since she had been discharged that she actually had no desire to return to the army, that she was a Liberty girl now through and through.

After storing her belongings in the staffroom, Mary made her way downstairs to the shop floor. Immediately she saw that Mr Button had already opened the doors and the first few customers were threading their way through the store, including one who was making a beeline for the empty fabric department.

'Were there any particular fabrics you were interested in?' she asked the tall, well-dressed woman walking towards an old paisley print.

'I do like this one,' the woman replied, turning to Mary, 'but I'm not sure if it will work all year round.'

'It's very versatile,' Mary said, taking the roll of fabric from the shelf and rolling it out on to the cutting counter. 'As you can see its durable, well made and the navy tones will work with any outfit, summer or winter.'

The woman ran her finger over the fabric thoughtfully. 'I do like it. I've got enough coupons for a pattern, if you're able to cut it out for me?'

Mary smiled as she reached for the scissors and measuring tape that always lay in the drawer. 'Of course.'

As Rose and Flo reached the shop floor she smiled at them, then got to work measuring and cutting the print.

As she did so she felt the woman's hazel eyes bore into her. 'Do I know you?' the customer asked finally.

Mary shook her head and smiled at the customer. 'I don't think so.'

The woman continued to stare at her. 'I do know you. You're Mary Holmes-Fotherington, aren't you?'

At the sound of her name mentioned by someone out of the Liberty's circle, Mary froze. Who was this woman and what did she want? Cautiously, she lifted her gaze from the fabric and ran her eyes across the woman's face. Her pale skin, close-set eyes and high cheekbones did look familiar but Mary wasn't sure. Just who was she and how much did she know about Mary's past? It occurred to Mary there was no sense denying it, Alice or Rose could easily call her name from across the shop floor. Not only that but if she denied it, then the woman could make a scene, drawing more attention to her, which was the last thing she wanted.

'Yes, that's right.' She smiled, putting down her scissors. 'I'm sorry I can't place you.'

The woman waved her concern away. 'You haven't seen me since you were a little girl so I'm not surprised. I'm Penelope Phillips-Thorpe. You used to play with my daughter Esme.'

Mary nodded. 'Of course. How are you, Mrs Phillips-Thorpe?'

'Fine,' she sighed, before concern flashed across her face. 'I must say I am rather surprised to see you working here. I saw your mother only last week and she didn't say a thing.'

'Oh, you know Mummy,' Mary said, feeling as if she were wildly grasping at straws.

'Only too well,' Mrs Phillips-Thorpe laughed. 'No doubt she's keeping your lovely staff discounts all to herself!' She tapped her nose conspiratorially before smiling gently at

Mary again. 'Although I was so sorry to hear about your father. Cancer is a terrible thing, Mary. I do so hope he makes a good recovery.'

Mary felt as if she was falling. Holding on to the counter for support she hoped that Mrs Phillips-Thorpe hadn't noticed how wobbly she felt as she tried to take in the enormity of this news and pretend that she wasn't hearing it for the first time.

Aware that the woman was looking at her waiting for an answer, Mary plastered a smile on her face. 'Yes, thank you. We are all praying for him.'

Mrs Phillips-Thorpe reached across the counter and clasped Mary's hand. 'I know that will help, dear. You always were your father's favourite; I'm sure that knowing you are here wishing him well will spur him on to get better. And we must all hope, mustn't we? After all, what this blasted war has taught us, if anything, is that we must have hope. And of course they can do marvellous things these days, dear, they really can.'

As Mrs Phillips-Thorpe droned on, Mary let the woman's words wash over her without really taking in anything that she was saying. Instead she tried to come to terms with the shock news that her father had cancer and, worst of all, she wasn't there to help him. She thought of her dad, so proud and strong, refusing help from anyone. He had built up his own empire from nothing. Mary cast her mind back to all the times he had sat her and her sister down to tell them how he had pulled himself up by the bootstraps to get on in life, making a name for himself at school and then going on to university on a scholarship before becoming something rather special in the City. Jeremy Holmes-Fotherington was not a man who accepted defeat, she thought wildly. He always got what he wanted, no matter what, and she knew that in this situation the powerlessness her father must be feeling was worse than any cancer he was faced with.

In that moment, all Mary wanted to do was find her father and hug him. Tell him that everything would be all right, just as he had done with her when she had fallen off her old horse, April, time after time. She thought about how good it would feel to wrap her arms around him, to feel the whiskers of his beard against her cheek and to tell him how much she loved him, and how much she would always love him.

Then with a jolt it hit her that her parents didn't want to know her any more. That they had told her in no uncertain terms that she was dead to them. That from now on they only had one daughter not two, and Mary was never to cross their path again. Sneaking a glance at Mrs Phillips-Thorpe, she realised that her mother was so ashamed of her that she hadn't told any of her friends what had happened. She wondered what her mother would say when she found out that she was working at Liberty? A flash of hope rose within her as she wondered fleetingly if her mother and father might find a way to forgive her and welcome her back. How wonderful it would be to be a part of the family again, and help her father through his illness. With a start she wondered if it was her fault her father had cancer. Had she done this to him? Had her behaviour caused her father to become ill?

Aware that Mrs Phillips-Thorpe had stopped speaking, Mary did her best to smile at the woman again as she began to parcel up the fabric for her to take home.

Writing out the order in her book, doing her best to keep her trembling hand steady, she handed the sheet along with the fabric over to Mrs Phillips-Thorpe. 'It was a pleasure to see you again, and thank you so much for your good wishes about my father. We all hope he makes a full recovery and it helps knowing so many friends and family wish him well.'

'Of course, dear,' Mrs Phillips-Thorpe smiled. 'I'm seeing your mother next week at the Charlingtons' bridge game. I'll be sure to say I saw you and I'll be having words with her for keeping your job here at this glorious store a secret. I say, though, it has to be more fun than the grotty army, doesn't it?'

'It's certainly different,' Mary smiled weakly. 'If you're in London again you must let me know and I'll be glad to introduce you to the rest of the girls here and show you around the store. It really is so beautiful.'

'I should be delighted, dear, thank you,' Mrs Phillips-Thorpe smiled in her turn. 'Now you take care of yourself, you young things always work too hard.'

Mary watched the old family friend walk back across the crowded shop floor, heels clattering against the wooden floorboards. Once she was out of sight, she gripped the counter for dear life and took a deep breath. She had always known it was a possibility that someone connected to her family might find her here, but she hadn't been prepared for this sudden blast from the past, or the effect it would have on her.

She suddenly felt very homesick, in a way she hadn't done for months. Mary took in another lungful of air and did her best to steady herself. She knew she was being silly, that she had begun to carve out a wonderful life here for herself, that she didn't need her family. But in that moment she missed them so much, and would do anything to help her father. Cancer, she thought. Cancer was horrible. She didn't know much about it, and she had been so shocked to hear that her father was sick in the first place that she hadn't tried to find out what kind of cancer he had. Mary realised that the chance of surviving cancer was minimal.

What if her father went to his grave hating her as much as he did now? She should write to him, tell her that she loved him. But then she felt a fresh burst of pain as she realised that her father hadn't written to her to tell her about his illness for the very simple reason that he didn't want her to know. For the second time since losing her own baby, she felt enveloped in a grief she couldn't fully understand.

Chapter Twenty-Five

The rest of the day on the shop floor was a quiet one for the Liberty girls and Mary was pleased. For once she didn't want to serve customers, preferring to simply think about her family and hope and pray that whatever had passed between them could be forgotten now her father was apparently battling for his life.

She was listless, unable to do anything but stare into space, so she was alarmed when, following her afternoon tea break, Mr Button gently tapped her on the shoulder.

'I wonder if you might like to help with the Christmas store prep?'

Mary narrowed her eyes in surprise. 'Is there much to do, sir? I mean do we have that much to prepare? Rations are scarce.'

'That they are,' Mr Button agreed, rocking backwards and forwards on his heels. 'But the Liberty family and the board feel very strongly that Christmas is an important part of the year for our wonderful store. Even though there may not be an awful lot for people to actually purchase by way of gifts and decorations, we want to do our best to make the shop feel as festive and jolly as possible.'

Mary frowned. 'So what would you like me to do?'

'Decorations might be very thin on the ground now, but we're in luck.' He smiled conspiratorially. 'Since we last spoke about this matter I have been told that we've got a couple of boxes of old stock in the basement. Obviously it was before my time and I'm not sure what's in them, but with decorations hard to find, I'm hoping that we can make enough of a display to ensure Liberty's is the place to come for those beautiful glass baubles that are the centrepiece of any tree.'

'But I thought you said we weren't having a tree. How will we display them?' Mary asked doubtfully, knowing that the gorgeous pines she had grown up with were even harder to come by than decorations.

Mr Button grinned and nodded. 'A friend of the store has made our Christmas wishes come true.'

Peering over his shoulder, Mary let out a gasp of delight. Supervised by Flo and Alice, two men from deliveries were unveiling a beautiful Christmas tree and placing it in pride of place right underneath the glass chandelier. 'It's gorgeous,' she breathed.

Mr Button followed Mary's gaze and grinned. 'It is, isn't it? Now, as the Ministry of Supply have ordered us not to sell paper of any kind we can't have wrapped presents, so we're hoping that the simple majesty of this lovely tree underneath the chandelier will be enough to get people in the festive mood.'

'We could make streamers and decorations,' Mary said suddenly, feeling herself getting into the Christmas spirit. 'We could ask little ones when they come in Christmas shopping with their mothers if they would like to make paper chains from gummed paper. We could theme it "A Home-made Christmas", and get everyone involved.'

Mr Button stared at Mary slack-jawed with awe. 'What a wonderful idea.'

Mary found herself blushing. 'Thank you, sir,' she said bashfully.

'No, I mean it,' he said sincerely. 'I would never have thought of something so inspired, this will be magical.'

Still smiling, Mr Button marched off towards Flo and Alice to tell them about her idea, leaving Mary with nothing else to do but go to the basement in the bowels of the building. Mary relished the challenge, grateful for the chance to throw herself into a task. She knew that everyone would be finding Christmas tough this year. The rations and scarcity of food, not to mention toys and gifts, would make it very difficult for anyone to have a merry Christmas but Mary was sure that where there was a will there was a way.

Perching on one of the boxes, she looked about her and decided to start in the corner and work her way around. Pausing for a moment, she couldn't help marvelling at the beauty contained in the stockroom. The attention to detail in every corner of the store was astonishing. She took in the carvings on the wooden beams on the ceiling, the ornate coving around the doorway, and even the little frogs and angels that had been carved into the wood. Nothing had been left or forgotten, every corner of the store had beauty at its core, and that was just one of the reasons Liberty's was so very special, and why it was adored around the world.

As she began to sort through the glass decorations, her thoughts turned to the famous Liberty sale that customers flocked to year after year. Judging by the lack of Christmas decorations she had a feeling it may not be as well stocked this year as it had in previous years. It was no secret that with so many goods rationed, supplies were limited. The Midland potteries such as Wedgwood could no longer fulfil demand and were therefore unable to sell new stock. Even the carpet department had taken to rearranging what it had to make it look as though there was more available than there actually was: buying trips to the Far East were on pause because of the war.

It was a shame, Mary thought, but she knew the store would survive and carry on; it was the Liberty's way, just as it was the army's way. It felt bittersweet that David was joining the very service that she had been discharged from.

No matter how hard she tried she couldn't stop thinking about her own family home. Mrs Phillips-Thorpe's visit had rattled her and left her with more questions than she knew how to answer. Never had it been clearer to Mary than now just how much her family had meant what they said: that she really was dead to them. Mary thought back to the last time she had seen her parents. It had been in the drawing room of their Cheshire home as she had told them the truth about her situation. Mary remembered how she had apologised over and over again for the mistakes she had made and the embarrassment she had caused, but a small part of her felt furious that they hadn't offered her help and comfort when she needed it most. All her family had seen was a girl who had let them down, not a daughter in pain.

Feeling her pulse start to race, she took a calm, steadying breath and pushed the unwanted thoughts from her mind. Her father was sick, and for the moment there was nothing she could do but hope and pray he got better. Returning her focus to the stockroom, she finished cleaning, labelling and pricing the decorations and then turned her attention to the rest of the room. The whole place needed a sort-through, she thought, and it was exactly what Mary was in the mood for, finding the process of sorting, tidying and labelling therapeutic. By the time the store closed, she was delighted with her progress.

'My goodness,' Flo marvelled as she came downstairs to see how Mary had got on. 'I can't believe you've finished.'

Mary shrugged. 'Once I got started, I couldn't stop.'

Flo looked around the stockroom admiringly. 'It looks like a palace down here now.'

'Well, I think it does say in the Liberty handbook somewhere that the stockroom should be a place you would be proud to bring customers inside to view.'

'I'll say it is,' Flo said, running her finger along a box and marvelling at the lack of dust. 'We could use this as a break room if nothing else.'

Mary got to her feet. 'Are you done with me then? I think we'd better get ready to go to Dot's. She'll be on tenterhooks.'

'I'll bet,' Flo smiled. 'Yes, come on, you've more than earned your supper tonight, and if you're extra good I'll even treat you to a port and lemon as a thank you for all your hard work.'

Together they turned and walked out of the stockroom. As Mary followed Flo back up the stairs towards the shop floor, she took a final glance at all her hard work and felt a flash of pride. Nothing beat the satisfaction of a job well done, she thought.

Yet when they reached the top of the stairs, she saw Flo hesitate for just a fraction of a second before she pushed open the door that led to the shop floor. A strange sense of foreboding washed over Mary. What was beyond that door?

A million and one thoughts flashed through her mind as she steeled herself for whatever came next. Had Mrs Matravers told David her secret? Had something happened to David, or one of her friends? Or, worse, had her mother arrived to tell her that her father had died, and was lying in his grave cursing the day Mary had ever been born?

Following Flo as she walked across the floor, Mary told herself that she was more than strong enough to deal with whatever came next. Then, reaching the fabric department,

Mary's hands flew to her mouth as she took in the scene before her.

Liberty-print fabrics in hues of orange, pink, green, red and blue were artfully arranged around the counter and shelves, while ribbons in every colour had been wrapped around the stairwell and bannisters. Elsewhere, bright silks fashioned into ornamental flowers lined bowls and vases, clearly borrowed from the gift department, while a long red rug that had seemingly been taken from carpets marked out a path that led to the atrium.

Mary felt as though she were spinning as she looked around the store and saw her friends wearing huge smiles on their faces.

'What is all this?' Mary asked, confused.

'Just look over there,' Flo said, gesturing towards the atrium.

As she followed her boss's finger, she gazed beyond the makeshift red carpet and gasped. There, beside the Christmas tree, underneath the chandelier, was David on one knee, hand outstretched, clasping a beautiful diamond engagement ring.

Chapter Twenty-Six

Mary couldn't believe what she was seeing as she gazed first at David and then the girls. The whole scene was so beautiful, and so clearly well thought out, she was overwhelmed that those around her had gone to so much trouble.

'Go to him,' Alice urged. 'He's going to get cramp if you leave it much longer.'

'Yes, the poor man's been there for ages,' Rose agonised.

Turning back to David, Mary caught the look of pure love in his eyes, and suddenly felt as if her legs were no longer her own as she flew towards him.

She couldn't miss the look of nervousness in his eyes as he wobbled on one knee in his three-piece grey suit. Standing before him, she saw the look of love and devotion in his eyes even more clearly, and Mary felt her heart sing with love.

'Mary Holmes-Fotherington,' David began, his voice calm and steady, the nerves he had seemingly been filled with moments earlier clearly gone. 'I have only known you a short time, but I knew from the moment I first laid eyes on you that I would never meet a more perfect girl. You're clever, witty, beautiful, loyal, caring and, most of all, just being with you makes me the happiest man in the world. Mary, would you do me the very great honour of becoming my wife?'

'Yes,' she gushed, eyes shining with tears. 'Oh David, a thousand times yes.'

Beaming, David got to his feet and slid the ring on to her finger. It was the perfect fit, Mary thought as she admired the beautiful diamond ring that sparkled despite the gloom of the candlelight.

Silently, David bent down, closed his eyes and kissed Mary with an intensity that left her in no doubt as to the strength of his love. The soft feel of his tender lips against hers was sweeter than anything Mary had ever felt before and she returned his kiss with all the love and passion her heart contained. She wanted to show him just how much she loved him.

As they broke apart, David looked adoringly into her eyes. 'I want to give you the world, Mary. I want to make all your dreams come true, and I can promise you that I will spend my whole life dedicated to making you happy.'

'And I you, David,' Mary replied, her voice cracking with emotion. 'I have felt we belonged together since I met you. You're the missing piece of my jigsaw and I would be honoured to become your wife and build a life with you.'

At that, there was a loud whooping and cheering from Rose, Flo, Alice and even Dot and Mr Button as they all rushed forward to congratulate the happy couple.

'When did you do all this?' Mary asked the girls as Mr Button stepped forward to pat David on the back.

Flo winked. 'When you were down in the stockroom. Once David told us his plans the other day, we leapt at the chance to help.'

'But we knew we needed you out of the way,' Alice grinned. 'So we sent you downstairs for the afternoon.'

Mary roared with laughter at the ingenuity of it all. To think she had spent the afternoon lost in thoughts of her past, when all along her wonderful friends were upstairs planning her future.

'How did you manage to get all of this ready with customers here?' Mary asked, the shock still written all over her face.

Rose smiled. 'We have Mr Button to thank for that. He agreed to let us say we were organising an event and so we worked around the customers.'

'I'm indebted to you, sir,' David said, giving the store manager a little bow.

'Nonsense,' Mr Button grinned. 'Nothing makes my old heart gladder than to see a pair of youngsters in love like the two of you.'

'Couldn't agree more,' said Dot, linking arms with Mr Button.

As Mary watched the two of them, she couldn't miss the look of adoration that flashed between them. She was thrilled that the store, on the night of her engagement, was filled with so much love.

Mary gazed in wonder at it all again. She couldn't believe what she was seeing. Liberty's looked absolutely wonderful. Suddenly there was the sound of a champagne cork being popped, and she whirled around and saw David had managed to produce a bottle of champagne from nowhere and was busy filling glasses.

'Where did you get that from?' she gasped.

David smiled affectionately. 'Would you believe I've been hanging on to this since I left medical school? My old professor gave it to me when I graduated, but I decided to save it for a special occasion.'

'And this is more special than completing your medical training?' Mary whistled, touched he had gone to so much trouble.

David looked at her lovingly as he handed her a glass of champagne, and softly chinked his glass to hers. 'Mary, you're the most special person I have ever met. You're worth a thousand medical exams to me—'

'Come on, you two,' Dot interrupted. 'Less talking, more drinking. Here's to Mary and David.'

At that everyone raised their glasses and chorused, 'To Mary and David.'

As the couple exchanged another kiss, the sound of a violin came from nowhere and Mary broke free, astonished to see Mr Button was standing under the chandelier and had struck up a tune. 'What is going on?' she gasped.

'We thought that we'd have a little party here first,' Dot said, 'before going back to ours for tea. Seems only right as you found love in Liberty's that we celebrate here too.'

With that Mr Button carried on with his ditty, a catchy song that soon had Mary's feet tapping as she linked arms with David and let him whirl her around the carpet that had now become a makeshift dance floor.

It wasn't long before the others joined in, and as Mr Button played tune after tune, they all danced in celebration of Mary and David's happy news.

After about an hour Mary pleaded exhaustion and begged David to sit the next one out. Together they perched on the bottom step of the old wooden staircase and watched as the girls whirled and twirled the night away.

'Happy?' David whispered above the din.

Mary turned to him and smiled as she clasped his hands. 'More than I have ever been.'

'Then I can go tomorrow knowing that once this war is over I've found my very own happy ever after,' David said gently. 'Being apart from you will be hell, Mary, but knowing you're here waiting for me will make it easier.'

Mary leaned forwards and kissed David softly. 'If I can't be by your side, then know there is nowhere I would rather be. I'm yours.'

'And you're mine,' he replied. 'Forever.'

'Forever,' Mary agreed, her eyes shining with happy tears.

Leaning her head against his shoulder, she took a deep breath and inhaled the very scent of her fiancé. He always had such a clean, citrusy fragrance and she closed her eyes, wanting to commit the smell to memory.

'Have you any thoughts on when you would like to get married?' David asked, jolting Mary from her reverie.

She shook her head. 'After the war perhaps? We don't know what's going to happen next, what with Japan threatening to get involved. I know many people want to marry now, but I would rather wait until the wretched war is over and we can be together properly.'

'I think that's a good idea,' David beamed. 'That way we can plan the perfect wedding and have something to look forward to when all this is over.'

'Does Mrs Matravers know about any of this?' she asked, gesturing to the ring on her finger.

David looked sheepish. 'I haven't told her we're courting yet.'

Mary's hands flew to her mouth. 'Why not? She'll be furious she was the last to know.'

'I was going to – I wanted her to see all this,' he said, gesturing towards the store, 'but I've been so busy getting everything ready, I haven't managed to see her. I thought we could tell her together at dinner tonight.'

'You'll have a job,' Dot called over the violin. 'Mabel's not coming. Says her Alf needs her for something.'

Mary felt a flash of disappointment. None of it would seem real until David's sister knew and accepted her into the family.

David caught her look of unease. 'Stop worrying. My sister adores you after you saved her life and the life of her baby. She will be thrilled we're getting married.'

'That might be true, but you won't see her before you go away. It'll be down to me to tell her.' Beads of sweat gathered on Mary's forehead at the thought.

David took hold of Mary's hands and tenderly kissed each one. 'I promise I will ensure I see her before I go and tell her the news.'

Leaning forward to kiss him again, Mary drank in David's words of assurance. She was being silly; Mrs Matravers had been a changed woman since Whitstable. Feeling his lips against hers, she was taken aback by a sudden need to cry. This could be one of the last kisses she would ever share with David.

'I hate goodbyes—' Mary's voice broke off.

David leaned his forehead against Mary's and wiped her tears away with the pad of his thumb. 'Me too. But we have something wonderful to look forward to. I know that's what's going to get me through the next few months without you.'

Nodding, Mary pulled away and looked up at David, drinking in every last detail of his face. She had no idea when she would next see his sparklingly blue eyes, the dimple in his chin or the angle of his smile. She wanted to cherish every detail for her to picture last thing at night just before she fell asleep.

Looking deep into his eyes, she could tell he was as lost for words as she was. There was so much to say, so much to long for, but here in this moment was not the time. All that mattered for now had been said. They had pledged to spend their lives together, and that had to be enough.

'Until next time,' she whispered.

'Until next time,' he echoed, drawing her in for one last kiss.

Mary tilted her chin upwards and pressed her lips against David's with a sense of urgency she never knew she possessed. Overcome with love, Mary felt lost in a world where it was just the two of them, where there was no war, no despair, no pain, just love. Pure and utter love that flowed between them as naturally as oxygen. Giving in to this final kiss, she could sense from David's touch, the feel of his skin against hers, just how much they belonged together, how much they adored each other and how this could never be goodbye.

Chapter Twenty-Seven

Mary stared into her cup of tea. She was sitting in the staff-room on her afternoon break thinking about David. It had been two days since the magical Saturday night where he had asked her to marry him, and she was missing him more than she could ever have imagined. Taking a sip of the scalding liquid, Mary thought back to the moment they had met just a few weeks earlier. How could she have predicted that in less than two months she would be sat here pining for him as her fiancé?

Holding her finger up to the light, she couldn't help but smile as the diamond sparkled in the winter sunshine. Was it possible that she was really going to find her happy ever after? Just then an image of herself walking up the aisle, with her friends and family filling her home church back in Chester, looking on in delight as she pledged her love to David, filled her mind. But just as quickly as the happy image had appeared did it disappear when she remembered with a sudden painful stab that would be something that would never happen. Not only had her family cut her from their lives but she had lost touch with all her old friends, too embarrassed by the events surrounding her discharge from the army to write to them and face the pain of more rejection.

Just then, Mrs Matravers burst into the staffroom. Mary lifted her chin to smile at her boss, only to catch the set jaw and steely glint in her eye.

'In my office now, Mary,' she said quietly, before turning on her heel.

Wordlessly, Mary did as instructed. Heart roaring in her ears as her heels clattered down the corridor, she could only imagine what Mrs Matravers wanted to talk to her about. It could only be David. He must have broken the news before he left for the army and now Mrs Matravers was here to read her the riot act, their truce over in an instant.

With barely a chance to say a quick hello to Rose, Mary went straight into Mrs Matravers' office and stood in front of her desk while her boss sat down.

'I can imagine you know what it is I want to talk to you about,' Mrs Matravers snapped. 'My brother David.'

Mary nodded as Mrs Matravers continued. 'Moments before he left to fight for our country, he came to say good-bye and informed me you and he are getting married. Is that right?'

Meeting her boss's eyes, Mary didn't shy away from her flinty and unyielding gaze. 'Yes, that's right. We're in love.'

'You've barely known one another five minutes,' she spat.

'But it feels so right, surely he told you that,' Mary said hesitantly.

Mrs Matravers rolled her eyes. 'He said something like that, but then he said so many things. You and him court-ing was just one of them. Naturally I told him I thought he could do better.'

The harsh reality of Mrs Matravers' words cut Mary to the core. 'But I thought after Whitstable ...' Her voice trailed off.

Mrs Matravers narrowed her eyes. 'Don't you dare bring up Whitstable now. Things have changed rather a lot since then. Whilst I will always be grateful to you for what you did for me that night I really cannot support any union between you and my brother. You're not good enough for him, Mary dear, and I think you know full well why I think that.'

Mary lifted her chin defiantly. She had known this was coming, that Mrs Matravers would not think her good enough for David, and she was prepared to attack. Yes she had made mistakes but she had paid a heavy price for them, losing her family, her home and her job. She wasn't about to start losing anything else. 'I rather think I'll have to disagree with you there, Mrs Matravers,' she said coolly. 'David and I belong together.'

The deputy manager threw her head back and roared with laughter. 'You belong together? I don't think so. You and David no more belong together than Churchill and Hitler. I bet you haven't even told him your little secret, have you?'

At that Mary's cheeks flushed with shame. She knew that one day she would have to tell him the truth about the baby she had lost, but it wasn't something she had been able to say aloud to anyone. The idea of saying the words, repeating the whole story, made Mary's body quake with terror.

'Thought not,' Mrs Matravers smirked, getting to her feet. 'Write to him and tell him it's off or I will. You are not to spend another minute with my brother, do you hear me?'

Mary said nothing. She suddenly felt very tired of being told what to do. 'And what if I don't? What if I tell David the truth instead?'

Mrs Matravers eyes widened in shock at Mary's outburst. 'You wouldn't dare. And even if you did, he'd run a mile.'

Leaning forwards menacingly over the desk, Mary met Mrs Matravers' gaze head on. 'And what if he doesn't mind? What if he says he adores me and that whatever's happened in the past doesn't matter?'

Mrs Matravers leaned in so closely to Mary that she could smell the milky tea her boss had enjoyed over breakfast on her breath. 'Then I'll sack you and I'll tell everyone your secret anyway.'

Walking around to the front of the desk, she stood inches from Mary, looking like the cat that had got the cream. 'I'll expect it done immediately. Now go.'

With that she stalked from the office, leaving Mary feeling sick to her stomach. Trembling, she turned around, preparing to walk out with dignity, when suddenly she heard an almighty crash next door.

Rushing into Rose's office, Mary gasped in shock as she saw the girl crouched over Mrs Matravers, who had fallen to the floor.

'What happened?' she asked, shucking off her cardigan and fashioning it into a makeshift pillow.

'I don't know,' Rose wailed in despair. 'She just walked over to the filing cabinet; then the next thing I know she had fallen to the floor.'

Concerned, Mary looked down at Mrs Matravers and saw she was sweating. Although she was no doctor, Mary suspected the deputy manager had lost consciousness and quickly reached for her wrist.

'What are you doing?' Rose begged.

'Checking for a pulse,' Mary replied, deftly holding two fingers against Mrs Matravers' flesh. Just as she expected, it was rapid. She glanced down to check the rest of her boss, and felt a stab of alarm at the blood pooling underneath Mrs Matravers. 'Rose, can you call down for Larry and tell him we need to get Mrs Matravers to the hospital and to bring a van around to deliveries immediately,' she said urgently.

Rose sprang into action and telephoned down to the stores. Larry was upstairs in minutes.

'How do we move her?' Larry asked, drinking in the scene.

'With great care,' Mary said, searching the room for something. 'We must also be careful not to let anyone see what's happened. She would be devastated if people saw her like this.'

Seeing what she was after, she picked up the old wool blanket Rose kept on the chair beside her desk and started to tuck it around Mrs Matravers' bottom half. Anxiously she checked her pulse again; it was still beating too fast. They had to get help urgently.

'I'll take her legs,' Mary ordered. 'Larry, you take her arms and support her middle. Rose, if you can go ahead and ensure all the doors are open and fend off anyone who happens to be in the corridors. We need to keep this to ourselves.'

'All right,' Rose agreed, rushing forwards to open the door.

Gingerly, Mary and Larry picked up Mrs Matravers as if she weighed no more than a feather pillow. As they carried her gently down the stairs, Mary kept an anxious check on her boss, waiting to see if she stirred or cried out in pain but she barely opened her eyes. As they reached the loading bay, thankfully without seeing a soul, Larry eased Mrs Matravers into the back of the van.

'Now what?' he asked. 'We can hardly leave her there to roll around like a sack of spuds.'

'I'll come with you, and sit in the back to ensure she's comfortable,' Rose said. 'Mary, you go back and tell Mr Button what's happened.'

'Are you sure?' Mary asked. 'I don't mind going with her.'

'I'm sure,' Rose said firmly. 'From the way she was screaming at you in her office earlier, I have a feeling that if she wakes up and sees you she'll only get more distressed.'

Mary knew Rose was right. She nodded. 'All right. Make sure her airways remain clear and keep checking her pulse. Make sure the doctors know she's pregnant. It shouldn't take Larry long to get to the hospital.'

With that, she slammed the doors shut and watched as Larry drove at top speed down the narrow street.

Chapter Twenty-Eight

Mr Button was stoic as Mary broke the news about Mrs Matravers. He sat behind his large oak desk, face grave, as he listened to all Mary had to say.

'It's becoming rather a habit for you, saving the life of your superior, isn't it?' Mr Button sighed.

Mary's face flushed with embarrassment. 'I hardly think so, sir. I just happened to be in the right place at the right time.'

'On two occasions,' he replied, steepling his fingers together as if thinking what to say next. 'I'm sure Mrs Matravers will be more than grateful to you when she returns.'

Privately Mary doubted it but, looking into Mr Button's eyes, felt that now wasn't the best time to say so. Instead she smiled as he dismissed her, and went downstairs to tell the girls in the haberdashery and fabric department.

'Poor Mabel,' Dot gasped as she broke the news.

'As if Mrs Matravers hasn't been through enough,' Flo agonised.

'I should cocoa,' Dot said, shaking her head in wonder. 'Mary, you're a marvel, you really are.'

'If anyone's a marvel, it's Rose,' insisted Mary. 'She's the one that went with her in the back while Larry drove.'

'The way Larry drives, that's a miracle in itself!' Alice chuckled, earning herself a look of disapproval from Flo.

'Anyway, I suppose all we can do is wait for Rose to come back with news,' Flo sighed.

As the girls busied themselves tidying the store, serving customers and displaying the new Liberty print fabrics that had arrived straight from Merton that morning, each of them remained quiet as they hoped Rose would arrive with good news soon.

The wait was agonising for Mary, who found she couldn't stop thinking about the day she lost her own baby. All too soon she caught sight of Flo gesturing towards Rose, who was walking through the store, her face ashen.

'Oh God! It has to be bad news,' Alice wailed, rubbing her own bump protectively. 'She must have lost the baby.'

'Don't say that yet,' Flo chided as Rose made a beeline for the fabric department.

'Well?' Mary begged.

'She's fine,' Rose said quietly. 'She and the baby are both fine. She's tired apparently and will need to take things easy.'

'Oh thank God.' Flo let out a sigh of relief.

'Will she be coming back to work?' Alice asked.

'Not for a few days, and if she does come back the doctors say she must only do a few hours behind her desk a week.'

Flo shook her head in sorrow. 'Poor Mrs Matravers. We must get her something to say get well.'

Alice nodded. 'Good idea. Why don't we send her some flowers? The florist down the road will have something suitable, I'm sure.'

'Excellent idea,' Mary nodded. 'Well, I suppose we'd better get back to work. Mrs Matravers wouldn't be happy if she could see us all nattering away like this.'

As the girls returned to their stations, the hours ticked by and Mary found that in between serving customers she became lost in her own thoughts. Life was so precious; you never knew what was around the corner or when you might lose a loved one. This fight between her parents seemed so senseless, especially now when her father was so sick.

More than anything, she wanted to get in touch with her family and try to make things up with them. But did she dare?

She continued to agonise over the decision until Flo ordered her on her tea break. Alone in the staffroom, Mary wrapped her hands around a lukewarm cup of tea and gazed out across the London rooftops. The scenes of devastation through the grimy, dirt-streaked windows only reminded her how fragile life was. In that moment she made a decision. No matter what her parents thought of her, she couldn't possibly let her father go to the grave without letting him know how she still adored him, no matter what had happened.

Reaching into her handbag, she pulled out the notepad and pen she always carried with her and began to write.

3rd November 1941

Dear Mummy and Daddy,

I do so hope you are all well. I'm not entirely sure how to start this letter, or even really what to say, so perhaps it's better if I get right to the point. Recently I saw Mrs Phillips-Thorpe in the department of Liberty's where I now work. She obviously had no idea that we no longer speak, as she told me, Daddy, that you have cancer. I know you haven't told me about your illness, and I also know there is a good reason why, but Daddy, please know, in fact Mummy too, I want you both to know how much I love you and how much I always will love you.

Daddy, I only ever want you to be happy and so I just wanted to say that I sincerely hope you get well and you are in my prayers.

I miss you both so much and have only ever wanted to make you proud. I know that this is the last thing I have done and nobody is sorrier than me. But if you had just given me the chance to explain then perhaps you would see me differently.

I won't dwell on that now; that is not what this letter is about. All I truly want to say is get well soon.

Your loving daughter,
Mary

As she put her pen down, Mary scanned through the letter once more. It was short, she decided, but to the point, and perhaps in this instance that was what was best. Folding it carefully into an envelope, she sealed it shut and then wrote her parents' address neatly on the front.

She had no idea if her parents would even open the letter once they saw her handwriting, but she couldn't think about that now. All she could do was affix a stamp, post it and hope for the best.

Checking her watch she saw there were still a few minutes left before her break ended; if she hurried she could make the last post. But as she got to her feet and walked out into the corridor she was alarmed by the sound of raised voices in the stairwell.

About to hurry past whoever it was as quickly as possible, Mary was astonished to hear that the raised voices belonged to Dot and Mr Button.

Alarm coursed through her. She didn't want to hear their private conversation, and she retreated as quickly as she could back to the safety of the staffroom. Only as she pushed the door shut she couldn't fail to hear Mr Button shout with finality, 'You lied to me, Dorothy, you lied. I will never forgive you for that.'

Chapter Twenty-Nine

It wasn't until the following week on the shop floor that Dot confided in the Liberty girls that she and Mr Button had argued. Mary had kept what she heard in the stairwell the previous week to herself, refusing to get caught up in Dot's business. Mary told herself that her landlady would choose to talk about it if and when she was ready. Now, as she looked at Dot's face, which was lined with worry, she could tell she needed a sympathetic ear.

'So what happened?' Flo asked, her tone rich with concern.

Alice frowned. 'Yes, you've never argued before, have you?'

Dot shook her head. 'No, and it's rather shaken me, to be honest. Me and Edwin never argued when we was kids, and of course me and my George never had a cross word.'

'Did you make it up?' Rose asked, clutching the paperwork she was due to deliver to Flo. With Mrs Matravers still in hospital and likely to be on sick leave for a little while longer, Mr Button had promoted Flo to deputy manager in her absence.

'No we didn't,' Dot shrugged. 'And that's what I can't stand. I hate feeling as though there's unfinished business between us.'

'Why don't you go and talk to him now?' Mary suggested. 'You could take him his morning cuppa and have a chat?'

'I will do no such thing,' Dot exclaimed. 'I've done nothing wrong.'

'But sometimes it's not about who makes the first move, it's about making things right,' Alice said kindly. 'Anyway, you haven't said what it's about yet. How can we help you if we don't know what the row was about?'

Dot shifted uncomfortably from side to side. 'I'd rather not say if you don't mind. It's private.'

'Oh, go on,' Alice coaxed. 'We're all friends.'

'If you must know, we had a row about something that happened years ago,' Dot sighed. 'It all came out that he thought I'd stopped writing to him, and I thought it was him what had stopped writing to me, and that's why my father insisted I break off the engagement.'

Flo raised an eyebrow. 'Blimey! Maybe someone's letter got lost in the post.'

'Perhaps,' Dot shrugged. 'I said I would never have dreamed of stopping my letters to him, and he accused me of telling fibs. He said I should have known how much his heart would have been breaking.'

Mary frowned. Having heard the exchange, she felt the row had been about a lot more than that ... but then again, perhaps that's all there really was to it. Dot had already been called a liar once in the last week; Mary wasn't going to insult a woman she had come to care deeply about by repeating the accusation.

Opening her mouth to say something soothing, Mary suddenly became aware of a telegram boy threading his way through the store.

As she watched him make his way towards the fabric and haberdashery department, Mary's heart banged against her chest as she remembered the letter she had posted. Was there more bad news for her?

Sure enough, within seconds the boy was looking straight at Mary.

'Can I help you?' she asked with a braveness she did not feel.

'Yes, are you Rose Harper?' he asked, holding out an envelope.

As Mary shook her head, Rose sidled up alongside her and smiled at the boy. 'Who are you after?'

'Rose Harper,' he said impatiently.

'Oh, that's me,' she said brightly, so the boy thrust the envelope into her hand, then turned and left.

'How exciting! I never get any post,' Rose grinned, ready to rip open the envelope when Flo appeared, frowning.

'Rose love, I don't want to tell you off on the shop floor but you know as well as anyone else we are not to receive personal mail,' she hissed.

At Flo's rebuke, Rose's face fell. 'I'm sorry, Flo. Truly I am.'

'Oh, never mind now,' Flo sighed. 'It had better be important.'

As Rose ripped open the envelope, Mary checked the colour again and breathed a sigh of relief it was blue. The buff ones were marked priority and usually contained important messages from the War Office. Mary had seen enough of her friends receive messages of horror in those envelopes and would hate the same fate to befall Rose.

'Who's it from?' Flo asked nosily, peering over Rose's shoulder.

'Tommy,' Rose said shyly. 'He just wrote to wish me a happy birthday.'

'Rose, you never said it was your birthday,' Mary gasped. 'And I can't believe Tommy sent you a telegram, that's so very thoughtful of him.'

Rose hugged the telegram to her chest. 'Tommy's always been thoughtful. He was a delivery driver here, and always used to bring me flowers on a Friday night before he was called up.'

'I remember only too well,' Flo smiled. 'But, Rose, you should have reminded us it was your birthday. I forgot and I feel absolutely terrible. I'm so sorry.'

'There's no need to apologise.' Rose's eyes crinkled with happiness as she stuffed the telegram back in the envelope. 'We're all so busy at the moment, it's easily done.'

Mary exchanged a look of despair with Flo. 'Well, I feel terrible too. How about we treat you to a fish and chip supper tonight to celebrate?'

Rose's eyes lit up at the idea. 'That would be lovely, Mary, what a treat, thank you.'

'Yes, we could take you for a couple of drinks after work, then go back to yours as planned for our stitching circle afterwards,' Flo suggested. 'That way we can include your dad in the celebrations, unless of course you had other plans?'

'Only sitting down to leftover Potato Jane with Dad,' Rose chuckled. 'This sounds much more fun.'

The rest of the day passed without incident and the moment the clock struck six, the Liberty girls raced up to the staffroom to collect their belongings.

'Where shall we go?' Rose asked excitedly as they gathered around the back of Kingly Street.

'Not Jimmy Allan's place,' Dot insisted.

'Well, wherever it is, let's make it somewhere near,' Flo grumbled. 'It's freezing out here.'

'Fair enough,' Alice agreed. 'How about the place at the top? We've not been there in a while and last time I checked his port and lemon was as good as anyone else's.'

'Good idea,' Mary said, leading the way.

Moments later the group was settled in the snug, a round of port and lemons and a whisky between them.

'Well, here's to you, Rose,' Mary said, raising her glass in a toast. 'Happy birthday.'

'Happy birthday,' the girls cheered in unison, clinking their glasses together.

'So how old are you, Rose love?' Dot asked.

'Twenty-one,' Rose said proudly.

Dot raised her eyes to the ceiling. 'Twenty-one, I think I can remember that.'

'And how old are you, Dot?' Alice asked playfully.

'Never you mind,' Dot said, draining her port and lemon and getting to her feet. 'I'll get us another round. Are you having another whisky, Rose love?'

Rose's eyes shone with delight at the idea of another. 'Oooh, yes please.'

'I didn't have you down as a whisky drinker, Rose,' Mary exclaimed.

'Just on my birthday,' Rose admitted. 'Dad toasted me with a glass when I was seventeen and it's been a tradition ever since.'

'How lovely,' Flo sighed. 'I wish me and my dad had a tradition, but the only thing he did on my birthday was get blind drunk and nick my wages.'

Alice leaned over and squeezed her friend's hand. 'And if it's any consolation most of my birthdays were spent bailing my dad out of a prison cell.'

Rose raised an eyebrow. 'Do you never hear from him at all, Alice?'

'Never,' Alice said vehemently. 'I wish I could say the same about my sister 'n' all.'

'Don't tell me she's after your bally money again,' Mary groaned.

226

'Nothing like that.' Alice shook her head ruefully. 'With Joy, it's like she's an annoying fly. I know she's there in the background just waiting to jump out and pounce at any moment.'

'Has she been in touch at all since your Luke went missing?' Flo asked quietly.

Alice gave a snort of disgust. 'Don't be silly. Joy only ever turns up when she's in trouble or she wants something.'

The girls looked at Alice sympathetically and Mary leaned over to wrap an arm around her shoulders. Although she had her own problems with her parents, she couldn't imagine an upbringing like Flo and Alice's and she felt grateful to have had the luxury of an untroubled childhood.

'Well, you'll have the opportunity to make sure everything's different for your child,' Mary smiled. 'You can ensure he or she never endures what you did.'

Alice patted Mary's hand gratefully. 'Thanks, Mary.'

Just then Dot returned with a tray full of drinks. 'For the birthday girl,' she grinned, setting the tray down.

As Mary reached over to help her with the glasses she recoiled at the size of the whisky for Rose. 'Oh my days, that's a large measure.'

'It's her birthday,' Dot giggled and turned to Rose. 'It'll put hairs on your chest, love.'

Rose eyed the glass nervously. 'Well, I don't want hairs, but I would like to make a toast of my own. I just want to say thank you so much, girls, not just for making this a very happy birthday but for always being there for me. I don't know what I'd have done without you these past few weeks. Here's to you, the Liberty girls.'

Chapter Thirty

The next day, during her lunch break, Mary found herself in the pleating room unpicking the stitches of some old net curtains alongside Rose, Alice, Flo and Dot. Thanks to the fact they had spent longer than planned in the pub celebrating Rose's birthday the night before, the girls had decided to hold an impromptu sewing circle during their lunch break so they could keep on top of Flo's wedding preparations, leaving two of the Saturday girls in charge.

The girls were conscious that there were just six weeks to go until Flo's wedding and they were more than a little behind.

'I'm sorry,' Rose wailed. 'If we hadn't stayed out for as long as we did then we could have finished this veil last night.'

Dot rolled her eyes heavenwards. 'Give over. It was your birthday.'

'Exactly,' Alice grumbled. 'If anyone should apologise it's me. I'm so tired at the minute it takes me twice as long as it usually does to sew.'

'At least you *can* sew,' Mary muttered. 'I'm still best suited to unpicking old garments.'

Shaking her head, Dot set down her stitching. 'You're a sorry lot, aren't you? How about less moaning and more stitching or we'll never make up for last night.'

Too tired to argue the girls carried on with their work, the silence only broken by Dot a few minutes later.

'I saw old Mabel yesterday. I meant to tell you yesterday but what with the birthday girl here it clean slipped my mind.'

'Have you heard how she and her baby are doing now?' Rose asked anxiously.

'She's fine. Discharged two days ago,' Dot said matter-of-factly. 'Edwin was popping along as well after I'd been so she was going to discuss things with him. She's got to take things easier until the baby's due in March, you see.'

'You two have made up then?' Mary remarked.

Doris flushed with embarrassment. 'You could say that.'

'Will she be back at work at all, do you think?' Alice asked, idly stroking her bump.

'Maybe for a few days a month when she's recuperated,' Dot said. 'She's still very weak.'

'Poor Mrs M,' Flo said sadly. 'I've been thinking I really ought to invite her to the wedding, especially as she's done us such a large favour. Do you think she'd come?'

Alice smiled. 'I should think she'd be delighted. We all will be; we can't wait to share your special day. Weddings are so lovely. It seems like only yesterday me and my Luke got married up the little church in Bermondsey.'

Alice's face clouded over at the memory and Mary clasped her hand over hers. 'I take it there's still no news?'

Shaking her head, Alice got to her feet. 'Not a word and I don't expect it now.'

With that Alice's bravery faltered and the tears she had been successfully keeping at bay began to flow. 'Sorry, girls, some days are better than others.'

'You've nothing to apologise for,' Dot said fiercely.

'I can't believe how well you're coping,' Flo whispered.

'Sometimes we just have to,' said Mary sadly.

As the truth of Mary's statement hung heavily in the air, she was suddenly transported back to that hospital in Ceylon, one hot summer's day in July when she had lost her own beautiful baby girl. The nurse had been kind enough to wrap her in a blanket so she could hold her and say goodbye. Mary remembered how tiny and perfect she had been, with a mound of thick black hair. She seemed as though she were just sleeping, Mary had thought as she kissed her daughter tenderly on the head and named her Celia, just as she always intended if she had given birth to a girl. Holding her close, Mary had whispered a silent prayer and apologised over and over for not keeping her safe.

Turning back to Alice now, and catching sight of her blank expression, Mary knew her friend would find her own way of learning to live with the constant worry; she would have to. She was about to say as much when the sight of Rose suddenly resting her head on the desk in front of her sent a wave of shock along her spine.

'Whatever's the matter, darlin'?' Dot asked in alarm.

'Are you all right, love?' Alice begged.

Rose closed her eyes and groaned. 'Girls, I feel ever so funny. It's been getting worse all morning.'

'How do you mean?' Mary demanded.

'I've just been feeling sick, and I can't see straight; I've not been able to see properly since I woke up.'

'How much did you drink, Rose?' Mary asked warningly.

'Not much,' Rose replied. 'Just a couple of whiskies in the pub with you; then I had barley water. But those whiskies were ever so strong, not like whisky I've had before.'

'I think you just need to sleep it off, love,' Dot soothed. 'One too many gets us all on occasion.'

'Dot's right, dear,' Mary agreed. 'Why don't you let me fetch you a nice cup of tea and I'm sure you'll feel much better.'

Rose nodded weakly. 'All right.' Only as she lifted her head, she let out a terrifying shriek. 'My eyes! My eyes!'

'What is it, love?' Alice begged.

'I can't see!' Rose sobbed.

Chapter Thirty-One

Mary shivered as she made her way along the Thames in the dark November evening. She had intended to take the Tube to Guy's Hospital, but when Mr Button had shut the doors and said goodbye to the last of the day's customers, all Mary had wanted was some fresh air before she saw Rose at the hospital, promising to meet the other girls there.

Flo and Dot had been wonderful the moment Rose announced she couldn't see, leaping into action immediately. Flo had encouraged her to sip water and take deep breaths, while Dot had calmed her down, repeatedly reassuring her that everything would be fine. As for Mary, she had raced upstairs to Mr Button's office and without waiting for permission had used his telephone to call the hospital. They had sent an ambulance immediately.

That was the last they had seen of their friend, and the Liberty girls had been worrying themselves sick waiting for news. Each one of them had tried to visit or call the hospital but were told firmly that unless they were family they couldn't release any information. That afternoon, Malcolm had called into the shop to tell the girls Rose was well enough for visitors but had refused to say anything more. The girls hoped for good news and had promised to gather for an impromptu stitching circle around Rose's bedside if she was well enough.

Not for the first time Mary found herself wishing David was here by her side. He would be able to help, she thought, and would know precisely what to say. At the thought of her fiancé, she felt a pang of longing. She missed him every day but the letter she had received from him that morning was just the tonic she needed.

She had been so delighted to hear from him that she had read it over and over, committing the entire note to memory. She could recall it all now as she walked through the dark London streets, the wind whipping around her ears, finding comfort in every word.

9th November 1941

My Darling Mary,

Well, here I am, I have finally made it in one piece, I can picture you here with me so vividly. So far army life has been just as you described. I have discovered I'm not bad at early morning latrine duty and the camaraderie of being amongst men all fighting for the same thing is a wonderful feeling. Although I have only been with my posting a few days, I have already made friends I would lay down my life for and now I understand now why you talked of your army days so fondly and why you miss your friends so badly.

So far, I have been kept exceptionally busy, just as you said, my love, but I think of you every day. Once lights out are called, I bring your beautiful face to mind, and in the silence I allow myself to imagine our future together once the horrors of this war are over. I picture us in a beautiful home – in Surrey perhaps, amidst the countryside, but close enough to town for you to keep in touch with the Liberty girls. And we'll have oodles of children, Mary, enough for a small school! I'm only teasing, but the idea of more of you to love is an idea I cannot shy away from and I cannot wait to become your husband, and love, honour and cherish you.

Quite simply you are my world, and I cannot wait for our lives to begin together. However, just as you are fighting the war on the home front, I am here fighting Hitler for our freedom in my own way. Together we are stronger, Mary, and together there is no war we cannot win.

Until next time, my darling girl,

Your David

Rounding the corner, she saw the outline of the hospital illuminated up ahead and quickened her step. Pushing open the heavy wooden door, she asked a nurse on duty where she might find Rose Harper and was directed to a room on the ground floor. Racing along the corridor, Mary couldn't help noticing the strong scent of bleach. The place was spotless, she thought, taking in the sparkling tiled floor and whitewashed walls. It was incredible that there was a war on, but standards hadn't slipped – just like in the army, she thought sadly.

Reaching Rose's door, she took a deep breath and drew back her shoulders. Now was not the time to be miserable: her friend needed her to be brave and strong, and that was precisely what Mary intended to be.

Stepping inside, she saw a ward filled with twelve narrow beds. It didn't take her long to find Rose at the far end. She was sitting up in bed, patches over her eyes and her face pale. She looked like a little girl, Mary thought, lost in the large bed and surrounded by pristine sheets and pillows. Yet despite her obvious discomfort she was bravely wearing a small smile for Dot, Alice and Flo, who were perched on chairs around her bedside, chattering nineteen to the dozen.

'Mary!' Flo exclaimed.

'We'd given you up for lost!' Dot chuckled. 'You must want your head testing walking about in this weather; it's freezing out there.'

'It is colder than I thought,' Mary admitted as she peeled off her coat and sat at the edge of Rose's bed. 'How are you, Rose?'

'I'm all right,' she said in a small voice. 'Better now you girls are here. Matron's been ever so kind, says I can have more than two visitors at a time if I like.'

'That is kind,' Mary smiled. 'And where's your dad?' she asked, looking around the room, half expecting to see him talking to one of the other patients.

'I sent him home,' Rose replied. 'He's been with me all night, and he needs his rest; his leg was playing up something rotten.'

'And how are you?' Mary pressed gently.

'She's doing brilliantly, aren't you, darlin'?' Flo smiled. 'Be out of here in no time.'

'Have you heard from Tommy or your mum?' Alice asked, rubbing the small of her back.

Rose nodded. 'They've both sent me a telegram. Tommy's going to try and get leave to come and see me but I've sent a message straight back to say he's to stay where he is. The army needs him more than I do. Mother sends her love and has told me to remain strong.'

Not for the first time, Mary found herself impressed by Rose's grace and selflessness. She was the last person that deserved this.

'What have the doctors said?' Mary pressed gently.

Rose took a deep breath, the words were clearly difficult for her to say. 'They say I've got methanol poisoning. It's what you get when you drink pure alcohol.'

Mary frowned. 'When did you drink pure alcohol? You just had a couple of whiskies.'

Dot squeezed the younger girl's hand and explained for her. 'It's also what you get when you drink hooch – booze that's not proper booze.'

'But we didn't go to Jimmy Allan's place,' Flo said, furrowing her brow. 'We made sure. We went to the pub in Kingly Street. Of course you got proper booze.'

'I think perhaps this bleedin' hooch ring's expanded,' Dot cautioned. 'Seems whoever's behind this has branched out across the West End and is making a flamin' fortune in the process. I've already had a word with the pub we were in last night and told 'em what's what. Someone wants flogging for this.'

At that the girls fell silent, each furious at the seriousness of Rose's situation. None of them were strangers to the pubs around Liberty's, and it could just as easily have been any one of them lying in that hospital bed.

There but for the grace of God, Mary thought.

'So have the doctors said anything else?' Flo asked.

'They say the blindness might only be temporary,' Rose said. 'But even if it's temporary it can take weeks or sometimes months for sight to come back completely.'

'But there is hope,' Alice said optimistically.

'There's always hope,' Mary agreed. 'Sometimes it's the only thing we've got to cling on to.'

Chapter Thirty-Two

It had been a little more than three weeks since Rose had been taken to hospital and life had taken on a new rhythm for the Liberty girls. They now spent most evenings at Rose's bedside, each taking it in turns to talk to her, read aloud or just sit and hold her hand.

She was still unable to see and doctors had warned that the longer it went on, the more likely her condition was to be permanent. Mary had expected the news to rock Rose, but she had been stoic, insisting that she had her family and the love and support of her friends.

Mary knew just what she meant. There were some things that could never be fixed but there were also some things that made life worth living. The regular stitching nights with the Liberty girls were something that continued to keep her going when she thought she would break with grief. There was something so simple about the way they came together, and Mary could feel the love they felt for each other embedded in each and every stitch they made.

Never more so than when the girls gathered around Rose's bedside. They had all decided that just because Rose was in hospital there was no reason for their stitching nights to stop and so Dot had suggested they simply move them.

Now, the girls gossiped and stitched at Guy's Hospital instead of the pleating room and although Rose couldn't sew – her eyes were still covered in patches – she was as involved as possible, making suggestions, advising on stitch technique as well as offering helpful hints to Mary who was still struggling to sew in a straight line.

Tonight was no different, with Mary continuing to labour over a romper suit for Alice as the rest of the girls gossiped about the day's events.

''Ere, I heard something earlier,' Dot said in a hushed tone.

'What?' Rose asked.

'Well, I reckon I might be able to shine a light on this hooch racket making its way around the West End.'

'What do you mean?' Flo gasped.

Dot bent her head forwards conspiratorially towards the girls, and whispered, 'I mean a lad from another pub in Soho has gone blind.'

'Oh my days!' Rose gasped. 'That's terrible. Will he be all right?'

'Same boat as you, love,' Dot said, patting Rose's hand. 'But it makes you think, don't it? Girls, keep your eyes peeled and if you see anything suspicious—'

'—or taste anything suspicious,' Rose cut in.

'Or taste anything suspicious,' Dot agreed, 'then we must go straight to the police. Whoever's doing this is downright dangerous.'

'You can say that again,' Alice said, groaning as she shifted her weight on the bed.

'Can I get you a pillow or something?' Flo asked, her eyes brimming with concern.

'I'm fine,' Alice sighed as she tried to settle herself next to Rose. 'I'm just uncomfortable and tired. I can't sleep properly because my belly is so huge.'

'Oh Alice, not long now,' Rose consoled.

'A week,' Alice groaned. 'And it feels like forever.'

Rose smiled. 'But that's only around the corner. And just think, you'll have a lovely baby to cuddle, all in time for Christmas as well. What a lovely present.'

'I know, I know,' Alice replied weakly. 'It's just the closer the baby's arrival gets the more I keep thinking about Luke and how he's not going to be here to see him or her.'

At that Alice's face crumpled and the girls immediately crowded around her to offer comfort.

'No news is good news, isn't that what they say?' Flo rallied.

'Yes, there's no point dwelling on what might or might not be,' Mary said sensibly. 'You've got to put your little one first.'

'Mary's right,' Rose whispered. 'Believe me, I know how hard it is to remain cheerful when you feel like the whole world's trying to bring you down, but you've got to have hope.'

At that Alice clasped Rose's hand. 'I'm sorry, darlin', if anyone has a right to be down it's you and here I am moaning about my problems.'

'Don't be silly. It's what friends are for: we're there for the bad times as well as the good.'

'Hear, hear,' Mary said loudly, just as the door to the ward opened.

The girls looked up and immediately saw an awkward-looking Mr Button standing in the doorway.

Flo immediately rushed from her position at the end of Rose's bed to find a chair. 'I didn't know you were coming, Mr Button. Can I get you anything? Cup of tea? Do you need to put your feet up?' she babbled.

'You can see that I am,' Alice chuckled wryly from her position lying next to Rose.

Mr Button lifted his hand by way of greeting, but Mary couldn't miss the sombre look in his eyes as he saw Rose in her hospital bed.

'I shan't interrupt your evening. I just wanted to see how you are, Rose,' he said, doing his best to rally and sitting in the chair Flo had found.

'Much better, sir,' Rose replied. 'I've been learning to walk with the help of a stick to guide me. It takes some adjustment but it has felt good to get out of bed.'

Mr Button smiled. 'I can imagine.'

'And doctors say she may well be home by Christmas,' Mary informed him.

'Wonderful news,' Mr Button exclaimed. 'We shall all continue to hope for a speedy recovery, Rose, but I want you to know I have spoken to the Liberty family and the board. We all agree we want to do as much to help you as we can.'

'That's kind,' Rose replied.

Mr Button waved her gratitude away. 'Not at all. The family care very much about their staff and want you to know that there will always be a job for you at Liberty's.'

As Mr Button finished talking, Rose let out a little sob. 'I don't know what to say. I had been worried about making ends meet, and fretting about Father too and how we were going to manage. This is a weight off my mind, Mr Button, thank you.'

'It's my pleasure, my dear,' he said quietly. 'How is your father? Is he coping all right without you?'

'He seems all right, doesn't he, Rose?' Dot chipped in. 'One of us girls has been popping in to see him every day with something warm to keep him going and to help him get about.'

'Dot and everyone have been brilliant,' Rose added. 'As Dot said, the girls really have been ever so good.'

'It's no problem at all,' Alice said. 'Your father's ever such a nice man.'

'Well, I think so,' Rose agreed.

The girls chuckled, but Mary saw Flo was looking nervous.

'Anyway, Mr Button,' Flo said as the girls fell silent. 'There's something I was hoping to ask you.'

Mr Button regarded Flo nervously. 'All right.'

Flo chewed her lip before she blurted, 'Thing is, Mr Button, sir, as you know I am getting married on Boxing Day and the reason I haven't given you an official sort of invitation yet is because I was hoping you would play rather a special part in the ceremony.'

'Go on,' Mr Button said, looking perplexed.

'As you know, my father and I haven't seen each other in several years, and to be honest, sir, he's no father to me, which is why I was hoping you would do me the very great honour of giving me away.'

As Flo finished speaking, the girls stared at Mr Button, who was gazing at Flo open-mouthed in shock.

'You would really like me to walk you down the aisle?' he gasped.

'Only if it's no trouble, sir,' Flo said quickly. 'But I've rather come to think of you as a father figure in recent weeks, and, well, these girls, sir, they are like my family.'

There was only a brief pause before Mr Button spoke again. 'In that case I should be honoured.'

At that the girls whooped and cheered, the delight clear as day across all their faces. It seemed that Flo's wedding was giving them all something to look forward to.

Chapter Thirty-Three

The following day was a Sunday and the wintry weather was in full swing. The moment Mary pulled back her blackout blind she had shivered and been tempted to hop back into bed. The ground was covered in a thick frost, the trees were bare and the skies were grey and full of drizzle. Mary was delighted she didn't have to do anything but put her feet up.

The worry over Rose and whether Mrs Matravers would tell David her secret was beginning to take its toll. Then there was the lack of staff on the shop floor, not to mention the days and nights fire-watching, as well as the staff Christmas party which she needed to finish organising. It was no wonder Mary was about ready to drop.

Knowing Flo had promised to visit Rose, and with Dot and Alice at the cinema, for once Mary had taken advantage of the chance to relax, and had spent the day drinking tea and devouring a paperback.

As she sat at the kitchen table, a pot of tea freshly made, she heard the sounds of her friend and landlady shuffling though the hallway and got up to reach for two more cups from the shelf.

'Oooh, you're a mind reader,' Dot sighed gratefully. 'I could murder the entire pot.'

Mary chuckled. 'Film not very good then?'

Alice sniffed, sinking into the chair. 'The B movie and the Pathé news reel were more interesting.'

'It was all right,' Dot grumbled. 'But it would have been better without Katherine Hepburn. I don't know what it is about her but she gets up my nose.'

Mary couldn't help herself and snorted with laughter, but when Alice let out a groan she asked, alarmed, 'Is it the baby?'

'Ssssh!' Alice hissed, cutting across her and jerking her head towards the wireless. The girls fell silent as the newsreader spoke across the airwaves.

Japan's long-threatened aggression in the Far East began tonight with air attacks on United States naval bases in the Pacific.

'Oh my days!' cried Alice as the newsreader continued his broadcast. 'The Japanese have had a go at the Yanks in Hawaii now.'

Messages from Tokyo say that Japan has announced a formal declaration of war against both the United States and Britain, the newsreader continued.

'We all knew it was coming,' Dot said quietly. 'Japan has been making threats for months.'

'I suppose that means the Americans will finally enter the war after all,' Mary added thoughtfully. 'It looks like we might get the help we need.'

'We don't need no help,' Dot grumbled. 'We didn't need 'em in 1914 and we don't need 'em now. All this means is more confusion and hard work for our boys and girls out there fighting.'

'But we do need them, Dot,' Mary urged. 'This war's dirtier than the last. If we ever want to see an end to this, we need a country with money and power to help us out.'

'So you think this is good news?' Alice asked doubtfully.

Mary nodded. 'I do. I know it might not seem like it now, but with America on our side we have every chance of getting the resources and supplies we need to help us finally get rid of Hitler once and for all.'

Dot got to her feet and washed her cup up in the sink. 'I don't know. What I do know is there are a lot of lives being wasted in the name of this damned war.'

With that she went upstairs to bed, leaving Alice and Mary with their own thoughts about the future.

Monday morning at Liberty's, all staff and customers alike could talk about was the attack on Pearl Harbor. Mary found herself on edge listening to the customers' chatter. She knew David was now more than likely in a lot more danger and she felt strangely terrified she would never see him again. She had woken up with a physical ache in her chest, the pain of missing him as real to her as any headache. As she brought his handsome face to mind she felt a flash of despair as she realised she still hadn't dealt with the problem Mrs Matravers had set her. She didn't want to break things off with David, she adored him with all her heart, and after everything she had been through, all the pain she had carried around for months, she had finally found a place she could start again. Did she really want to lose all that?

Mary knew it wasn't a problem that could be solved this morning and so she threw herself into sorting, tidying and cleaning to try and take her mind off the latest developments.

She had just finished serving a customer following the lunchtime rush when she spotted Flo heading towards her, a stern look on her face.

'I had to sneak this out of the office for you,' she said grimly.

'What is it?' Mary asked, puzzled, for the expression on Flo's face was filled with fury.

'A letter,' Flo said, pulling out a white envelope from her folder. 'How many times do I have to say it? We're not allowed personal mail here under any circumstances so you might want to tell whoever it is not to write here again.'

Mary felt a pang of guilt. Since Flo had been promoted to temporary deputy store manager in Mrs Matravers' absence Mary knew her friend had been working around the clock to prove herself. Something like this would have let her down. 'Sorry. Thanks Flo,' she said, taking the letter from her friend's hand.

Turning the envelope over, the sight of the handwriting made her gasp. She had been sure she would never see that familiar slope again, yet here it was in black and white – a letter from her mother.

'Are you all right?' Flo asked, seeing the colour drain from Mary's face.

Nodding furiously, Mary stuffed the letter under the counter to read later. 'Fine, just wasn't expecting anything. Think it's from an old friend I haven't seen for a while.'

'All right, well, if you're sure?' Flo frowned. 'I'll see you later and remember, don't tell a soul that you received that letter here.'

As Flo walked across the shop floor towards the stairs, Mary felt herself tremble. She was itching to open the letter and read her mother's words, but she also felt afraid. She had been desperate for a reply ever since she had written to her parents weeks earlier. Now the answer was here, she was scared. What if her mother had bad news? What if she was writing to tell her that her father's cancer had progressed? Or, worse, what if he was dead?

She couldn't open it here on the shop floor. Better to wait until after work when she was away from customers and prying eyes. Shoving it to the back of the drawer, Mary knew she needed a few moments to collect herself and was about to flee the shop floor when she saw Alice leaning against the window, beads of sweat trickling down her forehead.

'Alice, are you all right?' she gasped in concern.

'Fine,' Alice panted. 'I just need a minute.'

'I think you'd better sit down,' Mary said. 'Go upstairs to the staffroom and get some rest.'

Alice shook her head, and turned to Mary, her eyes wild with fear. 'I can't move, Mary. I'm in agony. I've got stomach cramps.'

Mary eyed Alice warily. 'Sweetheart, I really think you need to rest then we can get the doctor out to take a look at you.'

By now a couple of customers had appeared and were looking at Alice and Mary curiously while pretending to admire the prints.

Smiling in what she hoped was a welcoming and encouraging way to the customers, Mary turned back to Alice. 'Please, you've got to go to the staffroom at least to sit down. Customers are staring.'

Alice gripped Mary's hand and started to sob. 'I can't move. I'm terrified, help me.'

'What do you mean?' Mary gasped. 'Is it the baby? You're not due for another week.'

'I know, but I think my waters broke earlier this morning and for the past hour I've been blindsided by pain. It's like I keep getting kicked in the stomach.'

Horrified, Mary saw Alice's face was contorted with agony. Something told her that Alice's baby was about to make an unplanned appearance and become a part of Liberty's rich history.

Chapter Thirty- Four

Mary wasted no time springing into action. Calmly she turned to the customers and asked them apologetically if they wouldn't mind temporarily making space and giving them some privacy. Then she lay Alice down on the rug under the window and grabbed a roll of fabric from the shelf as a makeshift pillow.

'It's a good job Mrs Matravers isn't here,' Alice panted, 'she'd have your guts for garters if she could see what you've just done with that roll of silk.'

'I'm afraid needs must,' Mary muttered grimly. 'Now, I don't want you to worry. You're going to be fine.'

Alice eyed her suspiciously. 'Have you delivered many babies, Mary?'

'Enough to know what I'm doing,' Mary said, hoping Alice couldn't tell she was lying.

Turning then to shoo away the rest of the customers who were still stopping to look at what was happening, Mary took a deep breath. She knew that Alice did not want to hear at that moment how Mary had never delivered a baby in her life. However, she was sure that if she kept a level head she would get Alice through her labour.

Once the shop floor was clear, she reached for the room divider they used to display some of the fabrics on, and shielded Alice from the store. Then she knelt next to her. 'How are you feeling, sweetheart?' she asked gently.

'Never better,' Alice groaned.

Mary smiled. If Alice was cracking jokes, she had a feeling they had a bit of time. If she could get someone to phone for an ambulance or midwife there was a possibility that they might get Alice home in time to deliver this baby after all.

Peering over her shoulder, she looked for a member of staff to try and attract their attention, but there was nobody around. She turned back to Alice and reluctantly started to get to her feet. If she was quick she could make it up to the offices upstairs and ring for help. 'I'm just going to get help. I won't be long, I promise.'

Alice clutched Mary's hand, her fingernails digging painfully into her flesh. 'Don't leave me, please. I'm frightened.'

Stroking the hair away from Alice's clammy forehead, Mary did her best to reassure her friend. 'I won't be long. Can you imagine the mess if you go giving birth on all these fabrics? Mrs Matravers will sack the pair of us. Besides, some of these fabrics are so beautiful it would be a shame to damage them!'

Despite her agony, Alice managed a smile. 'All right. But please don't be long.'

Promising solemnly, Mary ran up the wooden staircase. However, she had only made it around the first leg when she bumped into Mr Button.

'What is all the commotion downstairs on fabrics, Miss Holmes-Fotherington?' he demanded.

'It's Alice,' Mary said breathlessly, 'I think her baby's on its way. I need to call for help.'

Alarm flooded Mr Button's features. 'Is there time?

Mary nibbled at her bottom lip. 'Honestly, sir, I don't know. I hope so. Her waters broke earlier this morning and I suspect she's having contractions every few minutes now so there isn't a great deal of time.'

'Dear God! The poor girl must be terrified. I'll go to her now. Mary, hurry,' he called, running the rest of the way towards the shop floor.

Mary raced up the stairs, but she couldn't fail to hear his shouts of 'Coming through' and 'Excuse me' as he pushed past shoppers in his hurry to get to Alice.

Making it to the office, she called the hospital and alerted the midwife who promised to attend as soon as possible and advised Mary to arm herself with plenty of hot water and towels just in case. Hanging up the phone she dashed to the staffroom and filled two tin buckets with hot water and found several clean towels in the linen cupboard. Heart pounding, she ran back down the stairs to fabrics, surprising herself at how much of the water she managed to keep in the buckets.

Peering around the room divider, Mary was shocked at the sight that greeted her. There was Mr Button, on his hands and knees, peering up at Alice; he appeared to be gently holding what looked very much like a baby's head in his hands.

'You're doing beautifully, Alice,' he called gently. 'Just another couple of pushes and I think you've got it.'

Alice shook her head. 'I can't. I'm tired.'

Mary and Mr Button exchanged looks of concern as Mary dumped the hot water on the floor and held her friend's hand. 'I know it's hard, Alice, and I know you've had enough, but your baby is almost here. Don't you want to meet him or her?'

Alice nodded. 'So much. But I just don't think I've got it in me, Mary. I'm not strong like you are.'

'Nonsense,' Mary replied firmly. 'And I hate to say it but you haven't really got a lot of choice in the matter. Either you push and have a beautiful, bonny baby, or you stay here forever as a Liberty exhibit in the fabric department. I'll model all the latest fabrics on you of course.'

Mary knew she was being cruel, but sometimes that was what the situation called for. And as Alice pushed again, she knew her tough words must have had the desired effect for seconds later the sound of cries could be heard across the shop floor.

'It's a boy,' Mr Button cooed delightedly. 'A beautiful baby boy.'

Alice reached her hands out to clasp the baby in her arms. 'Can I hold him?'

'Of course,' Mr Button replied. 'Let me just get something to wrap him in.'

Mary watched in amazement as he reached for a roll of Liberty silk that she knew to be worth a small fortune, ripped a large piece from the roll and swaddled the baby tightly.

'Congratulations,' he smiled, handing him to Alice.

'Oh my days!' Alice wept, cradling the little infant in her arms. 'I can't believe he's here.'

'Our very first Liberty baby,' Mary whispered, peering down at him.

He was gorgeous, Mary thought as she took in his full head of blonde hair and smooth skin. He was the spitting image of his mother.

'What are you going to name him?' Mr Button asked, getting to his feet.

'Arthur Luke,' Alice smiled tenderly up at him. 'After Arthur Liberty, founder of this precious store and in honour of you both, and Luke, well, so he never forgets his father.' She glanced at Mary. 'I would never have done this without you two, I don't know how to thank you.'

Tears filled Mary's eyes. Just being here for her friend was reward enough, and one she'd never expected to receive. When she left Ceylon she'd had no expectations beyond surviving. To be part of such a special milestone in Alice's life and to help deliver baby Arthur into the world was something she would never have dared hope for.

Looking across at Mr Button it was clear he felt something similar as he dabbed at his eyes with his pristine white cotton hanky. 'You have no need to thank me at all, Alice. This was a very great honour.'

The scene was one to treasure, Mary thought as they fell silent and watched baby Arthur snuffle contentedly in Alice's arms. It really was what life was all about and she felt nothing but happiness for her friend and the unexpected gift she had been given that day.

Just then, the sound of voices behind them brought them swiftly back to the present. Turning around, Mary saw Flo flanked by another woman she didn't recognise. Dressed in a brown uniform with matching hat, she had rosy cheeks and a kindly face.

'This is Joan, the midwife,' Flo explained in hushed tones.

'Although it looks like I might be a little late!' Joan cried, her warm smile filling her face with kindness. 'Let's have a look at you both anyway, dearie,' she said, gesturing to Alice and Arthur.

As Joan began her checks, Mary, Mr Button and Flo stepped behind the room divider to give them some privacy.

'I can't believe I missed it all! How exciting!' Flo squealed, her face flushed with delight.

'It wasn't so much exciting,' Mary sighed, 'more terrifying, to be completely honest. I had no idea what I was doing. Thank heavens you turned up when you did, Mr Button.'

'Yes! However did you learn to deliver babies?' Flo quizzed.

Mr Button blushed. 'I trained as an ambulance driver and worked with many of the army docs,' he said. 'I think baby Arthur is actually my fifth delivery.'

Mary stared at the store manager open-mouthed, suddenly seeing him in a completely different light. 'I had no idea.'

Mr Button shrugged. 'No reason why you should, my dear.'

'You must tell Dot,' Flo insisted. 'She'll throw you both a party when she hears about all this.'

'I think the only thing I'd like just now is a cup of tea,' Mary chuckled. 'And I've a funny feeling our new mum would love one as well.'

'I'll put the kettle on,' said Flo. 'It's the very least I can do after all the hard work you have both put in today.'

Chapter Thirty-Five

The next stitching night, held a week after Arthur's sudden arrival into the world, was something of an anomaly. It wasn't held in the hospital, or the pleating room, but for once in the Elephant and Castle kitchen, with Dot proudly laying on refreshments as much to welcome the latest addition to the sewing circle as to keep the girls going.

Dot was determined to get everyone in the Christmas mood. Not only had she made an abundance of pipe-cleaner decorations for the store but she had also made enough for the little house in Bell Street too. Reindeers and stars lined the mantelpiece, while a nativity scene Dot had kept since her own childhood took pride of place in the window. Although there was no tree, the coloured paper chains Dot had made from gummed paper hung from the picture rail, making the house feel very festive indeed.

As Mary watched Dot carefully press a pile of newborn baby clothes before the guests started to arrive, she felt a pang of regret for her landlady. Dot would have been a wonderful mother, and it was a shame she never got the family she longed for. Still, she thought grimly, Dot had been more of a mum to her these past few months than her own mother had ever been, and for that she would always be grateful.

Since Arthur's sudden arrival, she, together with Alice and Dot, had found the days had passed in a blur as they got used to another resident in the house. Once the midwife declared both mum and baby fighting fit, Larry drove them both home in style in a freshly valeted Liberty van, and Dot sorted out a drawer for Arthur to sleep in, as well as various linens.

It had been a good job that she and the rest of the girls had increased their stitching nights, otherwise Alice wouldn't have had a thing ready for the poor baby. Looking at him now, curled up in his mother's arms wearing the romper suit she had made for him, Mary smiled fondly.

A part of her had worried that she would find it difficult to cope when Alice's baby was born. Mary hated herself for it, but she had fretted that having Arthur around would make her remember all she had lost and the pain she had felt when her own baby's life had been snuffed out. But strangely, and thankfully, Mary hadn't felt like that at all. In fact, she found nothing but pleasure in spending time with Arthur, and loved helping Alice put him down for his nap. As for cuddles, she had plenty of those to offer; the sweet smell of his gorgeous head was like nectar and she loved nothing more than breathing it in, much to Alice and Dot's delight.

This baby might not have a father for the moment, but he would be surrounded by love, she thought, watching him sleeping peacefully while all hell broke loose outside. Just as Mary had predicted, Hitler had declared war on the United States, and America was standing shoulder to shoulder with Britain to fight the good fight. Mary didn't care what some people were saying about the Americans being too late to join in. It was good to have them on the side of the British and she felt more confident than she had in months that there was a chance this war would be over sooner rather than later.

Now, as she heard a rap at the door, she tore herself away from the sight of baby Arthur and went to answer it, finding Flo on the doorstep, bundled up in scarf, coat and gloves to keep out the chill.

'Ooh, let me in quick, Mary, it's parky out there,' Flo grinned, pushing past her friend and making a beeline straight for Alice and Arthur who were sitting at the kitchen table. 'Oh, he's so beautiful,' she gushed. 'I want one.'

'Only a matter of time once you and Neil are hitched. Less than a fortnight to go!' Alice grinned as she held Arthur close to her chest. 'I can't believe how quickly it's come round.'

Flo ran a finger along Arthur's cheek and sighed. 'I know. In a fortnight I'll be Mrs Canning. I can't wait. Just think, Mary, it could be you and David next.'

Mary flushed uncomfortably at the thought. She hadn't replied to David's last letter; she didn't trust herself not to say something she might regret. 'Here, Alice, give Flo the baby, she looks like she's going to inhale him!'

Alice chuckled and handed Arthur to Flo. 'Mary's been smelling him all afternoon. I think it's time someone else had a turn.'

'They should bottle whatever it is and sell it!' Dot chuckled, kissing Flo warmly on the cheek.

'He was the only reason I insisted on taking my half-day today,' Mary added good-naturedly. 'I said to Mr Button, I'm sorry, I know we're short-staffed but there's a newborn baby at home that I have to smell.'

'I still can't believe he helped you deliver Arthur,' Flo exclaimed.

'Man of many talents is Edwin,' Dot mumbled, setting down a pot of tea and cups for the girls.

Mary giggled. 'What I can't get over is the way he ripped up that roll of gorgeous Liberty silk.'

'I know. I'm going to have his christening gown made out of it though so it doesn't go to waste,' Alice said.

'What a lovely idea,' Dot cooed. 'We could start sorting that out at the sewing circle.'

Mary raised an eyebrow. 'As long as it's after Flo's wedding. We've still got so much to do.'

'We'll manage ...' Alice sighed, pouring a cup of tea for each of the girls.

'I'm just glad it was Mr Button that ripped that fabric rather than one of us,' Flo laughed as she began to peel off her many layers. 'Mrs Matravers would have sacked us on the spot, emergency or no emergency.'

Dot turned back to the table and laid out a plate of almond biscuits. 'Has anyone been to see Rose today?'

'I popped over to the hospital earlier,' Flo said. 'She's stable, but seemed ever so down.'

'Why?' Mary asked. 'She should be coming home soon.'

Flo sank into the chair nearest the window. 'She's worried about her dad.'

'Malcolm's getting on all right, isn't he?' Dot frowned. 'He seemed fine when I saw him yesterday at the hospital.'

'Rose says that he isn't.' Flo scratched her chin thoughtfully. 'She says he's barely bothering to eat.'

'Poor thing,' Dot whispered. 'I'll go round there later.'

'I'll come with you,' Mary offered. 'Perhaps I can give the place a bit of a clean and tidy too.'

'I don't know how they're going to manage when Rose comes home,' Flo said, taking a sip of the tea Dot poured for her. 'I mean it was bad enough when she was working all the time and had her father to take care of.'

'But now she'll need help taking care of herself *and* her father,' Dot finished.

The girls fell into silence then as they each pondered Rose's situation.

'We'll find a way to help them,' Mary said firmly.

Just then, Arthur opened his mouth and squealed. 'Looks like he agrees,' Alice smiled, getting to her feet. 'I'll just go and put him to bed, but before I do, there's something I want to ask you Mary.'

'Oh?'

'I was wondering if you would be Arthur's godmother,' Alice asked, failing to keep the excitement out of her voice.

Mary's mouth dropped open in astonishment.

'Please,' Alice begged. 'You helped deliver him. I dread to think what would have happened if you hadn't been there. Please say yes – it would mean so much to me.'

An unexpected wave of joy bubbled up inside Mary as she looked from baby Arthur to Alice. The last thing she had been looking for was to become a surrogate mother of any kind when she had lost her own baby; could she really cope with a permanent motherly role in Arthur's life? Gently she leaned over Arthur and kissed the grumbling baby on his forehead, savouring the softness of his skin against her lips. A wave of love engulfed her and she knew without a doubt that although she might not have her own baby any longer, she had more than enough love in her heart for Arthur too. Smiling at Alice through tear-filled eyes, she knew there was only one answer she could give.

'Yes, a thousand times, yes.'

Chapter Thirty-Six

Mary had become used to being woken by the sound of a crying baby now. In fact in a funny way she almost looked forward to it, she thought as she reached for her dressing gown. She didn't need to glance at the alarm clock to know that it was just after five in the morning. Baby Arthur had got them all into a firm routine since his arrival.

Creeping down the stairs to the kitchen she smiled for a moment as she allowed herself to drink in the scene. Alice was sitting in the chair by the window feeding Arthur, toast and a cup of tea beside her.

It was the perfect scene of domesticity, Mary thought. Arthur had changed their lives for the better, and Mary couldn't imagine a house without a baby in it now.

'Ah, look, there's your Auntie Mary,' said Alice as she finished feeding Arthur. Patting him expertly on the back to wind him, she handed the baby to Mary. 'Here. I'm gasping for my tea; you hold him for a bit.'

Mary eagerly reached for Arthur. 'My pleasure.'

Settling down in the chair opposite Alice, Mary looked down and smiled at the baby in her arms. After she lost her own child a part of her had wondered if she would find it too traumatic to be around babies. She fretted that she wouldn't cope and would find the memories too painful to bear, but much to Mary's relief she had found that the time she spent with Arthur was a sheer delight. She thought only of him when she held him in her arms and felt only joy when she rocked him to sleep or kissed him goodnight.

Lifting his head to inhale the sweet smell of his scalp, she cautiously allowed herself to imagine doing this with her own baby, should she and David be as lucky as Alice and have children of their own. She thought that would be enough to prove her worth in life, but now with the war stepping up a notch, she wondered if she ought to turn her attentions towards doing more to help the war effort.

'I thought I'd go to the labour exchange today, make myself available,' Mary said stiffly.

'Why? Because all single women are now being conscripted?' Alice remarked.

Mary nodded. 'Now that new Act's come in I think a lot of women will be called up. Thought I'd get ahead of them all, but I don't know if anyone will want me after I was sacked from the army.'

Alice looked at her quizzically. 'You never did say why you were discharged, Mary.'

Mary felt her heart bang against her chest in panic. Alice had never asked her outright why she had left the army and she had always hoped she never would. She paused for a moment as she tried to think what to say but her mind was blank.

''Ere, Mary, you're on fire-watch duty tonight, aren't you?' Dot said as she shuffled into the kitchen.

Never before had she felt so glad to see Dot. Nodding, she returned Arthur to Alice and poured her landlady a cup of tea from the pot resting on the table. 'Unfortunately. Still, it's just one night tonight as Mr Button has said that I need some time to finalise the party details. Plus we've got to finish sorting through the sale stock, ready for Christmas Eve.'

'I cannot believe Christmas is less than a fortnight away,' Alice grinned. 'And Flo's wedding the day after, not to mention the Christmas party.'

'We've a lot on,' said Dot as she reached down to kiss the baby. 'How are the plans coming along?'

'All right,' Mary replied. 'There's so much left still to organise though, not to mention putting the final touches to the sale prep.'

'But the store's looking wonderful, isn't it?' Dot smiled. 'That idea of yours to get the nippers making chains and decorations has really got customers into the Christmas spirit.'

'It has, hasn't it? Mr Button was thrilled with the response – little ones have been clamouring to decorate the tree.'

'And the aluminium drive is going ever so well too,' Dot went on. 'Rita in carpets was telling me how they're determined to collect more than the jewellery department.'

'Well, they're always showing off,' Alice grumbled. 'It's 'cos royalty always makes a beeline for them when they visit; they think they're better than the rest of us.'

Dot frowned. 'Has anyone sorted out the Christmas window yet?'

'Not yet,' Mary sighed. 'I think we're hoping to do something with the old decorations we've used in the past. New ones are so hard to come by.'

'I've offered to do the fabric department's window,' Dot smiled again. 'I love a good rootle about all the old things.'

'You are an old thing,' Alice teased good-naturedly, earning herself a playful swat from Dot.

The sound of a rap at the door broke up the giggles, with the girls turning to each other in surprise, the unexpected noise causing Arthur to grumble.

'Who's that at this hour?' Alice exclaimed.

'I'll go and find out, shall I?' Dot sighed, getting to her feet.

It didn't take long to find out as Mary saw her land-lady shuffle back into the kitchen closely followed by Mrs Matravers.

'Mrs M!' Alice cried in surprise. 'What are you doing here? Shouldn't you be at home resting?'

'That's what I said,' Dot added pointedly. 'Can I get you a cuppa?'

Mary hurriedly pulled out a chair. 'Here, sit down.'

Giving Mary a small smile, the deputy manager flung herself into the chair and took off her coat. 'No thank you, Dot. I shan't stay long – I know you all have to get to work. I just wanted to come and see you, Alice. Especially after I heard about little Arthur's dramatic entrance into the world.'

Alice chuckled as she held Arthur out to Mrs Matravers. 'You can say that again. He took us all by surprise. Would you like to hold him?'

'Of course. He's a beauty,' Mrs Matravers marvelled as she gently rocked the baby.

'And how are you, Mrs Matravers?' Mary asked nervously. 'Are you feeling better?'

The deputy manager nodded. 'I am. And I know I shouldn't be away from home, but I couldn't resist a little peek. He's a credit to you, Alice. Have you taken him into Liberty's yet to show him off?'

Alice shook her head. 'Not yet. I'm still finding my feet as a mum. There's so much to think about and do. I keep thinking I'm going to break him.'

'Don't be so silly,' Mrs Matravers admonished.

'You're doing a wonderful job, Alice,' Dot said comfortingly.

Alice smiled. 'Thank you. There are just times when I feel so overwhelmed by it all. Sometimes, much as I love Arthur, I think I'd give my right arm to get back to Liberty's. I know what I'm doing there.'

'The store really misses you, Alice,' Mary said, 'but your place is here with Arthur.'

'I know. And really I don't want to be anywhere else but with him,' Alice said, a guilty look flashing across her features. 'But with Luke still missing, I'm going to need to think about putting food on the table. The money the RAF pays us won't go very far for too long.'

'I'm sure the store would have you back part-time, Alice,' Mrs Matravers said helpfully. 'We could perhaps share childcare between us in time. Alf's sister has very kindly offered to take care of mine when I go back to work.'

'Really?' Alice said, brightening at the thought. 'What a good idea.'

'You'll be going back to work then?' Dot put in. 'Once the baby's born?'

Mrs Matravers nodded. 'Yes. We need the money. There's no two ways about it.'

'What about Alf? He still out of work?' Dot asked bluntly.

'Unfortunately,' Mrs Matravers sighed. 'He's been trying so hard to find something else since he was let go from the cinema. But of course with his leg it's hard to find someone that will take him on. That's why the cinema got rid of him. Said he was too slow at showing people to their seats.'

'That and customers were probably sick and tired of having their purses pinched,' Dot muttered under her breath.

'Anyway, have you been to see Rose?' Mary asked, shooting daggers at Dot as she hurriedly changed the subject.

At the mention of Rose, tears filled Mrs Matravers' eyes. 'Yes, poor dear. It's shameful what's happened to her. I hear the Liberty family have offered to pay her hospital bills.'

'It's very generous of them,' said Mary. 'It's so sad that this has happened.'

'I tell you, if I get my hands on 'em, I'll make 'em wish they'd never been born,' snapped Alice. 'I still know a few of my dad's old mates. Years ago, this sort of thing would have been snuffed out sharpish.'

'Now, now, dear, there's no need to get excited.' Mrs Matravers suddenly handed Arthur back to Alice and got rapidly to her feet. 'I must get on, leave you all to it. Mary, I shall see you at work later. No need to see me out.' The deputy manager turned on her heel and scuttled out of the house as if she had been burned.

'What do you think that was all about?' Alice frowned. 'She raced out of here.'

'Probably forgot to give Alf his breakfast, lazy good for nothing—' Dot snarled before Mary cut her off.

'I think it was probably my fault.'

'Why?' Alice demanded.

Mary sighed. She had kept Mrs Matravers' demands that she end her relationship with David to herself, believing that the deputy store manager might somehow change her mind. 'She doesn't want me to marry David,' she admitted. 'She wants me to write and tell him.'

Dot's jaw dropped open in astonishment. 'Why on earth does she want you to do that?'

'Because she doesn't think I'm good enough for her brother.'

'You're not serious?' Alice gasped.

'I'm very serious,' Mary sighed.

Now Dot shook her head in amazement. 'Would you like me to talk to her? I know Mabel of old; I'll tell her she's being a bleedin' fool.'

Alarm pulsed through Mary. Although she knew Dot had her best interests at heart, she also knew that there was a very real danger Mrs Matravers could tell her everything.

Mary shook her head and offered Dot what she hoped was a kind smile. 'I'll be fine. Thank you, Dot. She perhaps just needs a bit more time.'

'If you're sure,' Dot muttered doubtfully. 'It's not the first time Mabel's had ideas above her station. I don't mind putting her in her place.'

'Neither do I.' Alice nodded in agreement. 'After all you've done for her, she's got a nerve.'

Mary gave her friends a grateful smile. 'You two have enough on your plates. I can deal with Mrs Matravers.'

With that she went upstairs to finish getting ready for work, hoping against hope her past didn't catch up with her future.

Chapter Thirty-Seven

With Christmas just nine days away, the store was perpetually busy with shoppers searching for something to buy their loved ones. Although there had been no fresh deliveries for several weeks, Mr Button had ensured Liberty's pulled out all the stops so they could offer as much as possible. This meant every department had to go through their stockrooms and bring out everything they had, regardless of the season. As a result, ready-to-wear had displayed summer stock on their mannequins, marketing them as a perfect early gift for those summer parties. Elsewhere the gift department were offering parasols as that must-have accessory for winter trips to the sunshine, choosing to ignore the fact that commercial travel had been severely reduced since the dawn of war.

Nevertheless, the shop was in full swing, and so by the time Mary finished her day on the shop floor she found she was even more exhausted than usual for fire-watch duty.

Usually there were four staff on hand, and spotting her fire-watch colleagues all getting their stirrup pumps and buckets ready Mary was glad to see they wouldn't be short-staffed that night as they had been the last time she had been on duty, meaning she would be able to take a well-earned rest break later.

Initially Mary had been worried there would be a lot of training involved – after all, she'd had so much to learn about her day job – but the instructions were quite simple. Between the four of them they would keep watch for incendiaries and fires from the Liberty roof while one of the volunteers napped on a camp bed set up in the staffroom. If you saw a fire, you were supposed to raise the alarm and attempt to put it out but so far there had never been any fires and for that she was grateful.

Ensuring her tin hat was perched firmly on her head, Mary made her way out of the small wooden door Rose had shown her when she first started and clambered on to the roof. Out in the night air, she found herself saying a silent prayer for her friend. Of all the pals she had made in recent years, Rose was easily the most loyal, selfless and loving. To have lost her sight in the way that she had was unbearably cruel and Mary couldn't believe how well her friend seemed to be coping with the tragedy in such a small space of time.

Out on the roof of East India House, which overlooked the splendour of Regent Street, Mary shoved her hands into the pocket of her wool coat as she stalked around the perimeter. Even though it was a mild and clear night – perfect for a raid, Mary thought bitterly – she knew that she would be chilled to the bone if she didn't quicken her pace. Pausing for a moment, Mary looked up at the stars and smiled. She knew she was here to keep watch for fires, but she always found being on the roof incredibly romantic. There was something rather beautiful about being in the heart of the capital in the dead of night.

But after two hours of pacing up and down the roof, Mary had to admit she had lost her enthusiasm for the romance of it all. Instead all she wanted was to go inside and warm up. When she finally saw Albert from gifts lumbering towards her with his bucket and pump, she thought she had never been so glad to see anyone in her life and smiled at him gratefully as she hurried downstairs to the warmth of the staffroom for her couple of hours' rest.

Climbing into the narrow camp bed, she shut her eyes and hoped sleep would find her. But Mary was too cold and every time she moved to try and find comfort under the thin sheets, she was reminded of the fact she was missing out on vital rest.

In a flash she decided to pop to the pub on the corner for a drink. Her mind was too busy for sleep and she knew lots of the staff relied on a port and lemon to keep them going during their nights fire-watching. Mary hoped it might help her too.

Hurrying down the stairs towards the door with only her electric torch to guide her, Mary quickly found herself out in the cold night air. Hurrying towards the pub she knew was just a few doors along in Great Marlborough Street, she licked her lips, already tasting the port that would soon be coursing down her throat.

Pushing open the door, she saw the pub was teeming with people and so she weaved her way to the bar, ignoring the tuts and stares from some that thought she had no business as a woman being in a pub alone.

Reaching a corner that overlooked the courtyard out the back, Mary frowned. Bombs might not be dropping on the capital regularly at the moment but the blackout restrictions were firmly in place. Leaving the back door open like that was not only flouting the law, but also placing everyone in grave danger.

Leaning across the teak bar, Mary tried to catch the barman's attention, but he was so busy serving customers he didn't see her. Shaking her head in disbelief, she pushed her way through the crowds, lifted up the entrance hatch and made her own way through the bar and out to the back.

She was about to slam the back door shut and return to the bar when the sight of four figures in the court-yard, illuminated in the light, left her rooted to the spot in shock. There, just inches away from her, stood what looked to be Mrs Matravers, Alf, the pub landlord and another man.

They were talking in low voices and from her position she could see that the landlord's expression was furious.

'I won't tell you again, I don't want no more of your hooch after this lot,' he snapped.

'Now, now, Harry, there's no need for that,' Alf replied. 'I've already told you it won't happen again. We've got the mix all sorted now.'

'That's right,' the man Mary didn't know boomed in a deep voice. 'Just a bit of trial and error, you know how it is, Harry.'

'It was a one-off, that's all,' Mrs Matravers added, her natural cockney accent coming to the fore. 'Come on, Harry, you ain't gonna do no better on price, and we can make it quick as you like.'

'And I've already said I can't take the risk no more,' Harry insisted. 'There have been too many mishaps. Poor John's only just got his sight back and what about that girl what works at Liberty's? They say she's gonna be blind for the rest of her life, poor mare, and all because of your hooch. Nah, I'm sorry, I won't go back on a deal but I won't be buying no more off you neither. Now let's get this lot in off the van before we get caught, and we'll settle up.'

With that Mary heard the sound of footsteps crunch-ing over gravel as they walked away from the pub and she leaned her head back against the wall, trying to catch her breath. Had what she heard really been true? Were Mrs Matravers and Alf at the heart of the hooch ring that had made Rose blind?

Mary felt sick. She had to tell someone exactly what her boss and her husband had been up to, but first she had to return to safety. Glancing behind her she checked nobody was watching and then darted out into the pub court-yard where she raced across the gravel and back towards Liberty's for what she hoped was safety.

Chapter Thirty-Eight

Heart hammering against her chest, Mary could see the white clouds of her breath in the cold air as she raced like the wind across the pub courtyard. Pausing at the gate she looked to her left and right, trying to find the quickest way back to Liberty's, only to come face to face with two men.

Her heart sank; she already knew who it was: Alf and his friend, with Mrs Matravers bringing up the rear.

As Mary caught sight of Mrs Matravers, the moonlight highlighted the brief shock in her boss's eyes, before she recovered. Elbowing her way past the two men, Mary saw the woman's expression harden.

'What the hell are you doing here?' she hissed.

Mary ran her eyes over the trio. Mrs Matravers looked almost unrecognisable with her scraped-back hair and face devoid of any make-up whatsoever. As for the third man, he looked as mean as Alf, dressed in a battered camel coat and torn trousers. With an inch-long scar that ran down his cheek, the man radiated pure menace and made Mary's blood run cold.

'Who's she?' the man next to Alf asked gruffly. 'She ain't no grass, is she?'

Mrs Matravers shot Mary a frosty look. 'She's a girl what works for me up Liberty's, Bill. Don't worry, she won't say a word if she knows what's good for her.'

'You're that posh cow, ain't you?' Alf sneered. 'What you doing here, girl?'

'I was on a break from fire-watching,' Mary said hurriedly. 'Thought I'd get a quick drink to warm me up.'

There was a silence then as each of the trio weighed up the truth of what she said. As Mary looked from one to the other she couldn't ignore the stench that emanated from each of them. She couldn't put her finger on what it was but it was like overripe, gone-off hops. What on earth was Mrs Matravers doing here? The toxic smell of whatever it was couldn't be doing her or her baby any good.

'Make an 'abit of skiving off, do yer?' the man that appeared to be named Bill growled again.

Mary tried to swallow her fury. These three were clearly in the wrong, making and selling illegal hooch, blinding her poor friend in the process. For a brief second she wondered what David would think and whether he would object to her calling the police on his sister and brother-in-law, but then the thought of Rose lying in a hospital bed flashed into her mind and she knew that whether David minded or not was irrelevant, she had to do the right thing.

'I'm not skiving, as you put it,' she said coldly. 'I was just taking a quick break and now I'm returning to work, if you'll excuse me.'

She made to push her way past, only for Alf to catch her by the arm and hold her firmly in his grasp. 'You ain't going nowhere 'til you tell me what you think you've seen.'

Mary narrowed her eyes as she tried to yank her arm away. 'I haven't seen anything. Now if you'll excuse me ...'

Going to pull her arm away, she saw Mrs Matravers look warningly at Alf. 'Leave her, love, I'll deal with this.'

'I don't trust this one. Thinks she's too good for the likes of us,' he said, releasing his grip on Mary's arm.

'No I don't,' Mary snapped, rubbing her elbow.

'Alf, I said leave it,' Mrs Matravers hissed. 'I told you I will deal with it.'

'And I don't want this bleedin' mare ruining things for us with her big bleedin' mouth,' he snarled. 'We're in enough trouble as it is.'

Mary took a step back as she glanced at the pavement ahead. Whatever was going on, she wanted no part of it. All she wanted to do was get back to Liberty's and away from Alf and Mrs Matravers.

'Mary,' Mrs Matravers began wearily, 'I saw you lurking in the pub while we were talking with the landlord so I know you know that we are making hooch but you will say nothing.'

Mary's mind went into overdrive. Was it worth denying that she had heard anything or should she admit what she knew? 'I cannot believe you would stoop this low,' she spluttered. 'It's not only wrong, but dangerous. You must know that.'

'There's nothing dangerous about it,' Alf snapped. 'It's home brew, that's all.'

'Tell that to Rose,' Mary fired, stuffing her hands in her coat pocket.

Mrs Matravers blanched and Mary couldn't miss the look of sorrow in her eyes. 'I feel terrible about that, truly I do, Mary. But we had no idea that Rose would go blind.'

Fury poured through Mary. She had heard enough. 'Of course you wouldn't, you don't know how to make alcohol.'

Alf roared with laughter before his face turned nasty. 'I've been drinking beer all my life, love. I reckon that means I know what I'm doing.'

'We need the money, Mary,' Mrs Matravers explained simply. 'With a baby on the way, we need to find a way to make ends meet. My wages at Liberty's won't feed three mouths. You know how I feel about my family; they must always come first.'

Suddenly the penny dropped as Mary remembered how Mrs Matravers had come to her and Flo's rescue without warning. 'Was this the alcohol you could get your hands on for the Liberty dinner? And for Flo and Neil's reception? Were you lining up extra business for yourself?' Mary gasped. Without waiting for a reply, she added, 'Mr Button would have a fit if he found out where it came from. And what if someone else goes blind because of this hooch? How would you feel then? Well, you can forget supplying either event with your booze. I think everyone would rather go without.'

Mrs Matravers shrugged. 'If that's what you want, but I can assure you our colleagues at Liberty's won't thank you. What happened to Rose was an accident. It hasn't happened again.'

'What about that other man that went blind because of your alcohol?' Mary fumed. 'Was that a mistake as well? Then of course there's the rationing you're wasting. We're all going without so our soldiers can go on winning this war.'

'Load of old rubbish,' Alf sneered.

No longer afraid, Mary shot him a menacing glare. 'As someone who served in the army I can tell you that every ration we received was precious. People like you, only thinking of themselves and lining their own pockets, are going to cost us this war. Your brother's out there, Mrs Matravers, what do you think he'd say if he could see all this?'

At the mention of David, Mrs Matravers burst into tears. Alf suddenly grabbed hold of Mary by the arm and shoved her roughly against the wall. 'What did you say, you cheeky cow? I ought to give you a good hiding, upsetting my wife in her condition. And from what I gather the army didn't want you on account of your loose morals so don't you lecture me.'

Mary shrank back as the truth of his words hit home. Sensing he had hit a nerve, he ploughed on, tightening his hold. The pain of his grip sliced through her as if she were being torn in two. 'If you start telling people about what we're up to here, I'll make sure you pay, d'you understand?'

Nodding, she felt Alf relax his grip as he lifted her chin roughly and looked her in the eye. 'From what I know, you've got a few secrets of your own you don't want blabbing. If you don't keep your mouth shut and forget what you saw here I'll make sure everyone in the world knows your bleedin' secrets – and what's more I'll make sure that wherever you go next everyone finds out there 'n' all just what kind of girl you are. Your life'll be in tatters. I promise you that. Now are we clear?'

As Mary looked into Alf's soulless black eyes, she felt the menace radiate from him. He meant every word he said: Mary could see that. If she breathed a word she would be ruined forever. Reluctantly, she gave a short nod of her head. What else could she do?

The following morning, Mary felt absolutely exhausted by the time she arrived at work. Standing at the counter, ready to serve customers, she braced herself for the Christmas rush. Yet as she looked at every passing customer she couldn't miss the mixed expression of relief and worry etched across their faces at the latest developments of the war.

Something told Mary that meant it was only a matter of time before American soldiers started their descent on the UK as a whole, and she couldn't help wonder what that would mean for their country. With the Americans on side, it would undoubtedly mean a boost to their power, but would the US troops really be willing to fight like British soldiers? As usual her thoughts were never very far from

David and she wondered what this new development would mean for him, and she suddenly found herself hoping against hope that he would remain safe.

Stifling a yawn, she pushed the worry of war from her mind. She was far too tired to think about it, and instead turned her attentions to Flo, who was stacking fabric patterns neatly on the counter. You couldn't miss the smile on Flo's face as she worked, Mary thought. She was obviously looking forward to her wedding and Mary was delighted for her. Until she remembered that she had insisted Mrs Matravers didn't supply the party and wedding with any alcohol after all.

'I'm afraid I've got some bad news,' she said quietly.

Flo turned and looked at Mary in confusion. 'What is it? Oh, please don't tell me there are more paperwork problems? Doing Mrs Matravers' job as well as my own is hurting my head!'

Mary shook her head. 'Nothing like that. I bumped into Mrs Matravers last night. She told me she doesn't think she's going to be able to get her hands on any alcohol after all – for either the party or the wedding.'

'Oh no!' Flo groaned, crestfallen. 'What shall we do?'

'I don't think it matters,' Mary said kindly. 'Everyone at your wedding will be too busy celebrating your happiness to worry about whether they've got a glass of something.'

'I suppose so,' Flo said, looking forlorn. 'If that's the worst thing that happens, then I suppose it's not so bad.'

'Exactly,' Mary consoled. 'Not long now.'

Flo put down the patterns and leaned dreamily on the counter. 'I know, I'm counting the days. Neil wrote to me just last week telling me he couldn't wait to make me Mrs Canning.'

'There's still plenty to do in the meantime,' Dot said, joining them from the stockroom. 'I just caught the tail end

275

of what you were saying about booze, Mary. I take it Mabel can't make good on her promise?'

'Something like that,' Mary replied, yawning.

'How was fire-watch?' Dot asked, taking in Mary's drawn expression and pale face.

She sighed. 'Long. But I saw Mrs Matravers on my break, so that livened things up a bit.'

'I thought you'd seen her just now,' Dot frowned. 'She's in with Mr Button.'

Alarm coursed through Mary. 'She's here!'

Dot chuckled. 'She does work here, darlin'. Said she's here to pick up some more paperwork, and then she'll be down to see us— Ooh, speak of the devil.'

At the sight of Mrs Matravers walking down the wooden staircase Mary tried to swallow the rising sense of panic that threatened to envelop her.

'Morning, all,' Mrs Matravers said briskly. 'Any problems here, Flo?'

Flo shook her head. 'None at all.'

'Good,' the deputy manager said in a clipped tone. 'Then would you mind if I stole Mary for a moment? Mary, I would just like a brief word.'

Mary grimaced. 'Of course.'

Following Mrs Matravers down the stairs to the stockroom, Mary braced herself for her manager's onslaught. 'What can I do for you?' she snapped.

'You're getting to the point a bit quick, aren't you?' the deputy manager retorted.

Mary fixed Mrs Matravers with a pointed stare. 'I'm very tired and not in the mood for games. I'm sure you would like to get home, just as I would like to get back to work. If you want to ask me if I've told anyone about your little operation yet then rest assured I've kept it to myself.'

Mrs Matravers pursed her lips. 'Good, but that's not what I want to talk to you about.'

'Oh?' Mary felt wrong-footed. Although she hadn't expected to see Mrs Matravers today, she had been steeling herself for an argument since the moment the woman had walked into the department.

'No, Mary. I wanted to apologise,' Mrs Matravers said quietly.

Mary felt as if the ground had been swept from under her. 'I don't think I heard you properly.'

Mrs Matravers had the good grace to look ashamed. 'Alf should never have threatened you like that and neither should I. After you found out about our ... our freelance business, shall we say, Alf and I had a long talk and we decided that with a little one on the way we can't carry on, even though we really do need to find an extra income.'

'So what does that mean?' Mary asked.

'It means that we won't make any more hooch.' She sighed. 'We should have stopped after what happened with Rose.'

'So why didn't you?' Mary demanded. 'Because it wasn't just Rose that was hurt, was it?'

'I know it was wrong, but I don't think you understand, Mary.' Her tone was gruff. 'I didn't grow up like you in a world full of privilege. Everything David and I had we had to work for. There was never any money; what little my father brought home he spent in the pub, which meant that as soon as my mother left I had to go out to work and raise David. I was just twelve years old, Mary, and I was already scrimping and saving, working two jobs in two different cafés washing dishes just so I could feed myself and my brother. I don't want my baby to go through what I went through. I want my baby to have the best of everything, and with his or her father out of work, we had to find a way to make ends meet. I didn't want to do this, Mary, but I had to. After Rose went blind I told Alf we should stop but he and Bill had already made several more batches and they refused to be out of pocket.'

As Mrs Matravers finished, Mary found herself feeling a flash of sympathy for David's sister. She knew that she been given the sort of opportunities some people only dreamed of. Yet, Mary thought angrily, she had still been taught right from wrong and even when she had found herself cast out of the family that had given her so much privilege she hadn't turned to crime, because she knew quite simply that it was wrong.

Mary scratched her head thoughtfully as the draught from the staircase blew around her legs. She didn't know what to think any more. She felt weighed down by all the secrets she was carrying.

'I know I haven't given you a lot of reason to trust me,' Mrs Matravers said, interrupting Mary's train of thought. 'But I can promise you that you don't have to worry about this any more. So, Mary, I'm begging you: please don't call the police.'

For a second Mary was confused. She knew that she ought to call the police but what good would it really do? Mrs Matravers' intentions had been honourable, she had wanted to provide for her family, but had gone about it very badly. What had happened to Rose and the other man was an accident. Would Rose feel better knowing Mrs Matravers was locked away in prison, her baby growing up in a children's home? If the deputy manager had learned her lesson and really was going to turn her back on this life of crime to make ends meet then perhaps Mary could look the other way just this once. There was still one question on her mind, however.

'What about David?' Mary asked defiantly. 'Are you still going to tell him what you've done? Are you going to tell him what you know about me?'

At the mention of her brother's name, Mrs Matravers sighed in despair. 'I know you to be a loyal, dependable, capable girl, Mary. You saved my life, and I shall never forget that, but you are not good enough for my brother. I won't and will never change my mind about that, regardless of if you go to the police or not. David is my world, I would lay my life down for him – and I would quite happily go to prison for my crimes if it put a stop to any intention you and he have of marrying.'

Mary stared at Mrs Matravers and the look of determination on her face.

'While I am grateful you have come to my aid twice now,' Mrs Matravers said eventually, 'I simply cannot allow you to marry my brother. He will be back at Christmas. If you haven't written to him by then you can talk to him and tell him the truth in person.'

She was looking at her so earnestly and with so much fear in her eyes, Mary's heart went out to her for just a moment. She could of course understand why Mrs Matravers felt the way she did. To have been abandoned by her mother so cruelly while a drunk and abusive father ruled the roost at home must have been awful. No child should have had to go through that.

Mary cleared her throat nervously. 'Let me explain—'

Mrs Matravers put a hand out to silence her. 'I don't want to hear it.'

'But I want to say it,' Mary continued, determined not to be put off. 'I only want to say that I understand why you must feel very strongly over the reason why I left the army. I would probably detest unwed mothers too if I were in your shoes.'

'What do you know about it?' Mrs Matravers hissed, her face suddenly twisted with anger.

'I know what Dot and David have told me,' Mary said, lifting her chin in defiance. 'I know your mother left you when she fell pregnant with another child that wasn't your father's. I know she left you to bring up David alone and I know your father made your life hell.'

Mrs Matravers took a step towards Mary and jabbed her in the chest. 'You don't know everything, lady, and I've warned you several times now. Feel free to go to the police if you wish, but you will break it off with my brother, Mary, or I will tell the world your secrets.'

With that the deputy manager turned on her heel and stalked up the stairs, making it clear to Mary that the decision had been made.

Chapter Thirty-Nine

It was approaching lunchtime and Mary was standing in the atrium beside the modest, but beautifully decorated Christmas tree. Together with the rest of the staff, she had been ordered to attend an emergency briefing chaired by Mr Button.

As she watched him walk down the wooden staircase, his every tread causing the boards to creak, she felt a flash of fear. Did this last-minute meeting have something to do with Mrs Matravers? Had he found out about her involvement in the hooch ring, and in turn was Mrs Matravers about to blab Mary's secret to all and sundry after all?

'Thank you, everyone, for assembling so promptly,' he said. 'I can assure you it is nothing to worry about, but I wanted to let you know that we have a special customer this morning.'

'Is it Greta Garbo?' Judy, a young girl that worked in jewellery asked hopefully.

'Or Rita Hayworth?' asked another.

As the guesses came in thick and fast, Mr Button clapped his hands and demanded order.

'Not that any of those wonderful stars wouldn't be welcome in our store, but it's not them. It is in fact Princess Valentina who will be returning to us today.'

A collective gasp was let out amongst the staff at the idea. Although royalty often frequented the store, Princess Valentina was a favourite amongst the staff as she always made time to talk to as many of them as possible, bestowing a smile or kind word. It was a thrill for all of them that she would be visiting again so soon after the last time.

'We will of course be opening up the store to our other customers at this time,' Mr Button continued, 'but we would ask you to make sure that the princess receives your very best attention.'

An hour later and the entire store was primed and ready for Princess Valentina's visit. With every member of staff at their station, they all fidgeted nervously – if they weren't helping customers – until they saw the black car drive up to the door. Immediately, a liveried chauffeur hopped out of the front and then walked around to the back to open the door.

As Mary watched the princess step from the car on to the icy pavement below, she found she was holding her breath. Valentina was just as beautiful as she remembered, she thought as the princess took care to smile and greet the staff that welcomed her inside.

'Places, everyone, places,' Flo hissed as if she were giving a stage direction.

Quickly, Mary busied herself organising and straightening the rolls of fabric, while Dot pretended to go through some important departmental paperwork. Meanwhile, Flo focused on customers; she was enjoying the interaction and chatter about Liberty print fabric after spending so long in the office.

An hour later and the princess had completely disappeared, and so Flo, Dot and Mary returned to their normal work.

'Are we still going to see Rose tonight?' Dot asked.

Mary nodded. 'I think so. It feels like ages since I saw her. How is she, Flo?'

Flo smiled. 'In good spirits, surprisingly. Looking forward to going home.'

'Do you really think she'll be discharged before Christmas?' Mary quizzed.

Flo pushed a lock of hair behind her ear and nibbled the top of her pen thoughtfully. 'I hope so. She's a marvel for staying so strong, but I think being in hospital for so long must be eating away at her, even though her sight hasn't returned and with every passing day it's looking less and less likely. She wants me to tell her all about the party.'

Dot raised an eyebrow in surprise. 'Do you think that's a good idea? We don't want to upset her.'

'I think you're underestimating Rose's thirst for gossip,' Flo chuckled. 'Speaking of thirst, have you got over the lack of booze for the Christmas dinner now?'

'I suppose I'll have to,' Mary sighed. 'Everything else is in place for Saturday night. We've got some port that Mr Button sourced so there'll be a welcome drink for everyone; that will have to do, I suppose. There's a war on; this Christmas will be the hardest so far as there are so many shortages.'

'But it's being with loved ones that counts,' Dot said wisely. 'That's what Christmas is really all about.'

Flo nodded sagely. 'And that's what Neil will think as well when it comes to our wedding. Besides, it's not like we won't have anything. I spoke to Aunt Aggie at lunchtime when she came in with her dress for alteration. She said neighbours have been clamouring to help even though they've already donated coupons so Aggie can make us a cake. As long as people have something to toast us with, well, that's all that matters, isn't it?'

Dot nodded loyally. 'Of course it is, darlin'.'

'And Aggie's making us a beautiful cake. All our neighbours have been so generous,' Flo added.

'It never fails to amaze me how kind people can be,' Dot agreed. 'When me and George wed, all our neighbours donated bottles of beer and little sugared bags of almonds. We were so touched.'

'Besides,' Mary pointed out, 'nobody really drinks that much anyway at these things.'

'You wouldn't say that if you'd seen George's family at our wedding,' Dot giggled. 'They managed to put away more than their fair share and were so legless afterwards they fell asleep in the garden until morning.'

The girls roared with laughter – so loudly they didn't hear the sound of footsteps behind them.

'Good morning, ladies.'

At the sound of the princess's heavily accented tones the girls turned around in horror at the shock of being caught out gossiping.

Mary was the first to recover as she dropped her head and curtseyed before Princess Valentina. 'Your highness,' she said, as Dot and Flo followed suit.

Princess Valentina smiled and waved for them all to get up. 'Please, ladies. Let us not waste time with formality, I want to gossip about fabric, even if there is not much for me to buy!'

With that they started to pull rolls of print from the racks for the princess to admire, spreading them out on the counter so she could see them properly.

'It truly is amazing these prints on such functional fabrics,' the princess marvelled, stroking her fingers across the pretty teal cloth.

'We love the scarf that's been created to match this one,' Flo said longingly.

Mary and Dot nodded; the new print in the bright colour was a lively way of cheering up a dull winter's outfit that they had already made do and mended a dozen times over during their stitching evenings. Now they were all looking forward to getting their hands on one after Christmas.

'So, is this fabric available for me to buy in anything?' the princess asked cautiously.

Flo offered a shy grin. 'I am delighted to tell you that there has been a hat made to match this fabric and as they are not on ration you can buy as many as you like.'

The princess's face lit up. 'Well, that is wonderful news. Please point me in the direction of hats immediately.'

'We'll escort you,' Dot said earnestly. 'It's the least we can do.'

'Thank you.' The princess beamed at the girls. 'But before you do that, I was sure I heard talk of a party and a wedding?'

The girls looked at each other in panic. Of all the things they had been warned off, gossiping about their personal lives was right at the top of the long list Mr Button had issued.

Princess Valentina caught the expression on the girls' faces and gave them a reassuring smile. 'Please do not worry. I will not tell. But what are these party and wedding plans you are having trouble with?'

It was Flo who was brave enough to speak up. 'I'm getting married towards the end of the month, and it's our Christmas party a few days before that. We are a bit short on supplies, that's all, but we'll manage.'

'I think I see what you mean.' She paused for a moment, a flash of sadness passing across her pretty face. 'I remember my own wedding to Mishka many years ago.'

'I didn't realise you were married, your highness,' Mary ventured.

Princess Valentina offered the girls a whisper of a smile. 'He died seven years ago in a rail accident just outside

Moscow. I have never got over it, but the memory of our beautiful wedding, so perfect in every way, is something I continue to treasure. You girls are always so kind and patient with me when I visit this beautiful store that I would like to help you to celebrate and give you a wonderful day to remember.'

Flo's face flamed with colour. 'Oh no, Princess Valentina, we couldn't possibly ask you to do anything like that.'

'You didn't ask, I offered,' the princess said solemnly. 'I wish to do this for you. You girls are all so wonderful to me when I come in here, flinging your fabrics around, pointing out precious patterns, letting me take up all your time. And as for Liberty's itself, it's my second home. The place I always come to when I am here in London because it feels so comfortable. Everything and everywhere is just so beautiful, it is why I wanted to ensure you had a Christmas tree this year.'

'That was you?' Mary gasped.

Princess Valentina nodded shyly. 'It was. I love it here and have done ever since I was a girl. You ladies must love your jobs very much.'

'We do,' Mary smiled brightly. 'Working here is the best job in the world.'

'Well, then, there we are,' the princess said with finality in her tone. 'I shall send you cases of Russian champagne for your wedding and also for your Christmas party that I have heard the staff talk about all morning. It is the best in the world.'

'No, Princess Valentina ...' Flo trailed off as she caught the look of severity in the princess's dark eyes.

'It has been decided. Do not insult me by refusing my gift,' the princess said, before her face broke into a lovely smile.

'I don't know what to say,' Flo replied.

'Neither do I,' Mary offered. 'We can't thank you enough.'

'You can thank me by showing me the way to the hat department. It is my pleasure to do this for you, so please do not say another word.'

With that she swept past the girls, and Dot quickly trailed after her to show her the way.

Mary beamed. 'Well, that was unexpected.'

Flo shook her head. 'She's like a whirlwind. A very beautiful whirlwind.'

Mary chuckled, amazement dancing in her eyes. 'Alice will be sorry she missed her.'

'We miss Alice,' Flo smiled ruefully. 'But at least we'll have something exciting to tell her later.'

'I think I can honestly say that's more than enough excitement for one day,' Mary replied. 'I'll be happy enough just tidying fabrics.'

And in fact that's just what Mary did for much of the day. As she sorted, folded and tidied, she allowed herself to become lost in her thoughts and found her shoulders were a little less hunched thanks to the fact help had come from a very unlikely source. As she ran her hands across the fine prints and rare silks, she began to dream – for the first time since David had asked her – what her own wedding dress would be like. After all, Princess Valentina had just shown her that problems could suddenly and very easily be solved; perhaps her dilemma with David was going to be easier to fix than she thought.

By the time Dot brought her a sneaky cup of tea to drink behind the counter, Mary was so happy she suggested a night out to celebrate their good fortune.

'What about Alice?' Dot mused.

Flo frowned. 'I'm sure she won't object to a quick drink after work.'

'I just think she's been on her own with the baby all day,' Dot sighed. 'It's not easy for her. I think she's trying her best to care for Arthur but she's overwhelmed with worry over Luke.'

Mary nodded in agreement. Alice's face had been etched with concern over the past few days. She understood how helpless Alice must feel and now that Arthur was here, she would no doubt want the very best start in life for her son, and what better start than two parents who loved their child? With a jolt Mary realised how Mrs Matravers and Alice were facing similar problems: they both wanted their children to have the world. Sighing heavily, Mary leaned her head on the counter. She so badly wanted to help her friend, she just wasn't sure how, but perhaps the Christmas party would lift her spirits.

Chapter Forty

There were just five days to go until Christmas, and as Mary stood on the corner of Piccadilly looking up at the Lyons Corner House she felt a shiver of excitement. This was the night the whole store had been looking forward to for weeks, and now it was here she wanted to pause for a moment and drink it all in. Although it was pitch black and she could barely see a hand in front of her face, she could just about make out the happy faces of the staff all dressed up in their finery as they ventured inside.

The scene made for a happy one and, thanks to Princess Valentina, Mary was sure the event would now be a huge success. For a moment her thoughts turned to David. He filled her mind almost every minute of every day, and now she wondered where he was and what he was doing. Was he getting ready to enjoy a Christmas party of his own, or was he making his way back to London? Since Mrs Matravers had issued her ultimatum Mary knew she had to make a decision that would affect their future soon. But here in this moment, all she wanted was for him to return safely home for Christmas.

Shaking herself from her reverie, Mary continued to watch friends and colleagues walk through the doors; then she followed them into the foyer and gasped in delight at the sight before her.

A large chandelier, a little like the one hanging in Liberty's atrium, hung from the ceiling, while vases of fresh nasturtiums and lilies lined the tables. A huge red and green banner above the door, made by the sewing circle from scraps of scraps, read *Merry Christmas Staff of Liberty's* and underneath stood Penny, one of the girls from the ARP canteen, who was taking coats and ticking off names on a large sheet of paper. Elsewhere, Ernie from the counting house was dressed in his finest dinner suit and handing out glasses of sparkling Russian champagne, welcoming everyone inside.

As Mary reached for a glass, she slipped Ernie a grateful smile and took a sip. As the perfectly chilled liquid trickled down her throat, she had to admit that Russian champagne was gorgeous, and every bit as good as the more traditional French variety she had enjoyed in her old life.

It was a truly wonderful spectacle and Mary looked forward to sharing all the details with Rose the next morning when she and the rest of the Liberty girls went to visit. Together with Alice and Arthur, they had all gone to see her earlier and the doctors had confirmed that she was making excellent progress, and that they were happy to discharge her soon.

The girls were thrilled and for Mary it was also something of a relief. Since discovering the truth about Mrs Matravers Mary had felt a flash of guilt whenever she saw Rose in her hospital bed and had vowed to ensure her friend wanted for nothing when she came home to make up for the fact she hadn't done the right thing and called the police.

The sound of a piano broke Mary's train of thought, and she glanced across at Glenda from carpets playing her favourite 'Clair de Lune' by Debussy. Today Mary had been rushed off her feet ensuring everything was as it should be. She had liaised with caterers, organised the florist, checked the table plans and ensured that there was enough space for the speakers and of course the dancing later.

It had taken Mary much longer than expected to organise everything and she had fretted she would never have enough time to get ready. Thankfully Dot had taken pity on her and brought the green tea dress she had planned to wear to the party, so she could change and make up in the rather posh ladies' toilets.

Spotting Dot sitting next to Alice and Flo, she rushed towards her friends and kissed them all on each cheek. 'Isn't this marvellous?' she exclaimed.

'It's wonderful,' Flo smiled, her eyes shining with delight. 'I don't know how you pulled all this together. Look how happy everyone is.'

Mary flushed at the praise. 'I couldn't have done it without you girls.'

'Nonsense,' Alice exclaimed, 'you deserve all of the credit for this. And I'm grateful for whatever you and Dot said to Malcolm as well.'

Mary blushed. 'I don't know what you mean.'

'I mean out of the kindness of his heart he offered to look after Arthur for me tonight so I could come to the party,' Alice beamed. 'We only popped over to look in on him after visiting Rose, but the sight of Arthur put a big grin on his face, and before I knew it he had offered to take care of him this evening.'

'There's something about a baby that lifts your spirits,' Dot said. She looked beautiful in a crêpe-de-Chine emerald gown that brought out the colour of her hair.

'And there's something about that dress that makes you look wonderful,' Mary exclaimed. 'Wherever did you get it?'

'My mother made it for me years ago,' Dot admitted, smoothing an imaginary crease out of her skirt. 'George used to love me in it, but of course I've never had any-where to wear it until tonight.'

'Well, it suits you wonderfully,' Alice exclaimed, before her eyes took in the gorgeous tree in the foyer. 'How did you find time to decorate that tree, Mary?'

Mary looked sheepish. 'The lovely staff here did it for me. I was going to do it myself but I ran out of time.'

'Well, they've done a brilliant job,' Flo remarked.

Mary turned then to look at the tree properly and with a start realised that it had been decorated with the very same decorations she had seen in Liberty's window when she had visited the store as a child. In a heartbeat she was transported back to that wonderful Christmas almost twenty years ago when she had been so enchanted by the display. Mary's love of Liberty's had been cemented back then, and as she looked at the gorgeous glass shapes, an array of stars, icicles and snowflakes, Mary felt alive with magic just as she had as a girl.

Suddenly an image of David came unbidden into her mind as she pictured the two of them standing beside their own Christmas tree in the future, a brood of children between them. In that moment Mary knew that this was a dream she wanted to become a reality and, with one last look at the tree, found herself hoping for a little bit of Liberty's magic to help solve her problems with Mrs Matravers and David. She would fight tooth and nail to ensure she didn't lose him, of that she was sure.

'Is Mrs Matravers here yet?' she asked, sliding into her seat and noticing the empty chair beside her.

Dot shook her head. 'Not seen her yet.'

'She's there,' Alice said, jerking her head towards the door.

There, dressed in a sombre navy dress and heels, stood Mrs Matravers, the huge bump making her unmissable.

She made her way through the room towards the table and took her seat next to Mary's.

'Hello, girls,' she said crisply, 'how wonderful to see you all here.'

Mary said nothing, just gave her former boss a brief nod of the head. She was too tired to deal with Mrs Matravers tonight.

Dot sensed Mary's discomfort and shot Mrs Matravers a warning glance. 'Now, now, girls. We don't want no trouble. You girls are to keep your differences to yourselves.'

Mrs Matravers let out a tinkling laugh. 'What do you think I'm going to do?'

'I shouldn't like to guess.' Dot shifted uncomfortably in her seat. 'All I'm saying is folk here have made an effort and spent months looking forward to their Christmas party. It would be a shame if anything happened to ruin that just because you don't approve of Mary here marrying your brother.'

'Dot—' Mary began, only for her landlady to hold her hand up abruptly.

'Let me finish, Mary. Mabel, I've known you and your family a long time, we all know what you've been through, but David will find someone eventually and he won't always be clinging to your coat tails or be at your beck and call. You must see that? And frankly after the way Mary saved your life in Whitstable a couple of months ago, I'm amazed you think she's not good enough. She might have had a different upbringing to you and David, but he won't do any better – he'd be lucky to have her.'

By the time Dot finished her speech Mary felt overcome with gratitude for the way her landlady had stuck up for her. Yet turning to Mrs Matravers, it was clear Dot's impassioned pleas had cut no ice.

'Mary is quite simply not the girl you think she is—' Mrs Matravers began, only to be cut off by the sound of a large bell echoing throughout the hall.

As Mr Button got to his feet from his table at the top of the room everyone erupted into applause and Mary breathed a sigh of relief. It seemed the bell had literally saved her from whatever it was Mrs Matravers was going to say next.

'Thank you, everyone,' he said, waving his hands to signal for quiet. 'I won't take up too much of your time, but I would just like to say a few words. First of all I want to begin the evening by extending a heartfelt thank you to Mary Holmes-Fotherington, one of our newer members of staff, who has worked tirelessly to organise tonight's event.'

When Mary's name was mentioned, everyone broke into rapturous applause again and called for her to stand up. As she did so, she felt her face flame with embarrassment until she saw all the happy and delighted faces of her colleagues, who all appeared genuinely grateful for all she had done.

When the clapping died away, Mary sat back down and Mr Button continued. 'I also wish to thank you all for your hard work over the past twelve months and extend my heartfelt thanks and congratulations to the carpet department who collected the most aluminium for our Russian drive.'

At the announcement, everyone in the room began to clap heartily again before sensing Mr Button had more he wanted to say.

'This hasn't been the easiest of years and Liberty's has faced challenges we could never have anticipated,' he continued. 'Yet the spirit in which we have come together to honour the work and the lifelong ambition of our founder

Arthur Liberty has not gone unnoticed. The family along with the board have asked me to express their deepest thanks for all you have done for the store and to wish you a wonderful night here tonight. We must also thank Princess Valentina, our treasured customer, for her wonderful gift of champagne and this marvellous tree you see before you!'

As Mr Button paused and raised his glass to Princess Valentina the staff broke into another round of applause and echoed Mr Button's toast to the princess.

'We do not know what the future holds for this great store of ours,' he went on. 'We have been a lot luckier than many of our competitors, who have not fared well in the face of bombs thanks to Mr Hitler; yet fate appears to have smiled down on Liberty's, for reasons we do not understand but for which we are grateful. The coming year promises even more challenges, as it appears a greater number of our workforce will be called into full-time war work to do more in our fight against Hitler. Yet I know that the spirit of our wonderful store is strong and that Liberty isn't just its name, it is an idea that we carry in our minds and in our hearts. To Liberty's.'

At that everyone got to their feet and shouted, 'To Liberty's,' before giving Mr Button a deafening ovation as he sat down. With the main speech of the night now over, the sound of the piano could be heard again as the girls turned to one another and grinned.

The meal was declared a huge success by everyone, as big bowls of tomato soup, plates of fish with potatoes and mounds of vanilla bombe were devoured by everyone, alongside never-ending glasses of champagne.

By the time the petit fours and coffee had arrived, everyone was complaining of over-full tummies, something Mary was delighted to hear, making her feel more charitable towards Mrs Matravers.

Turning to look at her, she watched her former boss stroke her stomach with affection. 'It can't be long now,' Mary ventured.

Mrs Matravers smiled and shook her head. 'A little over two months,' she replied softly. 'Alf and I can't wait to meet our child. It's all we can talk about.'

'And how is Alf?' Mary asked nervously. 'Is he still out of work?'

Mrs Matravers face darkened at the question. 'No. He has his job back at the cinema.'

'Lovely,' Mary murmured, wondering what else to say, only for Alice to come to her rescue.

'I'm ever so sorry to interrupt, but I love this song,' Alice said pleadingly. 'I don't suppose you'll dance with me, will you, Mary?'

'Of course!' Mary exclaimed, before turning back to Mrs Matravers. 'Please do excuse me.'

Without waiting for a response the girls hurried to the makeshift dance floor that had been fashioned around the Christmas tree. A lively foxtrot was now being played by the Liberty band, made up of Penny on the harp, Albie from gifts on the violin and Ernie on the piano.

Mary took great pleasure in leading her friend around the dance floor. It was something she had frequently done in the ATS when they held impromptu dances in the mess hall, and Mary had forgotten how much she enjoyed whirling her pals around until they were breathless.

Now, as the band changed tempo to a waltz, Alice smiled with relief at the chance to get her breath back. 'How is there not even a hair out of place on your head?' she panted, feeling a bead of sweat trickle down her brow.

Mary giggled. 'Lots of practice!'

'Well, I'm out of practice,' Alice chuckled. 'The last time I danced was when Luke and I were courting years ago.'

'I'm sorry,' Mary said quietly. 'Have you had enough?'

Alice shook her head. 'No! It's nice to be here with everyone, and it's nice to talk about Luke. It keeps him alive in my head and my heart.'

'Have you spoken to Mr Button about coming back yet?' Mary asked, pausing in the middle of the dance floor to allow her friend a breather.

Alice smiled in gratitude and nodded. 'He's been wonderful. He says I can come back whenever I like now Alf's sister has agreed to help out with Arthur. I love the bones of Arthur, of course I do, but I miss Liberty's too.'

Yet another thing she and Mrs Matravers had in common, Mary thought ruefully as they carried on dancing for another minute or two, enjoying the beat of the music and the rhythm in their hearts. But soon Alice was begging for mercy once more.

'I'm sorry,' she panted. 'I'm out of shape.'

Mary chuckled in understanding. 'Another glass of champagne and you'll feel much better.'

Alice walked back towards their table and Mary followed until, in the dim light, she collided with a man who stepped into her path.

Startled, her hands flew to her mouth. She was unable to believe the sight in front of her.

'Oh my God!' she squealed. 'David, you're here!'

Chapter Forty-One

As she drank in the sight of her fiancé in his army uniform, Mary felt as though she was in some sort of dream; the power of the Liberty magic she had found herself wishing for was clearly a potent mix. In that moment, nothing seemed real, and for a split second Mary wondered if she had enjoyed too much champagne.

'Is it really you?' she asked, suddenly doubting herself.

David threw his head back and roared with laughter before reaching for Mary and pulling her into his arms. 'Of course it's me, you daft thing. I had to see you.'

As Mary buried her head in his chest, she savoured the scent of him. 'What are you doing here?'

'I've been given eight days' leave; there was a case at Guy's they needed my help with, so I was granted special dispensation,' he explained, pulling back to look at her. 'Oh Mary, I have missed you so much. I've been dreaming about this moment since I left you.'

With that he bent down and pressed his lips against hers. At his touch, Mary thought she might explode with the deliciousness of it all. How she had missed him. As she gave in to the sheer wonder of having the love of her life back in her arms, she felt a surge of happiness. This truly was the very best Christmas present she could ever have wished for.

'But why didn't you tell me?' she gasped, pulling away from him just to revel in the sight of her love.

'Because I wanted to see the look on your face. Besides, Mabel told me how hard you had been working organising everything and I felt you needed a surprise so I asked her not to say anything.'

Mary didn't reply. She didn't know what Mrs Matravers had told him about the hooch ring or her own secret. The last thing she wanted was to argue with David when having him here was such an unexpected treat.

Instead she leaned in towards him and kissed him passionately. Then she grinned. 'I think there are a few people here who would love to say hello to you,' she said, leading him back to the table.

It was Dot who saw David first, and she was on her feet to welcome him with a warm hug. 'You should have told us you were coming.'

'Yes, you daft sod!' Flo scolded as she playfully swatted him with her arm.

'I like surprises,' David laughed as he hugged the girls and perched on Mrs Matravers' empty seat while she was hobnobbing with other guests.

'Just as well' – Alice chuckled – 'as you've given us all the fright of our lives.'

Flo clapped her hands delightedly. 'Oh, this means you'll be able to come to the wedding! Please say you can come?'

'I would love too if I'm here. When is it?'

'Boxing Day,' Mary put in. 'We're all bridesmaids.'

'Well, you lot might be,' Dot sniffed. 'I'm matron of honour.'

'It sounds fantastic, I would love to attend,' David said. 'I can't believe you're marrying on Boxing Day! When does Neil get back?'

Flo made a face. 'Christmas Eve, so we don't have long.'

David chuckled. 'You really don't do things by halves, do you? Neil will be looking forward to getting back to the navy for a rest.'

As the girls laughed, David looked around the table in confusion. 'Where's Rose?'

The girls exchanged awkward glances.

'She's in hospital,' Mary said quietly. 'She's suffered methanol poisoning and lost her sight. The doctors say it may come back but so far—'

'You're not serious?' David gasped, interrupting Mary.

'Afraid so,' Flo muttered grimly. 'I tell you, if they catch whoever's responsible I hope they lock 'em up and throw away the key.'

'Quite,' David said, clearly staggered. 'I'll pop in and see Rose tomorrow if you think she'd like that. Try and find out a bit more about her sight, too, with the doctors at Guys. Often it can take a while to return.'

'So they told her,' Mary agreed. 'But she hasn't experienced any of her sight returning yet.'

'So where are you staying?' Dot asked. 'With your sister?'

David shook his head as Mary reached for a spare glass and filled it with champagne. As she handed it to him, he smiled gratefully at her then took a small sip.

'No, with an army chum, Michael. He's a doctor like me and been asked to work on the same case. He still has a small flat in the city which, unlike me, he hasn't rented out so rather than inconvenience my sister I'm staying with him.'

Mary's eyes shone with delight. 'So does this mean we get to meet your friend? Where is he?'

David scanned the room. 'He should be somewhere around here. Probably chatting up a pretty girl if I know Michael.'

Getting out of his seat for a better view, he paused and then waved as he obviously saw who he was looking for. 'There he is,' he exclaimed.

The girls turned expectantly towards a tall, figure threading his way through the crowds, and all got up to welcome him.

Only Mary remained rooted to her chair as she stared in horror at the man approaching their table with an easy smile. It couldn't be true, she thought, this simply couldn't be happening. How was it possible to go from such incredible joy to such incredible pain in just a few short moments? Because coming towards her was a man she had never expected to see again and in fact had prayed she never would. He was the man who had torn her world apart, destroyed her life and taken everything that had been precious. As he neared their table, Mary was terrified there was every chance that he was about to do so all over again.

Chapter Forty-Two

Trembling like a leaf, Mary watched as the scene unfolded before her like some sort of horror film. She felt trapped in a nightmare with no escape. Waves of panic engulfed her. She watched everyone shake the man's hand as if he were a long-lost friend, when in fact Mary knew him to be a monster.

Somehow, she got to her feet and felt David's hand on the small of her back as he propelled her forward to meet the man she despised with every fibre of her being.

'Michael, this is Mary,' David said.

She turned to the love of her life and caught the look of pride and delight in his eyes as he introduced her. She knew what she had to do, what was expected, and turned back to Michael.

'Mary,' Michael said cautiously. 'What a pleasure it is to see you again after all this time.'

Opening her mouth to speak, Mary found that no words would come out. She looked him up and down and saw how little he had changed. On the face of it he appeared to be nothing more than a good-looking officer. Tall, with dark hair peppered with flecks of grey, olive skin and black eyes.

As he extended his hand for her to shake, she did the same, for the sake of appearances. Only just as she felt Michael's flesh against hers she thought she was going to be sick and snatched her hand back.

'Excuse me,' she mumbled before fleeing from the room.

As she jostled her way through the throngs of people busy enjoying the night, she didn't turn back to see if anyone was following her. The only thing that mattered to Mary was getting outside.

Reaching the foyer, she didn't even bother to find her coat, she just pushed through the doors and went out into the street. Taking in great lungfuls of air, Mary tried to gather herself together.

She looked down at her hands and was horrified to see she was still shaking.

'You look like you've seen a ghost.'

Mary whirled around at the unexpected voice behind her, only to come face to face with Mrs Matravers. Her heart sank; even in the gloom she could make out her features and see the look of pleasure at Mary's obvious discomfort.

'What do you want?' Mary asked in a tired voice.

'I told David I'd come out here to check on you,' she replied. 'I said it would take a woman's touch.'

Mary laughed bitterly. 'Is that right?'

'Yes, because when I saw your face, I realised what effect that man inside had had on you. In my experience, girls usually only become upset like that when they see a former lover who broke their heart, and I'm guessing that perhaps my brother's new friend has done just that.'

Mary looked away as Mrs Matravers gasped in comprehension.

'You went to bed with him, didn't you? Let me guess, it's him that's the father of your child?'

'Don't be ridiculous,' spluttered Mary.

'I'm right, aren't I?' Mrs Matravers continued. 'You thought you would never see him again. Yet here he is, larger than life, about to tear your world upside down, all without any help from me.' She laughed loudly. 'I couldn't have planned it better. Now I no longer have to look like the bitter and twisted sister telling her brother to stay away from the fallen shop girl. His new army friend's going to do it for me.'

'You have no right to judge me,' Mary seethed, glaring at Mrs Matravers. 'I have made mistakes but you know nothing about me or my life. Yes, Michael was the father of my child, but you don't know how much pain he has caused me, or how he destroyed my life.'

Just then a face appeared out of the shadows. 'And now here you are destroying mine.'

At the sound of David's voice, Mary's heart sank. The moment she'd seen Michael and realised he was her fiancé's friend, she'd known that her time was up, and that this beautiful, magical fairy-tale she had hoped to find a way to enjoy was over.

'David, let me explain,' she began, only for him to shake his head.

Mary took a step towards him. 'Please.'

'No.' He shrank back and stood next to his sister. 'I have been a fool. I should have known that what we had was too good to be true. You're not the person I thought you were, Mary.'

Mary felt tears pool at her eyes. 'David, you have to listen to me. Please let me talk to you.'

'Did I hear correctly? Did Michael get you pregnant?' David asked quietly.

'Yes,' Mary whispered.

'Didn't you think I had a right to know that? Particularly when I asked you to marry me?' he blasted.

Mary hung her head in shame; she wanted nothing more than to turn the clock back. 'There was never the right moment, and it was hard to put into words. I never thought I would see Michael again. I did plan to tell you, of course I did; I never wanted you to find out this way.'

There was a pause before David sighed in sadness. 'This is too much for me, Mary. How can I trust you when you've lied to me like this? You and I are over. I can't see you again.'

Chapter Forty-Three

It was the day after the Liberty Christmas party and every part of Mary's body ached and throbbed. It was as if she had been put through an emotional mangle.

She was terrified that now her secret was revealed the life she had carved out for herself so successfully was gone. Mary had barely slept since she had fled from the party traumatised at the sight of Michael, and had locked herself in her room all morning, ignoring Alice and Dot's pleas to come out and talk.

Instead she had barricaded herself behind the door, unable to imagine what her friend and landlady must be thinking about her. Tears had rolled down her face as she thought of how disappointed they must be. No matter how much they begged she simply couldn't face the idea of having to listen to them tell her she was a disgrace. That was something Mary knew already. What a fool she had been to think she could start again without anyone finding out her terrible secret.

The question was what to do now? She already knew her future at Liberty's was over. Mr Button was no Mrs Matravers, but he would no doubt agree that her reputation would damage the store and she wasn't fit to continue.

Mary had tried so hard to make a new life for herself, to forget the past. She should have known it would all come crashing down around her ears. As for David, she was racked with guilt over the pain she had no doubt caused him. She had felt so elated to see him at the party.

That fleeting sense of joy had been utterly perfect and she tried to recall it now, finding it hard to believe she had experienced something so wonderful for just a few moments.

The contempt in David's eyes ripped her soul in two. She had never meant to cause him so much pain, and hated herself for having hurt yet another person she loved.

Then there was Michael. She had hoped that she would never ever have to see his detestable face again. The way he had treated her, the way he had made her feel, she wouldn't wish on her worst enemy. She felt a wave of nausea as she imagined him defending his actions to David, placing the blame firmly at her door rather than his own. Resting her head in her hands, she knew there was no sense raking over the past.

An image of her old governess, Mrs Adams, floated into her mind. She had been a tough old bird, Mary remembered with a smile. She had been unable to bear self-pity of any kind and Mary knew that as sure as the sun rose each morning Mrs Adams would tell her to jolly well pull herself together and get on with it.

Mrs Adams would be right, Mary thought, taking a deep breath to settle herself. The answer was simple: she knew she would no longer be welcome here, and it was time to move on. The best thing to do would be to gather her belongings and leave, thanking Dot and Alice for all they had done and ensuring she paid Dot for the room until the end of the week. Her landlady wouldn't be out of pocket because of her poor judgement, of that Mary would make sure.

As if fate was smiling down on her, Mary suddenly heard the sound of the front door slam. Peering out of the blackout curtain, she could make out the figures of Dot and Alice, together with Arthur in his pram.

Immediately she galvanised herself and pulled her suitcase from under the bed. Flinging it open she threw in her things, grateful that she had had the foresight not to bring much with her. In went her shoes, her clothes and the dress she often were when working at Liberty's. She had been so proud of herself the day she joined Liberty's. It had been a sign, Mary had thought, that she had turned a corner, as for the first time since losing her baby she had not woken in tears as she relived the horror of it all. Instead she had felt happy and alive as the alarm went off, eager to start the day and revel in the adventures working at Liberty's would no doubt bring.

But not now. Now it was time to go. Mary had no idea where she was going or even where she would stay that night, and with Christmas just days away she had a feeling she would struggle to find someone who would accept lodgers into their home. No matter, Mary thought resolutely, she would sleep on a park bench if she had to, for now she just knew she had to leave.

Opening the front door, she went outside, slammed it shut, then reached into her bag for the key she always carried with her, which she slipped through the letter-box. Spinning around, she bumped straight into Dot, who even in the darkness Mary could tell wore a face of thunder.

'Dot, I was ... er ... going to pop back and talk to you in a few days,' she lied.

'Like hell you were,' Dot growled.

'And why have you got your suitcase with you?' Alice spoke up now and Mary could see she wasn't alone as she caught sight of a grim-faced Flo.

Her heart sank; she had hoped to avoid another scene but with her friends here it looked as if that wasn't going to be possible.

'Shall we go back inside?' Dot suggested, her tone gentler now. 'We're all freezing, even if you're not. You don't have to talk to us, darlin', but I think it might help.'

Realising she was outnumbered Mary followed Dot back inside the house, and went into the front room. As Alice flipped on the lights, Mary shivered in her coat. Despite the warmth in the house she still felt cold and numb inside.

Dot went into the kitchen to make tea leaving Flo and Alice to sit on the sofa beside her.

Mary watched Alice rock Arthur in her arms. As his eyes fluttered open, the look of love written across her friend's face was evident. Alice might be worrying about the possibility of raising her son alone, but one thing was for sure, she had enough love for both her and Luke.

'Lovely party last night,' Flo began nervously as Dot reappeared with a tray of tea.

'Flo!' Dot hissed. 'Not now.'

'Sorry.' Flo went crimson. 'I told you I'd put my foot in it.'

Mary shook her head and smiled at her friend's attempts at small talk. 'You've nothing to be sorry about. It's me that should be sorry.'

'That's not what I hear,' Dot said, pouring the tea into cups. 'From the gossip doing the rounds last night I should say you've been through more than enough and sorry is the last thing you should be.'

Mary paled at the kindness of Dot's words. That was the last thing she had expected to hear. 'What happened after I left?' she asked gingerly.

'Well, David ran off into the night and Mrs Matravers came upstairs telling everyone that the father of your long-lost child had suddenly appeared out of the blue,' Flo explained.

Mary glanced down at her hands. 'And then what?'

'And then nobody believed what Mrs Matravers was saying because she'd had so much champagne, Michael ran off after David and everyone else went back to the dancing.'

'You're joking?' Mary gasped.

Flo shook her head. 'It's all true. Mabel told anyone that would listen how you'd lost a child out of wedlock but nobody was interested in what she had to say.'

'Spiteful old cow,' Dot said angrily, before catching the looks of surprise on everyone else's faces. 'Sorry, girls. I've always had a soft spot for Mabel, but last night a spiteful cow is just what she was.'

'So nobody believed her?' Mary continued, unable to believe this stroke of good fortune.

Flo shook her head. 'Nobody except us,' she said in a small voice. 'We've been worried about you.'

'Desperately worried,' Alice said insistently. 'We don't know if Mrs Matravers is telling tales, but we know something happened and we want to help you.'

'The look on your face when you saw Michael was horrible. You looked terrified, Mary,' Flo added.

'We're your friends, darlin',' Dot put in. 'You can tell us anything.'

Mary leaned back against the sofa and closed her eyes. More than anything she wanted to confide in someone and tell them the truth. The burden of all she had been carrying was weighing more heavily on her now than ever before. She took a deep breath. 'Mrs Matravers was right. She seemed envious of my upbringing, the fact I came from a privileged background. And later, when she got in touch with the army and learned I had been dismissed because I fell pregnant, she detested me even more.'

'But she changed her mind when you saved her life,' Dot said matter-of-factly, filling in the blanks.

Mary nodded. 'Then, when she found out I was going to marry David she said she would tell him everything even though she had only half the story.'

'Little madam,' Flo rasped. 'Who does she think she is?'

'She's forgotten where she came from,' Dot remarked. 'Now, are you up to telling us the rest of it, because, my God, darlin', you look like you need to tell someone.'

Smiling with gratitude at the girls as they all nodded in agreement, Mary carried on. 'When I joined the ATS my parents weren't pleased. Daddy wanted me to find a nice husband and Mummy insisted work in the army wasn't appropriate for me or my sister Clarissa. She had married Henry by then and moved to Ceylon to run a tea plantation north of Kandy. But I was determined and I eventually ended up in Camberley training some of the other girls how to drive and that was where I met Michael.'

Mary paused for breath at this point, as though the very action of saying his name was too painful. Recognising her obvious discomfort at the next part of the story, Flo reached over and squeezed her hand. 'It's all right, Mary. Whatever it is you want to tell us, we aren't here to judge you, we just want to help you.'

Nodding, Mary smiled gratefully at her friend and carried on. 'I never liked Michael from the outset. He had been posted to our battery and worked as a medical officer for the barracks. Because we had such a big driving base, we trained everyone to drive everything, ambulances included, and Michael helped with the ladies' first-aid training. He was brash, arrogant and always tried to belittle the girls. I had come across a sergeant like that before when I was training and couldn't stand to see these girls go through something similar, so I wouldn't tolerate it. One day after he had tormented one young volunteer so badly she broke down in tears I gave him a dressing-down in front of everyone and told him he was a sorry excuse for a man.'

'Good for you, Mary,' Dot said approvingly. 'Sounds as though he deserved it. Not many would have had the guts to stand up to a superior like that.'

Mary shot Dot a watery smile. 'No, and I very much wish I hadn't. Afterwards he told me I needed taking down a peg or two. He told me to be on the lookout because he would make me pay.'

At that Mary fell silent as she nervously chewed her lip. She didn't want to say what happened next, but casting a cautious glance at the concerned and supportive faces of her friends, something inside her told her she had to carry on.

'I didn't think much of it,' she said haltingly. 'Men like Michael didn't scare me very much. But one night at a mess dance, Michael had invited lots of his friends over from a battery nearby to mix with the girls. We thought it was a good idea and it gave the girls a night off. About halfway through the dance, I went out into the kitchen to refill the tea urn, when I suddenly heard a noise. I spun around, and there was Michael, standing behind me with an evil glint in his eye. Something told me he was there to punish me for making him look foolish so publicly and I was right. Before I knew what was happening he was on top of me, his fingers pawing at my flesh.'

Tears brimmed in Mary's eyes as she remembered that fateful party. She had thought that after so long the pain of it all had lessened, yet reliving it now, in front of her friends, brought it all back.

Dot leaned over and put an arm around Mary. 'Oh, sweetheart,' she whispered. 'He forced himself on you, didn't he?'

312

At that Mary nodded, the memory now all too real as she recalled the way she had tried to fight him off, but he had been too strong for her.

'I had never been with a man before, but he pushed me back against the kitchen worktop and then held me down as he whispered in my ear that he was going to show me just how much of a sorry excuse for a man he really was. I remember feeling terrified as I smelt the beer on his breath, and felt the rough stubble of his chin against my cheek. I wanted to be sick, but I could scarcely breathe. As he tore at my skirt, I felt his weight on top of me and I remember feeling as though I was floating out of myself, as though the only way to survive what was happening was to pretend I wasn't there. So I stopped struggling – I knew that would only make what he was doing last longer – instead I thought about riding in a point-to-point back in Cheshire or dance nights in the mess when I taught my friend Peggy how to foxtrot, anything to keep out the pain of what was actually happening.'

By now Mary was trembling, the image of it as fresh in her mind as if it had happened yesterday.

Flo gasped in shock as she took in the gravity of what her friend had just told her. 'Go on,' she coaxed gently.

'All the way through he told me it was my own fault, that I was a silly little girl and I had brought it on myself.'

Dot shook her head in disbelief. 'Surely someone heard something, could have stopped him?'

'Nobody heard a thing,' Mary whispered, 'or if they did they chose to say nothing. When it was over, he laughed and said if I told anyone then he would make sure my career in the army was over. So I said nothing. It was as though he had broken my spirit. All I wanted to do was forget about it.'

'But then you found out you were expecting,' Flo put in.

'Yes, a few weeks later I discovered I was pregnant. Michael was posted elsewhere after the dance. I never knew where.'

'Do you think someone found out after all?' Alice asked.

'I don't think so,' Mary replied. 'It's fairly common for people to move around quickly, so I didn't think much of it. It was a relief, as I didn't know how I would have managed seeing him day after day.'

'So did you tell him you were expecting?' Flo asked.

Mary nodded. 'I wrote to him through the army postal service. I told him that the baby could only have been his. I had never been with anyone else. Only somehow the letter must have been intercepted as a few weeks later, just when I was beginning to show, my commanding officer called me into the office. Said he knew I was pregnant and I had to be discharged.'

'Surely not,' Flo gasped. 'The cruelty of it!'

'What did you do then?' Dot asked gently.

'When I left the army, I went to my parents in Cheshire. I had a feeling that once they found out they wouldn't be happy, so I didn't even bother to unpack my suitcase. But they were so angry. They told me I had brought shame upon my family and that I was dead to them. I was stunned. I knew they would be upset and would perhaps throw me out, but I didn't think they would cut me off entirely. I went to my sister's in Ceylon, knowing Mummy and Daddy rarely speak to Clarissa and Henry because of the distance. I hoped that we could renew our bond as sisters and then when it was time for me to tell her she would be supportive. I didn't want her to know straightaway what had happened because I hoped a fresh start abroad would be the answer. Then there was the fact Ceylon wasn't in the war then so it felt like a safe place to bring a baby into the world.'

314

'However did you get there?' Alice asked.

Mary smiled. 'Because I had been in the ATS I had become chummy with some pilots and they arranged transport on various ships and planes to get me to Kandy.'

'Did Michael ever reply to you?' Flo asked.

Mary nodded. 'Yes when I was in Ceylon. I had been disguising my pregnancy pretty well with lots of layers. Then one morning I got a letter from Michael, obviously forwarded on through the army, and his words shocked me. He said he had heard I was pregnant and that there was no proof the baby was his, that he knew about girls like me, that no doubt I had been with every man on shore leave.'

'That filthy toe rag,' Dot growled. 'When I get my hands on him ...' Her voice trailed off as she saw the look of despair in Mary's eyes.

'When I got that letter I was working with Henry in the office. He'd popped out to make us tea. I ripped the letter open and read it. His words brought back the assault and I ... I fell to the floor. The pain – it was searing through me. Clarissa found me collapsed an hour later, the letter by my side. When she read it and realised I was pregnant she started screaming at me, telling me I had let the family down, brought our good name into disrepute, just like Mummy and Daddy did.'

'But surely you told her about Michael?' Alice gasped. 'About how he forced himself on you.'

Mary wept then, unable to hold back the pain flooding through her any longer. 'I tried but I was in so much pain, I couldn't get the words out. I told her what I could and she said it made no difference. Said that I must have done something to lead Michael on.'

'The heartless little madam,' Flo fired, her face contorted with fury. 'How could she say that to you, her own sister?'

'I remember she turned to leave, but as she did she saw blood all over my legs. She must have sent for the doctor but by then I was drifting in and out of consciousness. When I was awake I begged the doctor to save my baby, but it was too late, she was stillborn.'

'Oh, my poor love,' Dot gasped, pulling Mary in towards her as if she were no more than a baby herself.

'As I lay in hospital, Clarissa came to see me. I was pleased to see her at first as I thought it meant she had forgiven me for what happened, but it was to tell me that I was dead to her as well.'

'But you were attacked!' Alice gasped. 'Surely they could see that.'

'The Holmes-Fotherington name cannot be sullied by tawdry scandal,' Mary smiled weakly. 'Clarissa told me to leave Ceylon when I was better and never see them again. They arranged for a return journey and I came to London. Then I saw your ad in the paper, Dot, and you and Alice, well, between the two of you, you offered me salvation when my heart was breaking. It's thanks to you two that I've managed to rebuild myself. I understand that all this might be too much for you now, but you've helped me more than you will ever know and for that I will always be grateful.'

'Sweetheart,' Alice cried, 'you surely don't think we're going to abandon you?'

Mary shrugged. So far everyone else in her life that she had trusted had let her down. 'I assumed you would think I was bringing ill repute into the house. David told me he didn't want to know.'

'Oh Mary,' Dot moaned, releasing the girl and getting to her feet to pour more tea. 'Let's get one thing straight. You have done nothing wrong, you've been brave and you've had to cope with more than your fair share. David will come around, I'm sure of it.'

Mary shook her head sadly. 'The way he looked at me last night, I don't think so.'

'But he didn't know the truth,' Alice protested. 'You have to tell him.'

Mary swallowed back her tears. 'I just don't think I can tell him yet. It's been hard enough reliving it all to tell you. Not only that, if Mrs Matravers has got to him by now then he won't want to listen to my side at all.'

'If you really think that, Mary, then perhaps it doesn't matter whether David knows the truth or not,' Flo said quietly. 'Perhaps David isn't the one for you after all.'

Mary blanched at the truth of Flo's statement. Put like that, her friend had a point.

Dot clasped Mary's hand affectionately. 'Whatever else happens you are always welcome here. This is your home.'

'And we are your family,' Alice smiled, planting a tender kiss on Mary's head. 'So let's unpack that bag, forget about David, and get you settled back where you belong.'

Chapter Forty-Four

The next day Mary was up with the lark to get ready for work. She had been expecting to have to look for a new job again, but on Sunday night Dot had announced that she would go round and see Mr Button to explain what had happened.

Mary had tried to insist that she would speak to Mr Button herself. However, Dot said Mary had been through more than enough and this would be one less thing for her to worry about.

When she returned, Dot's face was a picture. She said she had seen Mr Button and he had assured her that not only would Mary be welcome to return to work on Monday morning as usual, but that he would have a word with David on her behalf.

Making her way down Argyll Street, passing the Palladium adorned with huge posters of its Christmas show, Mary still couldn't believe she was allowed to remain a Liberty girl. Now, as she reached the staff entrance, Mary suddenly felt nervous. What if the staff gossiped or called her names? She had been touched at her friends' unexpected kindness and generosity of spirit, but how would the rest of Liberty's behave towards her?

Walking up the stairs two at a time towards the staff-room, Mary decided to pop in on Mr Button to say thank you. Passing one of the assistants from the ornamental department in the stairwell, Mary almost felt nerves get the better of her as she wondered if the girl would say anything.

'Morning, Mary,' she said with a genuine smile. 'Lovely party. You must feel so proud; everyone had such a wonderful time.'

'Yes,' Mary smiled back. 'I'm so pleased you all enjoyed it.'

'See you later,' the girl trilled as she ran down towards the shop floor.

As Mary lifted a hand to wave goodbye she felt her nerves begin to subside. Reaching Mr Button's office she knocked gingerly on the solid oak door.

'Come in,' he called.

Pushing open the door, she smiled hesitantly at him. 'Mr Button sir, if you have a moment I just wanted to say thank you.'

Mr Button raised an eyebrow. 'I rather think it's I that should be thanking you for the marvellous job you did with the party on Saturday night.'

'You already did that on Saturday, sir,' she said, hovering in front of his desk. 'I wanted to say thank you for, well … I know Dot spoke to you.'

Mr Button took off his spectacles and threw them on top of the paperwork on his desk. 'You have nothing to apologise or thank me for. I heard what you had been through. You more than deserve your job here; you're one of the finest staff members we have. I am not concerned about the past and I don't think you should be either.'

Mary felt her eyes well with tears. She had never expected such kindness, never thought she deserved it, and yet within this famous store she had not only found love and respect, but a family as well. It was far more than she could have hoped for and she stared at Mr Button, lost for words.

'Now how about you get back down to the shop floor. Today is one of our busiest shopping days, so let's show our customers that Christmas starts here at Liberty's,' he said kindly.

Mary nodded, and left the office feeling happier than ever. Back on the shop floor, Mr Button was right. Despite Mary, Dot and Flo's best efforts there was still so much to do. She could feel her friends' eyes on her all day, but was grateful that they said nothing. Mary was feeling too shell-shocked to talk much about the events of the last few days and so she busied herself with customers throughout the morning, taking care to wish everyone a very merry and blessed Christmas.

As she went to walk back up the stairs to take her lunch hour, she saw a tall older woman wearing a bottle-green hat and coat stalk across the floor and walk up to Flo who was serving another customer at the counter.

'Mary Holmes-Fotherington,' the woman barked. 'She works here.'

At the sound of her name, Mary jumped in shock as she spun around. 'Mother!'

The woman turned to face Mary and grimaced. 'So it's true. You do work here.'

Mary walked towards the counter and smiled reassuringly at Alice, Flo and Dot, who were watching the woman with distrust in their eyes.

'What are you doing here?' she asked eagerly. Her mother hadn't changed since the last time she had seen her, she thought. Perhaps a few more lines around the eyes, but then with all the worry over her father, Mary wasn't surprised.

'Didn't you get my letter?' Mrs Holmes-Fotherington barked again. 'I told you I was coming and wanted to see you.'

Mary shook her head before remembering the letter that had come for her a little while ago at the store. She had forgotten all about it and, quickly, she reached for the letter now covered with dust.

Before Mary could rip it open, Mrs Holmes-Fotherington put a hand out to snatch the letter back. 'It merely says I would visit you in the store as I would be in London today. Your father is seeing a specialist.'

At the mention of her father Mary's eyes lit up with hope. 'How is Daddy?'

'Not well.' Mrs Holmes-Fotherington narrowed her eyes. 'And that's what I wanted to see you about. Your father isn't well enough to cope with any more shocks or embarrassments. That's why he cannot give you his blessing for your hand in marriage.'

'What are you talking about?' Mary asked in surprise.

'Your fiancé, David whatever his name is, wrote to your father a little while ago and asked for his permission for your hand. Your father was too ill to respond and frankly hearing your name again upset him greatly and only made him worse. It's not for us to decide what your future holds, Mary. If you want to marry this man marry him, if you don't then don't. We don't wish to know about it.'

Shocked at the cruelty of her mother's words, Mary jumped back as if she had been stung but her mother hadn't finished.

'We told you before and I'm telling you now that you are very much dead to us, Mary. You have only yourself to blame. You have brought shame upon this family and I will not have your father upset by any further correspondence either from or about you. You shouldn't have written to us, Mary, we do not wish to hear from you. It was bad enough Penny Phillips-Thorpe saw you in here. I will not embarrass you or our family by going into the details that we no longer talk to you, and in turn I expect you not to do so either should any of our family friends shop here. I should think that after all the damage you have caused the family this is the very least you can do.'

Mary's heart was pounding as she took in her mother's words, each one feeling like a more vicious blow than the last. Suddenly she became aware of Dot standing by her side.

'How dare you,' she hissed. 'Your Mary is one of the finest young women I have ever had the pleasure of knowing and more fool you if you want to cut her out of your life.'

'Now just a minute—' Mrs Holmes-Fotherington began sternly, only for Dot to hold up a hand and cut Mary's mother off mid-flow.

'I haven't finished with you, young lady!' she spat. 'You've got a flaming nerve coming in here telling your daughter she's an embarrassment that has brought shame on the family name. Is that all you're bothered about? Your daughter needed your help and what did you do? You turned your back when she was in trouble. Not a very motherly thing to do in my book, darlin'.'

'I rather think you don't know the facts,' Mrs Holmes-Fotherington said coldly. 'If you knew how Mary had behaved I'm rather sure you wouldn't be standing here defending her actions. How she is allowed to work at such a respected establishment is beyond me.'

'Liberty's is lucky to have her,' Dot snarled. 'Unlike you. You're a disgrace to motherhood, coming in here blaming her for your husband's cancer. If anything has given him cancer it's living with you, you poisonous old bat! And yes, before you start we all know what Mary's been through; unlike you though we see a girl in trouble and we help.'

'That's right,' Flo said quietly as she came to Dot's side, providing a protective shield around Mary. 'You may not want Mary in your family any longer, but she's very much a part of the Liberty family and we couldn't be more proud to have her here.'

Mrs Holmes-Fotherington stood there in shock. 'Well I never! Mary, are you going to allow these – these women to address me like that?'

Mary lifted her chin in defiance as she met her mother's gaze. 'Yes, Mrs Holmes-Fotherington, I am. Because you see, unlike you, they are my family.'

Chapter Forty-Five

Once the shop was closed it was Mary that offered to check the window display in readiness for the New Year sale. Although the displays were always blacked out once darkness fell, the Liberty family and the board felt it was important that the windows drew people in when they could be seen and Mary wanted to make sure that the fabric department showcased the very best prints they could offer to customers.

Checking her watch she saw it was almost seven. There would still be enough time for her to get to the hospital and join the girls for the final stitching circle before Christmas. They had a lot to get through before Flo's wedding, not to mention gossip to discuss, and Mary didn't want to miss a minute more than she had to.

Quickly she ran up the stairs to get her things, then raced back down and out into Kingly Street. Rounding the corner, she hurried past the pub where she had seen Mrs Matravers and Alf, and tried to ignore the fury of the memory building inside of her.

Just about to turn right and up towards the Tube, she saw something that made her blood run cold. Ignoring the blackout restrictions, the light from the back of the pub spilled out on to the courtyard and there, right in the centre, were Mrs Matravers, Alf and the man they referred to as Bill once more. They were standing next to what looked like twenty crates of bottled beer, and chuckling as the landlord handed Alf a wedge of pound notes.

Mary flattened herself against the brick wall by the entrance to the courtyard and listened hard to what they were saying.

'So when can you get me some more?' she heard the landlord ask.

Mrs Matravers let out a peal of laughter. 'What happened to your last order being the final one, eh?'

There was a pause before Mary heard the landlord speak again. 'You know how it is, Mabel, business is business and your last lot flew off the shelf. As long as you don't make a mix strong enough to blind anyone else then I don't see the harm.'

'I keep saying that was a bleedin' one-off,' Alf snarled.

'Yeah, and if you want more it'll cost you,' the man she thought was Bill added.

'What do you mean?' the landlord asked.

'I think Bill means that the price has doubled,' Mrs Matravers said haughtily. 'We have to consider supplies and so on. It's so much harder to get stock these days.'

'But you have your ways, I'll bet, Mabel,' the landlord sneered. 'All right. Got me over a barrel, ain't you? But we've got a deal.'

Mrs Matravers chuckled. 'You won't regret it. Come on, fellas, we've got booze to make.'

As the trio moved inside, shock and fury coursed through Mary like never before. Mrs Matravers had promised her that she wouldn't make any more hooch, that she had learned her lesson and that she wouldn't put the lives of anyone else in jeopardy. Now here she was not only making a deal with the landlord who had sold Rose alcohol toxic enough to blind her, but she was also doubling her money.

Moving through the streets of Soho, Mary knew what she had to do. It was something she should have done a long time ago and she hated herself for not doing it earlier.

Reaching Liberty's, she ran towards the staff entrance and once inside ran back up the stairs. Arriving at Mr Button's office, she knocked sharply, even though she knew he wasn't in, then went inside. Stalking over to his desk she soon found what she was looking for under the mound of paperwork and lifted the telephone receiver.

'Police please,' she said, 'it's urgent.'

By the time she had spoken to the police and told them the whole story about Mabel, Bill and Alf, along with the hooch ring, Mary was worn out.

Leaving work for the second time that night she had more of a spring in her step, as she felt that finally she had done the right thing. The police had been very helpful, promising to act on the information immediately.

By the time she reached the hospital, she saw the rest of the Liberty girls had gathered at Rose's bedside, armed with an array of threads, cottons and lace.

Perching at the bottom of the bed, Mary looked around her at the women who had fast become her family. There had been so much heartache in her life, but to think she had now found these wonderful women who genuinely loved her and looked out for her was more than she could ever have hoped for.

Clearing her throat, she got to her feet. 'I just wanted to say something,' she began.

Flo smiled tenderly. 'We've told Rose about what's happened with David.'

'And I want you to know how sorry I am for you, love,' Rose said gently. 'I hope you're not going anywhere, because you belong here now.'

Mary shook her head. 'Oh Rose, thank you. But you might change your mind once you hear what I've got to say.'

As a flicker of confusion passed across the girls' faces, Mary took a deep breath before she spoke again. 'There's no easy way to say this, so I'll just come right out with it,' she said, her voice shaking with emotion. 'But the fact is, Rose, it was Mrs Matravers and Alf who sent you blind. They were the ones making the hooch.'

Confusion passed across Rose's face. 'Don't be daft, Mary, you must have the wrong end of the stick.'

Mary shook her head. 'No, there's been no mistake. In fact I've known for a while now. That's why she wasn't able to supply booze for the party or your wedding, Flo, because I caught her and Alf selling hooch to the pub where Rose drank a few weeks ago. She swore me to secrecy when she found out I knew, said she would make sure I lost my job and that everyone would know about the baby. I was so afraid I agreed, and I'm sorry, Rose, I should never have been so selfish.'

'You weren't selfish, love,' Rose gasped. 'She put you in an impossible situation.'

'I can't believe Mrs Matravers would do such a thing,' Flo exclaimed.

Dot grunted. 'I can. She's turning out more like her good-for-nothing husband day after day.'

'And to think she blackmailed you like that.' Flo shook her head in disgust.

Alice nodded furiously. 'I'm stunned she did this. I feel like making her drink her own bloody hooch, see how much she values her sight.'

'An eye for an eye,' Dot said sagely.

'But Mrs Matravers ...' Rose sighed sadly. 'I know things have been hard for her what with Alf losing his job, but selling hooch ...'

As Rose trailed off, Mary reached over to grip her hand. 'The thing is, Rose, I called the police tonight, that's what I wanted to say.'

'You rang the old bill?' Dot gasped.

Mary nodded firmly. 'It was about time. She promised me faithfully when I caught her, Alf and the other man that they would stop. Tonight I discovered them selling more booze.'

'I hope they lock her up and throw away the key,' Alice fumed.

'No more than she deserves,' Dot said loyally.

Mary looked down at the floor, her cheeks flushed with shame. 'I'm just sorry I didn't do it sooner. I was too worried about myself to do the right thing. Can you ever forgive me?'

Rose gripped Mary's hand urgently. 'There's nothing to forgive, love.'

Chapter Forty-Six

Christmas Eve dawned bright and clear, and as Mary made her morning pilgrimage to work, excitement bubbled up inside her as if she were a child. Wishing everyone she passed a merry Christmas, Mary couldn't wait to get to work despite the fact she was exhausted from recent events. Even though the weather told her there was no chance of a white Christmas, she knew that every corner of the store would be filled with magic and that was precisely the tonic she needed.

Arriving on the shop floor, she checked her sales book was ready for the day ahead and found herself wondering what had happened to Mrs Matravers and the rest of the hooch ring. She hoped the police had rounded them up by now and prayed they would be charged. Her thoughts turned to David once more and she felt a pang of longing for the man she knew she still loved.

She had no idea what he would think of his sister's antics, and by rights she knew she shouldn't care. David had made his feelings about Mary perfectly clear but she couldn't help wishing things were different. When she met David she hadn't been looking to fall in love, but now she had, she was devastated at the way things had turned out.

'Morning, Mary,' Flo said brightly as she joined her on the shop floor. 'Are you ready for your first Liberty's Christmas Eve?'

Mary laughed in spite of herself. 'I can't wait! I know there aren't really any presents for people to buy this year, but the atmosphere here is still so lovely.'

'I love this time of year,' Flo said, her eyes shining with excitement. 'I wrapped Aggie and Neil's gifts this morning in some waxed paper from the butcher and put them by the fire. He's coming back tonight and I wanted to get everything all ready for him. We couldn't get a tree this year, but Aggie's made some lovely sugar paste decorations to put on the mantelpiece.'

'So what have you bought?' Alice asked.

Flo chewed her lip. 'I've got him a book about ships. Aggie was more difficult so I mended a dress for her and wrapped that. She's not much of a one for sewing. Have you got Alice and Dot anything?'

Mary shook her head. 'No, we said we'd save our pennies. We're all looking forward to Christmas dinner instead. Dot's made us a lovely-looking pudding with the special ration of block suet the government allowed us for Christmas and of course it will be baby Arthur's first Christmas so it will be all the more special.'

Hearing the footsteps of the first few customers of the day behind them, Mary spun around, ready to smile in greeting. Yet instead she came face to face with David, dressed in his army uniform, his blue eyes making him look heart-stoppingly attractive and his neatly combed hair as elegant as the rest of him. Mary felt as if she were falling and hated her heart for betraying her.

'How can I help you?' she managed to say.

David looked at her sheepishly. 'I just wanted to let you know I have been to see Rose today.'

'How did you find her?' Mary asked.

'She's doing very well,' David said flatly. 'She will be sent home tomorrow.'

Mary clapped her hands together in delight. 'That's wonderful.'

'Yes, it is rather,' he nodded. 'I also wanted to let you know that I visited my sister in a prison cell this morning.'

Mary's hands flew to her mouth. 'Mrs Matravers has been arrested?'

'Yes. She and Alf have both been charged.'

'And what about the third man?' Mary frowned. 'Where's he?'

'I don't know. Apparently he has fled from the area,' David said stiffly.

'So he's still out there?' Mary gasped. 'He's seen me, he could do anything.'

'I'm sure it won't come to that,' he replied, refusing to meet her gaze.

Mary looked up at him, suddenly unable to recognise the man before her. He was treating her as if she were little more than a stranger, not a woman he had proclaimed undying love for just a few weeks earlier.

'Yes, of course,' she said sadly.

'Right then, that was all I came for. Goodbye, Mary,' he said, lifting his cap.

As she watched him turn and stride across the shop floor, Mary felt her eyes fill with tears. Was this really how it was going to end?

'Wait,' Mary called wildly.

David turned and looked at her in surprise. It was as if somehow the notion of being in Liberty's would protect him from having to talk to Mary properly.

'Yes?' he said quietly.

Mary couldn't miss the anger that flashed across his features, but there was something else there too, a look of love that he couldn't erase from his dazzling blue eyes. It was that look, telling her there was still something between them, which spurred her on. Gazing up at him, her heart beating loudly against her chest, Mary willed herself to speak. 'I wondered if you might be free for a quick cup of tea sometime before you go back?'

There was a pause and Mary felt her insides churn as her gaze briefly fell to the floor. Looking back up at him, she couldn't tear her eyes from his, suddenly catching the look of longing that passed across his face.

And then as quick as a flash the moment was gone. 'I'm sorry, no. I've a lot to do before I return,' he said gruffly.

Mary nodded, stung. 'I just hoped we could talk.'

'I think everything that needed to be said was said on Saturday night,' he stated formally. 'I have spoken to Michael and he has told me what happened. That it was a silly one-off and that he had no idea of your pregnancy or of course he would have done the decent thing.'

Mary snorted in disgust, unable to help herself. 'Is that what he told you? Because he's lying, David.'

David said coldly, 'I'm sorry, I wish you well for the future of course but there really is nothing between us now and it's best forgotten. Now if you'll excuse me, I must be off.'

A heady mix of rage and sadness pulsed through Mary. Before she could stop herself, she took the ring she had continued to wear in hope that they might be able to work things out and thrust it into his pocket. 'Yours, I think,' she sobbed.

If David was surprised he didn't show it. Instead he nodded, then turned ready to leave when Mr Button appeared at his side.

'Before you go, David, I wonder if I might have a word in my office,' he said gently.

David looked at him in surprise. 'Yes, all right.'

'Thank you.' Mr Button smiled gratefully. 'It won't take long, I assure you.'

As Mr Button led David up the wooden staircase, Mary watched him go feeling nothing but sadness in her heart. She had told herself over and over again that David's reaction to her past shouldn't hurt her, that it was better in many ways for her to find out now just who he really was. But as she watched his broad shoulders, so handsome in his army uniform, disappear around the corner, she knew all her words of positivity were no help to her now. She still loved him, and she knew she always would.

As if sensing her distress, Flo and Dot sidled up alongside her, silently offering her their support.

'Let him go, darlin',' Dot soothed. 'If it's meant to be, he'll come back to you.'

'You should tell him what happened,' Alice whispered. 'Not just with Michael but Mrs Matravers too. He should hear how she blackmailed you.'

A lone tear trickled down Mary's cheek. 'I wanted to, but I can't. I haven't got the strength to fight another battle.'

Chapter Forty-Seven

Getting out of the Liberty van, Mary smiled as she saw a cloudless blue sky. In spite of all she had endured this year, there was so much to be grateful for this Christmas morning.

Together with Larry, who despite petrol rationing had been given special permission to use the van to bring Rose home, Mary made her way into the hospital. She smiled in delight as she saw how full of festive cheer everyone seemed to be. Doctors were rushing around corridors wearing novelty hats while nurses wore large grins, determined to dish out as much happiness as possible to everyone finding themselves in hospital on this very special day.

When the Liberty girls heard that Rose would be discharged on Christmas Day, Dot suggested they move their Christmas lunch to Malcolm and Rose's house. That way, she reasoned, Rose would feel as if she were surrounded by love and wouldn't miss out on the festivities. Everyone had agreed it was a marvellous idea, and so while Mary and Larry brought Rose home, Malcolm, Dot and Alice got the place ready for Rose's return. Flo had offered to help too, but the girls had refused, insisting she had too much to sort out for her wedding the following day.

'Which one's Rose's ward?' Larry asked as he walked along next to her.

'First on the left,' Mary said, gesturing towards the whitewashed door.

Poking her head inside the door, she saw Rose perched on the bed, already dressed in hat and coat, with her suitcase resting beside her, looking for all the world as if she were returning from a holiday rather than going home after a spell in hospital.

'How are you feeling?' Rose asked, sitting next to her and taking her hand.

Rose smiled. 'Mary! You're here.'

'Nowhere else I would rather be,' Mary whispered, choking back the tears at the momentousness of the occasion. Her friend was finally coming home. 'Come on,' she said, getting to her feet to help Rose up. 'Let's get you back where you belong.'

An hour later and Mary was pleased to discover her friend was the very centre of attention. Flo, Alice, Arthur and Dot, along with Malcolm and Flo's intended, Neil, were ready to welcome Rose back, seemingly having worked wonders. Not only had the front room been set up as Rose's new bedroom, but Dot had worked her magic, providing what appeared to be a richly fruited Christmas pudding along with an eggless Christmas cake in honour of Rose's return.

Meanwhile, the smell of Christmas dinner emerged from the kitchen, and Mary was delighted to see that her friend seemed for all the world as if she were enjoying herself.

'I think you're the only one getting any presents at all today, Rose,' Flo giggled as she pressed a package into Rose's arms.

'Yes, I've been told that my present is getting married tomorrow,' Neil grinned, kissing his wife-to-be.

As everyone laughed along with them, Rose tore excitedly at the waxy paper. 'Ooh, is this what I think it is?'

'If you think it's the gorgeous teal scarf we've all been gifted from the Liberty family as a wedding gift, then yes!' Flo grinned.

Rose's eyes shone with tears. 'I don't know how to thank you all, you've all been so kind.'

'There's a letter here from Tommy,' Malcolm said, brandishing an envelope. 'It came the other day but I thought I'd save it for Christmas Day. Shall I read it, love?'

The delight on Rose's face was palpable, Mary thought as her friend nodded, as excited as a child.

Clearing his throat, Malcolm ripped open the envelope and began to read.

19th December 1941

My Darling Rose,

Merry Christmas, my love. I hope that by the time you are reading this you are safely at home with your family and enjoying Christmas as much as you can. I wish I could be there with you but my request for compassionate leave was refused (I'm sorry, Rose, I ignored your telegram and asked my commanding officer if I could have a short pass anyway to see you) so I am writing this letter, wishing with all my heart I could be by your side. The thing is, Rose, I know you to be the strongest, bravest, most generous girl I have ever met. I am furious at what has happened to you and want with all my being to make whoever is responsible pay, but I know, my darling, that you will face this new challenge as you face every challenge, with dignity, courage and grace.

I could not be prouder to have you as my wife and I have never loved and adored you as much as I do now. Please know that I will be thinking of you this Christmas Day, my love, but also know that although this wretched war prevents us from being together, in my heart we always are. Every night I go to sleep imagining that I am holding you in my arms, and I am holding you right now, Rose, as you face this new world. I am by your side and you are forever in my heart.

Merry Christmas, my love,
Tommy

As the letter finished, the room fell silent as they drank in the words of love. Mary saw the tears streaming down Rose's face and wrapped an arm around her.

'Actually, I haven't given you my present yet,' Alice said, breaking the silence as she gently bundled Arthur into Rose's arms.

'Oh my days! You're not giving me a baby, are you?' Rose giggled, stroking Arthur's cheek as he gurgled contentedly in her arms.

As the others joined in the joke, Alice shook her head. 'No, but if you play your cards right you can see Arthur every day from now on.'

Rose frowned. 'What do you mean?'

'I mean that me and your dad have been talking over the past couple of days about how you're going to manage,' Alice began.

'And we will manage,' Rose said stiffly. 'We always have and we always will, right, Dad? Just because Mother's away in this blasted war don't mean we need charity.'

'Just listen, love,' Malcolm said gently from his place next to his daughter's side. 'I think you'll like what she has to say.'

'Thank you, Malcolm,' Alice smiled. 'The thing is, Rose, it's actually you that will be doing us a favour because things are getting a little cramped at Dot's.'

'Charming!' Dot snorted, wiping her hands on her apron.

'And as you have a bigger place, and might need a bit more help as you and your dad adjust to your new situation, well, me and your dad thought Arthur and I could move in here,' Alice finished.

'It really is the best thing for everyone,' Malcolm said. 'What do you think?'

Rose smiled. 'Oh Alice, that will be wonderful, what a treat to have you both here.'

Malcolm leaned over and kissed his daughter's head gratefully. 'I'm so glad you see it like that, poppet.'

'Of course,' Rose smiled. 'Thank you, Alice. But won't you miss her, Dot?'

Dot chuckled good-naturedly. 'Not likely!'

'And this morning we've already moved our stuff in,' Alice said, giggling, 'so I'm delighted you think it's all right.'

'So am I,' Dot snorted.

'And me,' Mary chimed in. 'We might get a decent night's sleep now without Arthur keeping us up all night.'

'And space to move about in the kitchen,' Dot added.

At that the whole group laughed before falling into a companionable silence. On days like this, when they were so grateful for the love they had in their lives, the war seemed a million miles away. But the truth was the war was far from over, and Mary knew each of them would be thinking of the absent friends and loved ones who weren't lucky enough to be at this table. She turned to Alice and guessed from the way she looked at Arthur that her thoughts weren't far from Luke, while Flo, she thought, watching her set the table ready for lunch, would perhaps be thinking about her aunt or her mother and wondering what they were doing on this very special day. As for Mary, she had lost a lot this year: her family, her baby and of course David; the experiences had been difficult crosses to bear. Mary hugged her knees into her chest as she sat on the sofa. There was a lot to be sad about, she thought, but there was also a lot to be grateful for. Here, amongst this eclectic group, she had found real love, and that was something worth celebrating.

Just after one in the afternoon, everyone sat down at the table to eat the Christmas feast Dot, Flo and Alice had lovingly prepared, and Mary couldn't help counting her blessings as she saw the spread before her. Yes, there was plenty that was wrong in the world but, looking at this table and all who sat around it, there was plenty that was right too.

There might not have been much money for food and gifts, but the homemade newspaper chains that dangled cheerfully from Malcolm and Rose's ceiling, along with the paste decorations that adorned the mantelpiece and homemade crackers at each place setting, gave off a sense of cheer, as did the goose Dot now laid on the table.

'Tah-dah,' she called excitedly.

Mary looked at it admiringly. 'Where on earth did you get that?'

Dot tapped her nose knowingly. 'Friend of a friend has geese up Stepney way. Let me have a bird if I taught his wife how to make a new frock from an old pair of curtains.'

'Well, you've done marvellously,' Mary breathed.

Neil nodded in agreement. 'We don't get anything like this in the navy.'

At that Arthur giggled in delight, and everyone laughed. 'See, even Arthur agrees,' Alice exclaimed.

Glancing around her at the table filled with people she had come to adore, Mary cleared her throat and got to her feet. 'Before we eat, I hope you don't mind but I just want to thank you all for what you've done for me. For believing in me, for taking care of me, for standing up to my mother, and most of all making me feel as though I have a home and a family. I never expected to find any of this when I rented a room from you, Dot, but thank you all, you'll never know how much this means to me.'

With that Mary sat back down and everyone smiled fondly at their friend.

'I'd like to say something now,' Rose said, her beautiful blue eyes alive with love. 'You have all been so good to me, coming to visit me over the past few weeks, helping me come to terms with what's happened. I couldn't wish for better family or friends. Obviously I'm sad Mother can't be here, but those of us around this table are blessed because we have the love and compassion for each other to help us, whereas some folk aren't so lucky. These are the things that really matter and it's these things we should celebrate today.'

Once Rose had finished her speech and sat down, everyone applauded as Alice shook her head. 'I don't know how you can be so brave, love.'

Rose took a sip of sherry from the glass Malcolm had pressed into her hands. 'I'm not brave, Alice. Every single one of us is going through our own private battle at the moment, but the one thing I've realised is that forgiveness is just as important as love.'

Dot sniffed. 'I hope you're not thinking of forgiving old Mabel. She don't deserve your forgiveness, Rose.'

'No, I hope they threw the bleedin' book at her,' Malcolm blasted.

'People make mistakes,' Rose said quietly. 'If we carry nothing but hatred in our hearts we're the ones that will suffer, not them. Anger will do nothing but churn up your insides.'

Mary shook her head in wonder at her friend. Rose had more reason than most people to be hurt and upset, yet here she was, choosing to forgive those who had wronged her. As everyone stood up to give three cheers for Rose, Mary felt a tug of emotion: was it time she took a leaf out of Rose's book and started to forgive? If so, then something told her that the very first person she should start with was herself.

Chapter Forty-Eight

Christmas lunch was a long but very happy meal with the perfect mix of food and conversation. By the time every last mouthful had been devoured, the little party in the Elephant and Castle was feeling very festive indeed.

'There are no leftovers whatsoever,' Alice wailed. 'I promised I'd save Joy some. She's coming over the day after tomorrow to finally meet the baby.'

Flo frowned. 'Doesn't she work in Claridge's?'

Alice nodded. 'She's waiting tables and serving the lunch there today, I think.'

Rose chuckled. 'Then I expect she'll probably be fuller than we are now.'

'I don't think that's possible.' Mary patted her slender stomach. 'I think I need a lie-down in a darkened room.'

'I'll join you,' Neil groaned, before clamping his hands over his mouth, realising what he had just said.

As the table broke into fits of laughter there was a knock at the door.

'Who's that?' Malcolm frowned. 'We're all here, aren't we?'

'Might be Edwin,' Dot suggested. 'He was going to pop round after he'd done his bit up the Underground canteen, you know, for those what have been bombed out. I said he could come here after if he wasn't too tired. I hope that was all right.'

'Course,' Rose grinned. 'It's Christmas. The more the merrier.'

Being closest to the door, Mary went to answer it, and grinned. 'Mr Button, merry Christmas, sir.'

The Liberty manager shuffled from foot to foot on the doorstep and smiled. 'Merry Christmas, Mary dear.'

Stepping back to allow Mr Button inside, she saw a flash of excitement pass across his features as he tipped his hat. 'There's a little something for you as well on the step,' he said, walking past her and into the front room.

Frowning in confusion, Mary looked outside and let out another gasp of surprise as she came face to face with David. Dressed in his army uniform, he appeared to have lost weight, she thought sadly, and the bags under his eyes showed how little he seemed to have slept.

'What are you doing here?'

'I rather think I owe you an apology,' he began.

'You think or you know?' Mary said coldly.

David's eyes glinted with sadness in the half-light. 'I know. Mary, I said some appalling things to you and I would very much like to apologise to you. I judged you without hearing your side of things, I'm sorry.'

Mary said nothing. She had wanted to hear these words for so long but now she felt hollow and empty.

'I mean it,' David said earnestly, reaching for her arm, only for Mary to snatch it away. 'I made a terrible mistake. You deserved my help, Mary, not my treachery. Will you ever forgive me?'

'What's brought this on?' Mary asked eventually. 'When I tried to talk, you refused and said there was nothing more to be said.'

David glanced at the ground before he returned his gaze to Mary. 'I was wrong, Mary. I should have listened. Mr Button told me what Michael did to you. I will never forgive myself for not believing you.'

'Thank you,' she said simply, otherwise lost for words.

'I mean it, Mary,' David repeated. 'I'm sorry I got it so wrong.'

'So why do you believe me now? What's changed?' Mary asked curiously.

'Mr Button didn't just tell me what Michael did to you, he told me that he too had seen how Michael had behaved when they served together some years ago. He said that when they were stationed in Guildford he got a young girl in trouble after forcing himself upon her. However, Michael's father stepped in and made the whole thing go away.'

Mary's hands flew to her mouth in shock. 'Oh my God! He did this before?'

'I got it all so very wrong,' David said sadly. 'I am now staying with Mr Button until I return the day after tomorrow and then the first thing I intend to do is alert my commanding officer over what Michael has done.'

Mary paled. 'But surely they won't believe you now?'

'That's why Mr Button has also agreed to go on the record and state he had grave concerns about Michael's behaviour when he served with him. With a bit of luck we'll have the monster court-martialled; then they'll lock him up and throw away the key.'

'And what about your sister?' Mary asked. 'Is that how you feel about her too?'

'My sister was stupid and cruel,' David snapped, his face colouring with anger. 'I am appalled at the things I have discovered about her. These last few days have been far from pleasant, but I am sure they are nothing compared to what you have endured.' David paused then, and reached for her hand. This time Mary let him take it. 'Please can you forgive me for everything I have done? I love you, Mary, you're my world, my future – please tell me I haven't destroyed that.'

There was a silence as Mary took in everything David had just said. Was it really possible that Michael had attacked someone else before her? She felt wretched: everything she had been through, everything she had lost was because of one horrendous man with no scruples. Looking into David's eyes, which were brimming with love, she found that the passion she had for him had never died; this was a man with principles and heart, but this was also a man who had let her down. She knew then that her heart couldn't take being let down again after it had already endured so much.

'David, I'm sorry,' she said gently. 'You're my world, and I know I made mistakes; I should have told you the truth right from the start, but I was so afraid. I had worked so hard to build a new life for myself after losing my baby, my family, my job, I couldn't risk it.'

'I understand,' David nodded. 'But say you'll give us another chance, please, Mary.'

Mary choked back the tears that were threatening to spill down her cheeks. 'The fact is you're a different person to me now, and I don't think I will ever get over that. Goodbye, David.'

Wordlessly she shut the door on him, and went back inside where the family she had found and now cherished were raising their glasses once more.

Chapter Forty-Nine

On Boxing Day, just three miles away from the Elephant and Castle, a small two-up two-down in the heart of Islington was playing host to a flurry of activity as the Liberty girls gathered to help Flo get ready for her wedding. The place was chaos, Mary thought with a smile as she perched on the edge of Flo's bed and took a sip of the tea Flo's Aunt Agatha had just that moment pressed into her hand.

Dresses were strewn across the bed, Flo's veil stood proudly on her dresser, while a pot of open rouge stood dangerously next to it. Neatly darned stockings dangled from the bed post while in the corner Alice and Dot discussed how Flo should wear her hair.

The only ones that were quiet were Rose and baby Arthur, who was sleeping contentedly in her arms. She hadn't worn her dress in the end. Instead Rose wanted to put on the skirt she and the rest of the Liberty girls had made during their stitching nights, saying that it was filled with more love than any other garment she owned. Everyone thought it a fabulous idea, and Mary was delighted that their friend was still able to take part, thanks to some special arrangements Flo and Neil had organised.

Watching them all now, Mary felt overwhelmed with happiness that she was able to take part in Flo's special day. She couldn't quite believe how fate had smiled down on her. Although she had lost a lot, today she felt as though she belonged.

'Oi, stop daydreaming and help me with this,' Dot said, nudging Mary from her train of thought and thrusting a necklace into her spare hand.

'All right, keep your hair on,' Mary grinned as she stood up to help her landlady. 'You're done.'

Dot checked her appearance in the mirror. The blue dress she had picked out looked wonderful, Mary thought, and was very in keeping with the British theme the girls had worked out together.

'You look stunning,' Mary said softly.

Dot smiled. 'So do you, love.'

Mary checked her own appearance. Her own blue dress fitted her a lot better than the last time she had worn it and she was pleased to see there was a flush of colour in her cheeks.

'You look a lot happier than when you first moved in with me and Alice,' Dot marvelled. 'You've come into your own.'

Mary felt her cheeks flame with colour. 'Don't be silly.'

'I'm not being silly,' Dot said seriously. 'I mean it. You've had some setbacks, love, course you have, I mean who hasn't in this damn war, but you're thriving. And all without David too. You were far too good for him.'

Mary smiled gratefully at Dot for the support. After dinner last night, they had all toasted Christmas with a bottle of champagne left over from the party that Mr Button had brought around. It was then Mary had explained how David had apologised.

Mr Button and the girls had fallen silent as Mary spoke, allowing her to express her feelings without prejudice or judgement. When she finished, nobody said a word about the tears brimming in her eyes. Instead they all agreed it was for the best, and now she was free to move forwards with her life without baggage or burden.

Just then Aggie walked up the stairs with a tray full of champagne glasses.

'Blimey, Aggie, I'll be piddled at this rate,' said Flo as she helped herself to a glass.

'Get away, it's Dutch courage,' Aggie laughed as she offered a glass to each of the girls.

Mary smiled and accepted a glass gratefully. She had never met Flo's aunt before but she already liked her. Stern, but with a good sense of fun, Mary could see why Flo was so fond of her.

Just then Mr Button walked up the stairs and gasped as he stood in the doorway. 'My word, you ladies look beautiful.'

Dot blushed as she turned to Flo. 'Pretty as a picture, ain't she?'

'You all are,' Mr Button nodded, looking resplendent himself in his best Liberty suit, before turning back to Dot: 'You especially, my dear.'

As he leaned forwards to give her a kiss, Mary felt a rush of fondness for the couple. Dot deserved to find love, she thought, after being on her own so many years and it was wonderful to see them so happy together again.

'Shall we make a start then?' Dot called, breaking away from Mr Button. 'How about me, Aggie and Rose get to the church; Mary can come along with Flo.'

Flo beamed. 'Perfect!'

As she bade farewell to the three women with a kiss and promises to see them in church, Flo turned anxiously to Mary and Mr Button. 'You do think I'm doing the right thing, don't you?'

Mr Button and Mary exchanged puzzled glances.

'What do you mean, Flo?' Mary asked.

'Is it right for me and Neil to be getting wed at all today, with Rose and Alice, I mean? It doesn't seem fair that we get to be so happy when they have lost so much,' she said awkwardly.

'My dear, has Rose or Alice said something?' Mr Button began.

Flo shook her head. 'No, of course not, and they never would. But Neil and I were talking last night and he said he was sure that neither one of them would be upset about our wedding but if I was that worried about it then we should postpone it.'

'Do you want to postpone it?' Mary asked quickly.

'No, of course not,' Flo whispered, her red-rimmed eyes meeting Mary's. 'But I don't want to hurt anyone.'

'Then get married today,' Mary said firmly. 'Rose and Alice will only hurt all the more if you put off your wedding because of them. We're at war, Flo, there's no such thing as the perfect time.'

'She's right, Flo,' Mr Button agreed, 'but, Mary, I have to ask, can you not choose to follow Rose's example?'

Mary narrowed her eyes in curiosity. 'I don't understand.'

'I mean if Rose can forgive everyone involved for her blindness, can you not forgive David? You two seemed perfectly well suited, and I know how sorry he is.'

Mary rested a hand on Mr Button's arm and smiled. 'I've been meaning to thank you for talking to David. I didn't realise you knew Michael Mason.'

Mr Button's face clouded over at the mention of his name. 'A thoroughly bad lot. I said so at the time but nobody could see what I saw. He was good at hiding his tracks. But I spoke with an army friend of mine last night at Mason's latest posting. Apparently he's been on their radar for a little while, but nobody has come forward to give their side of things. I am more than happy to give my account again from a few years ago, but, Mary, if you will tell the truth about what happened, then I can assure you he will end up behind bars for a long time. You could have your job back in the ATS and be rightfully reinstated.'

Mary sank on to the bed, her mind in knots. She had truly believed after she was discharged from the army that her career was over, that there was no way back, that the only way forward was to flee. Although it had finally worked out, she had to admit there was a part of her that felt guilty for not telling the truth about what had happened to her, for allowing Mason to get away with it. She had been so focused on her new life bringing up a baby alone, in a safe, warm and loving home, she had buried her feelings and her worries about Mason attacking others. Now was her chance to put that mistake right and ensure he never got the chance to hurt anyone else again.

'Very well,' she said stiffly. 'I'll do it.'

Mr Button smiled gently. 'I'll ensure you don't go through it alone.'

'And we'll be with you too, Mary,' Flo said earnestly. 'All the Liberty girls will.'

Chapter Fifty

It was the happiest sound in the world, Mary thought as she stood outside the church and listened to the peal of the bells. She had caught a few of the congregation moaning that the bells were only to be rung if there was an invasion, but thankfully Dot had set them straight in her own inimitable style.

Shivering in her blue dress, Mary stamped up and down to keep out the mild chill as she watched the photographer Flo and Neil had asked to capture their precious memories on a Box Brownie instruct them to turn this way and that.

She couldn't help smiling as she watched the couple gaze adoringly into each other's eyes. They were made for each other, anyone could see that, and even though they had no honeymoon to look forward to, Mary could tell that for Neil and Flo, the biggest prize in the world was simply becoming husband and wife.

As she had followed Flo down the aisle, she had felt a lump form in her throat; she was so honoured to have been a part of her friend's special day, Mary thought she would burst with pride. Now, as Flo beckoned her over for her own photograph, she rushed over, proud to stand shoulder to shoulder with the Liberty girls.

'Look at us, aren't we gorgeous?' Alice giggled, tossing her blonde hair over her shoulder for the photographer to catch.

'I certainly feel gorgeous,' Rose smiled. 'And although I can't see you girls, I know you all look beautiful.'

'We *are* all beautiful,' Mary said firmly, linking her arm through Rose's and smiling for the camera.

Once their photos were done, the bridegroom was called to the front of the church for his picture to be taken with his family, leaving Flo and the rest of the Liberty girls to their own devices.

'How does it feel, then, to be Mrs Neil Canning?' Alice asked, taking the baby back from Neil's arms to hold close to her heart.

Flo looked as though she would burst with pride. 'It feels lovely. Natural, as though that's who I was always meant to be.'

Dot smiled knowingly. 'Sign of a good marriage, that.'

'Oh Dot,' Flo shook her head. 'What would I do without you? You're like a mother to me, and you girls, well, you're like my sisters.'

'You know we feel just the same, don't you?' Alice gushed. 'You have been there for me when my family wasn't.'

'And me,' Mary admitted. 'I would never have got through the last few months without you girls.'

'Nor me,' Rose said in a small voice. 'I don't know how to thank you.'

'There's nothing to thank me for,' Dot said kindly. 'Family comes in all forms, girls. You are like my very own daughters and I couldn't be prouder of you all if I were your own mother. Now, Flo, are we all going back to your Aggie's now?'

Flo nodded. 'Mr Button said he would give us all a lift in the Liberty van.'

Dot rolled her eyes. 'Course he did! I swear that man lives and breathes that shop.'

'I think we all do,' Alice giggled. 'I had my baby there.'

'I got engaged there,' Mary added.

Rose smiled. 'I bought my wedding dress there.'

'And I found love again there,' Dot said shyly.

Mary winked at the girls as they walked down the frosty church path. 'I think we ought to start looking out for a hat, girls. And best of all you know they're coupon free.'

At that, they all giggled as they made their way into the Liberty van, with Flo and Neil up front as guests of honour. Mr Button had done the happy couple proud, decorating the van with streamers made from the spare Christmas decorations and a 'Just Married' sign made from Liberty signage. It made for a delightful picture, Mary thought as she saw the look of love flash between Neil and Flo which told her in no uncertain terms that this was a couple destined to be together forever.

Arriving back in style at Agatha's house, Mary let out a gasp of disbelief as she walked inside. The entire place had been transformed in the couple of hours since they had left to get to the church.

Inside the parlour, more homemade streamers hung from the walls, while a trestle table covered with a pure white linen tablecloth was teetering under the weight of not only a dozen plates of paste and Spam sandwiches, but also several bottles of Russian champagne, Mary noticed with a smile.

'Where did all this come from?' Dot gasped.

'Everyone was so kind,' Agatha replied. 'All our neighbours gave me some of their rations so we could lay on a spread, and even Mr Potter from next door lent us his piano so we could have a good sing-song later.'

'It's a good job it's on wheels,' Alice said, shuddering at the weight of it. 'If I'd had to carry that, I'd have dropped it straight on my big toe!'

'I can't believe how lovely people have been!' Rose exclaimed. 'Isn't it wonderful the way everyone comes together?'

Mary wrapped an arm around Rose and hugged her tight as she glanced around the room and felt a flush of happiness. Family and friends were packed into every space, laughing and joking as they ate and drank their way through the spread, celebrating Neil and Flo's union. Little ones ran between grown-ups' legs, shrieking with delight, while Neil's grandma sat in the corner, her own bottle of champagne at her side, which she used to casually top up her own glass when she thought nobody was looking.

It was just what a family occasion should be like, Mary thought. With a flush of shame she realised that once upon a time she would have looked down her nose at an event like this, thinking that a decent party could only be held in a grand hall, where everyone wore ball gowns and the finest food and drink was served.

But, Mary reflected, the one thing those occasions didn't have was love and it was very clear that in this room, love was the one thing that wasn't in short supply. Everyone was laughing, hugging and kissing, and she knew it wasn't just Princess Valentina's generous supply of champagne keeping everyone in the party mood. It was because there was a huge amount of genuine affection for this couple and Mary realised with a jolt of surprise that if she were ever to get married, she would love a wedding just like this one.

Just then she felt a tap on her shoulder. Spinning around, she came face to face with David. 'What are you doing here?' she gasped in shock.

'Flo invited me. Insisted I came, even though I said I shouldn't,' David admitted with a hint of steel to his voice.

'I see,' Mary nodded. As she ran her eye over him in his army uniform, she felt her heart bang against her chest. She was better off without David, he had proven that he was no good for her, and yet it seemed her heart had not quite caught up with her head.

'You look beautiful,' David said in a quiet voice. 'As I watched you walk down the aisle behind Flo, I couldn't help imagining what it would be like if you were to walk down the aisle towards me, if it were our wedding day.'

'David, no—' Mary began.

'Please let me finish,' he implored. 'I know that you will never forgive me. I know I behaved appallingly, and my sister made your life a misery. I wish I could do more than say sorry, but, Mary, please know that if you were ever to forgive me I would spend the rest of my life dedicated to ensuring you never had to forgive me for anything else again.'

Lost for words at the baldness of his statement, Mary was unsure how to reply when the sound of tinkling glass caught her attention. Spotting Mr Button get to his feet, she fell silent along with the rest of the room.

Mr Button cleared his throat and began. 'As some of you may know, I am not the father of the bride, but I am delighted to say that I was given the very great honour of walking this young lady down the aisle today,' he said, before taking a pause to glance down at the notes he had prepared. As he looked up to continue there was a sudden crash at the door. Everyone spun around to see who the unexpected intruder was.

In the doorway stood a man with a mean look in his eyes.

'Oh my word,' Mary gasped, recognising him immediately. 'That's Bill, the man from the hooch ring. What's he doing at Flo's wedding?

'Flo! Flo!' he shouted.

'What are you doing here?' Flo whispered, the colour draining from her face. 'It's my wedding day.'

'And that's why I'm here. I'm your father. It should be me up there giving your speech.'

Mary felt a surge of fury. This was Flo's father? The man wasn't anywhere near good enough to be Flo's father and he certainly shouldn't be anywhere near her wedding. Shucking David's hand off her shoulder she pushed her way through the crowd towards him.

'That's enough, Dad, you're not welcome here,' Flo protested over the crowd.

Bill swayed at the doorframe. 'How dare you cheek me? You want to show me some respect.'

'Now that's quite enough of all that,' Mr Button called, trying to engender some calm.

'Mr Button's right, Dad,' Flo began, her voice taking on a steely edge. 'You only ever come around to see me when you want something or you're in trouble. Last time I saw you was over five years ago when you gave me and Aggie a hiding for going to the police. Why would I ever invite you to my wedding?'

'Because I'm your father,' he snarled.

At this Neil drew himself up to his full height and glowered at the man who was now his father-in-law. 'How dare you come in here and upset my wife! This is our special day, and you're not welcome. Now get out now before I knock you out.'

At Neil's outburst, Wilson began to march towards the newlyweds. 'Looks to me like you both want a good hiding ...'

As the crowd gasped in horror, Mary felt white-hot anger rise up inside. She knew that men like this – weak, powerless men who only wanted to dominate and control others – would never understand reason, no matter how

355

hard you tried. You had to fight fire with fire, she thought, and now, as she reached the man who thought it was acceptable to ruin her friend's wedding, she was determined to stand up for what was right in a way she should have done with Mason.

'You want respect?' she hissed, drawing herself up to her full height and glowering at him with intent. 'Respect has to be earned! Give me one good reason why Flo should respect you. You've spent most of your life in and out of prison, and when you were around all you ever did was beat Aggie and Flo black and blue or take their money. You're a disgrace!'

Bill Wilson turned to Mary and fixed his gaze on her. 'Who the hell are you to tell me? Some jumped-up little shop girl who didn't have the common sense to keep her mouth shut.'

'You should be back in prison under lock and key,' Mary snarled. 'I'm proud I told the police about your little hooch ring, and now I know it was you that was the third wheel I'll make sure the police know all about you.'

'Is that true, Dad? You were part of the hooch ring?' Flo gasped.

Wilson shuffled unsteadily against the doorjamb. 'What if I was? Gotta make a living somehow.'

'You made at least two people blind,' Flo hissed.

'And one of them was me,' Rose said quietly.

As the room fell silent, Flo's father looked uncertainly at Rose before fixing his gaze back on Mary.

'You cow!' he snarled. 'Here you are again ruining things with your big mouth. I'll make you suffer, girl, like you've never suffered before.'

Just as Wilson lifted his hand ready to strike, Mary felt a pair of hands shove her firmly out of the way, and then watched in amazement as David landed a punch to

356

Wilson's jaw so hard the thug dropped to the floor like the last in a line of dominoes.

'I imagine that's something else that makes you think people respect you, Wilson, hitting women?' David snapped. 'It appears you've a long list of unforgivable crimes. Now get out before I hit you so hard you won't get up again.'

Mr Wilson got to his feet. 'Think you're the big man, do you?'

'I don't think I'm anything, but what I do know is you stand up for the people you love. *You* don't know what love is, that's bigger than any punishment you'll find in prison. Now go.'

Looking first at Flo and then back to David, the crowd stayed silent as Wilson seemed unsure what he was going to do or say next. Straightening his overcoat, he turned to leave. 'This is not over for any of you,' he roared, before disappearing as quickly as he had appeared.

Once he had gone, everyone in the room visibly relaxed and Mary watched as Neil held Flo close. Dot stood on the hearth and clapped her hands for attention.

'I think we've all had enough excitement for one day. How about we steady our nerves with another glass of champagne and have a sing-song.'

'Excellent idea,' someone called, already opening another of the bottles.

As the drink was poured into glasses, Agatha took up her place at the piano. 'Any requests?' she called brightly.

'"Only Forever",' David shouted immediately.

'Oooh, lovely!' Agatha struck up the first few chords and broke into song.

The moment everyone began to dance Mary turned to find David staring longingly at her. 'Can I have this dance?'

Mary paused, then met David's gaze. 'As you did save me from a black eye, I think that's only fair.'

Taking his hand, she allowed herself to be whirled around the dance floor as David whispered in her ear, 'Please give me another chance, Mary. This war is already costing us so much unhappiness; let's not allow it to take our love too.'

Resting her head against David's chest, Mary thought for a moment. She had suffered so much loss and pain, but she knew she wasn't alone. Everyone around her had suffered at the hands of this dreadful war, and still people could forgive and become stronger. She thought back to the magic and enchantment she had first found in Liberty's as a child. Back then she'd thought she would never know a greater happiness than to step inside that store and enjoy the magic. Now, with the David holding her in his arms, she knew that thanks to the wonderful store, she had found something far more powerful than magic: she had found love.

'Yes, David,' she said, stroking his cheek. 'I think we can try again.'

Joy lit up David's face as he bent down to kiss her tenderly on the lips. Mary gave in to the moment and felt as if all her Christmases had come at once. David may have made mistakes, but so had she, and together they could spend their lifetimes proving their love. Mary knew that in this kiss she had not only found real love but she had also found a home.

Want to know what happens next?

Look out for the next book in the series ...

Amid the hardship of war, their friends will become family

The Liberty Girls

Fiona Ford

16 May 2019

ORDER YOUR COPY NOW

Available in paperback and e-book

arrow books

Hear more from

Fiona Ford